I0825353

AN AWKWARD COLLECTION

VOLUME 1

RACHEL RHODES

INCLUDES AWKWARD BOOKS 1-4

- Awkward in Print
- Awkward Abroad
- Awkward Infidelity
- Awkward in Trouble

AWKWARD IN PRINT

BOOK 1 IN THE AWKWARD SERIES

1

George's office is so big that I feel like I've been marooned in an ancient leather chair on an island of mahogany hardwood. Citrus and Old Spice wage an aromatic war with the lingering cigar smoke in the air. I find myself flicking my foot so that my sandal flaps against my heel. Flap, flap, flap, a steady beat counting the seconds.

"Jojo." George peers at me over his glasses. An impatient smile, a small gesture toward my feet. "Would you mind?"

"Sorry." I stop flapping and start to bite the edge of my thumbnail instead. I should have known not to arrive on time. George never runs to schedule and so, thanks to the ingrained punctuality my father drummed into me from my first day at kindergarten, I have spent the last ten minutes trying not to fidget while he reads the final pages of my manuscript. I'm not a writer. If I were, I would probably feel a sense of pride instead of this crippling sense of anxiety. I can even pinpoint its source. It's tucked between pages 243 and 244.

George wheezes out a chuckle, a combination of thirty Marlboro a day, and what I hope is the joke I made in the final paragraph. He removes his glasses and fixes me with a watery-eyed smile. "Fabulous!" he announces, dropping the manuscript on the desk before him with a hefty thud. I can't help but think that if we'd stuck to the cold hard facts, it would be significantly less effective – possibly a single sheet of paper wafting gracefully down onto the broad surface. "Poignant, endearing and sincere," George continues, and I can practically see the dollar signs reflected in his pupils. "We'll release in six months, to coincide with the film premiere."

F u u u u u u c k.

George presses a pudgy thumb onto the PA system resting on his desk. The button is worn, greyed in the center where it was once black.

"Yes, Mr. Beresford?" Sally's switchboard-smooth voice purrs through the intercom. I try not to remember the time I walked past her unattended desk and into George's office to find her servicing George rather than the copier. I've not been able to look George's saint-like wife, Susan, in the eye since.

"Sal," George booms. I wonder why he bothers with the intercom when she can clearly hear him through the door. "Approve Jojo's proofs, the polish is perfect. I want a bound print proof on my desk next week."

"Absolutely, Mr. Beresford."

I suck in a breath that doesn't reach my chest.

"George," I begin tentatively, "I'm not sure if we're one hundred percent ready. Some of the stuff in this book has been exaggerated, and—"

George cuts me dead. "Of course it has. Nobody wants to read the memoir of a celebrity who hasn't done anything wild or crazy. Everybody does it." At the word 'everybody' he opens his arm to indicate the framed photographs behind him. Gina D, Lucy Cale, Harrison Wentz, all boldly emblazoned with signatures and messages of thanks. George Beresford: Agent to the Stars. Paula Power addressed hers to 'Big George'. I shudder to think what that means and make a mental note to send Susan a fruit basket the second I leave this office.

I take another deep breath and try again. "But say someone had to discover that the truth has been... tweaked. Wouldn't that be grounds for a lawsuit?"

"A lawsuit? Jojo, you've been watching too many movies." He bellows at his own joke and then flips to page two of the preliminary pages. He jabs at the text midway down the page. "This," he tells me, "is a disclaimer. It indemnifies you against any such claims. It also," he lowers his voice conspiratorially, "allows us to blend as much fiction into the memoir as we please, without consequence."

"Okay, but legal consequence aside, I have my reputation to consider."

"Reputation? Jojo, that's *my* job. Besides, there's nothing like a scandal to ensure a meteoric rise to stardom. Not that you need it," he adds quickly. He's right, I don't. Right now, I can command more money than Julia Laurence, a fact she pointed out when we lunched last week. I'm officially the highest paid actress in Hollywood, surreal as that is. George didn't choose me, I chose George. Because, in the shark-infested waters of Hollywood agents, George is a nurse shark. Still...

"I don't know if I'm quite comfortable with that..." I begin, but he cuts me off again.

"There's only one thing in this book that matters. We even built the title around it, for God's sake. Jojo, you are a *virgin.* A real-life, twenty-six-year-old, celebrity virgin, living in L.A. You're as rare as it gets. In fact, if someone discovered a living, breathing dinosaur, we'd still outsell them."

I'm pretty sure that's not true. I wonder if I could actually find a real-life dinosaur, while George continues. "The rest doesn't mean shit. So, unless you've gone and dropped your panties for someone between writing the first draft and getting engaged to Alex, we have hit pay dirt."

There's a pause as George waits for this to sink in.

"I haven't," I say truthfully. Then I flick my foot.

2

It's been six months since my last visit and Sally has put on weight. She's also put on a perpetual smirk, and she barely bothers with discretion when it comes to placing her perfectly-manicured hands all over George. I'm back in his office, marooned, terrified, and holding a copy of my book in my hands. It's gorgeous – all gold foil and embossed font. *Hollywood Virgin: the dazzling autobiography of Jojo Hudson*. George came up with the title. I wasn't so sure about the word 'dazzling'. There's a silhouetted photograph of me in the background. I'm looking over my shoulder, straight at the camera. The word 'Print' is reflected in my eye.

"I love it," I tell George, truthfully. I do love it – the cover especially. It looks like a book I would buy. That doesn't make me feel any better about it, though. For the thousandth time, I wish I'd never told George I was writing this damned book. He seized upon that announcement like it was the Academy Award of his professional life. Within a week, he'd found a publisher. Three days later I'd signed a contract. I've had nightmares ever since.

"I'm having two thousand copies delivered this afternoon. We're all set for the launch next week."

"Wonderful," I lie. "I can't wait." An air kiss later and I'm out the door. I step out onto the street and take a few gulps of fresh air. The tightness in my chest eases, but only marginally. Right on cue, my driver pulls up, double parking, to a cacophony of angry hoots. I rush forward as he opens his door.

"I'm going for a walk, Phillip, I'll call if I need you."

"Yes, Miss Hudson." Phillip slides back onto the cream leather and signals. He pulls out into the traffic without missing a beat, but narrowly missing a red Mercedes.

I keep my head down. It's become a habit but today more than any I need to be alone with my thoughts. I've managed to sweep my anxiety under the rug for the past six months, but now it's returned, with a vengeance.

"Oh my God." A low voice to my left draws my attention from the cracked sidewalk, and I turn to find a young woman behind me, hanging onto a neon-blue dog leash. I follow the line of the leash to find a squirming golden spaniel tying himself into knots.

"Are you...?" The woman frowns at me and cocks her head to one side. I wait for the moment that I know will come. Her eyes widen, and her lips part as her head snaps upright. "Oh my God, you are!"

I smile, having learned the hard way that to deny it will only lead to a scene. "I am." I keep my voice down, hoping she will follow suit. Unfortunately, today is not my lucky day.

"I can't believe it! Oh my God, I'm such a fan. Your biggest fan. Could you..." she trails off, digging inside her oversized handbag and practically throttling the spaniel in the process. "Aha!" she whips out her phone in triumph. "Would you mind if I took a selfie?"

I nod. Grit my teeth. Step forward. By the time she jabs the photo button, I'm leaning into her, a picture-perfect smile on my face.

"I'm Donna, by the way," she says, as she checks the photo.

"Hi, Donna." The smile is still plastered on my lips. I can hold it for hours; my cheeks don't even cramp anymore. "I'm Jojo."

She laughs at that. A manic, over-the-top laugh that implies my joke is the funniest thing she's ever heard. The spaniel whimpers.

"I think your puppy is in a bit of trouble," I say. Donna glances down, gives a start, and bends to untangle the puppy before it loses consciousness. I take the opportunity to slip into the crowd of pedestrian traffic walking down the street. I feel a bit bad for pulling a vanishing act on Donna, but I've learned from experience that it's easier to cut and run. At least she'll always have that photograph. As I walk, I tie back my hair with the elastic band around my wrist and pull a pair of enormous Prada glasses from my bag. I walk three blocks without a single person recognizing me. Dark glasses and messy buns have saved my sanity more times than I can count.

I'm almost at *The Office* when my phone rings. My smile is genuine as I answer.

"Hey, babe!"

"Good morning beautiful." It's his I-just-woke-up-and-I'm-horny voice, not to be confused with his I-just-woke-up-and-I-want-to-cuddle voice. Alex and I had been dating for two years when he proposed. We've been engaged for just over a month, and some days I still have to pinch myself to make sure I'm not dreaming. Only just turned thirty, handsome as the devil and one of the youngest people ever to make the Forbes World's Billionaires List, Alex Masters is quite easily Hollywood's most eligible bachelor. That is, he was, until he met me. Automatically, I glance at my ring finger, where a five-carat diamond flashes brightly in the sunlight.

"How did the meeting go?" Alex yawns down the phone. Up all night working again, I think fondly.

"It went well. George is happy with the final edits."

"So, you're still on for the launch?"

I fake an enthusiasm I can't bring myself to feel. "We are!"

A pause. Alex is nothing if not intuitive. I catch my bottom lip between my teeth.

"Well that's good news," Alex says eventually. "I'm proud of you, angel."

That familiar warm feeling washes over me. "Thank you."

"Where are you now?"

"I'm just popping in to see Jude."

"It's a bit early for a drink, don't you think? Must have been one hell of a meeting," he teases. "Don't fall in love with him." It's his standard response whenever I visit my oldest friend in L.A.

"I'll try."

"I'll see you later. I should be done by seven or so."

"Perfect, I can't wait."

I disconnect the call and step inside *The Office*, a singularly inappropriate name for the small, low-lit bar. At this time of the morning, it's completely empty.

"Well, as I live and breathe, if it isn't Miss Josie Hudson!" Jude's familiar grin flashes in my direction from behind the bar. Jude can't resist calling me by my real name, even though almost everyone else has adopted my stage name. Everyone but Jude, my sister, Teddy, and my parents. He's wiping down the counter, his blond bed-head sticking up in all directions. I dump my bag on top of the counter he's just cleaned.

"What can I get for you, Miss?" Jude asks. My chest relaxes completely at the sight of the familiar devilish glint in his eye.

"Don't you start." I whip off the dark glasses. "I need coffee."

"You know where everything is," he says, but I'm already moving behind the counter, toward the coffee machine.

"You want one?" I ask over my shoulder.

"Make it a double. I had a hens party in here last night which just wouldn't leave."

Jude goes back to his cleaning while I whip up two coffees with the skill and ease of someone who spent three years working behind this bar.

I carry the two chipped mugs back to the counter, slip back around it and take a seat on one of the well-worn bar stools. Jude drops the cloth to take the seat opposite me.

"So, how did it go with King George?"

I take a sip of my coffee. "We're all set."

"Nice. You must be excited."

"Mmmm," I mumble, non-committal.

"Do I get to come to this fancy launch party you're having, or will George have a shit fit if you bring in the help?"

"Of course you're invited! You *are* coming, aren't you?" I fix him with a hard look, daring him to say otherwise, and he holds up his hands in mock surrender.

"I'm coming, I'm coming!"

"Good."

Jude doesn't let me off that easy. "I don't really have anything to wear."

I throw the cloth at him.

We settle into a comfortable silence. *The Office* hasn't changed much in the three years since I stopped working here. When I first arrived in Los Angeles, Jude was the only person who'd give me a job. He'd treated me kindly, kept my chin up when I failed to land any roles, encouraged me to keep auditioning when I was ready to give up, and advanced my pay-check when I couldn't make my rent. Without him, I probably would've scuttled back to Bridgeport, Connecticut with my tail between my legs before the first year was up. As it turns out, it was a good thing I didn't. My breakthrough role was a small part in an indie film that went on to win two Independent Spirit Awards. One for Best Feature. The other for Best Supporting Female. The first was our debut director's first award. The second was mine.

Within six months I landed the role of a lifetime. Primera Pictures were looking for a female lead to play the role of Hollywood legend Greta Garbo, in a feature film based loosely on her life. I got the part. I also got myself an agent – George.

"Oh, before I forget," Jude breaks the pensive silence and rummages beneath the counter. He withdraws a magazine and slaps it onto the counter before me, narrowly avoiding upending my mug. "I saved you this. I'm sure you'll want as many copies as you can get," he adds.

Alex's handsome face stares out at me from the cover. It's not the first time he's been featured in Times magazine, but it is the first time he's made the cover. The black and white photograph doesn't capture the hazel of his eyes, or the lighter streaks in his dark hair, but there's no denying the hard line of his jaw or the bold chin.

"You're going to drool on it," Jude teases, sliding it away from me. I slap my hand on the cover, hindering his progress and he lets out a low chuckle. "Take it, please. If I catch sight of him staring up at me one more time when I'm digging around under the bar, I'm going to throw up. He's like the fucking *Mona Lisa*, those eyes follow me everywhere."

"Oh, stop it. You know you love him."

"I wouldn't go that far. But so long as he's making you happy, he's got my vote."

I finish my coffee and make to carry the cup around to the back, but Jude stays me with a hand. "Leave it, I've got it."

"You sure?"

"You don't work here anymore, remember?"

"You know, sometimes I wish I did. It's true!" I insist as he laughs out loud. "I had fun here. It was like spending every day with family."

"Speaking of family – how are your folks?"

"Good. Dad just upgraded his truck."

"He didn't!" I laugh along with him. Jude knows as well as anybody that my father is frugal to a fault.

"Mom broke down at the store, and he finally caved."

"And Teddy?" his voice changes when he asks after my sister and I give him a knowing smile.

"Teddy just broke up with Scott number 2, so if ever there was a good time to call her..." I let the suggestion hang between us, but Jude shakes his head.

"I've told you a thousand times. It's too complicated."

"And I've told you a thousand times that I have no problem with you dating my sister. God knows she could do with a good man in her life."

My sister's full name is Theodora. Mine is Josephine. Our

parents are as traditional as they come, but fortunately, in an act of extraordinary kindness, our extended family intervened and never called us anything but Josie and Teddy. Teddy has spent the past five years dating two men named Scott. Not at the same time, obviously. Scott 1 lasted three years, Scott 2 only two. Neither deserved even a second date, but Teddy is nothing if not determined. Jude has had a thumping crush on her since the first night they met, but he refuses to act on it.

"It's not just you," he says now, "although that's certainly a big part of it. There's also the fact that we live on opposite sides of the country."

"Teddy's a vet. She could move."

Jude laughs. "I own a bar, yet you expect your sister to give up a thriving private practice?"

"Teddy needs adventure in her life. She's too comfortable. That's why she sticks it out with losers, because she's allergic to change."

"Exactly. Now stop plotting. I'm perfectly happy being single." I know that he is, but that doesn't stop me constantly trying to play matchmaker. Realistically, I know that he and Teddy as a couple is never going to happen, so I'm constantly trying to set him up with people right here in L.A. Jude changes the subject pointedly. "When does filming start?"

"The week after next."

"How many people are coming to the launch?"

My heart quickens at the mention of the dreaded event. "I'm not sure."

"Any pretty single ladies for me to flirt with?"

"Actually, I do have a—"

"Don't you dare, Josie I was joking. I'm not interested."

"But—"

"But nothing. I'm not into those Hollywood types." He realizes what he's said an instant before my face falls. "Shit, I didn't mean it like that. You're... well, you're different. But could you really imagine any of your actress friends hanging out here, in this place?" He spreads his arms wide to encompass the entire bar.

I smile. "More's the pity for them," I say, leaning forward to kiss his cheek. "They don't know what they're missing. This happens to be my favorite place in the world."

I could swear he's actually blushing. I scoop up the magazine and fold it under my arm. "I'll see you later, Jude."

His reply reaches me as I reach for the door. "Later, Josie"

3

"Good afternoon, Miss Hudson." Frank, my doorman, greets me as I step into the air-conditioned lobby of my building.

I flash him a smile. "Hey, Frank. Any messages?"

"No, Ma'am."

I keep walking toward the elevator. "How many times have I asked you to call me Jojo?"

"Company policy," he reminds me, for what must be the hundredth time. "Have a wonderful evening, Miss Hudson."

I wave at him as I step inside the elevator and press the button for the penthouse. "You too, Frank."

Other than *The Office*, my apartment is my favorite place in the world. It spans the entire top floor of the building, and the roof access leads to a private garden, complete with rim-flow pool. After the initial viewing, I had been captivated, and my sister Teddy had talked me into making an offer.

"You deserve it," she'd insisted when I'd balked at the price, "and besides, you can afford it. You know you can."

And I could, so I did. Since then, my finances allow for me to move to any of the sprawling mansions in the Hollywood Hills, but I just haven't found the inclination to leave. I have purchased three additional apartments in the same building, two of which I rent out. I keep the third for private guests.

Alex and I haven't properly discussed where we will be living after the wedding, but from the way he speaks, I've gathered that we will be moving into his home in Calabasas. Whether or not he expects me to sell my apartment, I have yet to figure out.

I drop my purse on the table in the hall and slip off my sandals as a frenzied yapping erupts in the kitchen. A ball of caramel and white fluff skids around the corner and launches itself at me.

"Hello Noodle," I croon, scooping her up. Noodle is a mixed breed mongrel I found injured on a set two years ago. Her back leg had been badly broken, and she'd spent four weeks in a splint, after which I'd had to take her for hydrotherapy twice a week for another six. After going through all that, there was no way I was giving her up. Unfortunately, she's not an endearing dog, and she hasn't got the looks to make up for her bitchy nature. Not even her vet can hazard a guess as to her breeding, but he's pretty sure there's Pomeranian in there.

"I thought that must be you." Fenn, my personal assistant, is standing in the doorway to my office, smiling at Noodle, who is now running laps around my legs. At twenty-three, Fenn is four years younger than I am, but she's efficient and reliable, and I wouldn't survive without her. Even Noodle tolerates her, and Noodle hates everyone.

"How did the meeting go?" Fenn asks.

"It went well. We're all set."

"I thought as much. Should I go ahead and consolidate the RSVPs?"

"Do it tomorrow. Why don't you knock off early and surprise Seb?"

At the mention of her boyfriend, Fenn grins. "He's taking me to dinner. Alejandro's," she adds shyly. No matter how many fancy restaurants Fenn attends with me, she still seems overwhelmed when it occurs outside of her line of work.

"Oh wow. What's the occasion?"

"I have no idea."

My eyes widen. "You don't think...?"

"Oh, hell no! I'm only twenty-three, Jojo!"

"True, but you and Seb have been dating for a while. You never know."

"Trust me, *he* knows better."

"Well, whatever the reason, Alejandro's is no simple date. You should look your best." I give her a meaningful look.

Fenn grins. "Really?"

"I insist."

She follows me through the apartment to my bedroom. My walk-in closet is almost double the size of my bedroom. The upside of being a Hollywood star is that you are never at a loss for designer clothing. The downside is that you need somewhere to keep it all.

It takes Fenn twenty minutes to make up her mind, a steady pile of discarded satin and lace mounting on the pale grey carpet.

"It's perfect!" I announce when she finally stops long enough to admire herself in the full-length mirror. The Naeem Khan dress sits mid-thigh on Fenn's long legs, the stark black-and-white geometric pattern softened by the gauzy fabric. Shoulder cut-outs end in black-ribboned ties just below the elbows. It's not too formal, but dressy enough for Alejandro's.

"I love it," Fenn admits. I help her braid her auburn hair over one shoulder and with an expert hand, I touch up her make-up.

"Shoes," I say when we're done. Fortunately, we have the same size feet. She picks out a pair of black leather ankle boots, and I approve.

"Leave it," I say when she starts to clear away the mess. "I'll get Ursula to do it in the morning."

"Liar." Fenn knows me too well.

I roll my eyes at her. "You're going to be late."

"I promise I'll look after it," she says as I usher her to the door.

"You can have it. It looks better on you than it ever did on me."

She opens her mouth to argue, but I'm already closing the door. "Have fun!"

4

By the time Alex arrives, I've tidied up and poured myself a glass of perfectly chilled white wine. I hear his keys hit the table in the hall a nanosecond before Noodle begins her frenzied yapping from the safety of my lap.

"Hush!" I give her a gentle shove off the couch She gives a dramatic yelp and jumps right back up.

Alex breezes into the living room and gives her a wry frown.

"Not today then?" he says. My stomach drops as his eyes find mine. His dark hair is slicked back, still damp from a recent shower, and the olive polo-neck he's wearing brings out the yellow flecks in his hazel eyes.

"Not today," I agree, scratching Noodle behind the ears. Every time Alex visits, he claims one day Noodle will decide he isn't so bad. It's been over two years, and he's still confident. He reaches out a tanned hand and pats her head.

"You will love me, Noodle," he says in a hypnotic voice. Noodle growls at him.

"How was your day?" I ask, pushing Noodle aside as he flops onto the couch beside me. She gives him a baleful look and then leaps off the couch to settle in her basket with an air of martyrdom.

"Long," Alex says. "I had back to back meetings. Which reminds me, I'll be out of town next week. I have to fly to Munich on Monday morning for a bid meeting. Don't worry," he adds teasingly, catching sight of my horrified face, "I'll be back on Friday morning, in plenty of time for the launch."

"Oh, thank God. I need you there."

He pulls me against his chest. "As good as it feels to be needed, did you honestly think I'd miss it?"

I reply by kissing him. It's long and lazy, but too soon, my blood is thundering in my head, and my fingers are moving up and under his shirt of their own accord.

Alex pulls away, breathing heavily. "God, I can't wait to marry you." He shifts a little, obviously uncomfortable. I get to my feet and offer him my hand.

"Let me help you with that," I grin, my eyes flickering to the bulge of his pants. We may not have had sex yet, but I can certainly ease his discomfort.

Later, we eat at the kitchen counter. It's casual and comfortable.

"God, Ursula is an incredible cook," Alex sighs. "I never knew a simple salad could taste this good."

"I know." I pop another caramelized onion tartlet in my mouth, and the pastry dissolves on my tongue. "Why do you think I'm so intent on bringing her with me when we're married?"

"You better watch it, love. They say the way to a man's heart is through his stomach, you know."

"Really?" I tease. "And the way to a woman's?"

His eyes sparkle. "Through her pants, obviously."

Before he leaves, Alex asks me to play for him. The Baby Grand piano I picked up at Sotheby's after my first big paycheck has pride of place in the white living room, but I haven't touched it in weeks. I've played since as long as I can remember. It was the reason I'd been accepted into Julliard in the first place. After one year, I'd migrated into the four-year acting program, because I'd realized that while music was my first love, acting would be my last.

"I haven't warmed up," I moan, but Alex is merciless.

"You don't need to. I'm tone-deaf, remember?"

He's not tone-deaf. He never has been, but he loves to hear me play. I take a seat on the piano stool I had custom-made when I bought the Baby Grand, and flip open my songbook.

"No," Alex groans. He hates it when I play by the book. I stick my tongue out at him, but I close it anyway. My fingers rest on the ivory keys for only a moment before the first movement of Beethoven's *Moonlight Sonata* comes to mind. I've always found this particular piece heart-stoppingly beautiful. At some point, Alex gets up to stand behind me, his strong fingers trailing the very top of my spine, lifting my hair, which has long escaped the bun, out of the way, but I barely notice. The music carries me away, as it always does.

I open my eyes when the music ends.

"Beautiful," Alex whispers, leaning down to drop a kiss on the top of my head.

When he's gone, I play the third movement. It couldn't be more different from the first – the technical piece a true workout for my unpractised fingers. I cringe at every wrong note, but I play through to the end, and when I finally head to bed, I sleep like a baby.

CEECEE GETS to her feet when I arrive at our usual table. "Jojo!" My name becomes an entire song when CeeCee says it, and I disappear into her cloud of perfume as she pulls me in for a hug. CeeCee kisses both cheeks, even though she's not French. Her real name is Cecily, and she grew up in a trailer park near Pittsburgh, but God help anyone who mentions it. At five foot two, she's diminutive, but I've seen grown men cry when faced with her legendary temper. CeeCee likes things to go her way.

"I took the liberty of ordering champagne," she announces as we take our seats. Immediately, a hovering waiter steps forward to fill my glass.

"It's only ten o'clock," I point out, filling a second glass with iced water. The waiter frowns at me as though by not asking him to do it I've caused deep offense.

"Yes, just too early for wine," CeeCee muses sadly. "So!" Her braceleted hands clap together. "Fenn mailed me. Everything is ready for the launch? How divine, darling, you must be thrilled!"

I take a hearty slug of my champagne. "I am."

"Well, I sent out all the invites we agreed upon, and a few extra last-minute to press we hadn't considered before. Everyone is coming, obviously."

"I have no doubt." I pity the press who try to deny CeeCee Cooper.

"Now when can I get my hands on a copy of the book?" she asks. "You know I've been dying to read it. Stuffy old George wouldn't let me take even a peek at the unpolished manuscript, but you know I want a signed copy."

Slug. "You'll get one, I promise."

"Wonderful. Now, what are you going to have to eat?"

I already know what I'm having – fresh tuna salad with no dressing – so while CeeCee deliberates over the menu, I scan the balcony. Two women in matching suits are having a heated argument. A woman with a bouncing baby boy on her lap is giving the man across from her bedroom eyes. She's wearing a wedding ring, and he isn't. A blond man with a short, military haircut is...

"Shit!" I raise my menu so fast it slaps me in the nose.

"What?" CeeCee squawks.

"Nothing," I say, keeping the menu raised. "There was a bee."

CeeCee's hand snaps forward and yanks the menu from my grasp. I spare a quick look back at the balcony, but the man is gone. I must have been imagining things.

"A bee?" CeeCee asks dubiously.

"Yes." I take another huge swig of my champagne. "It must have flown away."

By the time I leave the restaurant, I'm wobbling on my legs. It takes me forever to locate my car.

"Are you alright, Miss Hudson?" Phillip asks as I fall onto the leather seat.

I wave away his concern. "I'm fine, Phillip." I reach into my purse and root around until I feel the expensive tissue-lined envelope. "Could you drop me at *The Office*, please."

It takes me three tries before I manage to open the door to Jude's pub. When it finally opens, it's so unexpected that I almost fall flat on my face. From behind the bar, Jude bursts into laughter.

"I thought you'd be stuck out there all day," he says.

"Oh, shut it." I make a concerted effort to walk in a straight line, but I still end up three feet to his left. I slide right. "Your invitation, Sir," I announce cordially. Jude takes the invite from my outstretched hand. "So, you have no reason not to attend."

"Where the hell have you been?" he asks as he tears it open.

"I had breakfast with CeeCee."

"Jesus, Jojo. You should know better. The girl grew up with truckers who ran an underground gambling ring. She could drink Old Man Farley under the table."

Old man Farley is one of *The Office* regulars. He comes in every day, Monday to Saturday and drinks until Jude cuts him off. He doesn't speak. Ever. According to Jude, the first time he'd come in, he'd simply pointed to the bottle of single malt on the bar, and that had been that. We started to believe he might be mute, until one Saturday evening when Jude refilled his whiskey, and out of the blue he'd asked why Jude didn't open on Sundays. Jude had been so shocked the whiskey had overflowed.

"Jude goes to Church on Sundays," I'd whispered gravely in Old man Farley's ear. It was easier to lie than to explain that even Jude needed one day off a week. He'd never spoken again, but he could drink for the U.S.A if ever they made it an Olympic sport.

"You're probably right," I say now. Jude taps my nose with a long finger.

"You need coffee."

I don't even offer to help as he sets about making us both a cup.

"You need to RSVP," I tell his broad back.

"To the invitation you handed me fifteen seconds ago?"

"That's the one."

"I already told you I'm coming."

"I thought you might change your mind. Once you've got the invitation, your RSVP is official."

He sets the mug down in front of me and grins. "Why are you so worried about me coming to this shindig anyway? I hardly come to any of your premieres anymore, and it doesn't bother you."

"This is different. It's my first book."

"Do I have to read it?"

I throw a metal coaster at him. It misses by a mile.

"I'm coming, Jojo. You can take this as my official RSVP."

"Thank you. And you're welcome to bring a date."

"Great! I'll ask one of the hundreds of women who beat down my door on a daily basis."

"Ouch."

The downfall of owning *The Office* and spending almost every waking moment keeping it running, is that it leaves Jude very little time to date. It also means far too much time being pawed by lady patrons who have had too much to drink. It doesn't help that he's incredibly easy on the eye.

"You could always bring Laurel," I suggest helpfully.

"I could," he agrees wryly, "if I was in the business of breaking the hearts of beautiful girls."

That's the thing about Jude – he's just all round too nice. Laurel was my replacement when I left, and she fell head over heels in love with Jude within the first two weeks on the job. Laurel is beautiful. An all-American girl with blonde bangs and a shy smile that can melt even the lowest tipper's heart. She's perfect for Jude, in every way except one. He's just not that into her.

"I guess it would give her the wrong impression," I sigh, then, in a flash of inspiration, "what about CeeCee? She's single! And you certainly wouldn't have to worry about breaking her heart."

"Because she doesn't have one?"

I slap his arm.

"I'm joking! But still, no. Thanks, Jojo, but I'd rather go on my own."

"Oh, come on! You and CeeCee get on fine. She's gorgeous, and I know she finds you attractive. You deserve a night of guilt-free, meaningless sex."

"Oh really? And what would you know about that?" He's teasing, but I blush to the roots of my hair. I've never actually told Jude the truth, but he figured it out anyway. At least, I think he did. It's hard to say for sure.

"Cat got your tongue, Jojo?"

"No. I'm trying to formulate an argument."

"Ah," he nods his head gravely. "Not so easy to do when you're tanked."

"True. I still think you should go with CeeCee."

"So I can have guilt-free, meaningless sex?"

"Yes!"

"You're adorable when you're shit-faced."

I stay with Jude until I'm sober enough to navigate the sidewalk without an escort.

"Home, Miss Hudson?" Phillip asks.

"Yes, please."

I rest my head against the window, the cool glass heaven against my flaming cheeks. Jude's right, CeeCee *is* a terrible influence. We take a left turn, and I watch the people waiting for the light. A streak of dark-blond hair, and then we're passed. I whip my head around, but it's impossible to see anything through the crowd gathered on the sidewalk.

"Are you alright, Miss Hudson?" Phillip asks, more amused than concerned.

"I think I'm seeing things," I mutter, and then, before he can ask me what, I quickly add, "I may have had a bit too much champagne at breakfast."

"That's nothing two Tylenol, a big glass of water, and an hour-long nap can't cure," Phillip replies helpfully.

I decide to take his advice. Fenn doesn't bat an eyelid when I tell her I'm not feeling well and that I'm going to lie down for an hour.

Noodle is less impressed, especially when I lock her out of the bedroom.

"I'll take her for a walk when I take my lunch," Fenn promises.

"Thanks, Fenn."

I lie on my bed and close my eyes, willing sleep to come. Sleep does no such thing. Instead, I replay the two sightings of the blond man over and over in my head, trying to recall if at any point I got a clear view of his face. *No,* I scold myself. *You didn't. You're just thinking of him because the book is about to launch. Go to sleep.*

"Jojo?"

I jerk awake with a start.

"Sorry!" Fenn apologizes sheepishly. She's poked her head around my bedroom door. "I just thought I should let you know I'm headed out." I glance at my watch. It's after three. I slept the entire afternoon.

"Are you feeling okay?" Fenn asks.

"Yes, I'm fine. I took some pills, they must have knocked me out."

"Okay, well I took Noodle for a walk. Ursula is still here, so I've left her in the kitchen. She's cooking something which smells heavenly. Do you need me to get you anything before I go?"

"No, I'm fine. I'm up."

"Then I'll see you tomorrow."

"Hey, you didn't tell me about your date."

"It was dreamy. No proposal, thank God, but the dress was a hit."

"I'm glad to hear it."

She flashes me a grin. "Enjoy your evening."

"You too."

I hear the receding click of her high heels on the tiled floor, and I slump back onto my pillows. I start filming the week after next. It's exactly the distraction I need. I just need to get through the launch first.

. . .

"OH MY GOD, Jojo, it's even better than I expected!" George booms in my ear. It's incredible how, when one is dreading something, time seems to fast-forward. The week leading up to the launch was a blur, and now, here I am, in a stunning black Vera Wang dress, my heart in my throat. George and I are crushed together in a sea of bodies, under an ambient light that makes everyone beautiful. "Everybody is here," George continues as a waiter struggling to hold a silver tray aloft squeezes past. George helps himself to a crab cake with one hand, while the other caresses the red satin of Sally's ample behind.

"Where is Susan?" I ask pointedly, trying not to look.

"She's here somewhere," George replies airily. "No doubt checking that the caterers haven't run out of crab."

"Isn't that *your* job?" I ask Sally. She gives me a look that could melt metal, but I hold her gaze defiantly. I'm an A-list Hollywood actress. She hasn't a hope in hell.

"Don't give Sal a hard time," George whines as Sally stalks off to stuff her face with buffalo wings.

"George, I love you, but I swear to God if you don't at least try to be discreet, I'm going to fire you as an agent. Susan is a saint."

"I never said she wasn't." He's so remarkably unapologetic and so naturally charming, it's impossible to stay mad at him.

I roll my eyes. "I don't know how she puts up with you."

"I'm incredibly well-hung. Now you better get your sweet ass over to the signing table, the queue is already halfway across the room."

"You've left grease stains all over Sally's ass," I say as I march off.

"You look like a woman on a mission." I raise my head at the sound of Jude's voice.

"I wondered where you were!"

"Did you think I was going to chicken out?"

I shake my head. "Never."

He holds up a copy of my book. "Can I get your autograph?"

"I was actually on my way to the signing table, but I suppose I could save you the wait."

He laughs as I scrawl across the title page. Jude takes it back and looks down at what I've written. He smiles when he sees I've signed it, *With Love, Josie* instead of Jojo.

"I like it," he says.

"Are you going to be around for a while?"

He looks over his shoulder at the length of the line. "You're going to be at it for hours. I'm probably going to head out."

"But you just got here! We haven't even had a minute to chat!"

"We can do that this week. You've got a busy night ahead."

"Fine," I grumble. "I am glad you came, though."

"I told you I wouldn't miss it." He kisses my temple and disappears into the throng.

I take my seat at the massive table and pick up the *Waterman* pen George gave me especially for tonight, my name engraved in the silver. George is a shit, but he's the best agent in the business, and I trust him. He gives his clients all the respect and attention he fails to give his wife.

"Jojo, look this way, please!" a reporter calls and then I'm off, posing for photographs and signing books until my wrists cramp. The line is never-ending.

"You look like you could use a break."

I look up to find Alex standing before me, a proud smile on his face, a copy of the book in his hand.

"You bought it?" I laugh. "I have a dozen copies at home!"

"I'm supporting my girl." He holds up the book. "And I want it signed, this is going to be worth a lot of money one day."

I take it and scrawl in the title page, covering my words with my free hand so he can't read them.

"Alex, Jojo!" A photographer calls. "This way, please!" Alex leans toward me, and the man gets his frontpage photograph.

"How much longer do you think I'll have to do this?" I ask.

Alex looks over his shoulder. "You're just about done. I'll buy you a drink after." A wink and a flash of white teeth and he's gone.

The line is definitely coming to an end, but if I never sign my name again, it'll be too soon. I barely look up as the next person in line steps forward.

"Could you personalize it?"

My head snaps up. All the air is driven from my lungs and my smile, which has never faltered in all my years in front of the camera, dies on my lips.

"Ace." It's a whisper, but he hears me.

"It's nice to see you again, Josie."

Oh God, that voice. That deep, husky, sex-is-mandatory voice. His face hasn't changed much. His blond hair is shorter, cropped close to his head, and a few lines crease the skin around his eyes when he smiles, but he is still staggering. His arms are broader, more tanned, and the blue silk shirt he's wearing is a perfect match for his eyes.

"You'll sign it, won't you?" I'm staring. I drop my gaze, cheeks flaming to find his hand on the table before me. He's holding my book. *Holy fucking hell.*

6

"Ace, what are you doing here?"

The book is still in his hands. I don't want to touch it.

"What, I can't support an old friend?" His eyes dance with amusement. He's enjoying the fact that he still makes me nervous. *Bastard.*

"I wouldn't exactly call us old friends."

"Then what would you call us, Josie?" It's a challenge, laid down bold and bare.

"Acquaintances. At best."

"Everything okay here?" George appears as if by magic and manages to smile at Ace and frown at me at the same time. "There are still a few people waiting, Jojo."

"We're almost done," I tell him. Satisfied, George wanders off in the direction of the food table.

I snatch the book from Ace's hands. My fingers brush against his, and I swear I feel sparks fly where our skin touches.

"You can't have this," I tell him firmly.

"And why is that?"

"I..." I lick my lips and stumble for an excuse. "I just don't want you to have it."

"I've paid for it."

"I'll reimburse you."

"Excuse me, is this going to take long?" A raven-haired woman leans around Ace to ask. Then she catches sight of his face. A red-taloned finger comes to rest on his shoulder. "Sorry," she purrs, "I don't mean to rush you."

Ace shrugs. "That's okay." He yanks the book out of my hands. "I'll wait until you're done."

The rest of the signing is a blur. All I am conscious of is the fact that Ace has moved to the back of the line and every autograph brings him closer to the table. My pen tears through paper as the raven-haired woman saunters to his side and engages him in conversation. Her lipstick is the same color as Sally's dress.

"I'm so sorry," I tell the person whose book I just ruined. I pull another from the display pile at the edge of the table and sign it. "Here you go."

"I can't wait to read it," the next person in line tells me. "I'm such a fan!"

"Thank you so much. I hope you enjoy it."

"Could you possibly sign it to Tiffany?"

"Sure." I scrawl her name in the top right corner. Red lips is smiling up at Ace, her body arched toward him.

Sign. I've lost sight of them.

Sign. He's smiling back.

"Who is Josie?" a man in a grey pinstripe suit frowns down at his signed copy.

"Sorry!" I snatch it back and pull another copy from the decorative pile. "Here you go."

Finally, there's no one left.

"Let's try this again," Ace asks, stepping up to the table. The woman stands just behind him, waiting for him to finish. Ace turns to her, and I catch a whiff of his cologne.

"Sweetheart," he drawls lazily, "why don't you go and get yourself a glass of champagne. I'll meet you at the bar."

I swear if a lioness looked at a stag the way she's looking at him right now, it would die a blissful, pain-free death of testosterone overload. She sashays off in the direction of the bar.

"Give it back," I snap, refusing to look at him.

His voice is nothing like it was when speaking to the lioness, all trace of charm gone. "Why don't you want me to read it?"

"I just don't." I feel pricks of shame in the corners of my eyes, and I swat them away.

Ace braces his hands on the edge of the table and leans forward, so close that our noses are almost touching. "Does it have anything to do with chapter twenty-seven, Josie?" he asks.

I can't breathe. I jerk away from him, my back slamming into the back of my chair.

"Jojo?"

Oh God, oh God. Alex. Alex is here. He's standing next to Ace, a concerned expression on his beautifully familiar face.

I try to sound normal. "Hi."

Wrong. He knows me too well. Alex is sizing Ace up, and Ace hasn't moved. He's still crouched over me, his hands splayed on the table. No wedding ring.

"I'm almost done," I say, giving Alex a reassuring smile. He hesitates, torn between his need to protect me and making a scene in front of the entire Hollywood press.

"I think George wants you to start the interviews," he tells me. "I'll wait right over here." He moves away, but not far enough that he can't keep an eye on me.

Ace still hasn't moved.

"Please," I whisper. I don't know what I'm asking.

"We're not done," he replies. "Meet me tomorrow at *Gerard's*. I'll be there at eleven."

He takes his unsigned book with him.

7

By ten thirty the following morning I'm a bundle of nerves. My deepest darkest fear has literally become a reality. I take a cab to *Gerard's*, rather than let Phillip drive me. The subterfuge makes me feel even worse. The inside of the diner hasn't changed. I haven't been here in years, but it's still a popular college hangout, judging by the patrons. I slip into the red leather booth at the very end. I make sure to sit facing the wall, but I still tug at my beanie.

A frazzled waitress sidles over. "What can I get you?"

"Coffee, please. Black, no sugar."

"Anything to eat?"

"No, thanks."

My untouched coffee grows cold on the table. I check my watch. It's 10:56.

"You want another?" the waitress asks, looking at my full cup with a puzzled expression.

"I'm okay for now, thank you. I'm actually meeting someone, so I'll order another when he arrives."

She gives me a knowing look. "Got it. Just call me if you need anything."

The bell above the door jangles.

"Hey stranger!" the waitress calls. "Where have you been?"

"Would you believe it if I told you I'd gone off coffee?" I'd know that voice anywhere.

"Not in a million years," the waitress laughs. "She yours?"

I cringe, imagining Ace looking at the back of my head.

"Sure is," he replies easily. "Could you bring us two coffees, please, Marla?"

He's getting nearer, I can sense him, and then a denim-clad leg appears beside me.

"Hello Josie," his voice is softer than it was last night, more coaxing. He drops into the seat opposite me, larger than life. He's wearing a black sweater, V-necked and form-fitted. I've never seen a simple sweater look that good.

"Why am I here?" I ask. I'd already decided the best defense is a good offense, especially where Ace is concerned.

He frowns at me. "You're not going to ask me how I've been? What I've been up to these past six years?"

"I don't care."

A cup thumps onto the table before me. Perfect timing that Marla should arrive just in time to hear me say that. I keep my eyes lowered, terrified she'll recognize me if I look up.

"Here you go," she says, setting Ace's cup down far more gently. "You want anything to eat, John?"

John. It was so easy to forget his real name. Ace had started the first week of college. There were three Johns in our class. Usually, the lecturers would simply call them by the last names, but in this case, King and Jackman had been too good an opportunity to pass up. Ace's last name is Logan, but he'd become Ace. Ace, King and Jack. The joke had led to the three becoming friends, and they were seldom seen apart for the remaining three years at Julliard.

"I wouldn't mind a big plate of French fries. You want anything, Josie?"

"No, I'm good."

"Just the fries, then."

As soon as she's out of earshot, I try again. "What do you want, Ace?"

He takes a swig of his coffee. "Hardly anyone calls me that anymore."

"You must be devastated."

He stares at me over the rim of his cup. "When did you become so bitter?"

"Bitter? I'm not bitter, Ace. You ambushed me at my book launch, threatened me, and now I'm here, with no clue why. Forgive me if I'm not thrilled about it."

"If you're not thrilled now, wait until I tell you why you're here." It's a threat – implied, but a threat nonetheless.

"You read my book."

"I did. Last week actually." I don't bother asking how he got his hands on a copy when the book was under a worldwide embargo until last night. What would be the point? I can hardly file a lawsuit against the person who leaked it, not without revealing how I know and the reason I care. "It was good," Ace continues, "you're a good writer. A better actress, and an even better pianist, but the writing was solid." I don't have anything to say to that, so I keep quiet. When he speaks again, his voice is like silk. "Chapter twenty-seven, Josie?"

"My name is Jojo."

"You're deflecting."

I slam my hands down on the table. "What do you want me to say?"

"I want you to tell me why you lied."

"That's none of your business."

"I think it's very much my business."

"Why?" I sneer, anger radiating off me in waves. "Because you screwed me once, six years ago, and now you want to cash in?"

He settles back in his seat, completely unperturbed by my outburst. A flash of pity and then he smiles. "Actually, that's exactly what I want to do."

I should have expected it, but I'm still stunned when I hear the words. Furious, I snatch up my purse.

"Fine," I say, rooting around for my checkbook. "Name your price. If it's money you're after, just tell me how much so I can get on with my life."

"I don't want your money. At least not directly," he taunts.

I stifle the urge to scream. "Then what do you want?"

He smiles again, and it turns my blood to ice. "The same thing every Julliard graduate wants. Fame and fortune."

I gape at him. Marla arrives with the fries, and he coats them in ketchup while I watch in stunned silence.

"Here's the thing, Josie. I have a feeling that this secret could seriously impact your reputation. Your fiancé doesn't know either, does he?" He stares at me in silence and I feel the blood drain from my face. "I'll take that as a yes. So... reputation, career, fiancé. All the things you stand to lose if I go to the press."

"Why are you doing this?" I would never have expected this of him. He might've been an asshole once, but he wasn't a bad person. In fact, he was probably the nicest guy I ever knew, until he wasn't.

"I'm actually doing you a solid. You have the opportunity to salvage two of those things."

Two of those things. My reputation and my career. The only two that go hand in hand.

"No." I get to my feet. "I'm not doing this."

"Sit down, Jojo." His voice is clipped, all trace of charm vanished. I don't miss the fact that he's spoken my instantly recognizable name out loud. It's another threat, clear as day. I sit.

"You want me to break it off with Alex. Why?"

He grins. "Why do you think?"

I shake my head in horrified disbelief. "Fuck you, Ace."

"Well, I didn't expect you to take it that far, but I'd hardly say no."

"You want me to dump my fiancé and become what – your girlfriend?"

"Not forever. Just as long as it takes for me to establish myself." He pops a few fries in his mouth. I feel sick.

"You couldn't cut it as an actor on your own, and you expect to make it by riding my coattails? Are you delusional? This business doesn't work that way."

"This business works exactly that way, and you know it."

"I can't make you a star, Ace. Hell, I didn't even make myself one, I just got a lucky break."

"You have a lot more power in this business than you give yourself credit for."

I give him a scathing look while I try to think of a way out of this mess.

"Fine," I concede with a sigh. "I'll help you. I'll take you to events, put you in touch with the right people... all of it. But I don't need to break up with Alex and fake-date you to do that."

"No deal. The dating part is mandatory."

"Why?"

"Remember Jack Danvers?"

Everyone remembers Jack Danvers. Second husband of mega-star Sarah Carter, Jack was a nobody. Until his raging affair with Sarah came to light.

"Jack isn't famous, he's infamous," I point out. "He may be a household name, but everybody hates him."

"Only because he broke up a marriage. Last I checked you and Mr. *Forbes List* hadn't tied the knot yet."

Inwardly, I curse having had to delay the wedding because of studio commitments. Outwardly, I give Ace the filthiest look I can manage.

"He'll never buy it," I say. "Alex won't just accept me leaving him."

"Then I suggest you make your performance believable."

I can't believe we're having this conversation. "How did you become this person? You were a good guy, Ace."

"Not good enough for you, apparently." There's a bitterness to his voice that jolts me.

"It doesn't have to be like this. We were friends, once. We can be again. I can help you, I'll do everything in my power to help you, but not like this. It's extortion."

Ace yawns.

"I love him, Ace."

"You'll get over it."

He is so cold, so cruel, that I snatch up my purse.

"Go to hell. Do your worst, I'll just deny it. Who do you think Hollywood will believe – America's sweetheart, or the bastard trying to get his fifteen minutes of fame?"

Ace picks up his phone. "I thought you might say that. Fortunately for me, I have evidence."

"You're lying."

His lip curls. "Check your email. I'll expect to read about your break up by the end of the week. And Jojo," he adds as I turn to leave. "I'm not a patient man. Don't keep me waiting."

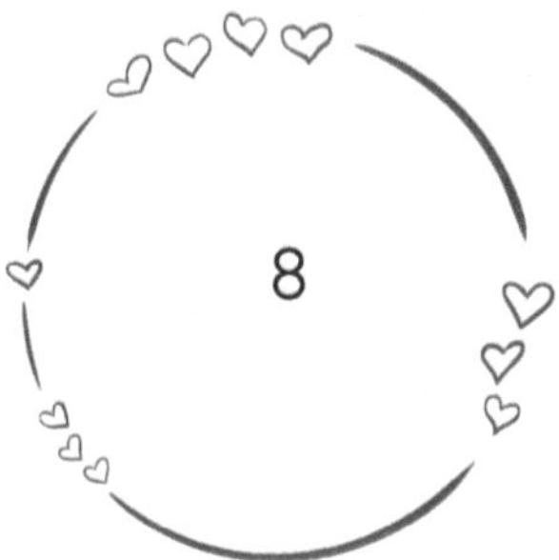

Oh my God. The photographs. We took photos. The memory comes flooding back and my face burns as I scroll through the images Ace has sent to my email. I'm lying naked in his bed, mascara smudged beneath my eyes. My hair is a dark mass against the cream sheets, and the empty Vodka bottle is visible on the bedside table. Ace is smiling down at me. The other images are taken at various times during the course of that night. We're half dressed, playing strip poker. We're doing Tequila shots, grimacing as we tear into slices of lemon. I'm dancing on a table, the result of a lost dare. In every picture, I'm gazing up at him through heavy-lidded eyes. The wanton look on my face is all the evidence he needs. I shove my phone back into my purse and lean back against the worn seat of the cab. One night. One stupid night and a handful of drunken selfies is going to destroy my entire life.

I'd been lovesick for John Logan from the first time I laid eyes on him. Even before he got given the nickname Ace. We shared a lot of the same classes, but he'd never noticed me in that way. He was always friendly – that was just how he was – but it wasn't until we'd landed the lead roles in a major production Julliard was putting on at a local theatre that I'd made any headway. We'd had to spend a lot of time together. I'd cherished every single moment. The night we wrapped, our entire senior class had turned up for the party, and I'd had far too much to drink.

"Miss?" The cab driver's voice yanks me back to the present. We're outside my building.

"Thanks." I hand him a crumpled bill. "Keep the change."

I go straight to my bathroom and splash cold water on my face. The eyes staring back at me in the mirror are hollow. My hair is lighter now, honeyed highlights softening the dark, and a smattering of faint freckles dusts my nose and cheeks. I find myself wondering if Ace still finds me attractive, and then berate myself for giving a damn.

He'd been so sweet that night. He'd taken care of me, made sure that I was looked after. He'd seen me safely home. Then he'd seen me naked. My roommate, Casey, had hooked up with John Kingman, and she wasn't coming home.

I still don't remember who made the first move. One minute we were saying goodbye, the next, his lips were on mine, and we were kissing as though we no longer needed air to survive. If he'd taken me to my bedroom, then and there, I would've let him. Instead, he'd led me to the couch, his wicked smile full of promise. We'd played strip poker. Slowly. Ace had refused to let me drink anymore. He'd taken my shots for me, until his beautiful blue eyes were crossing.

"Why?" I'd asked as I'd peeled off my top after a spectacularly bad hand.

"You've had enough," he'd said firmly. "I don't want you to regret this."

By the time I was down to my underwear, I was squirming with desire. Ace was wearing only his boxers and one black sock.

"You lose," he murmured, showing his hand.

I reached behind me to unhook my bra, but his hand closed around my wrist. His eyes bore into mine. "Let me," he whispered. It was my undoing. He was pretty drunk, and his fingers fumbled a few times, but under his expert hands, I'd unraveled.

"Jojo?"

At the sound of Fenn's voice, I whirl toward the bathroom door. I can picture her standing on the other side, checking her watch.

"Yes?" I croak.

"We need to leave now if we're going to make it on time."

THE DISTRACTION I've been waiting for is a hollow victory. Filming starts this afternoon, and this is a role I've been looking forward to for months. The movie is a dark thriller, and I play a woman who falls in love with her best friend's husband. It's my most dramatic role to date.

I spend two hours in hair and makeup and then check my phone to find a text from Alex, wishing me good luck and promising that he'll see me tomorrow morning before work. The filming schedule begins with two weeks of night work, so our schedules will be conflicting until then. I can't bring myself to reply to his text.

"Your eyes are watering Miss Hudson," my make-up artist warns. I blink rapidly a few times and close my eyes.

We work for eight hours straight, breaking only for drinks of warm water laced with honey to preserve our voices, and one light meal. The director, Harrison Garfield, is in the twilight of his career and has been around long enough that he still remembers a time when actors and actresses weren't prone to being spoilt. He's both brilliant and brutal.

"Cut!" he yells for what feels like the hundredth time. "Jojo, you are meeting the love of your life for a night of pure passion. Could you try to look pleased about it, sweetheart?"

My handsome co-star chuckles.

"You look a little too pleased for a man beginning to suspect his lover might be a psychopath, Blake," Harrison snaps. Blake gives me a discreet wink. We've worked together before. Blake is happily married with two kids, and Alex and I have had numerous lunches with him and his wife. I smile back, but both of us are far more somber as we get back to work.

Fenn is wilting on the drive home. She doesn't need to attend the set every day, but she always comes with me on the first day of filming, to check that every clause in my contract is being upheld.

"I'll see you tomorrow," she yawns when Phillip pulls up outside her house. Seb waves at us through the window and I wave back. I've always liked Fenn's boyfriend. He is unapologetically honest, and he adores Fenn.

It's well past midnight when I finally collapse into bed. I check my phone to find another message from Alex. *Goodnight, beautiful.* I pull my pillow over my head and sob until my chest aches.

When Alex arrives the following morning, I've composed myself. I've deliberately dressed down and left my hair loose, but I did apply a liberal amount of foundation to cover the angry red blotches on my face. That's what a night spent crying gets me.

I'm sitting at the kitchen counter, a cup of coffee in hand when he walks in. I don't lift my chin when he leans down to kiss me hello.

Ever perceptive, Alex picks up on it immediately. "What's wrong?"

I take a deep breath. "We need to talk."

He opens the refrigerator and pours himself some orange juice. "That sounds serious," he smiles.

"It is."

His smile falters, and I set down my cup.

"I need a break."

"What?"

"I know that sounds cheesy, but I've been doing a lot of thinking, and I just don't think I can handle us right now, not with everything else going on."

He's frozen in place, the still-open fridge sending a cool blast of air toward me. "Is this a joke?"

"No."

In an instant, he's at my side. "You can't be serious."

"I am. Very serious."

"Are you seeing someone else?"

Well, that escalated quickly. "No, of course not."

"Then what? You're not in love with me anymore?" I've never heard him sound so scathing.

"It's not that." I can't bring myself to say it. He knows me too well, he will see right through me.

"Then what is it?"

"I just... I need some time apart."

"Don't give me that bullshit! I'm leaving for South America in two days, you'll have ten days on your own. We barely see enough of each other as it is."

"I know. I'm sorry, I wish I could explain. I'm trying—"

He cuts across me, a whiplash. "Try harder."

"Alex, please. I just need some time to sort my head out."

"You're asking me for a *break*? What are we, seventeen?" He snatches up my hand and shoves it into my face until the five-carat diamond is all I can see.

"Ouch! Alex, you're hurting me."

"Good. Then you know how I feel. This is not a joke, Jojo. I proposed, you accepted. You don't get to just walk away from that."

I jerk my hand free and get to my feet. "I decide what I get to do," I snap. My hand tingles as the blood rushes back to my fingers. I rub at the red mark he left there. Alex catches sight of it, and all the fight goes out of him.

"Jesus, I'm sorry." He takes a step toward me, but I hold up both my hands, warding him off. I'm not afraid of him. I'm afraid of losing my resolve if he touches me, but Alex can't see that.

"I didn't mean to," he whispers.

"I know."

"You're making a mistake. You *know* you're making a mistake."

I swallow the lump in my throat and slide the ring from my finger. My hand feels naked without it. "Here."

"No." He shakes his head in denial. "Please don't do this. I'm leaving soon anyway. Take two weeks, get your head right. I won't contact you, and we can talk again when I'm back."

"I don't think that's going to happen." I'm dangerously close to losing it. I set the ring in his hand. "I'm sorry, Alex, but for now this is it. It's over."

On Saturday morning, without work to occupy my mind, I wander around the house in a depressed daze. I haven't heard from Alex. I hate myself for doing it, but on Wednesday I leaked a story to the press about our break up. I hate what this must be doing to him. For the thousandth time, I curse the day I started writing that book. I lied, that's the bottom line. After losing my virginity to Ace only to have him walk away without so much as a second glance, I wanted to forget it ever happened. I buried it and started fresh. He had taken something beautiful from me, so I had simply taken it back. I'd never told a single soul about Ace. Not even my roommate at the time had known. When I'd woken up in the morning to find Ace gone, I'd been gutted. I'd walked through the apartment looking for him. All I'd found was Casey, hungover and eating toast. She must have just got back; her hair was still wet from the shower.

At first, I thought maybe he'd just gone home for a change of clothes. It was probably best that Casey didn't see him. He'd been top of her hit list for a few months, and he'd rejected her on numerous occasions, which had only fuelled Casey's desire to have him. It was only when she told me that Ace was leaving for Paris that night that I realized I'd been played.

"You didn't know?" Casey had asked. "Where've you been all semester? He was offered a place in the theatre abroad program months ago. *Everybody* knew he was going."

BLINKING BACK TEARS OF ANGER, I fetch Noodle's leash from the hall.

"Let's go for a walk," I tell her. Noodle yaps in agreement.

I walk right into him in the lobby.

"I read about your break up," he says, "I'm sorry things didn't work out."

I grit my teeth and shove past him, but of course he follows me onto the street.

"Cute dog. What's her name?"

"Screw you."

"Interesting choice. I would've gone for something a little more fitting. Runt, maybe, or Street Rat."

Sensing my distress, Noodle growls at him. Ace drops to his knee and disarms her in five seconds flat. I watch his fingers kneading the tips of her pointed ears, and I feel a wave of hatred surge inside me.

"What do you want?"

"What do you mean? I'm here for our first date. I figured I wouldn't hold my breath waiting for your call." He stands and takes the lead from my hands. I jerk away as his free hand comes around my waist.

"What the hell do you think you're doing?"

"I'm giving them something to report." I don't know how he spotted the paparazzi, but he points directly at them. Two men in grey hoodies with long-range camera lenses pointed right at us.

"I only broke up with Alex four days ago," I hiss. "Can't we at least wait a few weeks?" All I can think of is Alex asking if I'd met someone else. I'd told him no.

"Sadly not," Ace says. His fingers brush the top of my buttocks as his hand returns to my waist. "Now, where are we off to? The park?" he gives a low whistle, and Noodle jumps on the spot. "Definitely the park," Ace laughs.

"I hate you."

He doesn't respond, only pulls me tighter against his side. He's enjoying this. I figure the paparazzi have enough photographs to last a lifetime by the time we make our way back home. My shoulders are aching with being tensed for so long, and my heart is in ribbons. Alex and I will never come back from this.

"What did you see in him, anyway?" Ace asks as if reading my thoughts.

"You mean other than the fact that he's handsome, successful, and the most considerate man on the planet?"

"You can't possibly know that for sure. Have you *met* every man on the planet?"

"You don't get to make jokes about it. This is my *life* we're talking about."

Frank narrows his eyes as we pass, but he doesn't say anything. My stomach curls as we ride the elevator up. Ursula doesn't work weekends, and the thought of being alone with Ace is terrifying. Who knows what he's capable of.

"What happened to you?" I ask abruptly. "You were voted most likely to succeed. You had the respect of every person in our class. You got into the abroad program, which is basically the fast-track to success. What happened?"

He meets my gaze. Something flickers in his blue eyes. "I had a change of heart. I dropped out after one semester."

"You stopped acting? Why?"

"I wanted to do something else. I was only in France for six months."

"What did you want to do?"

The elevator door opens, and his mask slips back into place.

"After you," he says, sweeping his arm out before him.

I snatch Noodle's leash and stomp to my door. "Before you get any ideas, you should know I studied martial arts for six months when I filmed *Heaven Rising*."

His cheek dimples. "Good to know."

As we move through my apartment, I can't help but see it through his eyes. Every luxury now feels like more motive for him to follow through with his revolting plan. To my surprise, he barely seems to notice his surroundings. Instead, he flops onto the cream couch in the living room and switches on the television.

"How long do you plan on staying?" I ask. "I have work to do."

His eyes don't leave the screen. "Go ahead, I'll be fine."

Noodle leaps onto the couch beside him and lays her head in his lap. I storm out of the room, but I can hear him chuckling all the way to my office.

Twenty minutes later, Ace sticks his head into the office. "Is something burning?" He catches sight of the flames coming from my bin and leaps into action. "What the fuck, Josie!" He scans the surface of my desk and grabs my water jug. The water douses the flames, leaving behind a haze of smoke and the acrid smell of burning paper.

"Are those your books?" Ace asks, peering into the bin. I smile sweetly, but my triumph is short-lived. Ace throws back his head and laughs.

"You burnt them? You think the truth is that easy to hide? There are hundreds of thousands of copies all across the globe. Besides," he adds, tapping a lean finger to his temple. "It's all up here, Jojo. Every sexy second of it."

"I wouldn't call your drunken fumbling sexy."

"Funny, because that's exactly what you called it that night." He raises the pitch of his voice and groans in a breathless whisper. "God, you're sexy. Don't stop, Ace. Please, don't stop."

All the blood rushes to my head as he repeats the words I moaned that night, almost verbatim. I gape at him, mortified. He taps his finger against his temple again. "All up here," he echoes.

I choke back a sob. "You're a bastard."

"And you're a spoilt brat."

My phone rings and we both jump. It's Alex. I can't answer it. I know exactly why he's calling. The rumor mill operates at lightning speed.

Tears well in my eyes. "Please leave," I beg. "I'll go through with this, but for now, please just go and leave me alone."

Ace walks forward and checks the screen on my phone. His face betrays not an ounce of sympathy when he reads Alex's name.

"You don't seem to understand how this works, princess," he tells me. "I live here now. I'm not going anywhere."

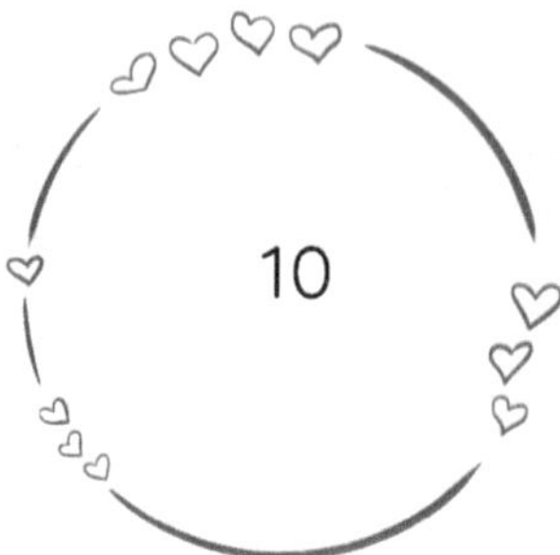

I spend the weekend hibernating in my bedroom and ignoring Alex's calls. I finally cave and listen to his voice mails. The fury and despair in his voice crucify me, but I don't call him back.

Ace has been quiet. I hear him moving around, but I don't see him again until Sunday evening when he barges into my bedroom without knocking.

"Get your ass out of that bed and into the shower. I've made soup, it'll be ready in ten minutes."

"I'm not hungry."

"I don't care. I've made it, and you'll eat it, even if I have to force feed it down your throat. God, Jojo, I never figured you for such a wuss."

"And I never figured you would turn out to be the world's biggest prick!"

He gives me an encouraging nod. "That's the spirit. Now get up. If you're not at the table in fifteen minutes, I'll be back to fetch you."

I take one look at the soup and push the plate aside. "I hate mushrooms."

"No, you don't. You love mushrooms."

"How would you know?"

"Because I watched you inhale a whole bowl after Hamlet."

It had been a first-year Julliard production. "You weren't even in Hamlet."

"No, but Kingman was. I spent a lot of time backstage with him."

"Do you still keep in contact with him?"

"I see him from time to time. He lives out in Vermont, teaches drama at his local college. Do you know he married Simone Wells? I think she played the clarinet."

I did know, but I'd never liked Simone. "Does Kingman know you've stooped to blackmailing women?"

"No. Although, considering his looks, I'm pretty sure he didn't land Simone the conventional way." Ace has a way of saying outrageous things in such a dead-pan manner I'm not sure when he's serious.

"Are you going to tell me why you quit acting?"

"I already did."

I shake my head and take a spoonful of soup. It's not bad.

"Where did you learn to cook?"

He gives me a wry look. "So you're speaking to me now?"

"I have staff, they'll be back tomorrow. I assume the sooner we get you in the spotlight, the sooner you'll be gone, so I guess it's in my best interest to make this performance believable."

"You see, that wasn't so hard, was it?"

There's a long silence while we eat.

"My mother taught me how to cook," he admits eventually. "She actually worked in a diner before she married my dad. She always wanted to have her own restaurant."

"Maybe when you're rich and famous you could set her up," I snap.

"She died, shortly after I left Julliard."

I wince. "I'm sorry."

"Why? It wasn't your fault."

"What happened?"

His face tightens. “She was in the wrong place at the wrong time.”

I can tell from his expression that the subject is closed.

“And your dad?”

“He moved to the west coast shortly after it happened. He has a brother out there. They play bowls.”

I open my mouth to ask him if his dad is any good but then decide against it. I don’t want to know. Hearing him speak about his family only makes him seem more human, and I don’t want to think of him as anything but the man intent on destroying my life.

“What about your parents?” Ace asks, seemingly oblivious to the turmoil waging war inside me. “Do they still live out in Connecticut?”

My spoon drops into the bowl with a clatter. “Enough. Stop acting as if we’re so close you remember anything about me.”

“But I do remember.”

“Why?”

“Why do I remember you telling me your parents lived in Bridgeport?” he seems genuinely confused.

“No, why do you care?”

“I’m just making conversation.”

I drop my chin to my chest and squeeze my eyes tightly shut. When I look up again, I’ve composed myself.

“I’m going to bed. I have to be on set early tomorrow.”

Ace gets to his feet and stacks my bowl on top of his. “What time are we leaving?”

“I am leaving at seven. You’re not coming with me.”

“I am, actually. What better way for me to start rubbing shoulders with the who’s who of Hollywood.”

I scramble for an excuse. “It’s a closed set.”

“Uh-huh. Sure it is,” he calls my bluff.

“Fine, it’s not a closed set, but I can’t have you wandering around getting in everyone’s way.”

“Don’t worry, you won’t even know I’m there.”

. . .

WHEN I GET BACK to my room, my phone is ringing. I glance at the screen, bracing myself for the gut-twisting pain that plagues me every time I see Alex's name. Instead, a new terror comes over me. "Jojo!" CeeCee yells the second I answer. "I'm your fucking publicist, and I have to read about your break up on page two! What the hell is going on?" Knowing CeeCee, she's as upset about page two as she is about me not telling her, but the death of a politician this week trumped my life events.

"I'm sorry, CeeCee. Everything happened so suddenly, I didn't even think."

"Jojo, you know how this works. We issue a joint statement, we protect your image. We get on top of things before the rumor mill spins it out of our control. What we *don't* do, is get caught on camera with our new boyfriend only days after a break-up."

I wince. "I don't know what to say. I'm sorry."

"Sorry isn't going to help." A note of pity creeps into her voice. "The public will crucify you for this."

"What do I do?"

"We need to issue a statement, immediately. I'll call it through to the newsroom tonight. Ray Jenkins owes me a favor, I'll get him to print it in tomorrow afternoon's papers. And none of this page two bullshit, either. It won't fix things, but it will soften the blow. In the meantime, you break up with that Tom Hardy wannabe and get back together with Alex. The only thing the public likes more than a nasty break-up is a romantic reconciliation."

I take a deep breath. "I can't do that."

"I'm not asking you, Jojo."

"It's over between me and Alex."

"I don't care. You're an actress, Jojo, so act. Alex won't want any bad publicity either, not with the foreign investments he's raking in. He'll play along. Just ride it out a few more weeks and then we can stage a mutual separation. You still have deep respect for one another, you wish each other only the best, et cetera et cetera."

"CeeCee you're not listening. I can't do it. You're going to have to find another way."

"There is no other way!"

"You're the best publicist in Hollywood. You'll find one. Say whatever you need to, I give you full permission to quote me."

I hang up before she can respond. I know CeeCee. Her ego is her downfall. If I say she can find a way, she'll damned well find a way, and I pray that she does because it looks like I might lose my reputation and my career along with Alex after all.

I switch off my phone and crawl between the sheets. I can't believe that in such a short space of time my entire life has gone right down the shit chute.

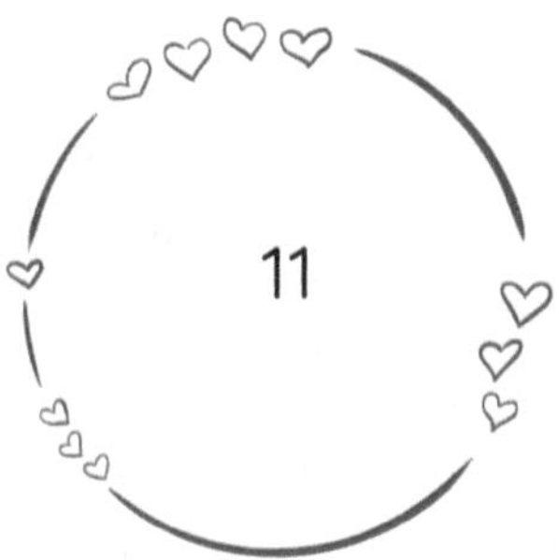

On set the following day, Ace is true to his word. I've barely seen him and, so far, no one has complained about him being there. By midday, I've almost forgotten that he's here until one of the make -up artists touching up my face asks me if the gorgeous blond man over there is one of my co-stars. I follow the line of her gaze to find Ace engaged in conversation with my stunt double. As we watch, she laughs uproariously at something he's said.

"No," I tell her firmly, "he's not."

I wave away her attempt to re-apply my lipstick.

"I'll come back. I need something to eat."

Ace joins me at the food table. "You're doing well," he remarks idly. "I was watching you earlier. You've come a long way from Julliard."

I pile salad onto my plate, refusing to acknowledge the compliment.

"How much longer do you have to stay?"

"We only have to re-shoot one scene. Probably an hour or so."

"Right, well there's something I need to do, so I'll just see you at home."

The casual way he says the word sets my hackles arise, but I grit my teeth. "Fine."

"I thought maybe we could go out for dinner tonight."

"I'm really not up to it. It's been a long day." I wait for him to reply but he doesn't, and when I raise my eyes to look at him, there's a resolute expression on his face.

"I'll book a table for seven," he says.

Fenn walks in as he's walking out. We'd left before she arrived for work this morning so this is the first time she's laying eyes on Ace. I'm surprised she doesn't give herself whiplash with the way she cranes her neck over her shoulder as he passes by. There's a newspaper tucked under her arm.

"Fenn, what are you doing here?"

"I tried you on your cell, but you didn't pick up."

"I'm working," I remind her pointedly. I never have my phone switched on during filming.

"I know. You don't have access to email either, and I thought you might want to see this before you go outside." She hands me the paper.

I flip it open and clap a hand to my mouth. The headline is enormous, taking up almost the entire front page. *JOJO FOLLOWS HER HEART*! Below is a black and white photo taken of Ace and I walking away from my apartment, his arm around my waist. With an expert eye, I scan my own face in the image. I don't look unhappy. In fact, my expression as I look up into Ace's eyes is one I never want to see on my face again.

"How did I not know any of this?" Fenn asks. That's the problem with Fenn. She's an excellent assistant, but she's too shrewd for her own good.

I ignore her and scan the article. Holy hell. I am going to murder CeeCee. It reads like a cliched rom-com. College sweethearts forced apart by circumstances. According to the article, I'm quoted as being the happiest I've ever been, although I regret the pain I have caused Alex and hope that one day he can come to understand that I had to follow my heart. I reach for my phone, realize it's stowed in my dressing room and hold out my hand for Fenn's.

"I need to call CeeCee."

"Uh huh." The look she gives me is pure 'I told you so' but she hands it over.

I'm just scrolling for CeeCee's number when Harrison barks. "Should we start without you, Jojo?" Given that the scene we're about to film features me exclusively, I take it that's a rhetorical question.

"I'll just wait in your dressing room," Fenn whispers, before hurrying off. She's always been terrified of Harrison. I take a deep breath and remove the dressing gown I wear during breaks to protect my clothing. The make-up artist darts forward and touches up my lipstick. Five minutes later, the camera is rolling.

When Harrison calls it a wrap for the day, I heave a sigh of relief. I can tell he's not impressed with my performance, but considering the day I've had, I don't feel as guilty as I should. I re-read the article on the way to my dressing room.

Wordlessly, Fenn hands me my phone.

"Is it true?" she asks while I wait for CeeCee to answer.

"Parts of it."

"Hello, lovely." I hear CeeCee purr down the line, "I gather you've seen the papers."

"I have. What were you thinking? When I said you needed to come up with something, this is not what I had in mind."

"Well, seeing as you didn't tell me what you did have in mind, I had to be creative," she counters.

"You've made it sound like I've spent the last six years pining for Ace!"

"I've made you seem less like a cold-hearted bitch who broke Alex's heart for the first cockafella who crossed your path." By her tone, I suspect that's exactly what she thinks I've done.

"Ace and I weren't college sweethearts. Anyone who went to Julliard with us will vouch for that."

"You were there at the same time. It's enough. I'm more concerned about what happened after college, to be honest."

"What do you mean?"

"I used every single resource at my disposal, Jojo, and believe me, I have plenty. You know what I found out about John Logan between when he left Julliard for France and the present day?"

Despite myself, my curiosity is piqued. "What?"

"Nothing. Absolutely nothing. It's like he fell off the face of the earth. There's no record of him anywhere. No employment history, no credit record, not one single social media account."

"That's impossible."

"My point exactly. How well do you know this man, Jojo? And why, pray tell, would you throw everything away for someone you clearly haven't seen in years?"

"It's complicated."

There's a long silence. "Should I be worried? Are you in some kind of trouble?"

"No. No, it's nothing like that."

"Look, this article is damage control. Your reputation should recover. I just hope you know what you're doing."

I hang up and shove the phone in my purse.

"I'm not even going to ask," Fenn says.

"That's probably best," I reply wearily. "Could you get Phillip to drive around back? I really am not up to any interrogation from the press right now."

By the time I get home, even my bones are tired. I'm not sure this day could get any worse. Then the elevator doors open and I'm certain of it.

"What the actual fuck is going on, Josie?" Jude thunders. He's standing in the hall outside my door, his hair a tangled mess as if he's been running his hands through it for the past hour.

"Jude," I sigh. "What are you doing here?"

"I closed the pub for the first time in twelve years so I could come and talk some sense into my best friend."

"You didn't have to do that."

"Yes, I did." He holds up a copy of the paper. "What is this shit? You've left Alex? For some guy I've never even heard of?"

"Yes." I hold my head high. Jude will see right through me if I so much as hesitate.

"Why?"

"Why do you think?"

"You're going to try to tell me that you're in love with this person?"

"I am."

He laughs, but it's an ugly, derisive sound. "Bullshit."

"Why do you care, anyway? You don't even like Alex."

"I liked him well enough. You love him, which is good enough for me."

"Maybe I didn't love him as much as you thought."

"You're not that good an actress, Jojo." It's a low blow and, combined with my stage name, which Jude never uses, it's probably the cruelest thing he could say to me.

"You should go. If you think I'm going to let you come into my home and insult me, you obviously don't know me as well as you thought you did."

"I'm starting to wonder if I ever knew you at all."

I press my fingers to my temple, trying to ward off the dull ache which has settled there. "Jude, please. Can't you just be happy for me?"

"Look at me." I really don't want to do that, but I tear my eyes upward. Jude takes a step forward, then another, until he's standing right in front of me. "What's going on, Josie?"

My eyes prickle. "I can't tell you."

All the fight seems to drain out of him. His face pales. "I knew it. You're in trouble, aren't you?" My eyes are swimming, and vision blurs. "Let me help you, please. Tell me what's going on."

"Josie?"

Horrified, I whirl around to find Ace in my now open doorway. The concerned expression on his face is replaced by anger when Jude steps around me to confront him.

"What have you done to her, you son of a bitch?"

I grab his arm. "Jude, please don't!" He shrugs off my hand, his fists white-knuckled at his sides. "And who are you, exactly?" Ace drawls, stepping outside the apartment and closing the door behind him.

"Someone who isn't going to stand by while you take advantage of Josie."

Ace manages to look bored. "And who says I'm taking advantage of her?" His eyes flicker to mine, brow raised in warning.

"Whatever you think you're doing, it ends now," Jude says.

"I'm not doing anything. Other than taking my girlfriend out for dinner," Ace replies. "Are you ready?" he adds, "I've booked for eight. If we don't leave soon, we'll be late." Jude may as well have left the room, for all the attention Ace pays him.

"She's not going anywhere with you."

"You don't speak for her," Ace reminds him.

Jude snatches up my hands. "Josie, please. We can figure this out."

I smile up at him. Jude is my best friend, and I'm very likely about to lose him too. I try to convey how sorry I am with one look, and then I gently pull away from him.

"I just need to change," I tell Ace. "I'll be ready in ten minutes."

Jude's face crumples.

"You should go," I tell him firmly. "Thank you for looking out for me, but it's really not necessary."

"In future, maybe you should call before you visit," Ace adds darkly.

Jude snaps. He lunges for Ace, swinging his arm in a powerful right hook. Ace ducks easily, grabbing Jude's wrist as his face thunders overhead and using his momentum against him. I rush forward as Jude crashes to the floor.

"Jude!"

"Don't touch me!" he yells, pushing me away as I reach for him. He gets to his feet, and we stare at one another, neither speaking a word.

Ace clears his throat. "The clock is ticking, Josie," he says. Jude gives me one last disgusted look and then shoves past Ace and into the elevator. The second the doors close, I burst into tears.

"You're going to ruin your make up," is all Ace says.

"I'm not getting on that thing," I insist fifteen minutes later when Ace leads me to a black motorcycle in the underground lot. He hands me a black helmet with a neon orange lightning bolt emblazoned on the side.

"I don't want to spend the night being blinded by camera flashes," he says, "and no one will recognize you with this over your head."

"I thought the whole point is to get you on the front page," I retort. "Isn't that how this works?"

"I think we've made enough headlines for one day." He pulls the dark visor on his own helmet down.

I expected Ace to have booked at *The Palms* or any of the celebrity-favored eateries on restaurant row, but instead, we weave through traffic and head downtown. I cling to Ace's waist, terrified with every lurch of the powerful engine.

When we pull up outside a quaint and quiet bistro, I'm begrudgingly relieved.

"You have helmet hair," Ace tells me. Self-conscious, I run my fingers through my hair, trying to fluff it up. "Don't worry, no one here will notice."

We sit at a table set for two at the very back. Ace offers me the seat facing away from the other diners, and I accept it gratefully.

I order a glass of wine, Ace a chocolate shake. I raise my brow at that. "I'm driving," he says by way of explanation.

I clutch my glass, missing the weight of Alex's ring on my finger.

"So, tell me about Jude," Ace begins once we've ordered.

I shrug, not wanting to discuss Jude with him. "He used to be my boss. Now we're friends."

"Did you and he ever…?" I throw him a filthy look which makes him chuckle. "No, then. Did he and Alex get along?"

"Not particularly."

"He fought pretty hard for a man he doesn't particularly care for."

"He cares about *me*."

"Point taken. And I assume that you haven't told him about our little arrangement?"

"What do you think?"

"I think that you're sulking and it doesn't become you."

"I'm not sulking."

He refills my wine with a deft hand. "What are you going to have to eat?"

"I'm not hungry."

"Are we really going to do this again?"

"Fine." I take the briefest look at the menu. The meals are simple and moderately priced. "I'll have a salmon salad." We both know there is no salmon salad on the menu.

Ace leans back in his chair, exasperated. "Why do you have to make everything so difficult?"

"You expect me to make this easy for you?"

"I expect you to admit defeat graciously."

The waiter returns to take our order and Ace orders two portions of calamari with chipotle mayonnaise. I don't tell him that I haven't eaten mayonnaise since college. The camera is unforgiving, and I've spent the past few years on a perpetual diet.

We lapse into an awkward silence. Well, I find it awkward. Ace looks completely content, lounging in his chair like God's gift to Calvin Klein.

I take a slug of my wine.

"What have you been doing since you left France?" I ask. "For work, I mean."

His eyes are dark as they cut to mine. "A bit of this and a bit of that."

I hold his gaze, refusing to let it go. Ace grins at me.

"I joined the French Foreign Legion. I even have a tattoo on my ass to prove it."

"You are so full of shit."

He takes a sip of water. "Yeah," he admits, to my surprise. "I am."

"You're really not going to tell me?"

"What does it matter? You're determined to think lowly of me, so why should I bother correcting you?"

"It's hard not to think lowly of you when you're blackmailing me for fame and fortune."

"As opposed to Mr. Forbes List, who only wanted to make you happy, I suppose?" There's a venom to his tone that is completely out of character.

"Don't you dare compare yourself to Alex!" I hiss. "And besides, he's rich and famous all on his own, without any help from me."

"Agree to disagree." He eyes me over his glass. "How did you meet?"

The abrupt question takes me by surprise. I sit back, my fingers fiddling with my napkin. "We met through a mutual friend. He set us up on a blind date." Ace doesn't respond. "We've been together for two and a half years."

"You think you can really know someone in such a short space of time?"

"Yes."

He pulls a face.

"Haven't you ever been in love, Ace?"

"Once," he replies darkly. "It didn't work out."

"What happened?"

"What do they say in the movies..." he pretends to think about it, "oh yes. She just wasn't that into me."

I flash him a wicked smile. "Smart girl."

"She was."

By the time our food arrives, the wine has relaxed me, if only slightly. I move onto water, not wanting to fall off the back of his motorcycle on the way home. I manage only a few bites before I push my plate away. Ace frowns, but I ignore him.

"Tell me more about this girl who broke your heart."

He looks at me as if I've just grown two heads. "Are you serious?" he asks when he realizes I'm waiting for an answer.

"Yes. I want to know. Call it morbid curiosity, not that there's anything morbid about it. In fact, I want to send her a congratulatory card."

"And what would it say, this card?"

I think for a second, tapping my finger to my top lip. "It would say, To the Woman who broke Ace's heart. You are amazing. We should be friends."

"Well, there you go then. Mission accomplished."

Now it's my turn to look confused.

"You really are an idiot, Josie," Ace sighs, calling for the bill.

"You're not making any sense," I snap. The combination of wine and mayonnaise is curdling in my stomach.

"Jesus Christ!" Ace shakes his head in disbelief. "Let me spell it out for you, then. It was *you*, Josie."

I blink up at him, all the air driven from my lungs.

"I wouldn't get worked up about it," Ace adds spitefully, "it was a very long time ago, and I didn't know any better."

"You were in love with me? When?"

Ace rubs at his jaw. "I'm pretty sure around the same time we made love, although it's possible it started before then." He arches his brow cynically. "You really didn't know?"

My fragile hold on my temper snaps. "You left me," I remind him. "If you had such strong feelings, why did you scuttle out before the sun came up and leave for Paris without so much as a text?"

"What?"

"You heard me. Do you have any idea how mortifying it was to wake up to an empty bed? I cried for a month, you heartless bastard!"

"Josie..." he shakes his head, his eyes wide with shock. "I didn't leave you. I came back."

"No, you didn't."

"I did. I went to get you breakfast. But when I got back to your dorm, your roommate told me you'd gone out, and that you'd asked her to give me a message."

"What message?"

"That you didn't really want to deal with the whole morning after drama. I was leaving, and I'd considered changing my flight so we could work out what was happening between us, but she said you didn't want to see me again."

"She didn't. She couldn't have..." I rack my brain, trying to recall the details of that morning. Casey had been home when I came through from my bedroom. She hadn't said a word to me about Ace.

"Hold on a minute. Are you telling me that all this time you thought I just up and left after that night, without so much as a second thought?" he doesn't wait for my reply before he continues, his voice stricken. "Well shit. No wonder you think I'm an asshole."

"Casey had a thing for you," I whisper, remembering. Ace looks disgusted.

"I'm sorry," he says, sounding sincere for the first time since this all began. "I should've known better."

I swallow down the bitter lump in my throat and gather my wits. "Like you said, it was a long time ago."

"Really? You're just going to brush this off?"

"What do you expect me to do? You might not have been an asshole then, but you're blackmailing me now. This doesn't change anything."

Something fierce and furious flashes across his face. "What if I wasn't the bad guy in all of this?" he asks.

I think of Jude's stricken face earlier, and Alex's emotional texts. "But you are."

The ride home is hell. I do everything in my power to avoid touching any part of Ace's body, but it leaves me feeling vulnerable and terrified that I might fall. We are almost home when a car pulls out in front of us, and Ace swerves violently to avoid a collision. I scream, feeling my body tilting dangerously to the left. His arm shoots out to steady me, and I cling to it, chest heaving. The second we stop in the underground lot, he's off the bike, whipping off his helmet.

"Are you okay?" he asks, helping me unbuckle my own. I nod, and his fingers brush the hollow of my throat.

I step away as if he's burned me. "I can do it!"

Ace curses. He waits while I fumble with the clip. "You sure you're okay?" he asks again when I'm finally free of the stifling helmet.

"I said I'm fine!" I shove the helmet at him. "But I am never getting on that death trap again."

He follows me into the elevator. The space is too small, and I press myself into the opposite wall, trying to get as far from him as possible.

"Stop that," he snaps.

I ignore him. Ace's chest rises and falls with every breath. He's furious, and he keeps his hands glued to his side as if he doesn't quite know what to do with them.

"Screw it." In the same instant he rams his finger against the emergency stop button, he rounds on me, blue eyes flashing. His hands are warm against my cheeks as he seizes hold of my face and before I can register what's happening, his lips crush down on mine. He doesn't wait for me to yield. His tongue sweeps into my mouth, hard and merciless. My head swims. I press my hands to his chest, intending to push him away, but somehow, I am gripping the front of his shirt and pulling him closer instead. Warmth blazes in my belly, spreading like wildfire through my body. My tongue clashes against his, and I arch my body into his, feeling the hardness of him press into me. The sound that escapes from my throat is barely human.

When he suddenly pulls away, I am left clinging to him, limp and breathless. Reality crashes over me. Tears of shame well in my eyes.

Ace turns his back on me, his shoulders heaving. I cover my traitorous mouth with my hand. I can still feel his lips on mine, worse, I ache for them.

Ace reaches over and releases the emergency stop, and the elevator continues upward as if nothing's happened. As if my life didn't just veer off its axis. Ace doesn't look at me once as he leads the way to the apartment door, and, once inside, I rush straight to my room to soak Noodle's fur with my tears.

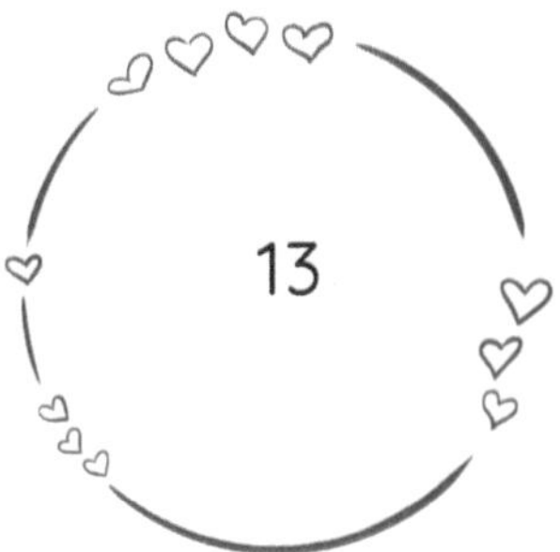

13

On Saturday, we take Noodle for a walk to the park. We've barely spoken since the kiss in the elevator, but that doesn't stop me reliving it over and over in my head. I kissed him back. After everything he's done, I threw myself at him. Every time I recall how I pressed myself against him, a deep blush shames my cheeks. I haven't heard from Jude, and my heart is heavy with his absence. I keep reminding myself that the only way out is through, and that the sooner Ace gets what he wants, the sooner he'll leave me alone. Maybe once all this is over, I can try to put the pieces of my life back together.

"Do you want a coffee?" Ace asks when I let Noodle off the lead. I nod, and he saunters off toward the mobile coffee cart. I take a seat on a dark green park bench and pick absent-mindedly at the peeling paint.

"Miss Hudson?" The man looming over me is dressed in blue jeans and a navy sweater. I don't like the look on his face. I've seen it once before, on an obsessed fan, and it ended with a restraining order.

I risk a glance at the coffee cart. Ace is in line, his broad shoulders towering over the girl behind him. "Can I help you?" I ask politely.

"I was wondering if I could get your autograph?"

"Sure. Do you have a pen?"

He shrugs, but the movement is too practiced, too obvious to be sincere. "I don't. Maybe we could go into that café over there and borrow one? I could buy you a coffee?"

I am not going anywhere with this man. "I'm sorry, I'm actually waiting for my boyfriend." I wave a casual hand toward the cart. The man's expression changes instantly.

"It's just a coffee," he says through gritted teeth.

"I'm really sorry, but I can't."

"Is this how you treat your fans?" he's dropping the act so fast I can barely keep up. "What, you think you're so high and mighty that you don't have a minute to spare for someone like me?"

I get to my feet. "I really think you should leave." Hearing the jangle of her lead, Noodle comes running.

"Is this your dog?" his eyes flicker. Before I can deny it, he's scooped her up. Noodle growls.

"Please put her down."

This time his smile is smug. "I will if you agree to that coffee."

"I'm not going to do that. Please put her down, or I'll call the cops."

He gives me a withering look and starts to walk off.

"Dammit!" I follow, throwing a desperate look over my shoulder. I can't see Ace anywhere. "Put her down!" I yell. I'm jogging now to keep up.

Realizing something is very, very wrong, Noodle starts to panic. I can see her tiny body squirming in his arms. *Please, God, don't drop her.*

"Put the dog down."

I've never been so relieved to see anyone in my life. Ace is standing a few yards away, blocking the path and cutting off the man's escape.

"And what if I say no."

"That would be your second mistake."

"Oh really?" A sneer. "And what was my first?"

"Forgetting that wherever Jojo goes, the press follows." He points toward the crowd of paparazzi that has gathered, their lenses trained on us.

"Please give her back," I say, sensing his growing agitation. He's got nowhere to go, and he knows it.

"You're a bitch," he hisses, shoving Noodle toward me. It's not the first time I've been called that, and it certainly won't be the last. I feel a rush of relief as Noodle leaps into my arms. "A filthy whore!" the man continues. Then he spits at me. Ace moves so fast it defies belief. In one rapid movement, he grabs hold of the man's hand and twists, jerking his body until he has his arm pinned at an unnatural angle behind his back. The man gives a yelp of pain.

"Apologise," Ace growls in his ear.

"Fuck you."

Another savage twist and I swear I hear muscle tearing.

"I'm sorry!" he howls.

"Let him go!" I yell at the same time. Ace does, but not before placing a well-timed kick in his arse, sending the man sprawling face-first onto the grass.

The click of the hovering cameras blurs into one long endless loop. I don't wait for Ace as I stalk off, but he appears beside me a second later, two coffees in hand.

"I shouldn't have left you alone," he says. It's the most apologetic I've ever heard him.

"It's fine. It happens all the time."

"How do you cope?"

I shrug. "It's part of the job."

SUNDAY'S HEADLINES must be exactly what Ace had imagined when he decided to blackmail me. The papers are all calling him a hero, one who saved me from the creepy stalker. I roll my eyes and toss them all in a heap on the couch.

"You can start a scrapbook," I tell him.

He barely looks up from the TV. "Nah, I'm okay."

He's wearing a pair of shorts and a T-shirt. My eyes linger on the powerful muscles in his thighs. I can see a faint line just above the hem, where his legs are a shade lighter than the rest of him.

"You see something you like, Josie?" I whip my head up to find him watching me, a teasing light in his eyes.

"You are so full of shit."

His eyes drift toward the Baby Grand. "Do you ever play anymore?"

"Not much."

"Why not?"

"No time."

He gives me an arch look and then swings his long legs off the couch. He's at the piano in three strides. I shake my head when he pats the small space on the stool next to him. His long fingers play a few test notes.

"It needs tuning," he announces cockily.

"It does not."

A few more chords and then he shrugs. I hold my breath as his fingers launch into action, playing a melodic ditty I've never heard before. He hits more than a dozen wrong notes, but he plays through them, not bothered.

"You're terrible," I say when he's done.

He grins. "Music was never my forte." Then, his face turning serious, "but I always thought it was yours. I thought this is what you'd be doing, in the end." He makes a sweeping motion over the keys to emphasize his point. "Not acting."

It's my turn to shrug. "Acting pays better."

"I'll take your word for it." He gets up and offers me the stool. "Why don't you play something now?"

I shake my head. "I'm going to get something to drink."

"Could you grab me a soda while you're there?"

"How positively domestic." We both jump at the new voice which cuts through the room.

"Alex!" I breathe. He's standing at the doorway to the living room, still wearing his traveling coat. He must have come straight from the airport.

"Hello, Jojo." His voice is pained, and dark circles shadow his eyes.

"What are you doing here?"

He stares at me, as if he's memorizing every inch of my face. "I don't know," he admits. "I thought you'd be alone."

"This is—"

"I know who he is."

Ace gets to his feet. Holds out his hand. "Nice to meet you... Alex, is it?"

Son of a bitch. It's a wicked move, as disrespectful as it is condescending.

Alex doesn't move a muscle and Ace lets his hand drop back to his side with a smug grin.

"Let's go into the kitchen," I say quickly, drawing Alex away from Ace. The second we're out of sight, Alex lowers his guard.

"What the fuck is going on, Jojo?" his voice is more venomous than I've ever heard it. "You end things with me, and a couple of days later this stranger moves into your house!"

"I know. It's a lot to take in, I get that. I don't know what to tell you—"

"Why don't you start by telling me exactly how long you've been seeing him?"

"I didn't leave you for Ace if that's what you're implying."

"Bullshit. What kind of a fool do you take me for?"

"I know it looks that way, but I swear to you, Alex, I wasn't seeing Ace before we broke up. We dated back in college, as you've probably read, and we bumped into each other at—"

"Your book launch. I know, I was there, remember?"

"Yes," I admit. "I'm sorry."

"Sorry?" he barks. "You've made me a laughing stock and all you can say is you're sorry?"

I've never seen him so out of control. He's always been so poised and perfect, and I hate that I am the cause of it. "I don't know what else to say."

"Are you sleeping with him?"

My mouth drops open. "No!" I exclaim, perfectly outraged, when all I can think is I'm so relieved he worded it like that and not 'have you slept with him'.

"Forgive me for assuming the worst," he snaps, "but it's hard to know what to think when your fiancé leaves you, and another man moves into her home a week later."

"He's sleeping in the spare room," I mumble. It's all I can give him. Alex slept in my bed every time he stayed over, and I hope that that means something, however small.

"Is that supposed to make me feel better?"

"No. In fact, I shouldn't be telling you any of this. We broke up, Alex. What I do with my time and who I spend it with, is no longer your concern."

He drags his hand across his face. "This is ridiculous. You don't just throw away two and half years for some deadbeat." At my look of surprise, his lips curve upward in a cruel smirk. "I did my research, Jojo. Your new boyfriend doesn't even have a job. He's obviously here for one reason."

"Oh really," I snap. He's absolutely right, but it still hurts to hear that he doesn't believe Ace could give a damn about me. "And what reason is that?"

"Your money, Jojo. In fact, I'll prove it." Before I can stop him, he strides out of the kitchen.

Ace is still lounging on the couch, but I can tell by his body language that he's not half as calm as he's pretending to be. He glances up as Alex enters, then shoots me a curious look.

"Logan is it?" Alex asks, and it's such a territorial thing to call Ace by his last name that I want to laugh, until Alex opens his mouth again. "Well, Logan, I have a proposition for you."

"You're not really my type," Ace drawls.

Alex's feigned laughter is grating. "I'll give you a million dollars to break up with Jojo."

I actually take a physical step backward. This isn't some romantic notion in a role I'm playing. This is my life. And Alex just put a literal price on my head.

"Are you for real?" Ace's voice is low, lower even than when he confronted the man in the park.

"You're obviously not here for any noble reason," Alex continues calmly, "so rather than waste all of our time, let's get to the point. A million dollars for you to walk away."

Ace gets to his feet. He's a full head taller than Alex. My feet are frozen in place, I couldn't move if I wanted to.

"A million dollars," Ace muses. His eyes meet mine over Alex's head. A storm is brewing. "What do you say, Josie?" Ace asks me, and his voice is so gentle I want to weep. "You think you're worth a million dollars?" His eyes pose a question, a challenge, and I rise to it beautifully.

"Alex," I say in a voice like honey, "get the fuck out of my house."

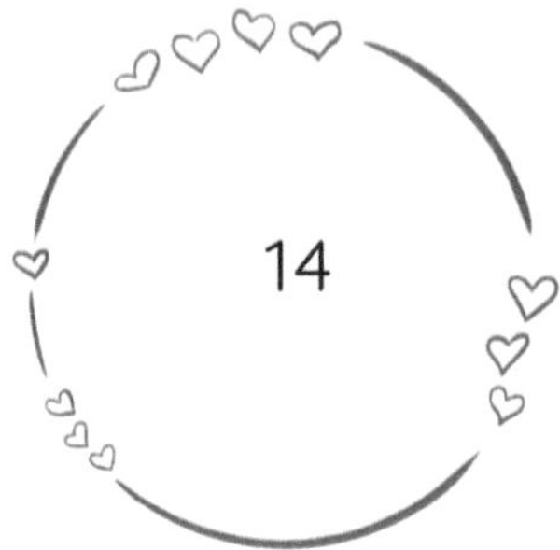

"I can't believe he offered me a million dollars," Ace muses, digging deep into the popcorn bowl for the burnt bits.

"I can't believe you turned it down."

He chuckles. "I think I could've pushed him for more."

"I think I could push you right down the stairs."

We're sitting on opposite ends of the couch. It took a full ten minutes for my heart rate to return to normal after Alex had left. Ace cocks his head to the side and fixes me in that intense stare of his.

"Can I ask you a question?"

"You just did."

"Why did you fall in love with him?" I arch my brow, and he holds up both hands in surrender. "I know, I know, he's perfect... God's gift to womankind and all that, but he just doesn't seem like someone you'd get involved with."

"How would you have any idea what kind of person I'd get involved with? You don't even know me."

"I know the girl you were. People don't change that much."

"I think you're proof that they do."

It's his turn to be silent.

"What happened, Ace? How did you go from being one of the nicest people in the world to this?"

"I wasn't that nice to begin with," he teases. "I did take advantage of you when you were drunk, remember?"

I blush crimson. I've become so used to denying it that any mention of that night turns me into a nervous wreck.

"Why did you lie?" he asks, "In the book, I mean. It would've sold no matter what you wrote, so why did you even say you were a virgin in the first place?"

"I guess I tried to forget it ever happened."

"Why?" his probing is gentle, but significant.

"You know why."

"Tell me."

"Because it hurt. I really thought... well, it doesn't matter what I thought. Once you left, I just wanted to forget it ever happened. I guess I considered myself a born-again virgin. It's very on trend at the moment," I add as his mouth falls open.

"Wait, so you haven't... I mean, since we...?"

I flush all the way down to my toes. "No, I haven't."

He whistles, low and loud. "Wow." His lip tugs upward. "And how did Mr. Forbes List feel about that?"

"I'm not discussing this with you. And wipe that smug smirk off your face."

I SPEND most of the following week on set, my emotions in chaos. Ace is a world-class prick, and yet I find myself enjoying his company. I even agreed to get back on his motorcycle after he called me out for being a wuss. And despite his claims that he wants to use me to further this own career, he hasn't done a single thing about it. Even Fenn is smitten. Once she got over her initial shock, she fell right under Ace's spell. She even offered to write up his resume and send it out on his behalf. Yesterday I overheard her telling him about a casting call downtown, and I had to take Noodle for an hour-long walk to calm down. George, of course, is thrilled, because with all the additional publicity I'm getting, the book sales have skyrocketed.

I have got to get out of this mess.

By Friday afternoon, I've started hatching a plan. I still haven't spoken to Jude but, as soon as filming ends, I make my way down to *The Office*.

"What are you doing here?" Jude asks when he sees me approaching the bar. It's happy hour, and a crowd of people fills the confined space. The only good thing about *The Office* is that the regulars have been around so long they knew me before I was famous, and they barely notice when I walk in.

"Can we speak, somewhere private?"

"As you can see, I'm a little busy."

"Fine." I slam open the hatch and move behind the bar.

"What the hell do you think you're doing?" Jude hisses.

"I'm freeing you up." I turn to the nearest crowd. "What'll it be?"

"Three beers, a scotch and soda, and a glass of red."

"You don't work here anymore, Josie."

"Don't worry," I say as I pull three beers from the cooler, "you don't have to pay me."

He curses under his breath. "Rachel!" a dark-haired girl taking a food order raises her head. "Cover for me, will you?"

The second she's behind the bar, Jude hauls me by my elbow to his tiny office down the hall.

"See, that wasn't so hard, was it?"

"I'm not in the mood, Josie."

I cave. "You were right. I'm in trouble."

He hesitates for only a fraction of a second before pointing to the chair behind his desk. "Sit."

Once he's perched on the desk before me, he instructs me to start from the beginning. So I do. His response is predictable as ever.

"Holy shit."

"I know."

"Why didn't you tell me. No, wait, don't answer that, I get why you didn't tell me. But why are you telling me now?"

"Because I have a plan."

"What is it?"

"George very clearly said that unless I'd slept with someone between getting engaged to Alex and writing the book, I was in the clear."

He pulls a face. "I really don't want to hear the specifics of your sex life, Josie."

"Bear with me. I was a 'virgin'," I put air quotes around the phrase, "when I wrote it."

"No, you weren't."

"I know, but you know what I mean. The point is, it doesn't really matter if I'm not a virgin after the fact."

"I literally have no idea where you're going with this. And please stop saying that word, it's freaking me out."

"I'm going to tell the world I had sex with Ace."

His expression is blank. "That's great, but I still don't get how it helps."

"I'm going to tell them I had sex with Ace *now*. That I'm not a virgin anymore. That way, I can control the story. If Ace tries to say we did it six years ago, no one will believe him, not after I make it front page news. It'd take the wind right out of his story. I'll be free."

"Okay, but you said he had photographs – evidence?"

"I haven't aged that much," I tease. "And they're not full-face photographs. He'd have a hard time proving when they were taken. I don't think he'd even bother, not when I've scooped his story. He'll run back to whatever hole he crawled out of, and I'd never have to see him again."

"Leaving you free to get back together with Alex?"

I hesitate. I hadn't even thought that far. In fact, Alex hadn't even crossed my mind.

Jude senses my distraction. "You *do* want to get back together with Alex, right?"

"Yes, of course I do."

"Don't sound so sure, you might hurt yourself."

"Alex offered Ace money," I blurt out. "To leave me."

"He *what*?"

"He came around, claimed that Ace was only in it for the money. He offered him a million dollars to walk away."

"Fuck me. What did Ace say?"

"He turned him down."

Jude steeples his fingers under his chin. "Why would he do that? A million dollars is a lot of money, and he wouldn't have to spend the next year of his life faking things with you."

"I have no idea. Who knows how Ace's brain works."

There's a pregnant pause, and then, "Alex really offered him money?"

"Yes."

"I never liked him."

I smile a small, sad smile. "I know."

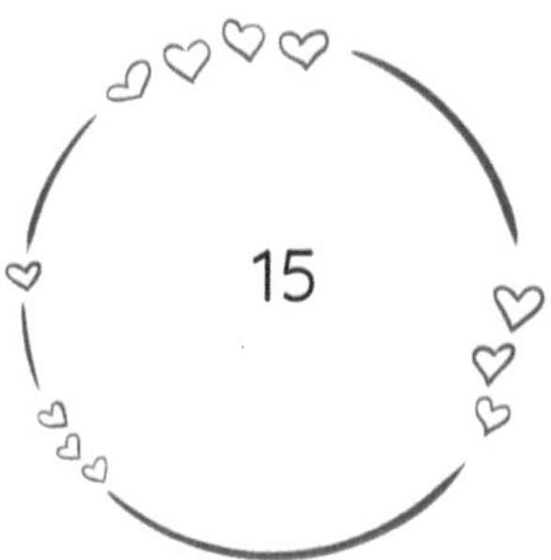

15

Buoyed by the idea that I have a plan, I practically waltz home. The only downside is that for said plan to have any chance of success, I'm going to have to actually sleep with Ace.

As luck would have it, we're attending a premiere this weekend in Vegas, the original Sin City. We're catching an early flight tomorrow, so I spend the evening closeted in my bedroom, packing everything I might possibly need to stage my seduction. I'm absolutely terrified.

"What's wrong with you?" Ace asks when I get up from the table to wash up after dinner.

"What do you mean?"

"You haven't insulted me in at least thirty minutes. Something isn't right."

"Maybe I just want an evening of peace?"

"Lies. You're up to something."

I cast around for a change of subject. "Have you packed for tomorrow? You know you can use my name at any of the designer stores if you need something to wear."

"I'm fine, thanks."

"It's a premiere," I remind him, "you need to look the part."

"Are you worried I might embarrass you by showing up in jeans?"

"Yes."

"Ah," he teases, his eyes sparkling, "there she is."

In the greater scheme of things, his outfit is the least of my concerns, but I do find myself worried that he's going to embarrass me in front of the world's press.

On Saturday evening, having been primped and preened by a crew of hair and makeup artists, I wait with bated breath for Ace to emerge from his room. When he does, I almost fall over in my six-inch stilettos. I don't know where he got the suit, but it's perfectly tailored to show off the breadth of his shoulders and his long, lean legs. His shoes are leather – Italian, I'd bet my life on it – and his blond hair is slicked back, exposing the smooth tan of his forehead and his wicked blue eyes.

"Good enough for you, princess?" he asks arrogantly. He looks incredible, and he knows it.

I narrow my eyes. "Where did you get that suit?"

"I had it lying around. Shall we?" He offers me his arm, and I link my own through his. Once again, Ace blows me away with his performance. When we arrive at the Orleans Arena, he stands tall at my side, smiling expertly for the cameras, but not once does he step forward and command attention in the spotlight. I am hyper-aware of him, standing always at my back, guiding me through the reporters and foreign press. Watching the screening, I find I am analyzing every move I make, trying to see my performance through his eyes. It's not my favorite film, but I want him to like it. I don't know why I care.

Ace doesn't say much. At the after party, there are a few instances where he disappears and, despite scanning the crowd, I can't find him. I think I catch him talking to a serious man in a black suit who doesn't look as if he belongs here, but then one of my co-stars steps into my line of vision and I've lost him again. All in all, he's attentive and charming, but he falls silent the moment we get into the limo for the ride back to our hotel. My heart is hammering at a hundred beats a minute in anticipation of what I need to do, but Ace appears utterly relaxed, draped over the leather seat.

"You're very quiet," he remarks as we take the elevator up to the penthouse.

"I'm just tired. It's been a busy night."

He nods, but I don't think he believes me.

"I enjoyed the film."

"Really?"

"Really." He chuckles. "Don't look so surprised, I've always said you were a good actress."

"You could've been a brilliant actor," I remind him, "if you didn't quit."

His lips press together in a grim line. "I guess it wasn't meant to be."

It all comes crashing back – the real reason that he's here, the blackmail, and I bite my lip to keep from snapping at him. "I guess not."

The lights are turned low inside the apartment. "I'm going to take a shower," Ace says with a yawn. "You need anything before I go?"

"No, I'm fine."

I wait until I hear the hiss of the shower in his private bathroom, and then I hurtle through to my own room. I turn the taps on full, letting the cold water pour over me. *You can do this*, I tell myself over and over in my head. *You've done it before, it's not a big deal.*

The smooth satin slithers over my skin. Pale cream, it stops a good three inches above my knees and is low-cut enough that only a thin strip of lace protects my modesty. The matching scrap of underwear is so small I wonder why it was even included. I leave my hair loose and take off all trace of the heavy make up that caked my skin. Barefoot, I walk slowly back to the kitchen.

Ace has a habit of taking a bottle of water to bed with him every night. It's only a matter of time before he pads into the kitchen, wearing only a pair of sleeping shorts. He stops dead when he catches sight of me.

"I thought you said you didn't need anything."

I hold up a bottle of Evian. "I was thirsty."

"That's an interesting choice of nightwear."

I glance down at my lack of an outfit and shrug as if I barely noticed what I'd thrown on.

Ace doesn't buy it for a second. "What are you doing, Josie?"

Screw it. I set down the water and cross the room to stand right in front of him. With his height, I know he can see right down my negligee to the scrap of lace beneath. I hear his shocked intake of breath, and my lips curve upward in a small smile. "What does it look like I'm doing?"

"It looks like you're trying to seduce me." His voice is ragged, and it sends a bolt of heat through my chest.

"Is it working?"

He squirms uncomfortably. "That depends."

"On what?"

"On why?"

I tug my bottom lip between my teeth. "Maybe I'm tired of waiting for you to make the first move. You can't pretend you haven't felt something between us these past few weeks."

"You should go to bed."

I inch closer until only a hair's breadth separates us. The smell of him wafts over me – expensive soap and the musky smell of him beneath. His body is rigid, his jaw tics. He's using every ounce of restraint not to close the distance between us. I notice a small silver scar near his shoulder, another just above his left hip.

"Don't you want me, Ace?"

He doesn't move. I lift my hand and run my nail down his chest, from collarbone to the dark hair below his navel. A small shudder runs through him.

"I don't like games, Josie."

"I don't believe that." I rise onto my toes and brush my lips across his, featherlight. "You've been playing one since you came to see me at that book launch." Another kiss, but this time I let my tongue follow my lips. "I'm only trying to even the score."

There's one part of his body that he cannot control, and it rises up to meet me. The touch of it sends an electric shock through my thighs. Ace is undone. His lips crash onto mine, his fingers knot through my hair. I gasp against his mouth, reaching for him, caressing him through the soft cotton of his pants. Ace groans, his tongue meeting mine in a frantic clash of wills. When he lifts me up, my negligee rises to my waist, and I yelp as my bare arse meets the cold marble of the kitchen counter. He pulls the shoestring straps down my arms, as his mouth trails my jaw, my neck, and then closes over one of my breasts. I curse in agony and ecstasy as he moves away, burrowing my fingers into his hair, and pulling him back to my chest.

His fingers dip lower, and my whole body stiffens in anticipation. When he brushes over my panties, it burns, a deep throb that sends me over the edge. I bite down on his shoulder, my hands fumbling for his pants.

"Josie," he growls, his breath hot in my ear.

"Yes!" I pant in encouragement, my body arching toward his teasing fingers. Only his arm prevents me from falling as I teeter on the very edge of the counter, my legs falling wide. He peels off my panties with one steady hand and then lifts me toward him. I wrap my legs so tightly around his waist that I don't know if I'll ever unravel them again. When he lowers me onto the couch, he stands back to admire my naked body. I close my eyes and reach for him.

"Josie," he repeats. His voice has changed. I open my eyes to find the wicked grin firmly in place. "What are you doing?" I ask, suddenly terrified.

He gives my body one last lingering look and then leans forward until our noses are almost touching. His eyes loom in my vision.

"This is not a game," he says. He straightens up, fetches my abandoned water bottle from the kitchen counter, and disappears out the door.

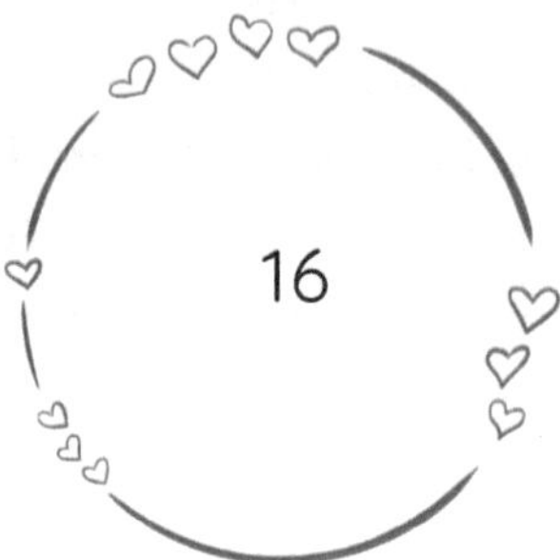

I spend the night cringing in despair. Not only did I fail, but Ace's rejection hurt far more than I expected. It's like that morning in college all over again. I don't cry. I refuse. This is my fault, because, as much as I convinced myself that my plan was all about escaping Ace, I'd wanted him. I'd completely let myself go last night. Even now, my body aches for him.

When the first light of dawn starts to filter through my window, I change my flight without telling Ace and catch a cab to the airport.

I don't go home. I send my bags with Phillip and spend the morning wandering through the park. I eat at the diner, the one place no one will look for me. When Ace calls, I don't answer. By the time his name shows up for the eighth time, I switch my phone to silent. Eventually, I'll have to go home and face him. I know I will, but I don't want to.

He's standing in the hall when I get home. His hair is disheveled, and a five o'clock shadow darkens his jaw. His expression is unreadable.

"Where have you been?"

"Out."

"Dammit, Josie!" He plunges his hands through his hair. "You can't just take off like that."

"I can do whatever I damned well please."

"This is about last night," he begins, but I shove past him, not letting him finish. I've just slammed my bedroom door when it bursts open. "Don't walk away from me."

"Get out."

"We need to talk about this."

"Get out!"

"No!"

I snatch up the lamp beside my bed and hurl it at him. He ducks easily, and it smashes into the wall behind him.

"Get the fuck out of my room!"

"You're behaving like a child!"

A book follows the lamp.

"That's enough!" Ace roars. He crosses the distance between us and seizes my hand before I can find my next weapon.

"Let me go!"

"Not until you've calmed down!" His face is so close to mine that I can make out flecks of green in the blue. My legs go out beneath me as my face crumples. Ace catches me as I fall. Heaving sobs wrack my body as I collapse against him, releasing all the pain and rejection I've been feeling since last night.

"Oh Jesus, Josie, I'm sorry." His arms tighten around me.

"You're not sorry," I cry, beating my hand against his chest. "You don't care, stop acting like you do!"

His voice is pained as he whispers against my hair. "But I do care."

"Stop it!" I plead. "Please stop it. I can't do this anymore."

"Why are you so upset?" His eyes are searching my face. "It was only a game."

I bite back another sob and shake my head.

"Josie." Firmer now. "It *was* only a game?" He's watching me closely. Something flashes in his eyes – triumph?

"It wasn't a game?" He's smiling now, and he's so beautiful it breaks my heart. "Josie, please, tell me. It wasn't a game?"

I squeeze my eyes together and shake my head again. Tenderly, he sets me down on the edge of my bed.

"Look at me."

I open my eyes.

"You're upset because I rejected you?" He sounds thrilled, and it drives home just how cruel he is.

"Please leave me alone," I whimper.

"No. You need to understand."

"Understand what, Ace?" I'm so tired, so very tired.

"I don't want to be a game to you. I thought... I never suspected..." he stops. Takes a deep breath. "Josie, I wanted you last night more than I've ever wanted any woman in my life. Except maybe you, six years ago." He wipes the tears from my eyes.

"But you left? You left me... naked," I add, and fresh tears spring to my eyes at the memory. "On the couch."

His teeth flash. "That was the hardest thing I've ever had to do in my life. Even after four cold showers, I'm pretty sure I've sustained a permanent injury."

I try not to smile and fail spectacularly. "You better not be screwing with me."

His face is the sun, blazing and triumphant. "Josie. There's nothing I'd rather be doing than screwing you."

This time, when he kisses me, there is none of the urgent frenzy of before. Instead, his kiss is tentative. I can feel him holding his breath, waiting for my silent approval. I lift my tear-stained face, allowing him easier access to my mouth, and he smiles against my lips. I part my own and slip my tongue into his mouth. Slowly, I explore every warm inch of it and Ace returns the favor. I close my eyes with a soft sigh, and he kisses my eyelids, tasting my tears.

His hands stroke my neck, my back, my thighs, sending tiny electric sparks along my skin. When his hands grip my shoulders and press me gently down, I lie back. He pulls off his shirt, giving me only a brief look at his muscular torso before his body covers mine. Every inch of him touches me. I feel light-headed, drugged, wrapped tightly in his arms.

We kiss, on and on, until my lips are swollen and sensitive. Until I think I might faint with desire.

Ace leans back, taking his full weight on his elbows, and I splay my hands on his chest. I trace the silvery scar with one finger.

"What happened?" I ask, my voice barely recognizable. He silences me with another lingering kiss. I already know every inch of his mouth, and I duck my head, letting my lips trace the strong line of his jaw. I breathe into his ear, and he stiffens. My hands move lower. This time, he lets me.

I WAKE up draped across Ace's bare chest. He's sleeping, the rise and fall of his chest marking every slow and steady breath. I trace the circular scar, feeling the twisted tissue, and then lift my head to check the matching scar near his hip. There's a long, thin scar in the groove of his collar bone, and another just left of his navel. I move my hand to touch it, but Ace's hand closes over mine. I look up into a pair of lazy blue eyes.

"What happened to you, Ace?" I ask.

"It's a long story."

"I'm not going anywhere," I say, but it's already too late. He's moved, twisting sideways to scoop me against him, his mouth meeting mine and I'm powerless to resist him.

When I finally drift back to earth, I bring it up again.

"Where did you get these scars?"

Ace sighs, realizing I am not going to drop it.

"I can't tell you."

I sit straight up in bed.

"What?" Somewhere in my addled brain, it registers that I thought this changed everything. That somehow after being intimate, all the walls would come down. Apparently, I was wrong.

Sensing that I'm about to bolt, Ace slides his arm around my waist, pinning me against him.

"Josie, I need you to trust me."

"How can I trust you if you won't be honest with me? What is going on? I know you're not here for fame, you've shown absolutely no interest in anything but me since you arrived."

"Can't you just believe that I want to be here and let it rest?"

"I need answers."

"I know. I just can't give them to you. Not yet, anyway."

"When, then?"

"I can't say. Soon."

I shrug out of his arms and scoot to the edge of the bed, as far as I can possibly get from him. "That's not good enough."

"Josie, please."

"I need something." I send up a silent prayer that he listens, because it's the truth. If Ace doesn't stop giving me secrets and lies, I have no choice but to end this. No matter how badly it crucifies me to do it.

"I can't," he says.

17

"Oh my God, Josie, what have you done?" CeeCee shrieks down the receiver.

"I told the truth."

"You can't do this! It doesn't work this way – you don't just go rogue on your publicist!"

I pick up the copy of *The Daily* which was delivered this morning. JOJO LOSES IT, the headline reads. The article is carefully worded, I know because I drafted it myself and sent it through to the newsroom yesterday. The accompanying photograph is one taken of Ace and I at the premiere. I'm smiling at the camera, and he's smiling down at me.

"I think I already have," I say, slamming the paper face down on my desk.

"Why? Why break *this*, of all stories?"

"It's the truth. I didn't want there to be any confusion."

"Christ Jojo, you lost your virginity. It's not something the entire world needs to know."

If only she were right. Sadly, this is the only way to get Ace out of my life. I haven't spoken to him since we made love two days ago. I'd left for work before dawn and stayed late on set both nights. He'd been asleep by the time I came home.

Tonight, I'd come home early, prepared to make my last stand, but he'd been out when I arrived. I pass the hours watching re-runs of old Hollywood movies and scratching Noodle's belly. When the front door slams with unnecessary force, I smile to myself.

"What the fuck have you done?" Ace is shaking with rage.

I stretch, deposit Noodle on the couch beside me and get to my feet. "Taking my life back. I've taken the liberty of packing your things," I add, gesturing at the Louis Vuitton luggage case beside the couch. "You can keep the bag, I have another."

"Dammit, Josie, this is serious."

"As am I. I want you out of my house. Right now, or I'll call the cops."

"You're bluffing."

I reach for my phone. Every muscle in my face is perfectly relaxed, displaying not a flicker of emotion.

"Don't do this."

"It's done, Ace. Get out."

"You have no idea what's going on. There's a bigger picture here, Josie."

"If I have no idea what's going on, it's no fault of mine," I reply pointedly. "And seeing that this," I lift the paper and wave it in his face, "leaves you with no bargaining chip, there's really nothing left to say."

"I won't leave you."

"Fine," I sigh. "We'll do this the hard way." I lift my phone and dial 911. I've barely hit the call button when Ace snatches my phone from my hand.

"Fine. I'll go, but this isn't over. I'll be back."

"No, Ace. You won't."

He leaves the bag. Granted, it only has a few of his clothes and a small toiletry bag, but still, I can't bear to have it in the apartment. I drag it downstairs and leave it beside Frank's station. When Fenn arrives bright and early the following morning, I ask her to make sure it's donated to charity.

I don't call Alex. For so long, all I could think of was getting back together with him, but now that I'm free to, I can't bring myself to do it. My only regret in running the article is the pain it must have caused him. A week passes, and I haven't heard a word from Ace. I throw myself into work. Filming will come to an end in a few days, and then we reconvene to shoot in Chicago in a few weeks. When I'm not at work, I spend hours at the Baby Grand. I haven't played like this in years, all raw emotion and vulnerability. Without any witnesses, I soak the ivory keys in tears.

The press is relentless. Noticing that Ace has been conspicuously absent, they are baying for blood. Cruel captions such as ONE NIGHT STAND? and WHAT A WASTE! dominate the headlines, but I pay them no heed. This will all blow over.

Avoiding the world's press, however, is far easier than avoiding my own family. Teddy arrives without warning ten days after I kicked Ace out. I find her waiting outside my door after the last day of filming.

"Sorry it took so long," she says. "I had to find a locum to fill in at the practice."

"Did mom and dad send you?" I ask.

She swipes a stray blonde tendril out of her eyes. "You bet your ass they did. And you should thank your lucky stars it's only me. It took me two whole days to convince dad not to get on a plane and come out here."

"I tried to call him to explain, but he wouldn't take my call."

"He's hopping mad." Teddy gives me a sympathetic look. "I'm assuming you have a good reason for all this crazy behavior?"

"You have no idea."

She scratches in her overnight bag and pulls out a bottle of wine. "Why don't you start at the beginning."

Teddy is my sister, and she loves me unconditionally. She also has the added benefit of having known me throughout my college life, and she clearly remembers the thumping crush I had on Ace.

"He just doesn't strike me as someone to do something like this," she says.

"I know. That's what makes it so weird."

"And he didn't offer any explanation. Or even a clue as to why he's being like this?"

I shake my head. "If he had, I wouldn't have kicked him out. Is dad really furious?"

"Josie, your cherry pop has been all over the news. What do you think?"

I bury my face in the couch cushion. "Oh, God."

"Yeah." She refills my glass. "And now you're not even together anymore, which isn't helping matters."

"You understand why I had to do it?"

"*I* do, but unfortunately no one else will. What really concerns me is that you don't look remotely pleased that your evil plan worked."

We've moved on to our second bottle when Jude arrives. It's his third visit since Ace left. He must be seriously worried about me to leave the bar so often. The sight of Teddy completely unnerves him.

"I didn't mean to interrupt—" he begins hesitantly.

"Oh, just come in," I snap.

He gives Teddy a look that is both apologetic and appreciative at once. "I need to speak to you," he tells me.

"About what?"

"Ace."

"Anything you say to me, you can say in front of Teddy. She knows everything."

He picks up my glass and takes a huge swig of wine. "I take it your plan backfired."

"My plan worked perfectly."

"Epic fail," Teddy counters with a small burp. Jude grins. "She's utterly in love with the handsome bastard."

"I knew it." Jude toasts her with my glass.

"Hey!" I snatch back the glass. "I'm sitting right here!"

"Pining," Teddy says.

"Miserable," Jude agrees.

"Why don't you just call him?" Teddy asks. "I'd like to meet him."

"You're pissed," I remind her. "You've forgotten that he's a liar."

"Oh, yes. He is a liar." Teddy gives me a narrow-eyed stare as if I'm playing Ace and she's practicing for when they meet.

"Don't waste it," I tell her solemnly. She straightens her face.

Jude fetches a glass, and we spend the evening curled on the couch. My head is on Jude's shoulder and, through squinted eyes, I see Teddy's feet in his lap. There are three empty bottles on the table.

"You know what I think would be a good idea?" I slur, after an extended silence.

"What?" Teddy yawns.

"You two should get married."

"Sure." Jude shrugs. "Why not."

"It's not like I have anything better to do," Teddy says.

"I can do it!"

Jude chuckles. "Not to take away from your impressive skill set, Josie, but I'm pretty sure it doesn't include marriage officiate."

"I'll be right back." I trip over my discarded shoes and bang my knee on the coffee table, but it doesn't deter me. Two minutes later I'm back, with my MacBook in hand.

"What are you doing?" Teddy grumbles. "I thought we were having a wedding."

"We are." A quick Google search and I hit pay dirt. "Ha! I knew it! I can get ordained in a couple of minutes."

Jude peers over my shoulder. "It can't be that easy."

"It is." I scroll down. "Some states require government registration, but California isn't one of them." I punch in my details and wait. Five minutes later, I'm ordained.

"Done." I grin at both of them. Then my eyes fall on Teddy's messy hair and her faded jeans and sweater combo. I frown. "Are you wearing that?"

She drops her chin to assess. "No. I'm going to raid your closet."

"Go wild. I'm just going to download one of these sample ceremony scripts."

Jude watches over my shoulder as I scan the different versions I could use.

"That one," he says, jabbing at the screen.

"Minimalist?" I ask, squinting at the tiny text. "Are you worried I might forget my lines?" We both find that hilarious. Trying to compose himself, Jude sets down his glass.

"I better get neatened up too." He's wearing a checked shirt over a white Tee, and black jeans.

"How exactly are you going to neaten up?"

He does up all his buttons with clumsy hands. "Tah dah!"

"Completely transformed," I giggle.

Jude laughs too, until Teddy steps back into the room. She looks exquisite in a dusty pink silk dress that I wore to the Golden Globes last year. She's left her hair braided, and is barefoot, but her cheeks are rosy and her lips shimmer.

"Gorgeous!" I announce, clapping my hands in excitement. "Now, what are we going to use for rings?"

We've run out of wine, so Jude pours us all a whiskey while we try to figure it out.

"I've got it!" Teddy announces after I've tried and failed to stuff Jude's man-sized ring finger into every piece of jewelery I own. "Tattoos."

"Tattoos?"

"Yeah. A friend of mine did it, it's awesome."

"There's a 24-hour tattoo parlor behind the bar," Jude offers helpfully.

"Perfect!"

The ceremony is short and sweet. I take my role very seriously and adopt a solemn expression as I recite the vows that they repeat after me. When it comes to the "with this ring" part, I skip ahead to "I take you," and both Teddy and Jude say, "I do."

There's a tense moment when I ask if anyone present knows of any reason why these two should not be joined in matrimony. All three of us look around my living room as if, at any moment, a guest might jump up and object. Nothing happens. Noodle doesn't even stir in her sleep.

"Then by the power vested in me by the American Marriage Ministry and the state of California, I now pronounce you man and wife!" I announce grandly.

I've forgotten something. I glance down at my phone, where I've stored the script. Jude clears his throat. I glance up to find him jerking his head toward Teddy.

"Oh yes! You may kiss the bride!"

Jude doesn't need to be told twice. He dips Teddy and plants a kiss right on her mouth. It goes on a lot longer than I expected and when he's done, her lipstick is smeared, but her eyes are sparkling.

I manage to unearth a bottle of champagne from the bowels of my fridge before we pile into a taxi and head for *The Office*.

"Are you sure you want to do this?" I ask when we enter the tattoo parlor. It's dark, and a little seedy, but the guy who greets us from behind the counter seems pleasant enough.

"Hey, Aaron!" Jude tries to give him a high five but just misses.

"What's up, Jude? You finally in the market for some ink?"

"Actually, yes." Jude steers Teddy forward proudly. "This is Teddy. My *wife*."

"Awwwwww," I croon as Teddy blushes to the roots of her hair.

"Congrats man!" Aaron pumps Jude's hand. "It's a pleasure to meet you, Teddy. So, what are you wanting?"

"Rings."

"Nice. I get that a lot. You want any initials, or just a band?"

Jude and Teddy exchange looks. "Just a band, I think," Teddy says.

Aaron gives Jude a quick once over. "You're not intoxicated, are you?"

"I know what I'm doing if that's what you're getting at."

"It's not just that," Aaron says. "Besides making a permanent bad decision, there could be other implications – excessive bleeding, for example."

"Will we die?" Teddy asks, winking at Jude.

Aaron laughs. 'no."

"We're not drunk," Jude lies. He holds Aaron's gaze, refusing to back down.

"Okay." Aaron seems satisfied, "but you're going to have to sign these consent forms."

I wander around while Aaron gets to work and flip idly through the heavy sketchbooks on every conceivable surface.

"Are these your designs?" I ask, holding up a thick book bound in black leather. Aaron takes a minute to finish what he's doing before looking up.

"Yeah, those are mine."

"They're really good."

Jude is almost done. Teddy looks a little green. Teddy is a vet, but she's never liked needles. Jude's touch does what the champagne couldn't. Only when he takes her free hand in his, does Teddy relax. The way he looks down at her makes my heart want to jump out of my chest.

"All done," Aaron announces after applying a liberal smear of ointment around Teddy's finger. He removes his gloves and moves over to the counter.

"It's on me," I insist, handing over my card. Jude starts to argue, but I cut him a warning look. "Maid of honor privileges."

"Technically, you're also my best man."

"Exactly. This is my wedding gift to both of you."

We walk over to *The Office* for the after party. Laurel has been holding down the fort, but Jude quickly joins her behind the bar. As busy as he is, he makes sure that mine and Teddy's drinks are permanently filled. Laurel looks utterly crushed.

By the time the last patrons leave, I'm wilting on my stool. Teddy is dancing on her own between tables. Every now and again she stops to admire her new tattoo or blow a kiss at Jude.

We head back to my place around two a.m. I don't even have the energy to find pajamas. Instead, I drop my clothes at the foot of my bed and collapse onto the cotton sheets.

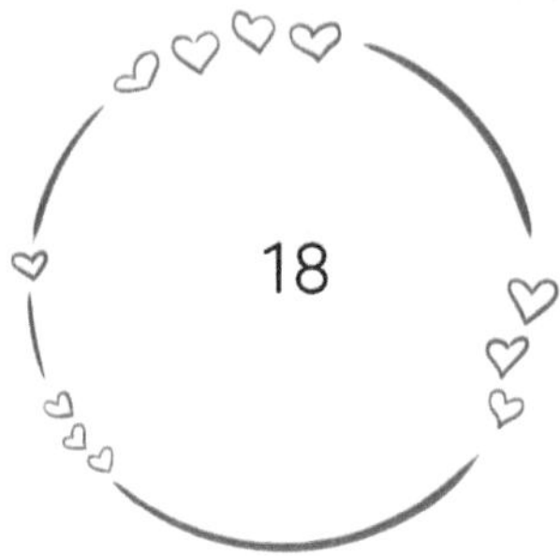

I wake with a dry mouth and a pounding headache. Wandering into the kitchen in only my gown, searching for Tylenol, I catch a glimpse of a bare ankle peeking over the edge of my couch. Curious, I round the corner and clap both hands over my eyes.

"Oh my God!"

Teddy sits bolt upright with a shriek of alarm, the sudden movement knocking Jude right off the couch. They're both stark naked.

I keep my eyes covered amidst the chaos of giggling while they search for their clothes.

"You can look now," Teddy tells me eventually. I drop my hand to find them both curled on the couch. Teddy is wearing Jude's checked shirt. Jude's white T-shirt is inside out. There's an empty champagne bottle on the floor.

Slowly, I piece together the fragments of last night. Teddy yawns, and as she covers her mouth with her hand, realization hits.

"Oh my God, Teddy!" I point at her finger, where the black band is visible through the clear dressing.

Teddy moves her hand away from her mouth and blinks at the

tattoo. Then her eyes cut to Jude's hand. Jude is staring at his own finger as if he's never seen it before.

"We got married," Teddy says.

"You got married," I confirm.

"We can't be married," Jude says. "There's no way Josie got ordained for real."

"Of course not," Teddy agrees quickly. Then she swallows. "Although, I'm more concerned about this right now!" she shoves her tattooed finger into his face as if he wielded the needle that put it there.

My MacBook is still open on the website I found last night. I scan it with Teddy breathing over my shoulder while Jude stumbles around in the kitchen making coffee.

"Okay, it says that I have a legal responsibility to complete a marriage certificate on the wedding day. We didn't do that, right?"

Jude sets down the mugs, and our eyes fall on the crumpled piece of paper below them. I recognize Teddy's signature at the bottom and Jude's jagged scrawl.

"That can't be legit," Teddy says.

"Look, it's going to be fine. I'll call them right now. Even if it turns out that this is official, we can just have the marriage annulled, right?"

"On what grounds?"

I rack my brain and then side eye Teddy. "You didn't consummate the marriage, did you?"

"We did," Jude answers easily. "Twice."

Teddy is dying. I try to keep a straight face, but I can't. "I'm throwing this couch out," I say. Jude starts to laugh.

"It isn't funny!" Teddy groans. "What are we going to do if we can't get this annulled?"

"It might not even be legal, Teddy."

"I have something to say," Jude interrupts. Teddy looks up at him, renewed hope flaring in her eyes. Jude, however, is frowning and I suspect what he's about to say isn't what Teddy is expecting.

"What if I don't want to have it annulled?"

It takes Teddy a moment to process. "What?"

Jude stares her down. "Yes, we were drunk, but that doesn't mean I didn't want to marry you."

"It's true," I concede. "Jude's loved you since," I try to come up with a date and settle for "well, since forever."

"He has not!"

"Actually," Jude says, without a trace of embarrassment, "I have."

Despite my hangover, I can't help but smirk. Teddy doesn't seem to know what to do with her face.

"That's... you're...," she sputters helplessly. She takes a deep breath and starts over. "You can't possibly expect this to work. We live on opposite sides of the country!"

"I'll move."

"What?"

"WHAT?" I echo Teddy's question. The thought of Jude leaving L.A is inconceivable, but his face is deadly serious.

"You'd move almost three thousand miles just to see if this might work?" Teddy asks.

"That's crazy," I snap. "Your whole life is here. What about *The Office*? You've spent years working to build something here and now that you have it, you're just going to up and leave?"

"I can find someone to manage the bar without me. Laurel's been there long enough, and she deserves a raise. I might even make her partner."

"But..."

Jude gives me a sad look. "You're right, Josie. I *have* spent years working. And do you know where it's got me? I'm thirty-four years old, and I haven't ever had a real relationship. Christ, I haven't even had a vacation in ten years." His gaze shifts from my face to Teddy's and his eyes soften. "Your sister is right. I've loved you since the first moment I saw you. So how about it, Teddy? I'd like permission from my wife, to date her."

. . .

I CAN'T BELIEVE I have to fly to Chicago this week. Teddy has extended her stay for a few days while she and Jude work this out, but I am quite sure that she's going to say yes. It's clear that they're crazy about each other. As happy as I am for them, watching them together only highlights how alone I am. It also makes me think of Ace, and I really don't want to be thinking about Ace. For someone who claimed to care for me, he made walking away look easy.

"You should call him," Teddy tells me on Tuesday evening. Fenn left half an hour ago, taking Noodle with her, and Teddy's been watching me pack. Jude is at *The Office*, getting things ready for his unexpected trip across the country.

"I wouldn't know what to say," I admit. I hold up a pale yellow shirt, and Teddy shakes her head.

I toss it on the discard pile and turn to find something else.

"You could start by telling him you made a mistake," she says gently.

"I don't think I did. He's been lying to me, Teddy."

"You don't know that."

"I know that he hasn't been telling the truth. And like dad says, omission of the truth is as good as a lie."

"I think after your big reveal, dad may have changed his mind about that."

"He's still not talking to me." I'd tried to call my father again this morning, but he'd let my mother answer.

"Look at the bright side. Once I get home and tell him I got drunk-married to a man he barely knows, your indiscretions will seem a lot less sordid."

I brighten. "That's true!"

Teddy laughs. "You could at least try to look less pleased about it. For my sake."

"He's going to love Jude. He already loves Jude. You'll be fine."

I pull out a few pastel tops and gather them in my arms.

"I better get going. I promised Jude I'd meet him for a drink,"

Teddy says. She gets up and gives me a meaningful stare. "Call him, Josie."

When she's gone, I slump onto the soft carpet and pull out my phone. I stare at Ace's name on the screen. My finger hovers over the call button. The phone pings with an incoming text and I almost drop it. *We need to talk.* It's from Alex. I stare at the words and a sob rises in my chest because it's not Alex I want to talk to right now. Decision made, I take a deep breath and dial Ace's number.

Ace answers on the first ring. "Josie?"

My courage evaporates.

"Josie, are you okay?" he sounds frantic.

"I'm fine."

"Oh, thank God."

"What's going on? Are you okay?" I ask, panicked.

"Hold on, give me a second." He mutes the phone, and I curse in frustration. It takes forever before he's back.

"What's wrong Josie? Why are you calling me?"

"I... I just wanted to talk."

"About?"

"About us."

I hear his shocked intake of breath. When he speaks again, he sounds stilted, as if he's trying to keep his temper in check. "What about us, Josie?"

He's agitated, and it's making me wish I'd never hit that call button.

"Never mind," I say quickly. "It was a mistake to call."

"You kicked me out," he says.

Without even thinking, the words pour out. "You said you'd come back."

He falls silent. I wait, cringing, the phone cradled against my ear.

"Do you want me to come back?"

That catches me off guard. "I don't know. I'm confused, Ace. I thought we... you just walked away, as if it meant nothing."

"Oh, Josie," he sighs, and I can hear the sincerity in his voice. "I was never far away."

What?

"What do you mean?"

He curses under his breath. I hear a man's voice, stern and berating. "Who are you with?" I ask.

"Hold on." He mutes me again, and I scream in frustration. "Josie, meet me downstairs."

Confusion, pure and simple, courses through me. I fly to my feet and out of my apartment. Has the elevator always been this slow? The lobby is empty. Frank smiles at me as I pass his station, and then I'm out the doors and on the sidewalk, scanning the street. Ace isn't here. A movement across the road draws my attention, and I frown in confusion as he steps out of the apartment block opposite mine. His face softens at the sight of me. His eyes never leave mine as he crosses the street.

"What are you doing here?" I ask when he's finally standing before me.

"Inside," he says. He's guarded, alert, and his shoulders are tense beneath his grey T-shirt. Behind him, through the door of his apartment block, I catch sight of a man standing just inside the door, watching us.

"Ace, you're freaking me out."

"Walk, Josie."

He follows me back inside. As soon as the elevator doors close, I let him have it.

"What the hell is going on? Who was that man? And why were you in that apartment block?"

"I'm going to lose my job for this," he replies.

"You don't have a job!"

"Let's get inside, Josie. I'll explain everything then."

We go to the living room. "Explain," I say.

Ace doesn't explain. Instead, he pulls a badge from his back pocket and hands it to me. I stare at the familiar crest. I've played an agent or two in my day. The seal is impossible not to recognize, nor is his name on the identity card beside it.

"FBI?" I whisper, my voice a croak. "Is this a joke?"

"No." he takes the badge back. "I'm going to hold onto this seeing as I'm about to lose it."

"You're with the FBI?" It's inconceivable.

"It's a long story, but yes."

"And you didn't tell me."

"I'm undercover, Josie. Not telling you is part of my job."

"But, why? Your being undercover has nothing to do with me – with us."

"My being undercover has everything to do with you."

A searing white pain shoots through my skull. "Oh, God."

Ace grabs my shoulders. "With you, Josie, not with us," he tries to explain, but it's too late. I yank out of his grasp.

"You needed me for a job, didn't you?"

"No, that's not what this is."

"Bullshit! What has this got to do with me?"

"It's complicated. For your own protection—"

"Don't you dare!" I roar. "I deserve to know!"

"Calm down!"

I slap him.

His head ricochets to the right. "Dammit Josie, calm down!" he yells just as his phone starts to ring.

"Hartley, this isn't a good time," he snaps. The person on the other end speaks rapidly, and the blood drains from Ace's face. "I've got her. Call it in, I want the full team ready to move." He ends the call and looks at me with real fear on his face. "Josie, listen to me. I don't have time to explain. You want to know why I'm here, why I've been watching you? It's Alex. This is all about Alex."

"Alex? Why on earth—"

"No time," he reminds me. "But you can't trust him, He's dangerous, Josie. You said I used to be the good guy. I still am. Please, you have to trust me, and you have to trust me *now*."

"Why?" I croak.

"Because he's on his way up."

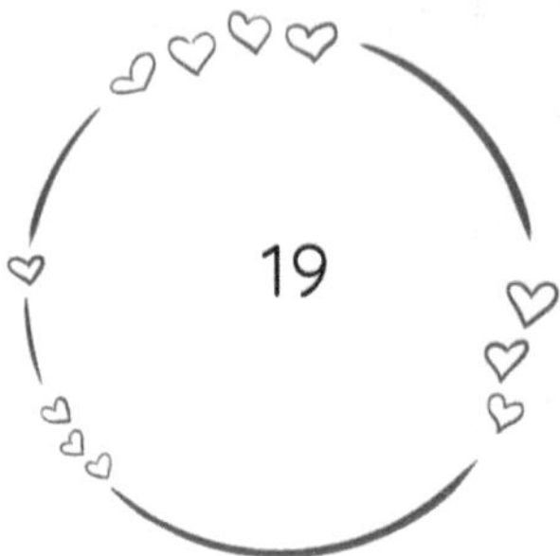

19

I barely have time to register his words when I hear the knock on the door. My blood turns to ice. Ace lifts a finger to his lips, warning me to be silent. My phone is still in my hand. I raise it to find another text from Alex, right after the last. *I'm coming over.* It must have come through while I was on the phone to Ace. I hold the phone up, and Ace reads the text.

"Just stay calm," he murmurs in my ear, "he's probably read about our break up and wants to try to get you back. Act natural, but get rid of him as soon as you can."

My heart is hammering in my chest, my saliva turned to acid.

"I'll be right here, Josie."

Another knock, louder this time. Ace slips into the kitchen and vanishes from sight. My feet are heavy as I walk toward the door.

"Hey." Alex smiles when he sees me, but it doesn't reach his eyes.

"Alex, what are you doing here?"

"I wanted to see you. I read about what happened." I don't ask whether he's referring to me having sex with Ace, or our break up. "Didn't you get my text?"

I shake my head. "It's not really a good time. I'm packing, I have an early flight."

"Chicago filming starting?" he asks fondly, reminding me that he knows my schedule as well as I do.

"Yes."

"Can I come in? I won't stay long." There's something different about his eyes. They're glittering, manic. After spending two years with Alex, I feel as though I'm looking at a stranger.

"I'm sorry, Alex, it's just not a good time." I start to close the door, but he rams his foot forward, jamming it open. I gape down at his shoe and then arch my brow.

"Alex?"

His smile changes. "I really do need to come in. I've done some digging, and I've discovered the most interesting facts about your new boyfriend. I assume *I'm* the reason he's been hanging around?"

"I don't know what you're talking about."

His eyes search my face, find the fear imprinted there. "You're a terrible actress."

A moment passes between us, one in which we both come to a decision. I throw my weight against the door. At the same time, Alex shoves it open. His superior strength wins out, and it bangs painfully into my shoulder.

"What has he told you?" Alex hisses in my ear. "What does he know?" His hand bites into my arm, jerking me toward him.

"Get your hands off me!"

"What, you don't like it rough?" he sneers. "You really had me fooled. All that time I held out for you, ever the gentleman, only for you to whore yourself to the next man to cross your path."

"Don't talk to me like that."

"I'll talk to you any way I damned well please. Now, you and I are going to sit down, and you're going to tell me *exactly* how much that bastard knows."

"And then what?"

His smile is pure malice, and a wave of nausea rises up in me. I try to shake him off with renewed energy, but he has me in a vice-grip. Desperate, terrified, I kick out at his shin. I'm barely able to appreciate the thud as my shoe connects, when he's hit me, hard, across the face. My vision swims, and I taste blood on my lip.

"Let her go." Ace's voice is a calm fury. He's standing in the kitchen doorway, his arm raised. The gun in his hand is trained on Alex, only an inch above my head. I feel Alex stiffen behind me. "Let her go," Ace repeats, taking a few steps toward us.

"Who the hell *are* you?" Alex asks, shifting so that I'm squarely between him and the gun.

Ace pulls out his badge. "John Logan, FBI. Now let her go."

"Not going to happen. Do you have any idea who I am? You're a dead man."

"Not yet, I'm not. And I know exactly who you are, you piece of shit. Now let her go, before"

Before Ace can finish speaking, Alex's free arm moves behind me. Too late, I call out a warning, but he's already pulled a gun. He presses it to my temple, the cold bite of steel nothing compared to the flare of terror in my chest. I let out a whimper.

"Drop it," Ace growls, his face a mask of fury. He takes another step toward us. Alex's only response is to twist the barrel more deeply into my skin.

"You first," Alex says. Ace falters.

"Don't!" I sob.

"Shut up!" Alex tells me. Then, glancing toward the door, he sidesteps, dragging me with him.

"You won't get away," Ace warns, keeping his voice level. "I have men stationed outside and at every exit."

"Please, Alex," I beg, "don't do this."

"I told you to shut up!"

He's so focused on me that he misses the quick look that Ace darts toward the door. It's still open, I realize. And the man that Ace spoke to on the phone – Hartley – knows Alex is here. If Ace told him to have the team ready to move, then that means...

I don't have time to think it through. Ace moves, launching forward as a gunshot rings out, so close to my ear, it's deafening. The boom renders me temporarily deaf as Alex jerks behind me, his arm tight around my throat. I see the glint of steel as he levels the gun. It all happens so fast, and then I'm screaming, watching helplessly as Ace drops to his knees and stares down at his chest in disbelief as blood blooms through his T-shirt.

A third gunshot and Alex's arm drops away. I lurch forward, falling to my knees beside Ace as men dressed in black pour into the room.

Ace is still conscious. I whip off my cardigan and press it to his chest to staunch the flow of blood. There's so much, my jeans are already soaked through.

"Ace!" I'm sobbing. His eyes meet mine, filled with relief.

"You're okay," he murmurs.

"Shhh, don't try to talk."

An agent appears on Ace's other side. He's yelling orders, calling for an ambulance. Firm hands pull me up, away from Ace. I kick out at the agent, but he steers me away. I twist in his grasp, see Ace speaking to the agent beside him. The man raises his hand. We stop. I'm free. I skid back to Ace's side. His smile is fading.

"Don't you dare die on me," I beg.

20

They let me ride in the ambulance, but I'm curled up in the far corner, staying out of the way while a team of paramedics works frantically to save Ace's life. Ace is so pale, deathly pale, and I keep my eyes fixed on the rise and fall of his chest. The agent who allowed me to stay – Ben Hartley, I learn – is with me, grim-faced.

"I told him not to go over there," he tells me. My heart pinches. If Ace hadn't been there, I don't know what Alex would've done, but I do know that Ace wouldn't have been hurt. "I don't need to tell you that this is confidential," Hartley says. I nod, not trusting myself to speak. "There's not much I can tell you, Miss Hudson, other than we've been investigating your ex-fiance for some time now. Let's just say he didn't make his money through corporate investments as he claims."

Past tense. Alex is dead. He was shot twice at close range. I should feel bad about it, but all I can think of is that he died too slowly. He managed to get a shot off at Ace before the team brought him down.

"How did he make his money, then?" I ask, even though I'm not sure I want to know the answer. Hartley casts a quick glance at the frantic medics.

"Not now," he murmurs, but I'm already distracted.

"Is he going to make it?" I whisper, gesturing at Ace.

"I've seen weaker men recover from worse."

They take Ace straight into surgery. I wait in the visitor's room, slumped in a straight-backed chair with my head in my hands. Black-clad strangers surround me, their collective concern palpable. They all know Ace so well – far better than I do, judging by the way they speak about him. I was so stupid. How did I not see that he was so much more than just a deadbeat wannabe actor?

"How long has Ace been an agent?" I ask the room at large. They all turn to look at me, seeming shocked to discover I'm there. A greying man with a scarred nose takes pity on me.

"Five years. He signed up right out of college and moved through the ranks faster than anyone else I know. It was just after his mother died."

His mother? I pull my phone from my purse and start to Google. It takes me a while, but I eventually find an article which mentions her, only briefly. Collateral damage of a drug bust gone wrong. *Jesus.* No wonder Ace dropped out and followed a career that would see justice served.

At some point, Hartley comes to stand before me. I see his black boots, but I don't look up.

"I'm going to need you to answer some questions, Miss Hudson."

"Josie," I say automatically.

"Josie," he acquiesces.

I lift my head. "Can it wait?"

He sighs and evicts the agent sitting beside me from his seat.

"Alex ran a drug cartel under cover of one of his subsidiaries. As far as we can gather, he's responsible for over a hundred million dollars' worth of heroin hitting U.S. soil in the past two years alone."

Drugs. Alex was dealing in drugs.

"How could I not know?" I spent two years with Alex, how could

I have been so blind to his crimes? I rack my brain, trying to think of a single instance that might have clued me in, but I come up blank. Barring the frequent travel, and the "meetings", which, admittedly, I never delved too deeply into, there was nothing out of the ordinary. No warning signs.

"He was a smart guy. Hell, it took us three years to build a case against him which might stick. And it gets worse. Over the past year, eight women have disappeared – prostitutes, runaways. Nobody paid much attention, until one of them managed to escape. The information she gave us led us to believe your husband was the abductor."

My mind reels. "Alex wasn't... he was never violent with me. Not once, in two years."

The look he gives me is pure pity. "Until he was," he says softly.

I blink back fresh tears. "Ace knew?"

"Yes. For what it's worth, Miss Hudson, I didn't want to bring you into this. I had no way of knowing whether you were involved in Mr. Masters' illegal activities. Logan went off plan when he contacted you."

"Why, though? Why contact me at all, why bring me into this mess?"

This time, the look he gives me is incredulous. "You really don't know the answer to that?"

"No, *Detective*, I really don't know the answer to that."

"Logan didn't want you tied up in this. He was concerned for your safety, especially when we discovered the missing women. He broke protocol when he made contact with you, to get you away from a man who is a suspected murderer. And he risked his badge to do it."

ACE SURVIVES THE SURGERY, but he's not out of the woods, not by a long shot. He's being monitored around the clock. No visitors are permitted, save for immediate family, and as far as I know, his father is still trying to find a flight out of Sacramento.

"You should go home and get some rest," Hartley tells me in the early hours of the morning. I'm slumped in my chair, and I have a plane to catch in six hours. He hands me a card with his contact details. "I'll have someone stationed outside your apartment until we're sure that all of Alex's accomplices have been brought to justice." He sees my longing glance down the hall. "You can come back tomorrow, perhaps they'll allow you in."

Reality asserts itself. "I'm supposed to be leaving for Chicago in a few hours."

"Can it wait?"

I stifle a sob. "I'm under contract."

"Well, I guess you've got to do what you've got to do. How soon can you get back?"

My mind draws a blank. I check the schedule on my phone, which is about to die.

"Not for at least ten days." Even then, I'll be pushing it. It'll have to be a day stop.

"He's going to need a long recovery, I'm sure he'll still be right here when you get back."

"I can't just leave him without even saying goodbye."

Hartley shrugs. I guess in a world of bullets and death, my feature film commitments must seem beyond trivial. I get to my feet, willing myself not to cry.

"I'll tell him you said goodbye," Hartley says. He doesn't meet my eyes when he says it.

21

Fenn is waiting in the lobby when I arrive home.

"Jojo!" She barrels into me, giving me the first real hug I've had since Ace left. I burst into tears. "I heard about the shooting. I've been desperate, but no one would give me any information and I couldn't get hold of Jude until just now..." she rattles this all off without pausing for breath. "He's on his way over, Teddy too. Oh my God, Jojo, I've been beside myself. What happened?"

"It's a really long story."

Fenn whips out her phone. "Reports are saying that Alex is dead."

"He is." I feel nothing when I say it. "I'm sorry, Fenn, but I can't tell you anything. There's an investigation and... well, I just can't say anything."

She shoves her phone back into her bag. "Understood. But you're okay?"

"I'm okay."

"What can I do?"

"Nothing, Fenn, honestly. All I need right now is a hot bath and to finish packing."

She steers me toward the elevator. "Well, I can help with that at least."

I'm soaking my weary bones in the sudsy water Fenn ran for me when Teddy barges into the bathroom, Jude hot on her heels.

I give a shriek of fright and try to cover myself with my face-cloth.

"What the hell happened?" Teddy asks furiously. Her lip is quivering and, before I can even get the words 'I'm okay' out of my mouth, she bursts into tears and drops to the floor beside the bath, drenching herself as she pulls me into a hug. I meet Jude's eyes over her shoulder. They're filled with concern.

"You okay?" He mouths the words. I nod as silent tears slide down my cheeks. Satisfied, he leaves the bathroom, closing the door quietly behind him. Teddy pulls herself together and helps me out of the bath. She dries my body, as gently as if I were a child, and then calls for Fenn to bring me something to wear. Ever-trustworthy Fenn brings me my most comfortable traveling outfit – soft jeans, sneakers and a cashmere sweater. I manage to dress myself, but that's as far as I get before I collapse onto my bed.

"I've put your phone on charge," Fenn says briskly, "and you're all packed."

Teddy gasps. "You're not seriously leaving?"

"Oh," Fenn adds, "and the press are here."

"Fucking bloodhounds," Jude growls, marching into my room in time to hear her last comment. "They've completely blocked the exit, Josie. You're not going anywhere for a while."

"I'm under contract," I whisper. The thing is, it doesn't sound like a big deal to anyone not in the know, but if I delay filming it costs the studio hundreds of thousands of dollars, which I'd be liable for. Not to mention the inconvenience to every single person who turns up. Not that I care about any of it, but this could ruin me. Legally, I have no choice but to go.

Fenn gives me a thoughtful look and darts out of the bedroom. A second later she's back with an enormous file. "There has to be a clause in your contract that covers extreme circumstances like this," she ponders out loud, flipping through the pages so fast it makes my head hurt. A tiny flame of hope flickers in my chest. I daren't let it kindle.

"George will know," I say. "He knows those contracts inside and out."

Fenn lifts her phone to her ear. "I'm on it," she says, striding out of the room.

Teddy sits down gently beside me and wraps both arms around my shoulders. "What happened?" she asks, keeping her voice down so only Jude can hear.

"Alex came over. He was bad news, Teddy. He..." my voice breaks and I feel her stiffen beside me.

"On a scale of one to ten, how bad?" she asks.

"There is no scale for people like him."

Jude curses. I manage a watery-eyed smile as I tell Teddy, "Jude never liked him."

Teddy doesn't smile back, but her grip tightens convulsively. "Did he hurt you?"

"No. He might have, but Ace stopped him."

"Ace?"

"I called him, like you told me to."

"No wonder the weather's all over the place. The last time you listened to me you were in kindergarten."

"It turns out Ace works for the FBI. They were investigating Alex this whole time."

"For what?"

I gaze helplessly at her. "I don't know what I'm allowed to say."

"Screw that. I'm your sister!"

"Leave it," Jude growls, uncharacteristically sharp with her. To my astonishment, Teddy takes a deep breath and leaves it.

"Where is Ace now?"

It's too much. I choke on my words. "He's in the hospital."

"The broadcast I saw mentioned an unidentified man was injured in the shooting," Jude says. "That was him?"

"Yes. He wouldn't even have been here if I hadn't—"

"Stop right there," Teddy cuts me off. "If he hadn't been here, you might've been hurt. Or worse. How bad is it?"

"He had surgery last night. He pulled through, but they wouldn't let me see him."

"George found a loophole!" Fenn bursts back into the room. "It's an unspecified clause, but he says in this instance it definitely applies." She pauses, catching sight of my stricken face. "He also said to tell you that if anyone gives you any shit about it, you let him know and he'll remind Garfield Harrison about the threesome in Cancun the night before his wedding." She shrugs. "I don't know if he means his or Harrison's wedding."

Despite everything, I smile through my tears. George always comes through. "I don't have to go?"

Fenn holds up the contract. "According to this, you may temporarily suspend filming for up to twenty-one days."

Three weeks. I leap off the bed and scramble for my sneakers.

"Where are you going?" Teddy squawks.

Jude is far more astute. "You're not going to make it through that crowd, Josie," he warns. I'd forgotten about them. I cock my head to one side and a small smile tugs up the corners of my mouth.

"Do you know how to ride a motorcycle?"

HARTLEY DOESN'T QUESTION why I want to know if Ace's bike is in the lot across the street. He even offers to have someone retrieve the keys from their base apartment. I don't know how much Ace has told him about me, but I gather he knows Ace wouldn't mind. The same man who followed me home and has been stationed outside my door jogs across to Ace's apartment block. The baying reporters barely give him a second look.

Ten minutes later, he pulls into the underground lot on Ace's bike. Jude gives me a wry look.

"Last chance to back out," he warns. "I'm more than a little rusty."

"I'm not changing my mind," I say. "The press sees what they want to. Jojo Hudson, Hollywood's darling would never be seen on the back of a motorcycle."

"Shows how little they know," Jude grins. "Because Josie Hudson, my favorite waitress, has got a lot more backbone."

I climb up behind him, and he guns the engine. I only have time to wrap my arms around his waist, and we're off, speeding up the ramp and out onto the street. I sneak a glimpse at the pack of reporters outside my apartment doors, baying for blood. Nobody pays us any attention, except for a lone, mousy-haired man a few feet away. I flip him the bird as Jude leans us into a corner and we disappear into the traffic.

22

My sneakers make no sound on the clinical white tiles. I feel a bit ridiculous carrying a helmet over my arm, but I'm so thrilled that we managed to evade the press, I don't even care. In fact, I might start biking everywhere.

Hartley is the only one left in the visitor's lounge. He gets to his feet when we walk in. "Miss Hudson?" His eyes fall to the helmet. "I guess you got hold of that bike, although I must admit I didn't expect to see you back here so soon."

"I found a loophole in my contract. How is he?"

"He's awake, or so the doctors tell me."

"Can we see him?"

"Not yet. I'm going to stick around until they give us the go ahead."

I take my familiar seat. "Well then, I'm waiting with you."

Jude brings us coffee from the machine down the hall.

"You should go," I tell him after the second cup. "Teddy will be worried. I'll call you if I need you to come back."

He hesitates, torn between wanting to stay with me, wanting to see Teddy, and wanting to escape the monotony of the hospital. I also think he's itching to get back on the bike, although he'd never admit it.

"You're sure?" he asks eventually.

"I'm sure."

"Okay." He gets to his feet. "You call me the second you want to leave and I'll come back and get you."

Hartley listens to our conversation without saying a word. Until Jude leaves.

"He the bartender?" he asks.

I imagine a board filled with black and white surveillance photographs and wonder just how much of my life this man has witnessed. "He is," I reply.

"Logan likes him. Says he's a good guy."

A movement at the doorway has us both on our feet, but it's not the surgeon. It's Ace's father. Even though I've never met him, the resemblance is impossible to miss.

"Mr. Logan." Hartley offers his hand, but Ace's dad pulls him into a bear hug instead.

"Ben. Thank you for calling me. How is he?"

"He's not in any immediate danger, but he's not out of the woods yet, either. We're expecting another update any minute now."

"Have you seen him?"

"No, Sir."

Ace's dad nods. His eyes fall to me.

"This is Jojo Hudson," Hartley begins, but Ace's dad holds up a hand to stop him.

"I know who she is." He takes two long strides toward me. "It's Josie, right?" he asks. I swallow the lump which has formed in my throat and bob my head. His eyes twinkle as he pulls me into a hug. "I wondered when I'd meet the girl who stole my son's heart," he says in my ear. Then, pulling back to look into my eyes, "I only wish it was under better circumstances." I start to laugh, dazzled by the fact that Ace told his dad about me, but it turns into a sob. "Oh, none of that now, girl," Mr. Logan says, pulling me back to his shoulder and thumping my back in what I assume is supposed to be a soothing gesture. "Logan men are made of strong stuff. You better toughen up if you expect to be with one."

I hiccup against his broad chest. "Yes, Sir," I mumble.

"It's Robert," he insists.

He finally lets me go when the surgeon arrives. I swipe at my eyes and nose, my face burning.

"Mr. Logan, I'm Doctor Thompson," he says, shaking Robert's hand. "I assume you've been brought up to date?"

"How is my son?" Robert asks, cutting through the preamble.

The Doctor smiles. "I don't like to make early predictions, but I think it's safe to say he's going to make a full recovery." He's barely finished speaking when Robert treats him to his own bear hug, lifting him clear off his feet. He doesn't seem to know what to do and flops around like a rag doll.

Once he's back on solid ground, he turns to Hartley. "I've moved him, as you requested. He's in a private ward. I'm sorry it took so long, but moving equipment out of ICU isn't as easy as it sounds."

"I appreciate everything you've done," Hartley replies.

"It's the least we can do, given the circumstances."

I blink at them in alarm. Hartley notices me and lowers his voice. "It's just a precaution, while he's incapacitated. I'll have a man stationed permanently outside his door."

"Can we see him?" Robert asks.

The Doctor hesitates, but Hartley clears his throat audibly, reminding him that this is not just any patient. I assume allowances are made for Federal agents who risk their lives for country.

"Of course," he replies smoothly. "But only one visitor at a time."

We follow him down the hall, through a labyrinth of twists and turns, until we reach a non-descript door.

"One at a time," the doctor reminds us, before returning to his rounds.

Robert goes first. He's inside a long time, and he's already apologizing on his way out.

"He's fallen asleep," he whispers.

Hartley sweeps a practiced look up and down the hallway and then pushes the door open. "Come on," he tells me with a jerk of his head. I don't need to be told twice. I slip inside, and he follows.

Ace is fast asleep, attached to so many machines it takes me a while to navigate my way to his side. Hartley settles for standing straight-backed at the foot of the bed. Ace's face is so pale even his blond hair looks dark. I find my eyes drawn to the bandage around his chest and my heart pinches. We stand in silence, watching over him. I'm happy just to look at him, but I suspect Hartley has no desire to examine every inch of his precious face because after ten minutes he excuses himself. At the soft sound of the door closing, Ace opens his eyes.

"I thought he'd never leave," he wheezes, a flash of mischief in his dulled eyes.

"You're awake!" I want to throw myself on him, to hug him, but it's impossible with all the electrodes covering his chest. I settle for taking his hand.

"Only just. I should've stopped him, but I wanted to talk to you alone first."

The word 'alone' makes me feel warm and fuzzy. "I was so worried about you," I say, "I didn't know if you were going to make it."

"Such little faith in me," he teases. Then he turns serious. "Alex?"

"He's gone."

"I'm sorry."

"For what?"

"I know he meant a lot to you."

"Not as much as I thought." Carefully, I take a seat on the very edge of the bed. "I can't believe I didn't suspect anything. All those terrible things he was doing and I was completely oblivious."

"You need to know that I didn't set out to ruin your life, Josie. I knew you were dating him, obviously. The whole world knew that, but it wasn't until he came under investigation for murder and abduction that I decided to do anything about it." I stay silent. "You should also know," he begins slowly, "that I have absolutely zero interest in becoming an actor."

I start to laugh and find I can't stop. "So you don't need me to advance your career after all?"

"I don't need you to advance my career." A pause, and then he says the sweetest words I've ever heard. "But I do need *you*."

"I need you too."

We lapse into a beautiful silence, our hands the only physical contact between us.

"Hey," Ace says after a while, "aren't you supposed to be flying out today?"

A grin splits my face as I recall how we started, and the road that brought us here. "I didn't get on the plane," I say meaningfully. Ace's answering smile is the sun coming out from behind a dark cloud.

"You didn't get on the plane," he echoes.

Screw it, I think, leaning toward him. I hear the electronic tempo of his heartbeat spike as our lips meet. By the time Doctor Thompson bursts through the door, a grinning Hartley behind him, neither of us is in any state to notice.

END OF BOOK 1.

AWKWARD ABROAD

BOOK 2 IN THE AWKWARD SERIES

1

I wake with a dull pain in my head and the all too familiar dry mouth that follows a night of heavy drinking. I lie as still as possible, knowing that when I move, it's going to bring a world of hurt. Only yesterday I'd sworn off booze. I was going to go dry for a month to give my liver a much-needed break. As it turns out, the road to hell truly is paved with good intentions. I'd lasted all of six hours before Lara suggested a Vodka tonic at *The Appaloosa*.

Tentatively, I turn my head, and a wave of pain cuts through my skull. I can only clutch my forehead until it subsides, cursing my non-existent willpower. In the kingdom of self-destructive assholes, I'm a queen. What I'm not, however, is a masochist. I avoid pain wherever possible, which is why I pull a pillow over my head and go right back to sleep.

The sun is high in the sky when I wake again. The silky softness of satin caresses my skin. I peer below the sheets and utter a low curse. I'm naked. And now that I think about it, I don't have satin sheets. My hand inches across the broad expanse of the bed, terrified I might encounter warm male flesh. I almost weep in relief to discover I'm alone. Through lowered lashes, I examine my surroundings. The hotel suite is impressive, even by my standards. Floor to ceiling windows stretch the length of the wall opposite the bed. Gauzy tulle curtains blow gently in the breeze at the open balcony door. I scan every inch of the room I can see without moving a muscle, and only when I'm almost certain I'm alone, do I lift my head. A discarded champagne flute lies on its side on a marble table. Beyond that rises an enormous white sofa, utterly devoid of any cushions. They're strewn across the pale grey carpet, along with my clothes. The Michael Kors dress I was wearing last night, lies in a crumpled heap next to an empty Moët bottle. The scrap of red lace a few feet away brings a flush to my cheeks.

I flop back onto the satin sheets and drape my arm over my eyes, willing myself to remember what the hell happened last night. I remember doing Tequila shots. I remember holding onto the bar counter when the room started to spin. I'd been with Lara, or at least I had been until that stag party had arrived. After that, everything is a bit of a blur.

"Good morning, Amber." The voice is curt, clipped, and to my horror, utterly familiar. I'd know that voice anywhere. I've heard it almost every day for as long as I can remember. I sit bolt upright and gape at the figure lounging against the balcony door. It feels like I left my brain behind on the pillow, but that's the least of my worries. I'm naked, and this is *his* room. The perfectly logical conclusion is one that I refuse to consider.

"I said good morning, Amber," Kent James repeats dryly, then, after an exaggerated look at his watch, "or perhaps good afternoon would be more appropriate."

Caught quite literally with my pants down, I go immediately on the defensive. "What's so good about it?"

"I guess not much from your position."

"Oh, go and nail your dick to a door."

"Always so eloquent. It's nice to see you putting that private school education to good use."

I'm distracted by the scent of coffee, only to realize he's holding a steaming mug. I glance pointedly at it and arch my brow.

"Oh, sorry," he says, sounding wholly unapologetic as he waves the mug in my direction. "I would have got you one, but I figured from the snoring you'd be asleep a few more hours."

I'm too hungover to think of a suitable response. "What the hell happened last night? Why am I in a hotel room? And why am I naked?" I add, throwing him a filthy look.

He chuckles, low and melodious.

"Firstly, you owe me for the room," he says. "There was no way I'd have made it across town with you in the state you were in when I found you last night." He gives me the stern look which stopped working on me years ago. "And secondly, don't flatter yourself. Every other guy in that club might've wanted a piece of your ass – including the groom to be, by the way, but I prefer my women with a little more self-respect."

It's a low blow, but I let it slide. "So, we didn't actually...?"

"Have sex?"

I grimace. "Ugh. God, Kent, could you be any more gross?"

"Hey, I'm not the one who was tearing my clothes off last night and claiming I'd take you to places you'd only ever dreamed about."

I risk a glance at my crumpled dress. "I didn't."

"Oh, you did. You also drank an entire bottle of Moët, which I'm going to have to pay for."

"You can afford it," I grumble.

"So can you. I'll send you the bill."

"Fine. Now can we just pretend none of this ever happened and go back to annoying each other to death? Throw me my dress so I can get the hell out of here."

An exasperated look crosses his face. It's a nice face, actually. Strong features, but with surprising softness to them when he thinks no one is looking. Those intense green eyes which always make me look away first. No matter how nice the face, though, Kent's been a bit of a dick since college. He's not someone I would associate with by choice, not anymore anyway. The fact that our mothers have been best friends since childhood means that we've known each other, unofficially, since the womb. We were born only two weeks apart and spent most of our childhood giving our mother's grey hairs. Now, Kent works for my father and seems set to become every bit as uptight and intolerant as he is.

My father, Peter Holland, is a property magnate who spends his days terrorizing his massive staff complement and making money. A harsh man who sees everything in black and white, he has never forgiven me for flouting his authority and opting to study language over property law. A strict teetotaller, with an iron will and impeccable self-control, my erratic and irresponsible behavior drives him demented.

In Kent, however, he has found the perfect ally. Not only does he add some much-needed modernism to Saber Development, the company my father started only a few years after I was born, he also dons a twin frown of disapproval every time I so much as set a toe out of line. Which, incidentally, only encourages me further. It wasn't always like this. Growing up, Kent and I were inseparable – the terrible twosome, our mothers had called us. Together, we had wreaked havoc in the lives of the endless slew of nannies charged with trying to keep us under control. In second grade, I'd pummelled the nose of a particularly revolting boy who had made the mistake of trying to bully Kent on the playground. When the teacher on duty had grabbed my hands, I'd landed a well-placed kick to his crotch for good measure. In our sophomore year, a boy that I harbored a thumping crush on had made a lewd comment about my chest in front of the entire cafeteria during recess. By the fifth period, he'd been sporting a spectacular black eye, and Kent was nursing two broken knuckles. I'd told him he forgot to tuck in his thumb, then hugged him until he'd complained he didn't want to add two broken ribs to the list of injuries.

We'd been a team, back then, equally wild and accountable only to each other. We'd set off for college in his trusty Ford, my father having refused to buy me a car after I'd crashed his golf cart into the shed, filled with optimism and excitement. Little did we know that everything was about to change. Within six months, Kent had met a gorgeous blonde undergrad named Erica, who ate tofu and spent her free time hugging trees. I'd laughed at her sanctimonious attitude, but for the first time, Kent hadn't laughed with me. It wasn't long before we began to drift apart. When I joined the most popular drinking club on campus, Kent had joined the student council. Erica didn't last long, but it didn't matter. The seed she had planted continued to bloom, and something between us had been irreparably damaged. By the time we graduated, we were barely on speaking terms.

I left college with a degree, a group of friends who promised to be a lifelong bad influence, and no intention of finding a job anytime soon. Kent, on the other hand, wanted to start working before the ink had dried on his degree. Determined to work his way up the ladder, he'd approached my father for a letter of recommendation, having spent three summers interning at Saber. My father had taken one look at his impressive results, added a healthy dose of nepotism, and offered him a job. He's been wearing tailored suits and oozing disapproval ever since. Daddy's right-hand man, I like to call him these days. Mostly to his face.

"Amber?" It takes me a moment to realize that Kent has been speaking for some time and I haven't heard a word. "Are you even listening to me?"

"I'm trying not to, as far as I can help it."

"You might want to start, this is important."

A sense of unease creeps up my spine. He's wearing the face – the one he only wears when he's about to deliver bad news. The last time I saw it, my dad had insisted I get a job. It only lasted one summer, but I still shudder at the memory.

"Be warned, you're probably going to hate me even more than you do already once you hear this," Kent says.

"Not possible," I grumble, but he's not even listening. He's too caught up in his own rhetoric.

"And just so you know, I didn't want to be the one to tell you this. Not that you don't deserve it, but I'm getting tired of being the mediator between you and your father."

Liar. I bet he enjoys it. "Spit it out, Kent."

He sets down his mug and comes to sit on the edge of the bed. His eyes are hard and determined.

"You've gone too far, Amber," he says simply. "And your father is no fool. You may think you have the wool pulled over his eyes, but he knows exactly what you get up to."

"And what exactly is it that I get up to?" I ask. Kent has never been comfortable discussing my sex-life, and I'll be damned if I make this easy for him. To my astonishment, he doesn't even hesitate.

"You behave like a whore." It's blunt, brutal, and stings more than I care to admit. "Hell," he continues, "if I hadn't hauled your ass up here last night and fended off your not-so-subtle advances, you'd be walking bow-legged this morning."

An ugly heat rises on my cheeks. "You wish. I'd never throw myself at you, and besides, I doubt you'd be able to 'bow' anything."

"Shut up!" he roars. He's off the bed and halfway across the room before I can blink, pacing like a caged tiger. "You give yourself far too much credit. Your father knows exactly what you get up to, your mother too, and you're acting like that's okay? That your parents shouldn't be concerned when you're meeting Lara at least three times a week at *The Appaloosa*. That you get wasted and leave every time with a different man? You're not even remotely selective, so long as they have a hotel room and a platinum card."

When he says it like that, it does sound rather awful, but I refuse to be shamed like some child, especially by him. "You're twisting everything around. I'm just enjoying my youth."

"You're twenty-three! It's time to grow up."

I open my mouth to argue, then remember that my twenty-third birthday was a few weeks ago, and I'd spent most of it in an alcohol-induced haze. "Fine," I snap, "point taken. I'll try to do better."

"It's too late for false promises."

There's that look again. "What exactly are you saying?"

"Your dad has had enough. He gave you a final warning weeks ago, and you haven't paid even the slightest bit of attention."

"I'm not an employee, Kent. A final warning? Please, it's not like he can fire me."

"True. But he can cut you off."

"He would never."

"You crossed the line when you started sleeping with guys from the office. Do you think they keep quiet about that? The biggest feather in their proverbial cap – screwing Peter Holland's daughter."

"That's not fair. I've only slept with a couple of guys from the office, you're making it sound like I screwed the entire IT department!"

"Stuart and Dave *are* the entire IT department."

"Oh."

Kent runs his hands through his all too perfect black hair and lets out an exasperated sigh. When he looks at me again, his face is weary, his eyes softer.

"You're killing him, Amber. The man has a business to run, and you're making him a laughing stock."

My eyes prickle. I pull the sheets higher to hide my bare shoulders. I know I can be reckless. I want to be more than just a party animal, but as soon as I have that first tequila, it's like Amber disappears, and this other person takes control of my body. She's fierce and afraid of nothing. And apparently always horny.

Kent clears his throat. "I'm sorry," he says softly.

Again, that sense of foreboding. Kent never apologizes.

"Sorry for what? What exactly does this mean? Is he sending me to rehab? Is he curbing my allowance?" I pray it's not the last one. I've become accustomed to a certain lifestyle, and I really don't want to have to give it up. Then Kent speaks again, and I wish having my credit card confiscated was the worst of my worries.

"He's sending you to Beijing."

It takes me a full minute to recover. "You can't be serious."

He doesn't falter. "You'll be given enough money for rent and food. The rest you'll have to work for."

"You're not serious," I echo, then, when he doesn't respond, "what the hell am I supposed to do in Beijing?"

"The thing you're qualified to do. I've set up interviews at three different schools. You'll be teaching English, and finally putting that degree to good use."

I want to laugh at the absurdity of what he is saying, but I can't.

"Don't be immature about this," Kent warns, sensing an argument brewing. "Peter has given you plenty of chances to sort yourself out, but you're only getting worse. The last few weeks have been like watching a slow-motion train wreck. Consider this an intervention before you land yourself in serious trouble."

"This is ridiculous. You can't just send me away, I'm not a child."

"Really? You certainly act like one." I don't dignify that with a response, and he relents. "You're a smart girl. You have everything going for you, or at least you did before you became so hell-bent on destroying yourself. Your dad only wants what's best for you. For once in your life, just take his advice and try to be responsible. Who knows, maybe you'll get off early for good behavior."

"I'm not going to Beijing," I insist. "I'm almost certain I have a date tonight, and I plan to keep it."

His face falls. "What happened to you, Amber?" he whispers, so softly I barely catch the words.

I hate it when he does that. Shows a side of him that reminds me of our youth, and acts like he gives a shit. In an attempt to gain some control over the situation, I get out of bed without saying a word, flaunting my naked, sunbed-bronzed body while I leisurely reach for my dress. When I turn to put it on, he's looking the other way. *Bastard.*

With his back still to me, he says, in a voice like flint, "Go take a shower. Make yourself look less like a hooker. There's a boutique downstairs. I'll pick up some clothes for you. Your car leaves for the airport this afternoon."

I throw him a filthy look, grab my purse, and stagger toward the bathroom. Once the door is closed behind me, I rummage for my phone. The battery is almost dead. I sit on the edge of the marble double sink and dial my dad's number. He answers on the first ring.

"Don't even think about trying to change my mind."

"Daddy—"

"Daddy nothing. I am done playing games, Amber. You need to know how seriously I take your future, even if you don't. You can go to Beijing under my terms, or you can give it all up and try to make a life for yourself here with no help from me."

I open my mouth to argue, but he's already cut the call.

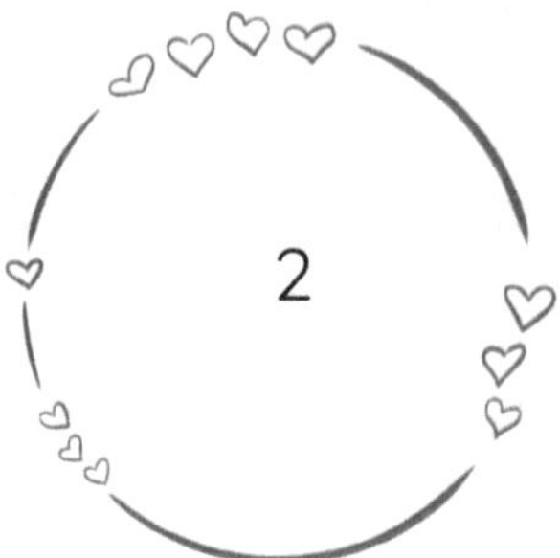

When I emerge from the bathroom, feeling marginally more human, Kent is nowhere to be seen, but fresh clothes are draped over the back of the armchair. I pick up each item, marveling at his keen observation. I could've picked this exact outfit from my own closet. Ripped jeans, a grey T-shirt, and an olive-green military style jacket, all a perfect fit. I scowl at the cheap white sneakers I wouldn't be caught dead in. *Asshole.*

Anticipating the glare outside, I don my Tiffany sunglasses before I leave the room. They're also perfect for hiding my bloodshot eyes. I need a plan. There's no way I'm going to China – I can't even hold a chopstick. As soon as I've recovered from my hangover, I'm going to find a way out of this.

I hit the sidewalk and spot a Starbucks on the corner. My pace increases automatically as my caffeine craving re-awakens. Five minutes later, armed with my usual Grande skinny vanilla latte and two bottles of water, my spirits are already lifting. I hand over my card, grateful that the gum-cracking cashier isn't keen on small talk.

She swipes my card and then gives me a look of bored annoyance when it's declined. I've already started on the latte.

"Impossible," I snap. "Try it again."

She does. Declined. Two different cards produce the same result. The cashier grows more tight-lipped by the second as the queue grows behind me. I scrabble in my purse for cash, but I only have five dollars.

"I'll just take the latte," I say, dumping the water on the counter and handing over the crumpled bill.

Humiliated and furious, I'm not even surprised when I walk out of Starbucks to find my father leaning against the black SUV parked across the road. His arms are crossed tightly over his chest. I drag my feet toward him. Not for nothing is my father known as the great white of the development world. Tall and barrel-chested, he oozes natural confidence and charm, but as those who have tried to cross him have learned, his bite is deadly. I fix my eyes on his chest. He's not wearing a tie. A very bad sign. I swallow on the lump which has formed in my throat and rise onto my toes to brush a quick kiss across his jaw.

"Hi, Daddy."

He takes in my wet hair, the dark glasses.

"Take them off," he orders. His voice is strained. I have no choice but to obey, and I wince as the sunlight stabs my eyes.

"Christ."

"Dad—" I prepare to start groveling.

"Get in the car."

"But Daddy—"

"Get in the car!"

I bolt around the SUV and leap into the passenger seat. I haven't felt so terrified since the day he caught me smoking weed behind mom's hydrangea bushes. He folds himself into the driver's seat, and we pull away from the curb.

We drive in silence for about ten minutes. It feels like a lifetime. I try to breathe out of the very corner of my mouth, so he won't be asphyxiated by tequila fumes.

I know the hammer will fall, but I'm not sure when. I sneak a glance across at him, but his face gives nothing away. When he finally speaks, I jump in my seat.

"Did you have fun last night?"

It's not a question which I can answer honestly and live to tell the tale, so I shrug instead.

"You reek of booze."

"I didn't have that much to drink."

"Your credit card bill begs to differ."

"It was Lara's birthday, I was buying rounds."

He spares me a disgusted look and shakes his head. "You're a lousy liar, Amber."

Feeling like I might burst into tears, I mumble, "I'm sorry."

He takes a left turn, his hands perfectly positioned at ten and two.

"Kent explained about Beijing?" he asks once he's straightened out.

"Dad, that's really extreme. I know you're mad at me, but you can't seriously expect me to just up and go to China?"

"I'm surprised you even know where it is."

He's definitely spitting. He's never been so cruel before.

"I'm not an idiot."

"So you only act like one?"

I slump back in my seat. "You're blowing this completely out of proportion. Mom will never agree to this." A few years ago, I might actually have believed it.

"Your mother supports my decision one hundred percent."

What? "Well, I don't! It's my life, and I'm not a child. You can't make me go."

He shoots me a stern look.

"Amber, I have entertained your bad behavior for over two years. At first, I was happy to accept it as a rite of passage after college, but enough is enough. I don't know why you have such a strong desire to sabotage yourself..." I try to interrupt, but he cuts right across me. "I have never discouraged you from experiencing life, and I was happy to foot the bill while you were studying. I even accepted your choice of degree, although you know it wasn't what I wanted. God knows I've given you enough time to grow up and start taking responsibility for your behavior, but you just keep pushing."

We've pulled into my apartment lot, the gorgeous studio apartment that he paid for. He kills the engine and swivels to face me.

"I have put my blood, sweat and tears into building this company so I could give you everything I never had. To offer you a future. And all you've done is take advantage. I wanted to raise an independent, strong-willed woman. Instead, I've raised a spoilt brat."

I flinch away from the hurtful words.

"Please," I whisper, mortification flushing my cheeks. "Please, give me another chance." I rack my brain to think of an alternative that would appease him. "I could come and work for you? I could come and work for Saber, if that's what you want."

He draws in a deep breath. It's what he's always wanted, but I turned my back on that path years ago.

"What I want," he says slowly, "is for you to lead a full and happy life. I want you to become the woman that I know you are, deep down inside. A woman who cares about more than just shoes."

"I do care about things!" I insist, casting a guilty look at the hideous sneakers.

"Like what?" he shakes his head again. "Do you even know what today is?"

"Friday?" I don't mean to say it so flippantly, but the damage is done. His eyes grow dark, and his hands clench into fists on his lap. I sense a storm brewing.

"It's October thirteenth, Amber!"

The significance of that date hits me like a bullet between the eyes. I clap a hand to my mouth. "Oh, God."

His mouth is a grim line and I can't blame him. I'd completely forgotten my mother's birthday.

This time when he speaks, I know there is no hope.

"You will go to Beijing, and you will turn your life around. This is your very last chance. And if I hear you've set one foot out of line, I will withdraw your food and accommodation allowance and let you figure it all out for yourself. I am done enabling you."

It takes me a long time to pack. I'd begged my dad to delay my flight by a day so I could go and see my mom before I left, but he'd refused. "She'll be at the airport to see you off," was all he'd said.

LAX never looked so depressing. I find them waiting for me at departures, my mom trying desperately not to cry. I go straight into her arms, tears of shame pricking at my eyes.

"I'm so sorry, mom," I tell her, and I mean it.

"Let's get you checked in," she replies sadly, "then we'll grab a coffee."

I've always been close with my mom. I certainly get my wilder side from her, although my father keeps hers in better check.

"I need to make a quick call," my dad says once we're seated, and my mother and I share a secret smile. We both know that there's no call – he's just giving us a few minutes alone to say our goodbyes.

"I'm really sorry, mom," I say again, once he's gone.

"You don't have to apologize. These things happen." She says it as if getting drunk and passing out is something that happens *to* one, and not something that one brings upon oneself.

"I don't want to go," I say softly. It's my way of testing the waters, but to my dismay, her lips tighten into a grim line.

"I hate to admit it, sweetheart, but I think your father is right."

"You agree with him?"

"I do." She fixes me with one of her signature glares. "And you *know* how hard that is for me to admit."

I do know. Like I said, my mother can be wild. Kent's mom, Janine, calls her Mustang Sally for good reason. Sometimes I think they allowed Kent and I to get away with murder when we were younger because we reminded them so much of themselves.

"Do you remember that wine tasting we went to at the country club?"

She tries not to smile. "It's hard to forget."

A couple of years ago, I'd joined my mother and Janine on a rare night out. It was for a good cause – all funds raised were donated to charity, although for the life of me I don't remember which one. We'd arrived early, and my mother had managed to charm a complimentary bottle out of the organizers, which we'd polished off in no time. Janine coaxed a second bottle out of them, and then like a lamb, they'd sent me out amidst the wolves to hunt for more. I'd come back with a bottle under each arm and the number of a very cute waiter named Chad. By the time the event was underway, the three of us were smashed. Still, it wasn't my idea to steal that golf cart. Oh no, that blame lay firmly on the shoulders of Mustang Sally and her trusty sidekick.

"It was hilarious, mom. One of the best nights of my life."

My mother's smile fades. "Do you remember how it ended?"

"Of course I do."

My dad and Kent had had to bail us out of the security office at the Country Club, who fortunately didn't press charges due to the fact that Peter Holland is one of their most generous benefactors. I'm still not sure who was more furious – my father, or the security guard who actually caught us removing the 'O' in Country Club from the sign at the main gate.

"Amber, honey, that's exactly what worries me."

"What?"

"That night wasn't something to be proud of. It was fun, sure, but I still cringe whenever I think about it."

"But mom, it was just a little innocent fun!"

"Oh, sweetheart," she sighs, leaning forward to tuck a loose strand of hair behind my ear. "It's all innocent fun. Until it isn't."

AN HOUR LATER, I'm waiting to board. I check my ticket. Economy, go figure. I've never traveled economy in my life. Sandwiched between an elderly man and a sullen teen with a pair of earphones draped around her neck, I resign myself to the fact that there will be no sleeping on this flight.

By the time we land, it feels like someone threw a bucket of gravel into my eyes. I switch on my phone to find a message from Kent: *I've arranged a driver to collect you and take you to your apartment. Safe travels.*

I know that none of this is his fault, but I need someone to blame, and considering this nightmare started in his hotel room, he seems like a worthy recipient.

My reply is a single emoji – the one showing the middle finger. Because I am that mature.

I walk through the arrival terminal to find a sullen Chinese man holding a sign with my name scrawled across it in neon green ink. Or at least I assume, it's my name. It actually reads Am Ba Hole And. *Sweet Jesus.* The man grabs my bag and pumps my hand in a bone-crushing handshake, but he doesn't speak a word to me. I rub at my eyes and follow him out to the waiting car.

The city streaks past in a blur beyond the window. There is beauty here, but it feels cold and unfriendly. When we pull up outside a high-rise apartment block, I gape up at it in alarm. It's hideous. The raw brick has been leached of all color and paint is flaking from the metal window frames. A few rusted satellite dishes hang limply from the wall.

"I think there's been a mistake," I tell the driver, but he only shakes his head and jabs his finger on his GPS device. I peer around, hoping to miraculously find a five-star hotel opposite, but there's only another awful block and a dingy restaurant. This is really happening. I want to turn around and go straight back to the airport. To catch a flight home and throw myself at my father's feet and my mother's mercy.

The driver, who still hasn't spoken a word, dumps my suitcase on the sidewalk and hands me a key. The tag tells me I'm the lucky new tenant of apartment 43.

"Could you...?" I start to ask the driver for assistance with my suitcase, but he's already back in the car. As it pulls away, I fight the urge to run after it. I square my shoulders, realize I can't pull my suitcase in that position, and stoop, admitting defeat. The lobby is empty, and the elevator takes at least four minutes to reach me. It then creaks ominously as it creeps to the fourth floor. I tremble all the way up, praying it doesn't break.

When the doors open, I bolt out of the elevator and onto the most hideous grass-green carpet I've ever seen. It hurts my eyes to look at it.

I see no one. The whole experience is unnerving, as if I've stepped into a cheap Hollywood horror movie. If I get axed to death in this shithole, I'm coming back to haunt Kent. As quickly as I can, I let myself into apartment 43. It's probably identical to every other apartment in the block and could fit into my apartment back home ten times over. I drag my bag into the tiny bedroom and give the miniscule closet a hateful look. I'm too tired to even bother unpacking. Overwhelmed and terrified, I fall onto the scratchy sheets, and try to swallow down the lump in my throat, vowing I won't cry. The past twenty-four hours barely seems real. I am all alone, over 6,000 miles from home. And I have no idea how I am going to survive the next few minutes, let alone a whole year. I close my eyes and try to imagine that I'm back home, curled up in my own bed. I dream of satin sheets.

I wake to a thunderous banging. It takes a few seconds to register where I am, another couple to force down the depression that follows. Stumbling to the door, I open it to find a short Chinese man grinning broadly up at me.

"Hurro, Miss Amber! I here to take you to Engrish."

My first impulse is to tell him to piss off, but if there is any hope of me getting my life back, I need to at least prove to my Dad that I tried. I step aside and wave him in.

"Mister Kent text you, yes?"

I check, to find that yes, Mr. Kent had indeed texted me. *I've arranged for transport to your interviews, he'll be there at 7.*

"I'm going to change," I say, gesturing at my rumpled clothes. He bobs his head twice, grin still firmly in place.

I'm showered and dressed in under twenty minutes, quite possibly a record. I've scraped my hair back into a ponytail and slapped some tinted moisturizer on my face, but I don't bother with any more make-up than a coat of mascara and smear of lip gloss.

My driver is waiting exactly where I left him, teeth in full view. How anyone can smile that wide for that long, is beyond me. I can barely see his eyes, they're so scrunched up in his face.

"I take you to interviews now, Miss Amber. I hope your Engrish better than mine, or you fucked."

Whoever taught him to speak English obviously missed a few very important rules. I burst out laughing but halfway through it turns into a sob. His smile vanishes, replaced by a look of alarm.

"Miss Amber, you okay?"

I give a groan of despair and press my fingers into my temples to ward off the headache I can feel coming on. "I'm fine," I mumble. "What should I call you?" He falters. "Your name," I say slowly, pointing at his chest.

He beams, understanding dawning. "Denri," he says, mimicking the gesture and jabbing at his own chest. "Denri Wu." Then, without missing a beat, "we go now, traffic bad."

Denri drives a compact Volkswagen. I find myself clutching the sides of my seat as he zips through downtown traffic. He wasn't lying about it being bad. Over the honk of horns, I try to catch a glimpse of my new home. It still doesn't look very welcoming. Every now and again, Denri mutters under his breath in Mandarin. For all his clumsy charm, he shifts the little car like a pro.

"How long have you been a driver?" I ask.

He flashes his teeth. "No driver. Favor for Mister Kent."

"How exactly do you know Kent?"

"Mister Kent do work."

Well, that sums it up. "He works with you?"

He shakes his head. Scrunches up his eyes in concentration. "You father?"

"My father?" Furious head bobbing. I try to recall a single time I've heard of Saber doing business in China but draw a complete blank. I'm embarrassed to admit how little I know about my father's company, especially considering that up until now it has funded my lavish lifestyle.

Denri pulls up beside a school playground and kills the engine. "You go. I wait."

A few kids wave as I walk past on my way toward what I hope is the administration block. I wave back, fighting down a growing dread. I can barely communicate with Denri, what if it's the same here? Plus, I'm still jetlagged. The whole experience feels surreal.

Fortunately, the principal speaks remarkably good English. I answer his questions as well as I can, and the interview goes by without a hitch. My lack of teaching experience is a concern, he tells me, but my credentials are perfectly acceptable. He promises he'll be in touch.

The second interview is a disaster. The Dean has been called away on an unexpected emergency, so I'm interviewed by a whippet-slim British girl who has been teaching at this school for over a year.

One look at her, and I know the instant dislike is mutual. She proceeds to fire a volley of questions at me, all of which feel more like an English exam than a job interview. Halfway through, I stifle a yawn and get to my feet.

"Thank you for your time," I say.

"We're not done," she sputters.

"Yeah, we are."

"It go good?" Denri asks as I slump into the passenger seat.

"It go great!" I lie.

The third interview is the most promising. It's an International English school, and the Dean is a petite Chinese woman in her mid-thirties who introduces herself as Bianca and speaks with an American accent.

"You're American!" I gasp before I can help myself.

"Born and raised in Chicago," she confirms with an easy laugh. "My parents moved there before I was born. They named me Bianca and figured I'd fit right in – as if it would be that easy. As if no one would notice my last name was Chen."

"How did you end up back here?" I ask, genuinely curious.

"I've been back and forth a few times, but China has always felt more like home. My grandmother lives just down the street, and my cousin's children come to this school."

"And your parents?"

"Still in the US," she shrugs. "They're divorced now."

"So much for the American dream."

"Tell me about it."

The rest of the interview is easy and natural. Bianca is more interested in my skill-set than any teaching experience I may or may not have had, and I can tell that she likes me. She promises to let me know the outcome within a week. I leave with a sense of pride that I haven't felt in years, and wave far more enthusiastically at the children as I pass the playground on the way to the car.

Denri drives me back to my apartment. Picking up on my positive attitude, he praises me for a job well done, and I don't have the heart to point out that he would hardly know given that he spent the entire time in the car. He walks me right to the elevator before he hands me his business card, with strict instructions to call him if I need anything, no matter the time, day or night. At least, that's what I think he said. He could well have been giving me a recipe for Dim Sum.

Upstairs, I decide not to tempt fate by texting my dad that I may have found a job. Instead, I Google the nearest takeaway restaurants and order in. My credit card payment goes through.

4

I sleep for fourteen hours straight and wake feeling better able to cope, but with a crick in my neck –a combination of cattle-class travel, and the rock-hard mattress adorning my new bed. Not just a new bed, but a new life. I still can't quite process everything that's happened in the past few days, but after a solid night's sleep, I feel a sudden need to prove myself, or at least, to prove everyone else wrong. I know I haven't got a job offer yet, but this might actually work out. Who knows, maybe I'll be home sooner than I think. I'm sure my father will see sense once he's over his latest tantrum.

I almost don't recognize the tone when my phone rings. Vaulting out of bed, I scrabble in my purse until I find it. Lara's name flashes on the screen. All thoughts of making it on my own vanish.

"Hey!" I answer, so excited to hear a familiar voice I could cry.

"Get your dancing shoes on, you sexy bitch," Lara commands. "We're going out."

I've never been great at math, but I'm pretty sure it's early evening back home. I frown at the morning sunlight streaming through the cheap curtains of my apartment and then slump back on the bed. "I can't. You're not going to believe me when I tell you this, but I'm in China."

"China?" she squawks. "What the hell are you doing in China?"

"It's a long story. Believe me, I'd rather be there."

"Well get your sweet arse on a plane and get back here, then!"

"I can't. My dad's put his foot down. I have to stick it out."

Lara wails. "How am I supposed to have any fun without you?"

"I'm sure you'll do just fine," I tease, thinking that we may start our evenings together, but we seldom end them that way.

"I'm serious, Ambs. I *need* you."

"Why?" I laugh. "You're perfectly capable of causing trouble all on your own."

"Yeah, but..." she trails off and it occurs to me that she might need me for a reason I haven't considered. In all the times Lara and I have partied together, she's never once picked up a tab. It never bothered me because I'd been spending my father's money, and people in glass houses shouldn't throw stones. But suddenly, it does bothers me. A lot. I choose my next words carefully, praying I'm wrong.

"Lara, I hate to ask but all my accounts have been frozen and–" I begin, but Lara is already backpedaling.

"Sweetie, I'm so sorry, but I have to go. I didn't realize you were abroad, this call must be costing me a fortune."

"Actually, I think I"

"Call me the second you get back! Love you madly, sassy pants!"

I blink at my phone, watching as the screen fades to black. She hung up. That lying, using bitch hung up on me. Deep down, I think I always knew that Lara wasn't a true friend, but it still stings to be proven right.

WITH NOTHING else to do and only my foul mood for company, I set out on my own to explore and familiarise myself with my new neighborhood. I discover a bunch of takeaway restaurants just a few streets down from mine, and a 24-hour liquor store, which I scurry past as fast as I can. I can't afford to make that kind of mistake, literally can't afford it, now that my father has set a strict limit on my credit card. It occurs to me that I didn't actually think to check what that limit is.

I walk until my feet hurt, determined to embrace the culture of a new and interesting city. The streets are buzzing with people, and the air is not as clean as I'm used to. When I stumble into an informal market, I'm assailed by the smell of fish and spices, cheap plastic, and cat piss. A grizzled woman with a leathery face offers me a plate piled high with chicken feet, and I bolt, weaving through stalls as though the hounds of hell are after me. I emerge on the other side of the market and take a few deep, steadying breaths. So much for immersing myself in the culture. Across the street, I spot a bicycle hiring stand. Perfect! My feet are killing me, and I'll cover far more ground on a bike. I navigate the docking station quickly, sparing only a fleeting concern for the sixty-dollar charge to my credit card. It's refundable, and besides, there's no way my father can find fault with me hiring a bicycle to get around, it's healthy cardio.

It takes me about half a mile and several near misses with startled pedestrians before I find my balance. I can't remember when last I rode a bike, but I guess it's true what they say about never forgetting. I coast down street after street, finding my rhythm and getting hopelessly lost, when suddenly the city begins to fall away. Gone are the high-rise buildings and, in their place, stand temple-like structures, with intricate artwork carved into their walls. It's greener here, the air thinner, easier to breathe. I pedal slowly, taking it all in, and then I follow a crowd of people who all seem to be walking in the same direction until I find myself at the southern gate of the Forbidden City, which I recognise from the tourist signboard I saw on the way from the airport. I stare in wonder at the stone expanse, the five arches, and the sight takes my breath away. Wordlessly, I park the bicycle in a designated area and join the queue. I hand over my credit card to pay the entrance fee, not caring if I don't eat for a week.

The massive entrance leads into a large area surrounded by the same beautiful buildings. There is an awed hush, a respectful silence as visitors simply stand and stare at the palatial architecture. And then, a loud, nasal voice shatters the quiet. I whirl around in a fury to find a portly tour guide wearing Ray-Bans and leather sandals, surrounded by a crowd of tourists kitted out with selfie-sticks and fanny packs.

"... used to be the imperial palace in the Ming and Qing Dynasties, and ordinary people were not allowed in without permission," the guide is saying now. He pauses, and I sense a punchline in the making. I cringe as he opens his mouth. "But don't worry, we won't kick you out. You all paid the entrance fee!" *What an asshole.* The polite half of the crowd forces fake laughter, while the rest pretend not to have heard. I meet the eyes of a blond girl about my age, and she rolls hers, displaying an alarming amount of white. I give her a sympathetic look and then can't help but grin. As the guide waxes lyrical about the history of the Meridian Gate, through which they've just come, I wander off in the opposite direction. It feels ironic, standing here in this hallowed place – the banished daughter sent to the Forbidden City for her sins – and yet, as far as punishment goes, this isn't the worst thing that could have happened. I'd never have made it here myself, never have experienced the beauty and wonder of this glorious place. I might even have to stop hating Kent.

"You seem quite in awe of the Forbidden City." A deep voice interrupts my thoughts. A cute, twenty-something, with a deep tan and a mop of curly brown hair, is standing beside me. My eyes come to settle on the loudest floral shirt I've seen since a trip to Hawaii a few years back.

I shrug. "I was just wondering why I bothered to climb the wall to get in when the gate is wide open." It's a joke worthy of the loud-mouthed tour guide, but to my astonishment, he throws back his head and laughs, as if he finds my response genuinely funny.

"Nice shirt," I tease, warming to him instantly.

He looks down at it. "It's amazing, right? I won it in a dare."

"Was the dare to wear it in public?"

He flashes me a grin and gazes up at the palace looming above us. "This place is amazing though, right?"

"It is pretty incredible," I admit. "I haven't been this still in a long time."

He turns to face me and thrusts out his hand. "I'm Ben."

I shake his hand. "Amber."

"That's pretty. Like the color."

I shrug. "If you like brown, I guess."

We fall into another pensive silence, only this time, my sense of calm isn't quite as zen as it was a few minutes ago. I'm acutely aware that there is a very handsome boy at my side who laughs at my jokes and is a serious threat to all my good intentions.

"So," Ben says, breaking the silence. "Are you here on a spiritual journey?"

"Something like that."

"Does this spiritual journey allow you any sabbaticals. A drink with me, for instance?"

He really is ridiculously cute.

"That depends."

"On what?"

I think of the splendor which awaits me if I continue to explore the Forbidden City. I think of my father's ultimatum, of Kent's haughty disapproval. I remember the ridiculous limit on my platinum card.

"On who's buying."

THE *JUICY BAR* is only a ten-minute drive from the Forbidden City and is already filled with people and buzzing with conversation and laughter. It seems to be a popular place for tourists because I see hardly any locals in the confined space.

I learn that Ben is originally from San Diego but is currently working his way across the globe with two of his friends, in search of the perfect wave. Josh and Garrett arrive a few minutes after we've settled into a booth and proceed to tear Ben apart for visiting the Forbidden City instead of joining them at the beach. They speak almost exclusively about surfing, which at least accounts for the ridiculously dark tans, but after an hour of *gnarly*, *dude*, and *right on*, I'm ready for something stronger than the beer I've been nursing.

Fortunately, Ben senses my discomfort and gently guides the conversation in other directions. The beer flows fast and furious, and after what must be my fourth draught, I excuse myself to go to the bathroom. I squint at the red tiles which stretch from floor to ceiling, broken only by a garish gold in the form of two enormous mirrors over the sink. The entire effect is revoltingly vulgar. As is my face, I realize in horror, when I catch sight of my reflection. My mascara is smudged beneath my eyes, and my hair is escaping its ponytail. I remove the hair tie and run my fingers through it, then smear a layer of concealer beneath my eyes. It's hot as hell in here. I use the paper towels to wipe my sweaty armpits, then weave my way back to the booth where another full draught awaits.

Ben is eager to know more about me, but I'm not willing to spill the daddy-cut-off-my-credit-card beans, so instead, I fabricate an elaborate story of how hard I've been working, building up my property development company, and how I just needed to get away from it all to center myself.

"You know what you need?" Josh asks, and I squint at his blond dreadlocks.

"What?"

"A tequila!"

Before I know it, the waitress arrives with four tequilas and places them in the middle of the table. I eye the lemon and tug my lower lip between my teeth. I know the right thing to do. I know I have to say no.

"Amber? You okay?" Ben's eyes are crossing, his tousled hair standing on all ends, but when he smiles, my heart flip flops in my chest.

"I'm fine." I snatch up a glass and hold it aloft. "Cheers!"

5

My mouth is dry, my head throbbing. A hangover. I have a hangover, but somehow it feels worse in China. Maybe it's the altitude. Or maybe I'm just out of practice. The sounds of the street below seem amplified, too, as if every resident of Beijing decided to use the street outside my apartment block as a thoroughfare today. Honking horns, people shouting, doors banging. It's a cacophony of pain, and I pull my pillow over my head with a whimper of frustration.

"Oh good, you're up."

I freeze at the sound of that low, melodious voice. I keep deadly still, praying I imagined it.

"Good morning, Amber."

Son of a bitch! I twist my neck and peer around the pillow. Kent's wicked green eyes gaze back at me. He's standing beside the bed, an open Manila folder in his hands.

"Please tell me I'm just having a really bad case of déjà vu," I groan.

He closes the folder with a snap and shoves it into the laptop bag beside my bed. "No such luck, unfortunately," he says. He looks tired, his suit rumpled as if he slept in it. A five o'clock shadow darkens his jaw, and his face is creased.

"Amber," he begins wearily. "Do you remember anything that happened last night?"

I close one eye, racking my brain, but there are holes in my memory. I remember the Forbidden City, and Ben of the revoltingly loud shirt.

"The Juicy Bar!" I announce in triumph as the name comes back to me. "That's where I went last night."

"Uh-hmm," Kent drawls, sounding far from impressed. "And what time was that?"

"I don't know, around six?"

"I found you wandering around down the street at 4 am," Kent says.

"That can't be right." I do the mental calculation. What in God's name could I have been doing for over eight hours?

"What are you doing here, anyway?" I snap, going on the defensive. "Spying on me?"

"Actually, I had absolutely no intention of even letting you know I was here. I flew in yesterday morning and had back-to-back meetings. You weren't on my list of priorities."

"And yet here you are," I reply smugly.

"I'm here," he thunders, "because the accounts department called me about irregular activity on your credit card. I told them not to tell your dad," he adds menacingly, "until I could get to the bottom of it."

I sit bolt upright in bed, clutching the sheet to my chest.

"What? That's bullshit. I've hardly spent a cent since...." I trail off, the details of yesterday coming back to me.

Kent's nostrils flare, inhaling the scent of victory. "You want to tell me where I can find the bicycle that Shu Cycles claim you stole?"

A COUPLE of Tylenol and a cold shower later, I emerge from the bathroom to find Kent flipping through the Manila folder, his foot tapping in irritation. He's made the bed, which he's sitting on. I don't think I'd ever be able to get it that straight.

"Feel better?" he asks, taking pity on my pale-faced shakiness.

"A little."

He gets to his feet and puts the folder back before shouldering his laptop bag.

"Let's go."

The plush interior of his hired car is heaven, and I melt into the dove-grey leather.

"How come you get a car, and I have to taxi everywhere?"

"Because I'm here on business," he snaps. "It's called a perk, and it generally comes with earning your keep. You should try it sometime."

"God, can you just not," I grumble. "Why do you always have to turn everything into a life lesson? You used to be fun, you know. About a hundred years ago."

He shoots me a warning look. "Fun? Is that what you call what you were up to last night?"

Given that I can't actually remember what I was up to last night, I wisely stay silent.

"That's what I thought," Kent says. He indicates left, makes a perfect turn, and then glances across at me. When he speaks again, there's something different in his voice, a cold fury that I shrink away from.

"I found you wandering the streets, out of your mind, Amber. With three men who seemed thrilled at the prospect of spending the night at your place."

"They were just friends. It wasn't like that."

"You were hardly in any state to be sure of that."

"How did you find me, anyway?"

"I tracked your phone. When I couldn't find you at the apartment, I got worried. Especially knowing you'd hired a bike and hadn't returned it."

"You tracked my phone?" I'm outraged.

"Saber pays your bill," he reminds me darkly. "And before you get on your high horse, I was worried. For all I knew you'd been hit by a car."

"Well, I wasn't. You must be so disappointed."

"God, you're impossible."

"And you're an asshole."

His jaw tightens. "Maybe, but at least I give a shit about you, which is more than I can say for the company you keep. I don't even know why I bother. I should just call your father and tell him you're a lost cause so he can stop wasting his time and money."

"Go ahead. At least I'd get out of this crappy country. It's awful here."

"Bullshit! You're in one of the most beautiful cities in the world, if you'd only take the time to appreciate it."

"I tried," I retort, as we round another corner and the Forbidden City looms into view. "I came here yesterday, in case you've forgotten."

I'm out of the car the second Kent parks, and I scan the area for the bicycle.

"There it is," I say, spotting it amongst a group of bicycles in a nearby stand. "Exactly where I left it."

Kent loads the bike with difficulty into the backseat of the car and we drop it back at the vendor. He pays the fine with his platinum credit card.

"You're paying me back," he says. "The second you get your first paycheck. Now come on, I'll take you to breakfast. We're going to do some straight talking."

"Do we ever do any other kind?"

"Only when you're dead drunk and making inappropriate advances."

He half-smiles, and I can't help but marvel at how it completely transforms his face, so different from the permanent scowl he usually wears in my presence.

"You should smile more," I tell him. "It makes you seem almost human. You might even find yourself a girlfriend."

THE RESTAURANT IS SMALL, a quiet place with rickety wooden tables and chairs upholstered in a cat-sick yellow velvet, and to my delight, the menu is in English. Dark blue paneling lines the walls, and the ancient candelabras cast a soft, warm light over us. Kent clears his throat, and I look away from the ceiling to meet his green eyes.

"They serve vanilla lattes," he tells me wryly. "You want one?"

"I want four."

Kent orders eggs – poached – on rye, but I need grease. He raises a brow when I order a double cheeseburger with fries, but I ignore him, giving a soft sigh of satisfaction as I take a sip of my latte.

He watches me intently, waiting, and eventually, I cave. "I'm sorry," I mumble, setting my mug on the table.

"For what, exactly?"

"You're really not going to make this easy on me, are you?"

He shrugs and crosses his arms over his chest.

"For finding me last night," I admit. "I guess I got in a little over my head. But," I add, throwing him an indignant look, "I wasn't planning on taking anyone to bed. I just... well, it was nice to have company."

"You're lonely?" he asks. "Amber, you've barely been here two days."

"You know me. I don't like being on my own."

"I won't deny that you're a social creature." He's teasing me now, and I roll my eyes.

"You used to be social too, remember?"

"Can I ask you something?"

"You just did." It's my standard reply.

"You're always reminding me of what I used to be. Why does it matter so much?"

"I don't know." I chew on a fry while I think. "I guess because we used to be friends."

"You don't think we're friends anymore?"

I laugh at that. "We haven't been friends since you started dating Erica Gilmore in freshman year and turned into a pretentious prick."

His mouth twitches, but he doesn't comment.

"What did you see in her, anyway?" I ask, through a mouthful of bun. "She was awful."

"She was interested," he replies enigmatically. "And I like how you've turned it all around in your head. Typical Amber, always the victim."

"I *was* the victim. You're the one who changed."

"I'm surprised you even noticed."

"What's that supposed to mean?"

He shakes his head. "It doesn't matter. It's in the past. What I'm concerned about right now is how you plan to get yourself out of this mess."

"Would it help if I said that I genuinely want to prove that I can do it?"

"It might. Depends if you're serious. Last night wasn't exactly reassuring."

"Last night was a mistake. A lapse in judgment. And I can't even promise it won't happen again."

"Well, at least you're being honest," he concedes. "How did the interviews go? Denri said you seemed positive."

"I won't know until I hear."

"Well, keep me posted. If none of those work out, I have a few other contacts I can call in favors from."

It grates me that he'd need to. In that moment, I decide that I'm going to find myself a job if it kills me, with no help from Kent.

"That won't be necessary. I'll do this myself."

"You're so stubborn," he says, but there's a hint of something almost like pride in his voice.

He drops me back at my apartment, and I savor every mile of luxury transport.

"Do you want to come up?" I ask. The words are a surprise, even to me. I guess I just can't face the prospect of spending the rest of the day alone. With myself. "We can watch a movie. They have subtitles, although, I guess you wouldn't need them," I add, recalling that Kent speaks fluent Mandarin.

"I can't. I have a plane to catch."

"You're going back so soon?" I feel a flare of panic at losing my only contact with home.

"Yes. Your father needs my report, and I actually do have a job to do. One that doesn't entail fireman's lifting your drunken ass up four flights of stairs." He winks at me to soften the blow, and I shake my head in mild amusement.

"There's an elevator," I point out.

"Yes, I'm aware." He doesn't offer any further explanation and leaves me standing on the pavement, perplexed, as he drives away.

6

I hate subtitles, I discover, as I lounge on the ancient brown sofa, which is as uncomfortable as it looks. I'm just dozing off when my phone rings with an incoming Facetime call. My mother's face takes up the entire screen on my iPhone. I smile at the sight of her sharp platinum bob and cornflower blue eyes, narrowed in concentration.

"Hi, Mom," I say. As always, she looks astonished to see my face, as though she can't believe the call actually worked. Video calling is definitely a millennial thing.

"Hello, darling!" There's a slight delay and then, "You look exhausted, are you sick?"

There's no way I'm admitting to a hangover. "No, just tired. I think I'm still jetlagged."

"How are you enjoying your trip?" she asks, as if I'm off on some exotic vacation, and haven't been banished to the ass end of the world.

"It's been great so far," I say, knowing better than to correct her. "I've done some sight-seeing, and I've been to three job interviews."

"How did they go?"

"Good, I think. It's hard to tell."

"I'm sure they loved you."

I force a smile. "I hope so."

"Did Kent come and see you? Janine mentioned he was over there on business."

"He did!" I say brightly, knowing it's what she wants to hear. "We had lunch today, it was great."

Her smile is dazzling. "Oh, good! I'm so glad he could find time to fit you in. Your father said he probably wouldn't be able to, with the amount of work he had to get done in such a short space of time."

I ignore the twinge of guilt I feel that Kent had to come to my rescue when he obviously had so much on his plate.

My mother's face disappears as an incoming call shows on my screen.

"Mom, I have to go, I've got another call. It might be from one of the schools."

"Okay," she sounds disappointed. "Let me know if you hear anything positive! I'll be holding thumbs!"

"I will, I promise. Love you, bye!" I switch calls. "Hello?"

"Hello, is this Amber Holland?"

"Yes, speaking."

"Hi Amber, it's Bianca, from the International English school. We met the other day," she adds, unnecessarily. "I was just phoning to let you know that your application was successful."

"What?"

She gives a low laugh at my stunned tone. "We'd like to offer you the teaching position," she says, "that is, if you're still interested?"

"I am most definitely still interested," I say, barely taking in her explanation that I will be starting on Monday morning, and will undergo a brief induction before diving right in. Lesson plans will be provided, thank God.

"The kids are so excited to meet you," Bianca finishes.

"Not as excited as I am," I lie. The prospect of managing a bunch of six-turning-seven-year-olds leaves an oily slick in my gut.

"Thank you," I say before she ends the call. "I really appreciate you giving me the opportunity."

"You're most welcome," she says. "I won't see much of you, except at faculty meetings, but we have some wonderful teachers, and I'm sure you'll fit in well."

The second she's off the line, I text my mom to let her know the good news. I pull up Kent's number, remember that he's on a plane, and set my phone aside.

DENRI ARRIVES twenty minutes early on Monday morning, bursting with excitement as if my landing this job is a personal triumph.

"You knock them down dead, Miss Amber," he grins when he drops me at the school.

"Thanks, Denri." I grin right back, then smooth down my black pencil skirt and square my shoulders.

The school is made up of simple rows of classrooms, situated behind the administration building, and a few playing fields. Bianca meets me in the reception area with a polite but brief apology that she has meetings to attend, and then hands me over to an Australian woman named Mandy, who has been teaching at the school for six months. Her sandy-blonde hair has a gorgeous natural wave and her eyes are a light hazel, warm and welcoming. She's almost my height and has the toned, compact figure of a woman who's been blessed with good genes.

She speaks so quickly that I can barely understand her accent, but I learn that the teaching staff is a mish-mash of foreigners from all over the world, some who joined only a few weeks ago and others who have been here for over five years. I can also tell, within five minutes of being in her company, that Mandy and I are going to get along. She's easy-going, with a wicked sense of humor, and she doesn't take herself too seriously. While we talk, she strides around the admin building, giving me a whirlwind tour.

"God, I hate orientation," she announces, opening a door halfway down the hall. She waves me in first. "Let's get this over with, shall we? I'm sure we don't need to cover *everything*. If you come unstuck, you can just ask."

We spend only about half an hour going through the educator's handbook, which covers teaching methods, the code of conduct, and disciplinary procedures, and then Mandy breathes a sigh of relief. "Time to dive in." She deposits a heavy file intro my arms. "Syllabus." And then, at my look of alarm, "you'll figure it out."

I almost make a run for it when we reach my classroom. Children are tearing around inside, all talking at once. As I watch through the window, a cherubic-looking girl with curly blonde hair and enormous baby blues gives her classmate – a slight, dark-haired boy, a savage pinch. The boy rounds on her, wide-eyed and furious, and then promptly tackles her to the floor. A frazzled looking woman, who must be a temp, hauls him off and sends them both to opposite corners of the room for time out.

"Oh, God," I breathe, watching the chaos unfold from behind the relative safety of the louvered window.

"They're a treat, right?" Mandy laughs, rolling her eyes. "Whoever said teaching is a gift was on meth."

I try to look amused and fail dismally.

"You'll be fine," Mandy says. "Just don't let them know you're terrified. They can smell fear."

"Good to know." I straighten my shoulders and put on my strictest face. Mandy cocks her head to one side.

"Nailed it. I'll see you at lunch!"

"If I survive that long."

"You'll be *fine*," she repeats, and then she's sashaying down the hall, her long skirt flapping behind her.

THE TEMP'S CRY OF, 'Oh, thank God you're here!' the second I step into the classroom, does little to boost my confidence.

How is it possible that there are only twelve children, I think hysterically, trying to do a head count.

An hour later, I'm already frazzled. Being an international school, most of the students are European – children of ex-pats currently living in China. But I do have two native Chinese students – a shy, serious little girl called Li Na, who seems most comfortable in the storybook corner of the room, as far from the other kids as she can get, and Wei Li – the dark-haired, beautiful and unruly boy who tackled the blond girl this morning. Wei is wild, with a capital W. He also spends the entire morning conversing with me exclusively in Mandarin, much to my shock and horror. It's almost lunchtime when I overhear him carrying on an entire conversation with another student in perfect English and realize I've been had.

Fortunately, lunch is provided by the school. It's the same food the children are served in the cafeteria, but I at least get to eat in the staff room, which is mercifully child-free.

"Amber!" Mandy flags me down, and I weave through the tables to sink gratefully onto a chair beside her.

"Hungry?" she asks, eyeing my plate, which is piled high with chicken and noodles.

"One less meal to budget for," I tell her gleefully.

"Clever." She offers me a wicked grin and then turns to a tiny, delicate woman with pale skin and a Halle Berry haircut, who is sitting opposite me.

"Kate, Amber," Mandy says, bits of spinach flying from her crammed mouth. "Amber, Kate."

"Hi!" I extend my hand, and Kate takes it shyly. If first impressions are anything to go by, this girl is as mild as milk. "Have you been working here long?" I ask.

"Just over a month," she replies, her accent instantly recognizable.

"You're British?"

She nods. "I'm from Windsor."

"I adore the U.K," I say, "but only in summer. I can't bear the cold."

"We get that a lot. And you're American?" she asks politely.

"Yeah. California. I love it, it's warm," I tease, and I'm rewarded with a small smile.

"How's your first day going?" Mandy interrupts.

"So far, so good. A few of the kids are..." I try to find a suitable word and fail. "Energetic," I finish, lamely.

Mandy laughs out loud and gives Kate a pointed look. "She's got Wei."

Kate's look of sympathy is utterly genuine.

"Did he pretend he couldn't speak English?" Mandy asks.

"Yes!"

"It's his favorite trick. He's an absolute shit."

"I feel sorry for him," Kate interjects softly, and Mandy rolls her eyes.

"You're such a drip." She's teasing, though, and Kate doesn't look offended. Their dynamic is relaxed, with the easy banter of two people who clicked instantly. Mandy is extroverted and easily bored, whereas Kate seems more shy but self-assured in her own quiet way.

"Wei's parents are super successful," Mandy explains. "You know the type – investment banking and international travel, corporate dining, Louis Vuitton, and rubbing shoulders with the who's who of high society, but taking absolutely zero interest in their own kid."

I feel slightly less hostile toward the little boy who, an hour ago, I was ready to throttle.

"He plays up to get attention," Kate adds, "but admittedly, it's exhausting. I think he just needs someone to pay an interest in him."

"He needs someone to pour some Ritalin in him," Mandy corrects, before turning back to me. "How are you enjoying Beijing so far?"

"I haven't really done much, I've only been here a couple of days. I did go through to the Forbidden City, though," I add, purely to impress.

"Godawful shite," Mandy says, at the same time that Kate lets out an appreciative "Ah, isn't it beautiful?"

"A bit of a culture-vulture is our Kate," Mandy explains. "I, on the other hand, prefer to spend my free time doing *fun* things."

"Sight-seeing *is* fun!" Kate insists, but she's laughing.

I sit back and feel the thrill of possibility wash over me. I like these girls. I *really* like them – they're hilarious and just straight up *nice.* Is it possible I might actually make some friends here? Friends who don't need a platinum card to buy their loyalty?

"We should go out after work," Mandy is saying now. "To celebrate surviving your first day. I know an amazing little pub just down the road."

My first instinct is to balk, but I don't. I might be wanting to turn my life around, but that doesn't mean I have to stop having fun. If anything, this is a chance to prove to myself that I can control myself. An exercise in moderation.

"Sounds good," I say. Mandy grins, and we both turn to face Kate just as the bell rings, signaling time to head back to class.

"Well, obviously I'm in," Kate says, giving Mandy a sidelong glance. "I mean it's not like you're going to give me any choice."

"I'm not," Mandy says, giving a whoop. "I'll meet you both at the main gate after school. Good luck, Amber!" she adds, giving me a wink.

Back in the classroom, I find myself watching Wei far more closely than before. He truly is a beautiful child, with thick, sooty lashes and a cupid bow mouth, but his eyes are hooded, solemn, and his destructive behavior is even more obvious now that I'm paying attention. Twice, I catch him striking out at other children with sharp fingers when he thinks no one is looking. More specifically, when he thinks *I'm* not looking.

"Wei," I call, once I've settled the class with their sentence blocks, and his angry eyes cut to me. "Could you come up here, please."

His small body is stiff as a board as he approaches, but I keep a calm smile plastered on my face until he comes to a halt before my desk.

"Wei," I say, speaking softly so the others won't hear. "We don't use our hands to resolve conflict, we use our words." I catch myself, wondering if he even understands the big words I'm using, given his age and the fact that English is his second language. "If I catch you hurting the other children again, I'm going to have to report you to Principal Chen," I finish. I'm sure the word Principal is easy enough to grasp.

He shrugs as if he couldn't care less. Almost as if he's daring me to do it. I don't rise, and I wave him back to his seat. Not a minute later, Joshua, a sweet little boy sitting on Wei's left, gives a howl of anguish. Wei keeps his eyes fixed on his work as I rush across, only to find a red mark blossoming on Joshua's ribs.

"He did it!" Gabby, the curly-haired blonde points an accusatory finger in Wei's face. Wei slaps it away, then kicks out at Gabby's chair legs, sending her crashing to the floor. Gabby bursts into tears.

"Wei!" I scold, lifting Gabby and her chair and setting them upright. "Outside, right now!"

I settle Joshua and Gabby as quickly as I can and then stalk outside. I walk right past Wei, who is perched on top of a low wall, swinging his legs so hard that his sneakers ram the wall with every kick.

"I'll deal with you in a minute," I tell him over my shoulder as I pass. He doesn't even acknowledge that I've spoken, and I hurry down the hall, peering into every classroom along the way. I heave a sigh of relief as Kate's familiar face comes into view.

"Amber?" she asks when I open her classroom door. "Is everything okay?"

I wait until I'm right beside her before I speak, so her students won't overhear our conversation. "Could you keep an eye on my class for a few minutes? I need to take Wei to Bianca's office."

"That didn't take long." She winces. "What did he do?"

"He physically attacked two kids, after I'd warned him not to."

"Sounds like Wei. Sorry," she adds, catching sight of my stricken expression, "it's just that he generally does the opposite of what he's told. Telling him *not* to do something is basically a guarantee that he will."

"Should he even be in this school? Why hasn't he been expelled, if his behavior is so deviant?"

"It's a long story, but let's just say his parents aren't the kind of people you want on your bad side. Bianca tried to address Wei's issues when he first started here, and they threatened to report her to the education board."

"For what?"

"Racism, would you ever believe?" She shakes her head. "The woman is Chinese, for goodness sake, but Wei's parents claimed she's too westernized and doesn't understand Wei's culture. It got pretty ugly, and eventually, she had to let it go. You should still take him," she says, sensing my determination wavering. "You have to report it."

"Okay." I nod, feeling unsure and in way over my head.

She claps her hands, and every child in her classroom sits up straight in their chair and waits for her instruction. "Follow me, children, we're going to be visiting Miss Holland's classroom. Single file, please, and no running in the corridor." They do exactly as they've been told, shuffling past us in neat, orderly lines.

"How do you do that?" I whisper.

"Years of practice," she whispers back.

BIANCA'S OFFICE door is closed, but the bright-eyed secretary outside it lets her know that we're here to see her and promises she will only be a few minutes.

"Miss Holland?" Bianca gives me a curious smile as soon as she opens her door, which falters as her eyes fall on Wei.

"I'm so sorry to bother you. I know you said you had meetings today, but we had an incident in class."

"Well, in that case, you better come in. Wei, you wait here with Miss Candice, I'll call for you when we're ready."

Wei simply slouches deeper in his chair.

Bianca's office is a safe haven for parents. Every detail, from the pale cream upholstered sofa to the dozens of framed photographs of past students adorning the walls, makes you feel as if you could tell her anything.

She gets straight to the point. "What happened?"

I tell her, trying to narrate the incident from an objective point of view. When I'm done, Bianca presses her fingertips to her temples.

"This isn't the first time this has happened, I'm afraid. I feel bad that you're the one having to deal with him, being so newly employed, but he was placed in that class at the beginning of the academic year and I didn't want to move him. He doesn't cope well with change."

"It's fine, I can handle it," I insist. "If you could just tell me *how* to handle it."

She smiles. "Wei is a very difficult case. His parents are, unfortunately, almost impossible to get hold of, and, when we do manage to get them here long enough to discuss anything, they simply deny that their child is the problem." She gets to her feet and riffles through an orderly filing cabinet behind her desk. "Here," she says, handing me a hefty Manila folder. "This is Wei's file. You should read through it, so you know what you're dealing with. It's quite a tome," she adds, apologetically, "it might take you a while. If, after a few weeks, you feel you can't handle him, I'll re-allocate him to a different teacher." I can tell that she really, really doesn't want to do that, and I suspect it's because of how Wei's parents would react. Silently, I vow that I won't complain, no matter how bad things get. Bianca gave me a chance, despite my lack of experience. I'm not about to let her down, not if I can help it.

"What do we do now, though?" I ask.

"We call him in and explain again that there are rules to be followed. It's about all we can do at this point. We'll also have to let the parents of the other children involved know what happened – you'll find their email addresses in your class register. You mentioned Gabby was one of the children who was hurt?"

"Yes."

She grimaces. "Gabby's mom isn't exactly a walk in the park. Let me know how she responds. If need be, I'll get hold of her myself."

"I'm sure it'll be fine," I say, my fake confidence improving in leaps and bounds.

"Thank you," Bianca says, and she sounds like she means it.

"I BET you could use a stiff drink about now," Mandy says when I catch up to her and Kate at the front gate after the final bell.

"You have no idea," I say, automatically. In truth, I could go home and sleep for days. "Are kids always this exhausting?"

"Every. Single. Day." Each word is a sentence on its own as she drives her point home.

"Don't scare her off," Kate warns, "we can't afford another Fenn."

"Who's Fenn?" I ask as I fall into step between them.

"She's the teacher you replaced," Mandy says. "She said she was going back to South Africa, but we're pretty sure she had a nervous breakdown. Kate swears she saw her waiting tables in a pub downtown."

I look to Kate for confirmation, and she nods sagely in agreement.

"I'm too young for a breakdown." I grin. "I've got my whole life ahead of me."

"Miss Amber!" The sound of Denri's horn almost sends all three of us off the sidewalk and into the bushes beyond.

"Denri!" I squawk, my hand clapped to my chest. With everything that had happened today, I'd completely forgotten to let him know not to fetch me. I hurry to the car, idling beside us. "I'm so sorry, I forgot to text you. I'm going for a drink with my friends." I gesture at Mandy and Kate and Denri waves enthusiastically.

"You go drinky drinky?"

"Yes," I laugh, "we go drinky drinky."

"In, in. I give you lift!"

I feel too bad to decline, given that he's come out especially for me. We pile into the Volkswagen, Mandy grumbling that it's only a minute away, and Denri whips away from the sidewalk, redlining the little engine in first gear.

We take a left turn, hit second gear, and Mandy yells for him to stop.

"We're here," she explains, pointing at a low-roofed building on our left and I burst out laughing.

AT FIRST GLANCE, I gather that what Mandy deems to be amazing, and what I deem to be amazing are two very different things. *Calico's* is a grimy little pub with bad lighting and stale peanuts. Then I discover that cocktails are half-price on a Monday night, and I find the appeal. A teaching salary and an entertainment budget are not synonymous. I'd offered for Denri to join us, but he'd driven off quite happily, promising that he'd pick me up for work in the morning. He'd even gone as far as to say he'd collect me when I was done having 'drinky drinkys', but I'd told him I was perfectly capable of catching a bus. Or a taxi. It turns out Kate lives only a few streets down from me, so at least there's no chance I'll get lost.

Armed with Mojitos and a bowl of salted peanuts, we navigate our way to an empty table. It takes about twenty minutes, as Mandy stops to say hi to almost every person in the pub.

"You come here often?" I tease, as we finally take our seats.

"What can I say, I'm a friendly girl."

"Mandy knows everyone," Kate interjects. "You'll get used to it."

"A toast," Mandy announces, raising her glass, "To Amber's first day."

"To Amber's first day," Kate echoes.

"To you two," I interject, "for helping me get through it."

"So, Amber," Mandy says after downing half her Mojito in one impressive gulp. "What's your story?"

"My story?"

"Yes, your story." She rolls her eyes. "Amber Holland in thirty seconds or less. Why are you here, where have you been? Are you single, married, divorced? Straight, gay, bi? The possibilities are endless."

"Okay." I've never been one to back down from a challenge. "It's probably easier to tell you where I haven't been – Australia springs to mind, actually." I frown, ticking her questions off one by one. "Single. Definitely single. And straight – although there was this one time at college that I seriously considered the alternative. As to why I'm here, we're going to need another drink, and a hell of a lot longer than thirty seconds."

Mandy grins and raises her hand to flag the nearest waiter. "Challenge accepted," she says.

It takes two cocktails and almost an hour before I'm done talking.

"Holy shiiiiit," Mandy drawls, after a long silence. "You really are a poor little rich girl." I'm fast learning that one of Mandy's many charms is the ability to turn an insult into an endearment.

"I am," I say, dropping my head.

"Look, to be fair, it sounds as though you might've needed an intervention. Not that it doesn't suck," she adds graciously, "but it'll probably do you the world of good."

"I can't argue with that."

"You mean you wouldn't dare," Kate teases. Her eyes are sparkling, and her cheeks are flushed. Now that I think about it, I'm feeling quite tipsy myself. I order a sparkling water and, to my relief, neither of them passes comment.

"Enough about me. I want to hear your stories."

Kate goes first.

"I'm engaged." She holds up her hand, and I notice for the first time the delicate diamond ring on her finger. "My fiancé, Tim, is flying out to visit the week after next."

"He's still in England?"

"Yeah. He'd just started a new job in banking, something he's been wanting for ages, when I was offered this post."

"Kate has only white picket fences in her future, and she won't admit it, but she's already named all three of her children," Mandy says, with absolutely no underlying judgment and a heavy trace of admiration in her voice.

"Oh, shut it, you."

"How long have you and Tim been together?" I ask.

She blushes. "Ten years, since I was fourteen."

"Childhood sweethearts," Mandy says. "It's so sweet it hurts my teeth."

"That is seriously impressive," I say. "Do I get to meet him? When he comes over, I mean?"

"Of course!"

"Have you met him?" I ask Mandy.

"No, but I've witnessed enough of their video calls to know that he's perfect for our Kate."

"Isn't it hard being apart?" I ask.

Kate twists her engagement ring around her finger. "Very. Tim had been retrenched when we started the process to come over here, but then he got this other offer, which was too good to refuse, and plans changed. I'm going to stick it out for the year. I think it's been good for us. We've never been apart, so I see it as a true test of our relationship."

I meet Mandy's eyes, and she gives me a pointed look. "What did I tell you? Adorable."

"What about you?" I ask her. "Is there a handsome Aussie waiting for you back home?"

She looks horror-struck. "Hell no! Treat 'em mean, keep 'em clean and all that. Besides, I'm far too indecisive to be stuck with one guy. No offense, Kate."

"None taken."

Mandy waves her hand in a lazy circle. "The world is too big, and men are far too interesting to commit to just one."

BY THE TIME our shared cab drops me outside my apartment building, I'm well and truly ready for bed, but I force myself to open Wei's file. It's exactly as I suspected – endless reports of anti-social behavior, rule-breaking, bullying. He's bright though, well above his grade average. This kid is going to be a serious problem, is my last conscious thought before I collapse face first on my pillow.

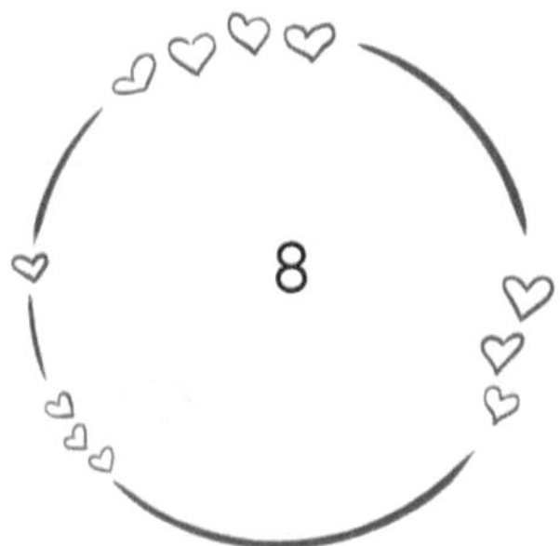

8

Gabby Martin's mother blows into my classroom the following morning like a hurricane intent on vengeance.

"I want that boy expelled!" she roars, pointing a red-taloned finger at Wei. Her plump face is contorted in an ugly scowl, her flabby upper arm exposed and quivering as her shirt sleeve hitches up.

"Mrs. Martin!" I exclaim, shocked to my core. "Can we speak outside, please? This is not the time, or the place to discuss this."

"You're the new one?"

"I am yes. I'm Gabby's new teacher, Amber Holland." I extend my hand, and she blatantly ignores it. Her icy blue eyes narrow beneath her platinum fringe as she takes me in.

"Exactly how new? When did you graduate?"

"I..." Caught off guard, it takes me a moment to find my words. "I don't think that has anything to do with the issue at hand."

"When *my* daughter comes home covered in bruises after being in *your* care and all I get is an unsatisfactory email in explanation, I think I have the right to voice my concerns."

I'm hyper aware that every one of my students has frozen in their tracks, listening to every word. Wei has gone rigid, his entire body tensed. Even Gabby looks miserable, head hanging at her mother's side.

"That may well be, but I am not discussing this in front of the children."

She relents and follows me outside into the hall. Before I step out of the classroom, I give Wei an encouraging smile, and I'm astonished to find he's close to tears.

I don't give Gabby's mom the opportunity to build up any more steam.

"Mrs. Martin, I understand that you're upset, but I have the situation under control. Both myself and Principal Chen have spoken to Wei and I'm keeping a strict eye on him. I do think," I add, knowing that this isn't going to go down well, "that he has some issues at home, and I think we need to keep in mind that sometimes children lash out when they are under emotional strain."

"If he's mentally unsound, that's even more reason he shouldn't be in a classroom with normal children." This woman's capacity for compassion is non-existent. I take a deep breath.

"Mrs. Martin, before the incident where Gabby got hurt occurred, I witnessed her pinching Wei. It was earlier in the day, and she did it without any provocation."

Shonda Martin may be blonde, but she isn't stupid. The second the full implication of my words hit home, her brows shoot up, and her shoulders go rigid.

"Are you trying to imply that my child is responsible for what happened?"

"I'm not implying anything, I'm simply giving you the bigger picture," I say quickly. My brain is whirring, trying to find the right words to appease this woman without insulting her. I dig deep and channel every ounce of my father's diplomacy. "I don't think we should overreact just yet. I'm new to this classroom, and I don't know the children well enough to have an informed opinion, but I can promise you that I won't tolerate bullying, Gabby is in good hands." I can't believe how easily that came out of my mouth. Oh my God, I almost sounded like a real teacher. If only Kent and my dad could see me now, I think, beaming with pride.

My moment of triumph lasts about two point seven seconds.

"Do you find this amusing?"

I snap back to reality to find Shonda Martin glaring at me.

"No, of course I don't." *Please just let it go, please just let it go*

"I want to speak to Principal Chen."

Shit.

I gather myself and give her a brief nod of understanding. "I can arrange that."

"Don't you dare! You're not to leave my child unattended with that boy. I know where her office is, I'll see myself over there."

"I hope you trip," I growl under my breath as she clacks off in her high heels. Then I paste a smile on my face and head back into my classroom.

FORTUNATELY, nothing comes of Shonda's visit. Bianca sends me a brief email to say that it's all sorted and that I handled it perfectly. I reply with an apology that it had to be escalated to her, but that I am keeping a strict eye on Wei.

By the second week of school, I've tentatively adjusted, and more or less found a routine. I wake up, go for a quick run to a coffee shop two blocks down, where I reward my efforts with a small vanilla latte. I take a far more leisurely walk back, shower, and slurp down a peanut butter and banana smoothie while I wait for Denri. I told him that I'm more than capable of finding my own way to work, but he insists that the school is on his way and he doesn't mind at all. Well, at least that what I think he said. With Denri, it's hard to be sure. He looks happy about it, though.

Week two goes by with no incidents. Wei is sullen but keeping mostly to himself. I find it hard to believe that Gabby's mom frightened him enough to curb his bad behavior, and in my more optimistic moods, I wonder if he feels bad that he got me into trouble. I've treated him with nothing but kindness and encouragement, and I've praised his work wherever possible. Still, he is a closed book. I try to talk to Kate and Mandy about it during our daily lunches, but Mandy shoots me down, and Kate has no words of wisdom to impart. Friday arrives faster than I anticipated, and despite it being an uneventful week, I'm exhausted.

I'm packing up after school, dreaming of a good movie – even if it does have subtitles – and a hot bath, when Mandy bursts into my classroom, Kate right behind her.

"Amber, do you know what rhymes with Friday?"

"Duvet?"

"No." She lifts her hands theatrically. "Champagne."

"That doesn't rhyme at all." I stack the last of the chairs so the cleaners won't bitch and moan – a lesson I learned after last weekend, and catch Kate's eye. She winks. "I'm beat," I tell Mandy half-heartedly.

"Shake your ass, we're going to my place," she says as if I haven't spoken.

"Is it worth arguing?" I ask Kate.

"Not even a little bit," she replies.

"YOU LIVE HERE?" I can't keep the disbelief from my voice as I gaze up at the palatial apartment block.

"I do. And don't look at me like that, Miss *Thang*. From what you've told us about your life back in the States, you should feel right at home." Mandy breezes saunters inside. and we follow her into an exquisite foyer, complete with gleaming marble floors and fresh flowers on every surface.

The elevator hisses open, and Mandy jabs the button for the 15th floor. The *top* floor.

"You live in the penthouse?" I'm still slack-jawed, and Kate stifles a giggle. "What are you not telling me?"

"If I told you, I'd have to kill you," Mandy replies, non-committal.

My entire apartment could fit into Mandy's cream and gold living room. The west wall is comprised of enormous concertina glass doors which open onto a wide balcony. I catch a glimpse of a hot tub – a hot tub! – and two pool loungers, but before I can look any further, we've passed into the kitchen. It's monochrome heaven – stark black and white broken only by the sleek silver of top-end appliances. Black lamp shades hang above the vast white Caesarstone island in the center. I rotate on the spot, taking it all in, and then I round on Mandy, who is rummaging in the fridge.

"Is there something you want to tell me, Mandy?" I ask, and then when she glances over her shoulder to look at me, "the name of your sugar daddy, perhaps?"

"Actually, I'm just a responsible adult who manages her finances well." She grins before turning back to the contents of the fridge. She retrieves a chilled bottle of champagne and starts to open it. Kate has already fetched three glasses from a cupboard on the opposite side of the island.

The cork pops, missing my head by less than an inch.

"You're seriously not going to explain all of this?" I ask, raising a brow.

She only hands me a glass and wags her finger at me. "Drink up."

"A toast," Kate says, "to Friday."

"Which rhymes with champagne," I add, and we clink glasses. I take a long sip and then give a sigh of pleasure. "Man, that tastes good."

Kate, I notice, has downed half her glass in a single swig.

"Rough week, Kate?" I ask

She shakes her head, wiping champagne from the corners of her mouth. "I just really enjoy champagne. Especially the expensive kind."

"You can see why we became friends," Mandy says.

To my delight, we head for the balcony. Mandy and I sink onto the loungers, while Kate takes a seat on the edge of the hot tub, her feet in the water.

"It's like a free massage," she explains, moving her foot over the jets.

"I'm never leaving this spot," I tell them, closing my eyes and feeling the late afternoon sun on my face.

Mandy tops up my glass. "Don't you dare fall asleep. I'm not carrying you back inside."

"When does Tim arrive?" I ask Kate.

"Next Friday." Her voice is honey and light. It's the same voice she always uses when she talks about Tim.

"How long is he here for?"

"Only a week. He can't get any more time off work."

You must be so excited."

"I am. And I can't wait for you guys to meet him."

"Never ever have I ever met Kate's fiancé," Mandy drawls. Kate tips her glass and drinks.

"You know that game?" I adore it. Lara and I used to play it all the time.

"Never ever have I ever played never ever have I ever," Mandy says in response, and we all drink.

When the sky darkens and the night air begins to chill, we move inside. Mandy sits on the floor, on a soft cream rug, while Kate and I take opposite ends of the sofa.

"Never have I ever been caught doing it by my parents," Mandy says. We both take a sip of our champagne, but Kate remains still.

"Seriously, Kate? Your parents must be blinded by that halo floating above your head," I say.

"Never ever have I sexted," Mandy prompts, giving Kate a knowing grin. When she raises her glass, Mandy laughs and offers her the bottle. "You may as well drink it all."

Kate takes it. "Well, I am in a long-distance relationship."

. . .

WHEN I DISCOVER that Mandy has Netflix, I call the game to a halt.

"No subtitles!" I shriek, bouncing on the couch like a schoolgirl.

"You don't have Netflix?" They're both horrified.

"Cut off, remember?" I say, making scissor movements with my free hand.

"You can log into my account," Mandy offers. I give her my phone, and she sets it up. Seeing the familiar icon on my screen brings me insurmountable joy. I'm still staring at it when a text comes through from Kent. *How's employed life? You hanging in there?*

I squint at the screen through champagne goggles and send a reply: *Better than hanging in, I've even made friends.*

"I need a selfie," I announce. "Mandy, get up here."

She grumbles but gets off the floor to join us on the couch.

"Who are you sending it to?" she asks, once I've snapped six photos - three were blurred, and Kate had her eyes closed in two.

"Kent," I say automatically, forwarding the photo. I can see that he's typing, so I stare at the screen, oblivious to the fact that they've fallen silent.

That looks like trouble with a capital T ;)

I'm so stunned he's used the wink emoji that I drop my phone to find Mandy and Kate staring at me.

"What?"

"Who," Mandy begins.

"Is," Kate adds.

"Kent?" Combined, their voices are amplified.

"Did you guys plan that?"

My phone pings again, but before I can reach for it, Mandy snatches it up.

"I'm glad you're having fun," she reads aloud. Her fingers tap the screen in rapid succession, and then she zooms in. "Holy shit! Who *is* he?" she swings the phone around so the screen is in my face. Kent's profile picture fills my vision. It's a good picture. He's even almost smiling.

"Kent," I say, confusion setting in. *Surely I've told them about Kent?*

Kate leans into my shoulder to get a better look. "Woah!"

I groan. It's easy to forget how attractive women find the bastard.

"If this is what California men look like, I'm booking the next flight out," Mandy says.

"Stop it," I snap, grabbing my phone. "Trust me when I say, it'd be a waste of money. Although," I add, giving Mandy a wry look, "apparently you can afford it."

"Nice try," she says, reaching for the open bottle on the table and pausing the movie. "But I'm not pressing tit until you spill the beans."

"Honestly, there's nothing to tell. He's an old friend. A very old friend. As in, we used to swim naked in the pool together old."

"Kinky bitch."

"Very funny. But seriously, you guys, it's not like that. So, can we please get back to the lovely, no subtitles, movie?"

"He sent you a wink emoji," Mandy says as if that settles the matter.

I frown. That *was* weird. Kent doesn't use emojis, certainly not with me, anyway. I pick up my phone to check. It's definitely a wink. Still, I scroll up to show them our entire thread, which is a few short lines.

"See?" I say. "It's nothing."

Mandy actually puts her finger to my screen, as if calling my bluff, to see if there's more. When she discovers there's not, her face falls.

"What a waste."

"Not really. He's nice to look at, but he's a pain in the ass. You wouldn't like him."

"Methinks the girl doth protest too much," Kate says, and then lets out a spectacular burp.

9

I wake with a crick in my neck and a Kate-sized hot water bottle curled into my back. I blink a few times, testing my head, but I feel fine. After two bottles of champagne, Mandy had made a pot of coffee, and we'd stayed up later than we should have, but all in all, it really was just an innocent girls' night in. I can't remember the last time I did that. Lara would rather have been burned at the stake than admit to spending an evening at home. My lips curve upward as a rare sense of pride rises in my chest.

"Please don't tell me you're a morning person." Mandy hands me an enormous mug, steaming caffeine fumes. "The sun's barely up, and you look far too happy for my liking."

"*You're* up," I point out, carefully extracting myself from Kate, who is snoring softly.

"I forgot to close my curtains," she says, "the sun almost singed my eyelids."

Not even the heavenly smell of coffee can rouse Kate. "Should we wake her?" I ask, jabbing her with my toe when the snoring stops, to see if she's still breathing.

Mandy grins. "I have a better idea."

Kate wakes as we're applying the finishing touches to her face.

"You are both assholes," Kate groans five minutes later as she surveys the damage in the bathroom mirror. "And how do you even own a lipstick that red?" she demands.

"That wasn't mine," Mandy admits. "That was all Amber."

Kate wipes futilely at her clown-painted face.

"It's a stay-on," I manage, through peals of laughter. "Twenty-four hours of Moulin *Rouge*, or your money back. But look on the bright side. By this time tomorrow, you'll be fine."

"I am not leaving this apartment until it's off!"

Mandy catches my eye and shrugs. "I guess we'll have to watch a shit-ton of non-subtitled movies."

I GET HOME in the early afternoon. It turns out even expensive stay-on lipstick is no match for MAC Pro make-up remover, so Kate left at the same time. Mandy has plans for this evening, though she refused to tell us what they were, or, more importantly, with whom.

After a quick shower, during which I lament the fact that I keep bumping my elbows on the tiled wall while washing my hair, especially after the luxury of Mandy's double-wide, I settle on the sofa in a t-shirt and shorts, with a towel wrapped around my wet hair, and a cucumber sandwich which, thanks to Kate, is my new favorite thing.

I've just taken a bite when my phone beeps.

I hope your evening ended well?

The sandwich loses all appeal. It's not hard to read between the lines. Kent wants to know if I got out of hand last night. I reply with another selfie we'd taken shortly before bed, coffee cups on clear display, and the caption: *Wild Night.* Now that I look at it, I notice Kate's eyes are closed again.

No getting lost, then?

I don't dignify that with a response, and his next text comes through a few seconds later.

I'm flying in on Tuesday. Dinner Wednesday night?

I'll have to check my schedule. Oh, screw it. Who am I trying to fool? *You better be paying.*

Saber can pay ;) That damn emoji again! *I'll pick you up at 7.*

I reply with a champagne emoji, just to piss him off, but he doesn't check his phone again.

ON MONDAY MORNING, I find Mandy in the staff room with the biggest pair of sunglasses I have ever seen perched on her face. She's clutching a steaming mug of coffee as if her life depends on it.

"Rough night?" I ask primly as if I haven't been in her situation a thousand times before.

"I feel like I've been hit by a 10-tonne truck. Please tell me I at least look a little better than I feel?"

"All I can see are those glasses. Are those Prada?" I add, catching sight of the familiar logo. "Honestly, girl, you have got to let me in on whatever, or whoever, it is you're up to. Or at least introduce me to his brother."

Kate breezes in, a veritable ray of sunshine. "Morning! Ooh, I like your dress, Amber."

"Thanks." I smooth down the bright floral skirt. "I had a productive afternoon yesterday. I found an absolute gem of a market, only a few blocks down from my apartment." I'd been thrilled to discover it was cheap as chips, too, but I don't mention that.

"It hurts my eyes," Mandy groans, but she reaches out and rubs the fabric between her fingers. "Very pretty, though. Your legs look fantastic."

Kate frowns, noticing Mandy's glasses. "Are you okay?"

"No. I'm dying."

"We have a fire drill in twenty minutes," Kate warns. "I heard Bianca telling maintenance on my way over here."

"This is going to be the longest day ever. I didn't get a wink of sleep last night. I don't know how much longer I can carry on doing this without keeling over."

"Doing what?" I ask, pouncing on her moment of weakness.

She feigns ignorance, but not before I catch the flash of guilt on her face. "Just balancing my busy social life and this lousy paying job."

I open my mouth to tell her she needs to spend a few nights at home, catching up on sleep, realize it's exactly what Kent would say, and shut it.

"I hope the kids take it easy on you today," I say instead.

"I'd never get that lucky," she moans. "If I go missing, don't forget to check under my desk in case I've passed out underneath it."

THE CHILDREN ARE impossible after the fire drill. In an effort to calm them down, I read a storybook – *Three Billy Goats Gruff*, and then I allocate them an independent task, to write their own fairy tale, my only requirement that it be at least a full page long. That should keep them quiet for at least half an hour. I sit at my desk, surreptitiously watching Wei. To my surprise, he barely lifts his head from the page, his face close to the paper, tongue sticking out between his teeth in concentration.

I collect every paper before the lunch bell rings and, on impulse, shove them into my bag before dismissing the children.

To my surprise, Kate is alone at our usual table.

"Where is she?" I ask, peering around trying to spot Mandy.

"She's not here. She went home. Stomach flu, apparently," she adds loudly, as one of the other teachers passes close to our table.

"Do you know?" I ask Kate the second he's gone. "Where she gets the money?"

Kate gives me a long look. "No," she admits finally.

"You haven't asked?"

"It's none of my business. If she wanted us to know, we'd know."

Sensing she doesn't want to discuss it, I change the topic by asking about Tim. I've already learned that nothing perks Kate up quite like the mention of her man.

Before the next class starts, I send a quick text to Mandy: *All ok?* And then I hurry into my classroom and put my phone in my desk drawer. I whip it out the second the children have filed out at the end of the school day and am relieved to see she's replied.

All good, just feeling shite! I blame no sleep and bad sushi.

That brings a smile to my lips. Bad sushi – even I've used that one. Mandy and I are far more alike than she believes. I hastily type out a response. *Let me know if you need me to bring you anything. Hope you feel better x*

My phone pings almost immediately. *I should be good by morning, thanks x*

I READ through the children's stories with the TV on low in the background and a bowl of stir-fried vegetable perched on my knees. The stories are sweet – utter plagiarism and peppered with 'and thens', but all in all, I'm proud of the work they've put in. I save Wei's until last. I have no idea what it is about him that intrigues me so much, but he's like an enigma I need to solve. His behavior since the incident has improved, but I've noticed he hardly ever interacts with any of the other children anymore.

The forkful of food goes cold halfway to my lips as I read Wei's piece. Then I drop it back into the bowl and read it again.

Wei's story is simple. He's retold the story of the three billy goats, but he's done something remarkable – something I'd never have expected a seven-year-old mind to consider. He's told it from the troll's point of view.

I snatch up my phone and call Kate.

"Hey!" I say, the second she answers. "Sorry to call so late, you weren't sleeping, were you?"

"No, not at all," she says, in the high-pitched tone that someone adopts when they're trying desperately to sound like they haven't just woken up.

"I'm sorry, I just had to talk to someone about this. Have you ever taught Wei?"

"Wei Li?"

"Yes. Have you ever taught him?"

"No, why?"

"He's a genius. I mean, I think he might be really gifted. I set the kids a task today, to write me a story. I read *Three Billy Goats Gruff* to them first, as an example, and they were all pretty much the same thing – rehashing of common fairy tales. But his story was... hang on, let me read it to you."

"Wow," she says when I'm done.

"I know, right? And he's only seven!"

"That really is brilliant," she murmurs, sounding lost in thought.

"It's genius! And his writing – spelling, grammar, punctuation – it's incredible, especially seeing that it's not his first language."

"What are you going to do about it?"

"Besides give him a big fat A? I'm going to speak to Bianca. I told you I majored in English literature, right?" I don't wait for her confirmation, "well, anyway, I took a bunch of creative writing courses on the side, and I really think this kid has serious talent. Who knows, he might even find it a creative outlet for all that pent-up anger he's holding on to."

Kate is silent a long moment. When she speaks again, her voice is gentle. "Are you sure you're not blowing this out of proportion? I know you've got a soft spot for him."

That takes me by surprise. "No, I don't."

Her soft laughter tinkles through the phone. "Amber, Wei has been in trouble more times than I can count. Not a week goes by at school that someone isn't lodging a complaint about him, but other than that first day, you haven't spoken a bad word about him. Teachers bitch," she adds, "it's what we do."

"I'm not really a teacher," I remind her. "I don't know how it works."

"Bullshit. You're a fantastic teacher. You even have a soft spot for the troubled ones."

I THINK LONG and hard after we hang up. I can't deny that when Kate had called me a fantastic teacher, I'd felt a surge of pride so intense it made my chest hurt. I've only been doing this job a few weeks, but I already feel like it's what I was meant to do. For the first time in my life, I have a sense of purpose, and a feeling of complete responsibility. These twelve children are on my watch, and I find, to my utmost surprise, that I really don't want to let the little shits down.

I'm in such a euphoric mood that when Kent texts me in the middle of the night, oblivious or uncaring of the time difference, to confirm dinner on Wednesday night, and instructing me to dress up, not down, I send him a hug emoji without even thinking.

10

Mandy is back at work the following morning, looking more like her old self, if a little pale. Her sandy hair is pulled back into a messy bun, but her hazel eyes are on full display - no dark glasses in sight.

"I swear I've lost about five pounds," she tells us, looking thrilled.

"And all of it ego," Kate teases.

"I'm glad you're feeling better," I say, glancing at my watch. "I've got to run, I want to catch Bianca before the bell. We'll catch up at lunch?"

"Why are you going to the principal's office?" Mandy asks. "Did I miss something? Did something happen?"

"Nothing to worry about," I say, already halfway out the door. "Kate can fill you in. See you later!"

BIANCA IS SITTING at her desk, intent on her computer. When she spots me over the top of the screen, she waves me in.

"Amber! What brings you to my door so early?"

"I wanted to catch you before class," I explain, hurrying over to sit opposite her. "It's about Wei Li."

Her face falls. "Please don't tell me I'll be dealing with Shonda Martin today. I'm neck-deep in budget reviews, and I don't think I have the energy."

"No," I smile. "There will be zero difficult parents on the agenda today. In fact, this is *good* news." I slide Wei's story across the desk toward her. She arches a perfect black brow.

"I don't think I've ever heard the words 'Wei' and 'good' mentioned in a single conversation before." She picks up the sheet of paper. "What am I looking at?"

"It's a task I set for the children yesterday. I asked them to write a fairy tale, after reading one to them."

"Nice," she murmurs approvingly, while her eyes scan the page. She's referring to the task, not Wei's work.

"Thanks," I murmur, and then I hold my breath. Bianca's reaction is not quite as enthusiastic as mine, had been, but her lips curve upward as she scans the page again.

"He's a very smart little boy," she finally acknowledges, passing it back to me. I feel oddly deflated. It's a positive response, but not the one I was expecting. I try to remember that Bianca's been doing this a lot longer than I have, she's probably seen her share of talent over the years.

"It's fantastic," I say, my confidence draining by the second.

"Indeed. What I'm wondering though, is why you've brought it to me?"

"I..." I trail off, not sure what to say.

"You can speak freely, Amber."

"Well, it's just that he's obviously talented, and I think with a bit of encouragement and some work, he could really excel in class – not just at English, but in general."

Now her smile blazes.

"What?" I ask.

"I'm impressed. I knew Wei was something special within a week of him starting here, but unfortunately, as principal, there wasn't much I could do about it. Not without a teacher who was prepared to invest in him. And, as I'm sure you know, none have been particularly fond of the boy. I have been waiting for two years for someone to recognize his potential. The question is, what are *you* going to do about it?"

"I was kind of hoping you'd tell me."

She smiles, leans forward over her desk and clasps her hands together.

"If you're up to it, I'd like to speak to his parents about private tutoring. Possibly enrolling him in a new school – one for children who might match his intellectual level. Wei needs to be challenged," she adds quickly, catching sight of my crestfallen face. "There is no doubt that he's a bright boy, but if I were to hazard a guess, he is also borderline autistic. Being bored and completely understimulated isn't a healthy environment, but unfortunately, his parents refuse to acknowledge it."

"You want me to encourage them to move him?"

"Right now, I just want you to give him something he hasn't had before. A chance."

"If I agree," I say slowly, my mind racing, "would his parents even consent to me working privately with him?"

"It would mean his school hours would be extended, twice a week. Yours too," she adds, almost as an afterthought. "It would mean less time they'd have to worry about actually parenting. I'm quite certain they wouldn't have an issue with it." Her tone is acid, and for the first time, I catch a glimpse of just how much she dislikes Wei's parents.

"Ultimately, though, you want him to move schools?"

She smiles at that. "I don't want Wei moved because he's a nuisance," she says firmly. "I want him moved because it would be the best thing for him. Quite frankly, he deserves better."

. . .

BY WEDNESDAY AFTERNOON, Bianca still hasn't confirmed whether Wei's parents have agreed to extra tutoring or not, and I'm grateful for the distraction of dinner with Kent. I'm also absurdly excited to see him. I may be settling in well to my new life, but that doesn't mean that I don't miss home. I'd prefer my mom, but in her absence, I'm quite happy to take Kent instead. I'm also not so changed that I'm not thrilled at the prospect of dressing up.

I rummage through my closet, ignoring the more conservative outfits that have come to the fore as suitable work attire, and pull out one of my staple favorites – a simple, fitting black dress with a neckline high enough for anyone born after 1960, and low enough that Kent is bound to disapprove. I slip on a pair of strappy black heels, which were once my favorite pair, and find them oddly uncomfortable. At least my legs look good, thanks to weeks of running, and living off rice and vegetables. My mouth salivates at the thought of a rare steak dripping in garlic butter.

By six, I'm dressed and ready, with an hour to spare, so I send Kent a text to tell him I'll meet him at his hotel. Of course, he's 5-star accommodated over at *The Ritz-Carlton.*

THE CAB RIDE is only a few minutes, but as early as I am, I still find Kent waiting at the downstairs bar, his broad-shouldered back to me.

"I hope I'm at least getting a bottle of Moët for putting on these heels," I tease before he sees me.

"I thought you preferred tequila straight from the bottle," he replies easily as he turns around. His eyes drop to my chest, then keep going, taking in every inch of the dress before they rise to meet mine. His lips twitch upward in approval. "You look good." He puts a warm hand to my cheek and brushes his thumb below my eye. "The shadows are gone. You must be getting more sleep these days." The gesture is platonic, but it leaves a trail of fire across my cheek.

"I'm the poster girl for morals and virtue," I say, trying to keep my tone light as I duck away from his hand.

"No Moët," he says, turning back to the bar. "The last time we drank it together, you broke three bones."

IN OUR SENIOR year of high school, unbeknownst to my parents who had taken a short trip abroad, Kent and I had successfully pulled off the party of the summer. We'd managed to smuggle in copious amounts of alcohol, mostly beer, but Kent had (and I'm still not sure how he did it) managed to secure four bottles of Moët & Chandon. We'd shared the beer. The champagne, we'd kept to ourselves.

By the end of the night, I was dancing on the table, barefoot, with Kent on the floor beside me, mimicking my moves. I still don't know how I slipped, but I'd ended up in a heap on the floor. Mortified, I'd stumbled to my feet, only to find, as I attempted a dignified walk away, I couldn't put an ounce of weight on my left foot.

"It's fine, it's only a sprain," I'd argued when Kent insisted on taking me to the emergency room. Two days later, the swelling had reached epic proportions, and the pain was so bad I could barely move my leg without crying out. Kent had bravely confided in his mother, and Janine had taken the two of us to the hospital, with a dire warning that my parents would be hearing about the party. The X-rays showed I'd broken three bones.

I'd been on crutches for twelve weeks. Worse, the boot I'd had to wear resulted in the most horrendous suntan, which Kent had ridiculed the rest of the summer.

"WHERE DID YOU GET THAT MOËT?" I ask him now. He'd never told me.

"I bought it. Well, I got Alan Kirby's older brother to buy it. I blew my entire savings on that champagne."

"Why? We had enough beer that night to start our own pub."

He shrugs. "You said you'd always wanted to try it."

I lift my head in surprise.

"What, you don't remember?"

"I do. It's just... well, it's hard to remember that you used to do things like that for me. We're so different now."

"We grew up."

I throw him a wry look. "Well, you did."

"You look pretty grown up right now," he says, and then a devilish glint comes into his eyes. "Ah, screw it. Let's get the Moët."

"Kent James! I'm shocked. Look at you, living on the edge."

Kent orders a bottle to be sent to our table and we make our way through the crowded restaurant to be seated.

"What are you going to do if I break a bone?" I ask as the waiter pours us each a glass. It's ice cold and delicious, and the bubbles tickle my nose when I take my first sip.

"I'll drive you to the emergency room. I won't even need to call my mom in for back-up."

"*So* grown up." I laugh.

Kent picks up his menu. "What are you having?"

"Steak. Definitely steak."

"I'll have the same." He closes his menu with a snap, and the waiter appears as if by magic to take our order.

"Tell me about your job. How are you enjoying teaching?"

I tell him about Mandy and Kate, and the children in my class. When I get to Wei, I'm so caught up in the topic that I speak, non-stop, for a good ten minutes. Kent doesn't interrupt me once. He only refills my glass and waves the waiter away when he approaches to check on us.

"Why are you looking at me like that?" I ask when, at long last, I run out of steam.

"I'm a little stunned, actually. It sounds like you're *actually* enjoying yourself. And given that you're having fun which doesn't include partying all night and sleeping all day, you're going to have to give me a minute to process."

"Shut up."

"I'm not insulting you, Amber. I'm proud of you."

"I'm actually quite proud of myself."

"Are you really going to tutor Wei? If his parents agree, I mean?"

I nod. "I'd like to. He's a special kid."

"He's lucky to have you."

"That's the third compliment you've given me this evening. Be careful, it might even become a habit."

"I have no problem giving praise where it's due."

"Ouch." My light-hearted mood deflates slightly. It's a stinging reminder that he hasn't had much to praise me for in a while. Before either of us can say anything else, the food arrives.

"Why are you spending so much time in Beijing?" I ask, the second the waiter departs. If Kent knows I'm trying to change the subject, he doesn't argue.

"We just closed a major development deal. I'm back in four weeks, and I'll be staying a while. At least until all the preliminary work is finalized."

"You're going to be staying here? In Beijing?"

He chuckles, low and melodious. "Do you have a problem with that?"

"No, actually. It'll be nice to have a familiar face around."

His brows arch. "You expect me to believe that Amber Holland might find my company tolerable?"

"Well," I tease, holding up my glass, "you do have your charms."

"It's nice to see that you haven't completely transformed. I thought I might have to book you into a convent."

"I'm still me. I may have taken things a bit too far for a while, but I was never exactly convent material."

"No arguments there," he concedes, clinking his glass against mine.

. . .

WE ONLY HAVE the one bottle of champagne, but even so, conversation flows easily. We talk about his parents, my parents, mutual friends. When I ask him more about the development here in Beijing, his face becomes more animated than I've ever seen it. I realize how much of himself he's invested in Saber and how much he adores his job. It's nice to know that my father's legacy is in such good hands.

"This was... nice," I say, as Kent walks me out onto the sidewalk to hail a cab. "Thank you." I'd almost forgotten how easy things are with Kent, how comfortable we are with one another.

"I'm glad you came. I thought maybe you wouldn't."

I can't really blame him. "I'm sorry I've been such a bitch. I don't know what happened – when I became so selfish and spoiled."

"You got in with the wrong crowd. It happens. And let's not forget your father's the one who spoiled you. You, my angel, suffer from only child syndrome."

"You're an only child, too, in case you've forgotten."

"That probably explains why we're both always convinced we're right." He grins. "Come on, let's get you home, before you freeze to death."

Once I'm safely ensconced in the cab, he leans into my window.

"Do you think you can keep yourself out of trouble for the next three weeks?"

"I'll do my best." I'm about to tell the cabbie where to go when over Kent's shoulder, a flash of scarlet catches my attention, and I spot a couple emerging from the Ritz.

The man is elderly, grey-haired and slightly overweight, with a badly fitted suit, and the woman in the gorgeous red dress with the gorgeous wavy hair is – oh my God, it's Mandy!

"Amber?" Kent's eyes are filled with concern. "Are you okay?"

I bob my head, too afraid to move in case she sees me. Kent's body is blocking her view, but Mandy's attention is fixed entirely on her date. She rests her hand on his chest and leans in to listen to something he's saying. Her hair cascades down her back as she throws her head back in laughter, and then they move off down the street and out of view.

"Amber?"

"I'm fine." I splutter, too stunned to comprehend what I just witnessed.

11

My first thought when I wake up in the morning is of Mandy. Okay, technically, it's of Kent – the lingering remains of a very disturbing dream – but I shove that aside. I don't know what's gotten into me. It must be all these weeks without any male attention. I decide that the best way to handle the situation with Mandy is to keep my mouth shut. As Kate said, if she wanted us to know about it, we'd know, and besides, who am I to judge. Instead, once we've gathered in the kitchen for bacon and eggs, which Kate cooks, I fill them in on my dinner with Kent.

"Where did he take you?" Kate asks innocently.

My eyes cut automatically to Mandy, who is wolfing down a piece of toast.

"Some restaurant downtown," I say quickly. "I can't remember the name."

"Isn't he staying at the Ritz?" Kate frowns. Mandy's toast stops midway to her lips.

"He is, but he picked me up."

Pacified, Mandy finishes her crust in one bite.

"Are you ever going to admit you have a thumping crush on this man?" she taunts.

It hits too close to home. "Are you sure you're over the stomach flu?" I ask lightly, "because it sounds to me like you might be delusional with fever."

She and Kate exchange a look, and Mandy grins. It's a smug look.

I HEAD for Mandy's classroom after the final bell. She'd promised to pick up my lesson plans from the admin office, and I want to go over them before tomorrow. On the way to lunch, I hear the sounds of an argument coming from behind her door. Peeking through the glass, fear clutches at my chest. Mandy and a blond man who looks vaguely familiar are head to head having a heated conversation. While I watch, he seizes her wrist, and without any care for the consequences, I barrel through the door.

"Get your hands off her!"

They both whirl to face me, and a look of horrified alarm comes over my friend. The man drops her arm, but he doesn't step away from her.

"Amber," Mandy says, sounding shaken, "this is Mr. Davies... Ryan. He's Jack's dad."

It sounds as if she's expecting me to introduce myself. I don't.

"We'll talk about this later," Ryan tells her. He gives me a brief nod on his way past, and then he's out of the door.

"What the hell was that about?"

Mandy slumps back against the wall, tilts her head back and lets out a frustrated sigh. Then, like a puppet whose strings have been cut, she slides down the wall until she is sitting on her haunches, her head in her hands. I walk over and take a seat beside her.

"You need to tell me what's going on, Mandy."

She sniffs, keeping her face hidden.

"Did he hurt you?"

"No." A soft mumble.

I take hold of her hands and pry them apart. Haunted eyes peer up at me.

"What. Is. Going. On?"

Another low sigh.

"Ryan and I are... we've been seeing each other."

"You're dating him?" The thought of Mandy dating anyone is mind-blowing. I remember the old man she was with last night and a horrible thought occurs to me. "Did he catch you cheating?" I ask, as gently as I can.

"What? No! Why would you say that?"

"I saw you last night," I admit sheepishly. "Outside the Ritz. That wasn't Ryan Davies you were with."

"You saw me? Why didn't you say anything?"

"I figured you must not want me to know. Who was that man? *Are* you cheating? You can tell me. I'm not here to judge you, but I do need answers, especially after what I just witnessed. Are you in some sort of trouble?"

She licks her lips. "It's complicated."

"I'm going to need a little more than that."

"Ugh!" she groans. "I'm an idiot. I thought I had everything all figured out, and then Ryan came along and now it's all gone to shit. Turns out I'm not so good at leading a double life."

I smile. "I'm not one to jump to conclusions, but when you say *double life*, I can't help but think undercover FBI agent. There's no way I can go into witness protection, I've seen the movies, they have bad stylists and get given names like Olga or Peggy."

Mandy bursts out laughing. "Maybe double life is a bit of a strong term."

"Look, you don't have to tell me, but you do have to talk to someone. Trust me, keeping things bottled up is never a good idea. Maybe Kate"

"No." She shakes her head frantically. "Kate isn't like us, she wouldn't understand."

I wait while she deliberates. Then, in true Mandy fashion, she shakes the slump from her shoulders, leaps to her feet and grabs my hand. "If we're doing this, we're going to need Vodka."

TWENTY MINUTES LATER, we are sitting at our usual table at *Calico's*. Mandy orders a double, and downs half of it the second it hits the table. She hasn't said a word since we left the school, but now she gives me a wry grin. "Dutch courage," she says with a shrug of her shoulders, "it's a genuine thing".

I mirror her actions, feeling the burn of too much soda down my throat, and hail the waiter to bring us each another.

Mandy gives me a grateful look. "There is no judgment in this circle, right?"

"We agreed on that a few days into this friendship, and we haven't deviated yet."

"Okay." She bobs her head. "I'm an escort."

My jaw drops. "An escort? Like a prostitute?"

"Oh, God, no! An escort like an *escort*. I accompany people who can't find a date, or who are just plain lonely. I provide company - *nothing* more."

"Okay."

"It sounds odd, I know, but you'd be surprised how many men are craving female companionship."

"That doesn't surprise me at all, but I find it hard to believe they wouldn't want any more than that."

"Oh, some of them do," she admits openly, "but they don't get it. And if they aren't happy with that, they get banned from my books."

"Your books?"

She downs the last of her drink and starts on the second.

"It's sort of a business."

"Mands. It sort of sounds really bad when you put it like that. How did you even get into something like this?"

"I took it over from a girl I met shortly after I arrived here. Cindy worked at the Prada store, and we became friends. She was killing it here – always wearing expensive clothes, lived in a penthouse apartment – well, you know the drill."

"I certainly do," I say, recalling Mandy's lavish lifestyle.

"At the time, I was struggling to afford my rent, let alone designer clothes."

"I know that struggle well."

She grins. "Anyway, one night she said she was leaving Beijing. Her visa was expiring, and she couldn't extend it. Plus, I think she was ready to go home – she lived in the States, too – and she offered me the business. I jumped at it. I was tired of living on cabbage and beer."

"You certainly don't live on it anymore," I point out, with a pang of envy. I may be feeling more fulfilled than I ever have before, but that doesn't mean I don't miss life's creature comforts.

Mandy gives me a knowing look, which tells me she knows exactly what I'm thinking.

"It's not even difficult, honestly. Just a small list of exclusive clients prepared to pay a ridiculous amount of money to spend time in the company of a beautiful woman. When Cindy left, I took over the lease on Cindy's apartment, the list, and that was that. I've been doing it ever since."

"If it's so simple, why are we here? I assume meeting Ryan wasn't part of the plan?"

"Got it in one." She takes another sip of her drink. "I honestly didn't mean to fall for him, but the heart wants what it wants."

"Is he making you give it up?" It's an educated guess, but, to my surprise, Mandy shakes her head.

"Not in the way that you think. Ryan is fine with the business. You really need to believe me when I say it's not sordid in any way," she adds wryly. "Most of my customers are genuinely nice people who lack the social skills to interact with women. I feel sorry for them. I like to think I help – it's like a training course. I equip them so that they're better able to handle women in the real world."

"You're a bona fide saint, Mands."

"Laugh all you want, but it's the truth."

"Ryan?" I remind her to get back to the point.

"Yes, Ryan. I honestly didn't mean to fall for him, but he's so damned charming, and a widower – his wife died when Jack was two – which breaks my heart, and he treats me like a princess."

"It didn't look like that from my perspective." My mood darkens as I remember how he had grabbed hold of her wrist. "He was manhandling you."

She waves my concern away. "It looked worse than it was. We've been going through a bit of a tough time, we're both cracking under the pressure."

"What pressure?"

"Ryan's contract here is coming to an end, and he's moving back to Canada. He wants me to go with him."

I sit back in my chair, stunned. "How the hell have you been in a relationship this serious and yet Kate and I know nothing about it? I mean, I get why you didn't tell us about the business, but why would you keep having a boyfriend a secret?"

"I don't know. I guess I figured when I finally admitted it, it would make it real, and I'd have to make a decision one way or another."

"You're a freaky little weirdo, you know that, right?"

"I am," she concedes. She takes another swig, and I join her. "What do you think I should do?"

"It's not my call."

"I know, but I'd like your opinion."

I think about it. Try to find the right words, and then settle for the most obvious question. "Do you love him?"

She bobs her head, almost embarrassed to admit it.

"Then I think you should go. You'll regret it if you don't."

"Shit. I was worried you were going to say that."

"Then why'd you ask?" I laugh. "Besides, what's the worst that could happen? If it doesn't work out, you could always come back here, or go home."

"I don't think I'd want to come back." She gives me a look more solemn than anything I've ever seen on her face. "I think this is the real deal, Ambs."

"Then you should *definitely* go. What's really holding you back?"

"You're going to laugh at me."

I hold up my hand." I swear I won't."

"It's the business. Not the money," she quickly clarifies, "but the people. Some of these men have become real friends. I'd hate to let them down."

"I'm sorry, Mands, but I can't help you with that. But at some point, it's okay to be selfish and put your own needs first."

"I guess." She doesn't sound convinced.

"Tell me more about Ryan," I say, and the frown lines on her forehead smooth instantly, as I knew they would.

12

Thankfully, the following morning, Kate is so distracted by the imminent arrival of her fiancé, that she doesn't notice that Mandy and I are unusually quiet. After last night's revelations, my head is still spinning, and after the copious amounts of vodka we'd consumed I have my first real hangover since the night I'd met Ben at the Forbidden City.

Around mid-morning, I receive a summons over the communications system to please see Principal Chen during lunch, so as soon as the children have left the classroom, I make my way to her office.

"Wei's parents have agreed to the private tutoring," Bianca tells me the second I walk through her door. "You can start tomorrow. I proposed Tuesday and Thursday afternoons, right after school, as we discussed. Are you happy with that?"

"Absolutely."

"They're happy to reimburse you privately for your time, rather than through the school, and I think logistically that would be easiest. They're hardly struggling, so I'd recommend you put in a decent fee."

"I wouldn't have a clue what a decent fee is."

She frowns, thinking. "I have a few contacts who are private tutors. Let me get in touch with them and find out. I'll drop you an email as soon as I know."

"Perfect."

I float on air for the rest of the day. Not only am I thrilled that I'll be working with Wei, but my finances just improved significantly. I might even be able to buy myself a little car to get around in.

Mandy throws me a few meaningful looks at lunch, but I have no idea what they mean, and Kate is in a state, constantly checking on Tim's flight details to see if there's going to be any delay.

"When do we meet him?" I ask as she checks her app for the tenth time.

"I was thinking maybe dinner next week? We're going away for the weekend." Her grin stretches from ear to ear.

"No doubt you have a lot of catching up to do," Mandy teases.

"Dinner next week sounds great," I add, as Kate blushes to the roots of her dark hair.

Mandy, I presume, must have a date scheduled tonight, though whether with Ryan or a client, I couldn't say, because she doesn't propose any Friday night plans. I'm happy to get takeaway, which I eat with chopsticks, and go to bed early.

I WAKE up to a loud banging on my apartment door and yank it open to find Mandy on the other side. She's wearing jeans and a Cheshire-cat grin, and her eyes are glittering with ill-concealed delight.

"What did you do?" I ask, catching sight of my watch as I wipe the dried drool off my cheek. She breezes past me.

"I've got it! I've got the solution to all of our problems!" She is speaking so fast I can barely make out what she's saying. "It just came to me, in a moment of brilliance! I, my friend, am a genius!"

"Whatever you've been smoking, I want some," I grumble, as I make my way to the living room and sink onto the couch.

"I'm high on life and wisdom," she replies gleefully, taking a seat beside me. She sits for only a few seconds before she's back on her feet, pacing the small space.

"You're giving me whiplash." I throw a cushion at her. "Sit down, you raging lunatic, and tell me what's going on."

"I think you should take over the business!" she blurts it out without preamble.

I blink, twice. "I beg your pardon?"

"It's the perfect solution! I don't want to let anyone down, and you need the money – no offense."

"None taken," I mumble, intently aware of my abysmal apartment.

"I've given this a lot of thought," Mandy continues, "and I'm deadly serious. You're perfect for this. You're like me... only less glamorous." I look up to find her grinning. "Just checking you were paying attention, you looked like you'd fallen asleep."

"I'm flattered, Mands, I really am, but I don't think I can"

"You can! I know you can. It's a shit ton of money for minimum input. You get free dinner, free drinks. We can even scale down, so you're not overwhelmed. There are a few men in my list who are ready to fly solo, and I'm just spoiling them."

"I can't just pretend to date a bunch of strangers. What will we even talk about?"

"To be fair, they do most of the talking. You just need to sip on champagne and look pretty."

"You admitted yourself that this lifestyle was taking a toll on you – all those evenings out."

"That's because I had Ryan to take into consideration too. And let me tell you, that man knows how to keep a girl up at night."

"Mandy," I groan, covering my ears.

"Sorry, too much information. My point is, you're *not* seeing anyone. And if I'm gone, you're not going to have anyone to party with anyway. You'll be at a loose end most nights." That much is true. Kate never instigates our evenings out. It suddenly dawns on me that

Mandy might actually be leaving Beijing and I feel an inexplicable pang of sadness.

"Have you told Ryan you'll go?" I ask.

"I said I'd try. I'm going to give Bianca my notice on Monday, and I'll leave with Ryan at the end of the month. I'll be back in a few weeks though," she says, catching sight of my crestfallen face. "I have a bunch of stuff to wrap up, and I've told Ryan that if I'm not happy, that'll be my dramatic exit. I just won't go back."

"You'll go back," I say, with complete confidence. She has that look in her eye – one very similar to the one Kate gets when she speaks about Tim.

"Obviously, but it never hurts to keep them on their toes."

"I'm happy for you. But I still don't know if this is a good idea."

"Amber." She sits down and puts her hands on my shoulders "I am doing you a favor. This is a pay-it-forward scheme and you're lucky number three. You've got to get through the year, right?"

I nod. My father was very firm on that. One year, not a day less.

"So, you do this until you're ready to go home. You make a bunch of money, live in a great apartment, and then, when you're ready to go, you hand it over to someone else. Someone *deserving*," she adds, as if this is a great honor.

"Do you have any idea what my father will do if he finds out about this? He'll send me to social Siberia, for the rest of my life."

"Why?"

"What do you mean why?"

She shakes her head. "You still don't get it. You're not doing anything wrong. You've got to get your head around the fact that it's not an *escort* agency, not in the way people think. You're blowing it out of proportion."

I tug my lip between my teeth. She's got a point. I have evenings free, and I can make some real money. It's not like I'm going to be expected to have any physical contact with these men. Mandy pounces on my moment of weakness.

"Just give it a shot," she says. "Go on one date. If you don't believe me after that, we'll call the whole thing off."

"And you'll leave it at that?" I ask, but I'm pretty sure she can already tell by my tone that I'm going to do it.

"I'll never mention it again," she vows.

"Okay, fine. One date, that's all I'm committing to."

"Yes!" she fist-pumps the air. "I knew you'd come around." A wicked grin. "Which is why I already set it up. You better dust off your heels, Miss Holland, because you start this evening."

13

"I am not wearing that."

Mandy and I are in her bedroom. She insisted I get ready at her place, so she could make sure I looked the part, and I'm coming straight back here after my date. Apparently, 'looking the part' requires me to wear an orange and white striped shift dress with a statement gold zipper running down the front. Mandy holds it up against me, checking the size.

"I said I'm not wearing that."

"Orange is Basil's favorite color," she says, not caring in the slightest. "Part of the job is knowing what the client likes, and dressing and behaving accordingly."

"You also said he likes cats. Do you expect me to drink wine from a bowl and meow at him during dinner?"

"Amber," she groans. "Just trust me, okay?"

"I'm not wearing it." I stride across to the closet and start rummaging through it. I've brought nothing with me except my pajamas and a comfortable change of clothes for tomorrow morning. My hands fall on a soft, coral cocktail dress. The color is only slightly more orange than pink, but the fabric is heavenly.

"I'll wear this one."

Mandy tries to stare me down, but I hold her gaze, unflinching.

"Fine," she sighs. "I guess it'll do."

We agree on minimal make-up, though she insists on a bright coral lipstick. I pick out a pair of gold hoops for my ears, and Mandy finishes off the look with a pair of tan heels.

"Fabulous," she announces, after giving me a head-to-toe inspection.

My palms are sweating. "You said he's a doctor?"

"He's a vet. The animal kind."

"Right." I rack my brain, trying to remember everything she told me about Dr. Basil Mitchell in the past few hours. "And he's British?"

She narrows her eyes. "American. Did you even listen to a single thing I told you?"

"Remind me."

She glances at her watch. "We have half an hour. Come with me."

I follow her through to the dining room.

"What on earth is that?" I ask as she dumps a thick file onto the ebony table.

"This," she announces proudly, "is *the book.*"

"The book?"

"The book. It's a record of every client – their personal information, likes, dislikes, everything."

I move to open it, but she yanks it out of my reach. With one hand firmly on top of it, she stares me down. "This is the holy grail of this whole business," she says solemnly. "After each date, you should add to it so that the next time they're in town you remember even the small details. That's what makes all the difference."

I try to keep a straight face and fail miserably.

"Okay, A, you sound like a mad woman. And B, when the hell did you become so organized? You can't even keep track of your whiteboard markers."

She throws me a look that clearly tells me I'm not taking this seriously enough.

"Cindy set it up, but I'm not kidding, it's important." She opens it to the front page, and I see a scribbled note right on top.

"What's that?"

She peers at it. Her lips move, and her brow furrows in concentration as she tries to decipher her own writing. Then she rips it out and crumples it in her hand. "Okay, fine, so I'm not as meticulous as Cindy was, but I do keep track of what's important." She flips through to 'M' for Mitchell and finds Basil's profile.

"Here, see," she says, showing me the contents. "Dr. Basil Mitchell."

"Mind if I test you?" I ask. Mandy waves her hand in agreement, and I snatch up the file.

"Hometown?"

"Chicago."

"Favorite color?"

She rolls her eyes. "Orange, obviously."

I run my eye further down the page. "Dislikes?"

"Peas, Celine Dion, and jokes about short people. He's only five-one," she adds, and then, without any further prompting, "Basil has a PhD in Veterinary Science. He visits Beijing every second month to give lectures at the China Agricultural University on his favorite subject – cats – and is actively involved in setting up mobile clinics in impoverished areas to provide basic health checks, vaccinations, and sterilization of domestic felines. He also eats dessert after every meal, even breakfast, and the last time he had a girlfriend was in college. She left him for a plumber named Stan."

I gape at her. "How the hell did you do that?"

"I told you. My clients are nice people. Most just need someone to talk to." She takes the book back. "Oh, and you won't find this in the book, but between you and me, I suspect Basil is gay. He was raised strict Roman-Catholic, so he'll never come out of the closet, but I think he's about as unhappy as a person can be."

"Mandy," I saw slowly, my stomach curling. "I don't think I can do this."

"Don't you dare! You're not backing out on me now."

"Yeah, but... you know these things. You care about these people. I can't do that - I forgot my own mother's birthday, for shit sakes!"

Mandy draws herself up to her full height and gives me a look of pure steel. "Pull yourself together. You are going to meet Basil, and you are going to be charming, and lovely, and so help me if you aren't, I'm going to rip out your arm and beat you with the wet end!"

We're both silent for a long moment.

"That's disgusting."

She grins. "I know. Now move your ass, sunshine, you're going to be late."

WHEN I WALK into the restaurant, I ask for the reservation under Dr. Basil Mitchell. A tall, distinguished-looking maître d, dressed in the customary white shirt and black pants, leads me to the table. I feel like a lamb being led to the slaughter. Fortunately, Basil Mitchell seems just as nervous. He scrambles to his feet as we approach, his round, chinless face creasing into a smile.

It's obvious why he doesn't like jokes about short people. His eyes are dead-level with my nipples as I extend my hand to his in greeting. If mine are clammy, Basil's are slicked with sweat.

"Please," he says, in a surprisingly smooth voice, "take a seat." To his credit, he waits until I'm seated before he takes his own, and then we simply look at one another for a long moment. I try not to stare at the tufts of greyed ginger hair, meticulously combed to hide a horizon of bare flesh.

"I'm Amber," I say eventually, to break the awkward silence.

Basil seizes on this like a lifeline.

"Yes, Mandy mentioned that. Beautiful name, Amber. Like the gem."

"Actually, it's fossilized tree resin."

"Oh." He deflates, and I scramble to recover.

"I always thought it was a gem, too, until my friend Kent informed me otherwise."

He smiles. "Basil is an herb. So I guess we're both named after nature."

I try to laugh, but it's just not funny. Basil's face falls.

"I'm sorry, I'm just nervous," I admit.

"Me too. I know this is a bit unorthodox."

I don't know whether to deny it, or be honest and agree wholeheartedly, but fortunately, Basil seems to have found his tongue.

"When Cindy left, I was so nervous to meet Mandy. Our first dinner was a disaster. She spent the entire evening making derogatory comments about short men," he adds, and I try to look suitably outraged. "But she turned out to be more fun than I ever imagined. She's probably one of my closest friends."

"You must be devastated that she's leaving. I know I am," I say, and, just like that, we find common ground. We both adore Mandy. Her leaving affects both of us, in our own way. Before I know it, the waiter has returned to refill our drinks, and I've all but forgotten that this is supposed to be uncomfortable.

I figure we've exhausted the topic of Mandy, so I switch gear.

"Tell me three interesting facts about yourself, Dr. Mitchell."

"Basil, please. Unless you have a cat at home who needs attending to, I'm Basil to you."

I smile. "Okay, Basil, then."

"Three interesting facts," he murmurs, rubbing his hands together in anticipation. "Let me think. I'm a cat person, but Mandy's probably told you that. Back home, I run a cattery – I look after cats when their owner's travel – and I usually have about twelve or so with me at any given time." He pauses suddenly, his eyes narrowing. "Do you like cats?"

"Love them!" I lie.

"Wonderful creatures, cats," he says, satisfied. "Did you know they're one of – if not the most – popular pets in the world?"

"I did *not* know that."

"Five hundred million people can't be wrong, eh?"

I laugh, and this time it comes out the adoring tinkle I'd planned. Basil warms to his topic.

"Right, next fact. I was born with not one sweet tooth, but an entire mouthful. As you can probably tell." He gestures at his straining waistband.

"Nonsense. You look absolutely fine to me." I know it's the right thing to say by the way his lips curve upward. "Chocoholic," I say quickly, needing to get off the topic. "Got it. What else?"

"I have a deep-rooted love for Asian culture. The art, the architecture, the tradition... I'd spend a lot more time here if I could. If it wasn't for the cats. They need me."

MANDY OPENS the door before I've even knocked. It's only nine-thirty, but apparently, dinner with Basil is never a late affair. I'm feeling pretty good. I've eaten a fantastic meal, had relatively decent conversation, when we weren't talking about cats, and Basil was a true gentleman. He'd walked me out, shaken my hand, and seen me safely into a cab. Not one inappropriate comment or attempt to touch me in any way.

"How did it go?" Mandy asks, bouncing on the balls of her feet.

I dump my purse on the table in the hall. "It went well."

"You didn't screw up?" she follows me into the living room, where I kick off my heels and sink onto the couch.

"I hung onto every feline-related word. He said he was looking forward to seeing me again. Happy?"

She frowns, thinking it through. "You didn't make any short men jokes, did you?"

"Oh my God. No! And that's an improvement from your first date, or so I heard."

"I wasn't warned. So, how are you feeling about it all?"

"I can't actually believe how easy it was. I had fun. And I'm getting paid for it. I *am* getting paid, right?"

"Yes, of course you are! Do you think I'm going to keep taking the money even though you're doing the work?"

"Just checking."

"So, you'll do it? You'll take over?"

"It can't be this easy. What are you not telling me?"

"Oh, stop being such a Debbie Downer. I've handed you the world on a plate, Amber. You should be kissing my feet."

"I feel so sorry for Basil."

"Right? He's a beaut."

"If I could learn to love that nasal laugh, and overlook his height, I'd marry him tomorrow and be Mrs. Amber Mitchell, mother of every ginger cat that exists."

"Don't get too excited, you've only just scratched the surface. And admittedly, Basil is a super easy client."

"Who's next?"

"You're really doing this? You can't back out once you've agreed."

"I'm really doing this." Earning a fortune for being wined and dined? Living in this apartment, with Netflix and no subtitles? I'd be an idiot not to. I run my hand across the satin cushion beside me. "It will be my precious," I say, in my best *Gollum* impersonation.

She grins. "Wait right here. I'm getting the book."

THIS TIME, I'm allowed to examine it. I flip through the thick white cardboard dividers, briefly scanning profiles at random.

"Each profile is filed alphabetically, under the client's last name," Mandy explains. "Don't worry I'll text you the broadcast message list, which has every contact number and name in it. It'll be easier than trying to go through this one by one and adding them to your contacts."

"They'll just text me if they want to see me?"

"Yes. Some will try more often than they're allowed, but don't be shy to get firm with them."

"What do you mean, more often than they're allowed?"

"Oh." She waves her hand in a lazy circle. "The rules. I haven't explained that to you yet. No kissing, no sex, no sleeping over, or even going back to their place. Trust me, it can land you in a whole heap of trouble."

"Are you speaking from experience?"

"Actually, yes."

"You're joking!"

"I wish I was. I slept with one of my clients. I fell for him, hard – thought he was the one and everything."

"What happened?"

"The asshole was married. Trust me, Cindy knew what she was doing when she set the rules." She doesn't wait for me to respond before she continues ticking them off her fingers. "Texting is limited to arranging dates only. And no more than two dates a month. Any more than that and one or both of you might start catching feels, and that's a complication you don't want. Men fall in love faster than they fall asleep, especially when faced with a woman who is literally being paid to agree with everything they say."

"That makes sense." I turn another page of the file to discover a bright red divider. "What's this?"

"That's the red list. Anyone beyond that is a tried and tested asshole. They're either married, or perverted, or both. We don't take on married men, but sadly it's only too easy to take off a ring. If you find out a man has a wife, or a girlfriend, or if he tries anything with you, you shove him in that folder and cut all ties immediately. Don't worry," she adds calmly, "it almost never happens."

While Mandy goes to fetch us a drink, I flip idly through the folder. It's easy to see where Cindy's entries end and Mandy's begin. Cindy was meticulous, her neat, tight handwriting easy to read. Mandy's illegible scrawl, on the other hand, is almost impossible to decipher.

"I have a feeling you're going to be really good at this," Mandy announces as she breezes back into the room with two flutes of champagne.

"I hope you're right. When's my next date?"

"Wednesday, if you're up for it. I can schedule it for you, but after that, I'll send everyone your number and leave it up to you."

"Who's it with?"

"Frank Gunner."

"Sounds like a douche," I say, without consulting the book.

"Oh, you're even better than I thought," Mandy replies and then takes a long sip of her champagne.

The next three weeks are a whirlwind. Between teaching, tutoring Wei, and my new business, I barely have time to think, but all too soon, Mandy is leaving and my heart is broken. Kate, who is still coming down from the high of her week with Tim, even now, is taking it surprisingly well. Mandy and I had met Tim during his visit. He was nice. He was Tim. I could understand what Kate sees in him, but he's not my type.

"I can't believe you're leaving," I tell Mandy for the fourth time in twenty minutes. The three of us are standing at departures.

"I'll be back in a few weeks! You won't even notice I'm gone. Besides, you guys at least still have my apartment to drink in. It'll make you feel better." She gives me a discreet wink.

We'd explained to Kate that Mandy would be keeping her apartment, but that I'd be living in it while she was gone. Kate hadn't questioned it. She'd seen my hovel. She sympathized.

"You girls better not get up to any trouble without me."

"As if that would be possible," Kate smiles.

"Right, I'm not into goodbyes, so I'm just going to say see you later and be off, yeah?"

I nod, then, on impulse, I throw my arms around her. Kate does the same.

"Oh God," Mandy mutters, but she hugs us right back.

I'M SO depressed that evening that not even Netflix on Mandy's enormous flat-screen can cheer me up. Kate and I had gone for mandatory drinks after the airport, on Mandy's orders, but our hearts hadn't been in it and we'd left after only two rounds. I'm flipping idly through channels when my phone beeps.

Hi Amber. I'd like to schedule an appointment for Wednesday at 7pm. The Bill and Trout. Please let me know if that works for you. Chase Crawford.

I fetch the book and flip to C. No Chase Crawford. He must be a referral. I haven't had any yet, but Mandy had mentioned this might happen occasionally. Most new clients were sent to us through existing clients.

I don't have anything planned this week, and Kent is only flying in on Saturday, so there's no chance he'll want to catch up before then. Chase's profile picture shows only a man with his back to the camera, swinging a golf club. Hastily, I type a quick reply.

Sure, I'll meet you there at 7.

He sends a thumbs up.

"WEI, THIS IS EXCELLENT!" I exclaim on Tuesday afternoon, as I review the poem he's written. "Really good job, I love how you've compared the sky to a blanket.

Wei smiles. He's been smiling a lot more since we started our private lessons, and it melts my heart every time. Bianca couldn't have been more right when she said that Wei was craving attention. Now that he has it, he's like a different child.

"What do you prefer," I ask him now. "Stories, or poetry?"

"Stories," he answers sheepishly, not wanting to admit this hasn't been his favorite lesson.

"Me too. We'll do another story on Thursday, okay?" I hand him a worksheet. "Now, before you go, can you put these sentences in order for me?"

We are so engrossed in the task that neither of us notices a diminutive, dark-haired woman enter the classroom. When she speaks Wei's name, I almost jump out of my skin.

"Oh my goodness, you scared me!"

"My apologies." She looks to Wei and gives a curt nod of her head before extending her hand to me. "I am Jia Li, Wei's mother."

I scramble to my feet. "I'm sorry, I wasn't expecting you." Looking down at her, it's easy to see where Wei gets his good looks. Jia is beautiful, her thick lashes framing eyes that are so dark they seem to be all pupil. "It's wonderful to finally meet you, Mrs. Li."

She doesn't return the pleasantry, but I plow forward.

"Wei is doing so well. He's really talented. I can show you some of his work, if you'd like?"

"I'm sorry, I'm in a rush." She speaks impeccable English, with no trace of an accent. "Wei, get your things, quickly, please."

"Maybe we could reschedule?" I ask, desperate to engage with her.

"I'm sorry, that won't be possible. My husband and I are moving. Wei won't be coming back."

"What?" My knees threaten to buckle beneath me.

"I've spoken to Principal Chen," she says, as if that settles the matter.

"When? When are you leaving?"

She gives me a pointed look, but I don't give a shit if I'm overstepping.

"It's been quite sudden," she concedes. "My husband's business requires him to go immediately, and I've accepted a transfer."

I glance to where Wei is standing, his backpack over his shoulders. He looks resigned.

"Perhaps I could tutor Wei online? We could continue our lessons remotely. It wouldn't be a problem, most of the syllabus I've set up doesn't require me to be"

"You will be remunerated in full for the notice period," she snaps, and I feel my temper fray.

"This has nothing to do with money, Mrs. Li. I genuinely want to tutor your son. I think he's got an exceptional gift, and I'd love to continue to work with him. You don't have to pay me." I hear myself add.

Jia Li looks at me as if I just crawled out of a block of cheese.

"You would tutor him for *free*?"

I stand my ground. "I would."

She turns to her son. "Would you like Ms...." She trails off, not having a clue what my name is.

"Miss Holland," I say quickly.

"Miss Holland to continue to tutor you?"

Wei bobs his head nervously, unsure whether the honest answer is the right one. Jia gives me an appraising look.

"I'll think about it," she says eventually. "I'll be in touch with Principal Chen if we decide to take you up on your offer." And with that, she turns on her heel and walks out. I reach out and grab Wei as he makes to follow her and crouch low on my haunches.

"You be good," I tell him softly, fighting back tears. This is too soon, too sudden, and I can't quite believe it's happening, but the least I can do is say goodbye. She's not going to contact Bianca. I know it, and Wei knows it too. "You be a good boy, because you *are* a good boy," I say quickly. "And work hard. You're the smartest seven-year-old I know. Don't let me down, okay?"

Wei nods. His dark eyes shimmer but he stands tall, shoulders back. "I won't let you down, Miss Holland," he says.

I sit on the floor, unmoving, for a long time after he's gone.

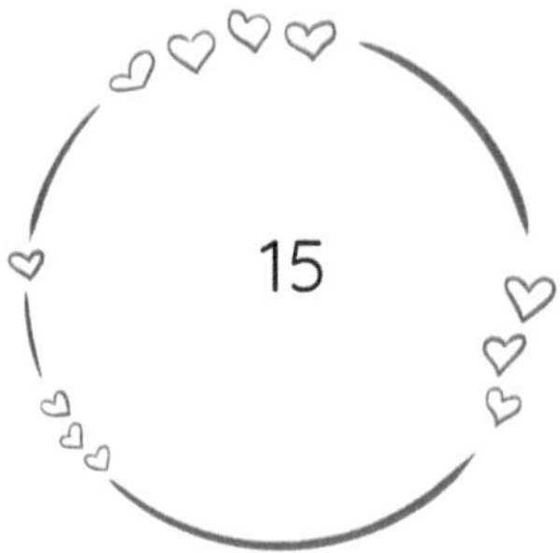

15

The following evening, I get ready for my date with Chase Crawford. It's the last thing in the world I feel like doing but, mindful of the exorbitant rent on this apartment, which won't pay itself, I slip on a little black dress and pull up my big girl panties. Bianca had been just as upset by the abrupt turn of events as I was but, sadly, it was completely out of her control.

"His parents have the right to move him wherever they want," she'd said. "And I know this isn't going to make you feel any better right now, but I had to send Wei's transcripts over to the new school. They listened, Amber – it's an exclusive private school with a high-level entrance exam. He's going to be fine."

She was right. It didn't make me feel better.

I CATCH a cab to The Bill and Trout, a cozy little restaurant uptown. The sound of sixties blues wafts through the open door, and I almost walk into the live band.

"Mr. Crawford?" I ask the waiter who steps forward to greet me.

"Right this way." He leads me to an empty table in the far corner of the restaurant. "Mr. Crawford hasn't arrived yet," he says, unnecessarily. "Can I offer you something to drink while you wait?"

"A bottle of red wine, please. The most expensive." I may as well set a precedent for my new client.

"Make it two," a low voice purrs. My head jerks up and my mouth drops open as I catch sight of the breath-taking man standing just behind the waiter. He gives me a crooked smile. "Amber, I presume?"

I recover my composure as quickly as I can with the answer to every woman's fantasy standing before me.

"Chase?"

"Last time I checked." He gives the waiter a wry look. "Just the wine for now." And then steps around him to offer me his hand. "It's a pleasure to meet you, Amber."

I meet his sapphire blue eyes and extend my hand, barely conscious of the waiter scuttling off, dismissed.

"You too."

He takes his seat, draping himself over it like a cat, all lithe grace.

"How did you hear about me?" I ask. "My services, I mean." Even I cringe at the word 'services', but Chase doesn't bat an eyelid.

"Frank."

"Frank Gunner?"

"Do you date *many* Franks?" he asks teasingly.

"Only the one right now."

I don't know if it's losing Mandy, or losing Wei, or just the charisma radiating off him in waves, but I throw caution to the wind. The old Amber opens a sleepy eye and stretches. I know I'm flirting with Chase, which is not against the rules, exactly, but probably not the best idea, given how attracted I am to him. Considering most of the men I'm attracted to end up being the wrong kind, I suspect Chase may not be being entirely truthful.

Half an hour later, my suspicions are confirmed. Not only is he ridiculously good-looking, but he's charming as the devil. We've moved on to our second bottle of wine when I call him out.

"So what's the catch?" I ask, during a rare lull in what has otherwise been scintillating conversation.

"The catch?" he smears a liberal amount of butter onto a bread roll and tears a chunk off with perfect white teeth.

"I wasn't born yesterday, Chase. I've gone on five dates before this one, and seen men so completely unalike they may as well be different species. But do you know the one thing they all have in common?"

"Excellent taste in women?"

I ignore the compliment and fix him with a pointed look. "*None* of them look like you."

He scans his menu. "I should hope not. I pride myself on being the only person who looks like me."

"You know what I mean. Do you really expect me to believe that a man who looks like you can't find himself a date the conventional way?"

"I never said I couldn't."

"Then why am I here?"

He sets the menu down on the table. "I think I'm going to have the salmon. And as to why you're here," he adds, conversationally, "it's simple. I have what I would assume is the opposite problem to your regular clients. I have no problem finding a date. It's finding someone to spend time with who *doesn't* want anything more that's a problem."

I burst out laughing. "You have a problem with being objectified? With women wanting to get you into bed? How very metrosexual of you."

"What can I say? I want to be able to go out with a beautiful woman for once, and make conversation, without it ending in meaningless sex."

"Is that what usually happens?"

He shrugs.

"That must be so hard for you."

"It's a curse."

I steeple my fingers and lean toward him. "Well, Mr. Crawford, I can assure you that won't be happening on my watch. You're quite safe with me."

"And *that*," he drawls, raising his glass in a toast, "is why you're here."

DESPITE CHASE'S CLAIMS, and my best intentions, there is an undeniable chemistry crackling between us. If I lit a match, I'm pretty sure we'd both burst into flames. I drink more than I should, skirt the line between courteous and cute, serious and sexy, and Chase takes it all in his stride. Over and over in my head, I recite the rules Mandy laid out. For all Chase's talk of wanting a platonic friendship, I call bullshit. I don't know what his deal is, but I've been with enough men to know that the way he's looking at me is not the way a man looks at a friend.

"Well, I guess this brings our evening to an end," Chase says softly, as he settles the bill. For the first time tonight, he won't look at me.

My tongue darts out to lick at dry lips. "I guess so."

Chase puts his hand on the small of my back to guide me through the tables but drops it the second we emerge into the frigid night air. For a second, we stand awkwardly, facing each other on the sidewalk.

"Well," I say, brightly, as I extend my hand. "This was fun. Thank you."

His eyes gleam in amusement as he eyes my outstretched hand. I drop it.

"Okay, that was weird. Sorry. I'll just..." I eye the street for a cab. "I'll just go."

Chase's hand catches my arm as I pass.

"Amber"

Our eyes lock. Time freezes. Mandy's warnings fly out of my head faster than a canary out of a cage.

"I don't want to objectify you," I whisper.

"Please, do," he groans, and then his lips crash down onto mine.

WHEN I WAKE up on Thursday morning, it takes a few seconds before the events of last night come rushing back to me. I kissed Chase. I kissed a client. Mandy would be furious, but I don't feel too bad about it. That's all we did. We only kissed. For fifteen minutes, and in full view of the street, but it hadn't gone any further than that. I brush my fingers across my lips. They feel bruised. I haven't done that much kissing since college. Still, it's a good thing that I won't be seeing Chase for another two weeks. That's the rule, and he knows it. It'll give me time to talk some sense into myself. It's not as if I'm falling for him, but who can blame a girl who's been on her own for so long from wanting a little physical affection?

I check my phone to find a message from Mandy, asking how things are going. It's like she knows. I haven't told her about the date with Chase yet, and I decide I'm not going to. It's safer if I don't. For me, anyway. I reply that everything is absolutely fine and ask her how Ryan's doing. *Dragging me to every God forsaken tourist attraction in Toronto*, she replies, but then she sends a heart-in-the-eyes and an eggplant emoji, and I burst out laughing.

ON FRIDAY AFTERNOON, I'm tidying up my classroom, singing Tracey Chapman's 'Give me one reason' softly under my breath, when I hear a deep voice behind me.

"I'll give you one reason to stop singing."

"Kent!" I gasp, my hand flying to my chest. He's lounging against the door frame, looking outrageously casual in a pair of dark blue jeans and a branded T-shirt. He's even wearing sneakers. "What are you doing here? I wasn't expecting you until tomorrow."

"I got an earlier flight. I had an unexpected meeting this morning, so I flew in yesterday."

"How did it go?"

"It went well. What *are* you doing?"

While we're talking, I've started stacking the chairs as I do every Friday.

"Tidying up. The cleaners throw a fit if they have to do more than absolutely necessary."

He smiles, and I know exactly what he's thinking.

"The irony isn't lost on me, either," I remark wryly.

"So this is the place that's tamed the untameable Amber Holland," he says, pushing off the door frame to come toward me. His eyes scan the walls, taking in the children's drawings, and the weekly theme board, which is currently decorated with planets. I stand tall, proud of the work my kids have achieved.

"It's awesome," he says eventually, his eyes coming to rest on me. "What you're doing here is incredible, Amber." I don't want him to see how much it means to me to hear him say that, so I turn my back to him and round my desk.

"You haven't seen anything yet," I say, then adding a hint of my teacher's tone to my voice, "please take your seat, Mr. James."

Kent grins and strolls casually to the desk right in front of mine. It takes him a few seconds to wedge himself into the tiny chair, and I have to bite my lip to keep from laughing.

"You, Sir, are very predictable. Always demanding front row seats."

"Well, I am a star student, so this is where you would place me, not so Miss Holland?"

"That is, in fact, Gabby Martin's desk. Gabby is by far the naughtiest child in my class, possibly the entire school, so you're definitely in the wrong chair, Mister Perfect."

"I'll have you know I was a terror at this age. I blame my best friend. She was always getting me into all kinds of trouble."

"I would've separated you immediately," I say sternly, trying not to smile.

Kent's face softens. "No, you wouldn't have."

"You're right. I wouldn't have."

He scans the other desks. “Where does Wei sit?”

I don’t reply.

“Amber?”

“His parents pulled him out.” My voice is tiny, fresh pain washing over me.

“Oh, Jesus, I’m sorry.” He’s trying to get up, but he’s having difficulty extracting himself from the chair. “I know how much he meant to you.”

“I’m fine. There was nothing we could’ve done, and he’s gone to a really good school. I was just... I wasn’t prepared.”

“I’m sorry,” he says again. He’s managed to free himself, but I don’t wait for him to get any closer.

“I’m fine, it’s over now.” I don’t want to talk about it. “How would you like a tour?”

To my delight, Kent pays a genuine interest in everything I show him. He asks questions about the children, the teachers, and even asks after Principal Chen’s grandmother, who had been ill when he visited three weeks ago.

“She’s fine. Bianca was super stressed because they couldn’t find what was wrong with her, but it must’ve been a bug because she bounced back.”

We wander back to my classroom door, and Kent looks up at the colorful sign on the door. “Miss Holland’s class,” he reads out loud.

“That’s me.”

This time, when he looks at me, it’s like he’s seeing someone else.

“I haven’t seen you this happy in a long time, Amber. I’d forgotten how good it looks on you.”

A blush rises on my cheeks. “I am happy.” Then, with an arched brow, I add, “but I like to think I always look good.”

A low chuckle rumbles from his chest. “That you do.”

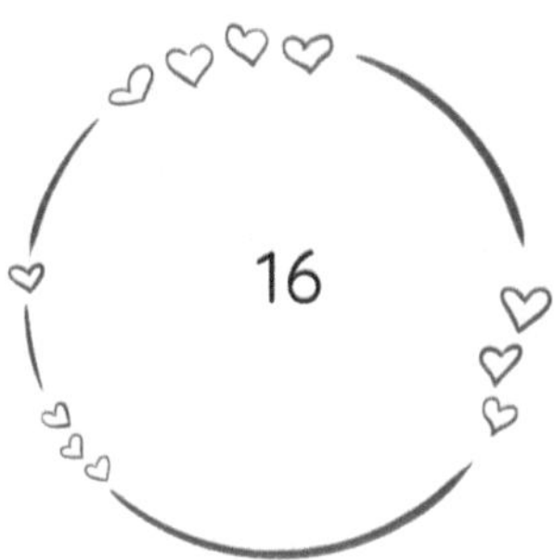

I take Kent to *Calico's*, regaling him with the story of how Denri drove us girls here that first time. Given that his hired BMW makes the journey in under a minute, he can't help but laugh either.

"Do you still see much of Denri?"

"No. It took me two weeks to convince him that I was perfectly capable of getting around on my own, but he finally accepted it."

"Do you come here often?" Kent asks as I find us seats at the table I usually share with Mandy and Kate.

"Hey, don't knock it 'til you've tried it," I tease. I try to remember how I saw the dingy little pub the first time I came in here, but I can't. Now, all I see is the cozy wallpapered interior and a bunch of familiar, friendly faces. "You're going to die when you taste the burgers," I add, confidently. "They're the best in town."

It takes Kent ten minutes to get us a beer at the bar, after striking up a conversation with Lorenz, the regular barman.

"Sorry," he tells me, setting two rapidly warming beers on the table.

"Making friends?" I tease.

"I'm a friendly guy."

"You definitely look more approachable than usual. I don't think I've ever seen you in jeans."

"I wear jeans all the time! You wouldn't know because you've only seen me a handful of times the past few years."

I start to tick them off my fingers. "My mom's birthday, my dad's birthday, *your* mom's birthday." I don't mention his father. I haven't seen Kent's dad since his parents split up when we were twelve.

"Christmas Eve," he adds.

"That's at least four times a year."

"My mother would kill me if I wore jeans to one of her functions. Yours too, probably."

Thinking of my mom brings a fond smile to my lips. "I miss her."

"She misses you too. I saw your mom just before I flew out. She said you call her twice a week, which seemed to make her happy."

"I think I talk to her more now than I did when I lived just a few minutes away," I admit. "It's true what they say. You really don't know what you've got until it's gone."

Kent averts his eyes and sips his beer. I'm about to ask him whether he's seen my dad, when my phone beeps. It's a text from Chase, and it catches me so unaware that I almost fall off my chair.

I can't stop thinking about you. It's too soon. He shouldn't be contacting me.

"Everything okay?" Kent asks as I frown at my screen.

I set my phone to silent and shove it back into my purse. "Everything's fine."

We eat our burgers in silence. Kent admits that he's never had better, which gives me a smug satisfaction, and then we head back to his hotel for a few drinks. On the cab ride over, I point out a few of my favorite places – the street-side market which sells the best wontons in town, the holistic center, where Kate, Mandy and I had medicinal leech therapy, which, I add, is as gross as it sounds.

"I got this," I say, holding up my arm to show him a small, fresh scar on my elbow, "in that park. I fell off my bicycle," I add, as he scans the flash of green to our left.

"Were you drinking?" he asks, but his voice is filled with humor.

"I wish. Mandy insisted we race down to the river. My only consolation is that she fell off, too."

"She left, right?"

"Yes. It's not really the same without her."

"Sounds like you've had a bit of a bad time. First Mandy, then Wei."

"That's life, I guess."

We walk into the airconditioned lobby of his hotel and make our way to the bar. A few finely-dressed patrons give us odd looks, and it takes me a while to realize that they're offended by our casual clothing.

Kent orders us each a beer, and then he deliberately raises a toast to a blonde woman who is still openly glaring.

"You're terrible," I laugh. "Maybe you should go upstairs and put on a suit."

"Screw that." He gives me an appraising look. "Actually, I have a better idea. I'm not in the mood for this pretentiousness. Let's both go to my room." He orders a bottle of wine to be sent up, while I stand stock still, mixed emotions barrelling into me. I know he means nothing by it, but the thought of being alone with him in his hotel room does something to my stomach.

"You coming?" he asks when he realizes I'm not following him.

"Right behind you!" I shake myself and step into line behind him.

KENT IS HILARIOUS. I'd forgotten how funny he is. Away from the prying eyes of fellow guests, we lounge on the enormous twin couches in his room, drinking wine and gossiping as if we're back in high school. The wine warms me from the inside out, but it's Kent who keeps the heat in my cheeks.

"God, I've missed you," he says after I've performed an Oscar-worthy impersonation of Erica Gilmore, his college girlfriend, which included a deep and meaningful conversation with the potted plant beside me. He's laughing as he says it, but it makes my heart flip-flop in my chest. I don't know what's happening to me.

"I need to use the bathroom," I say, grabbing my purse.

Once I've locked the door safely. Behind me, I. whip out my phone.

I'm with Kent, I text Mandy. *And I'm having feelings. Help*!

I stare at the screen, frantically trying to calculate the time difference, and almost weep in relief when I see that she's typing.

I'm not understanding your problem.

It's Kent!

The hottie from the photograph?

Yes.

And you're with him now?

Yes.

Is there a bed in the general vicinity?

I frown. *Yes.*

I'm still not understanding your problem.

I should've texted Kate.

"WOULD YOU LIKE A REFILL?" Kent asks when I walk back into the living room. He's sitting exactly where I left him, but the TV is on, volume turned low.

"No, I'm good, thanks."

He switches the TV off.

"Actually, I think I should go."

"Go?" he blinks at me. "Why? It's still early."

"I know, but I have a busy day tomorrow. Lesson plans and all that jazz."

"Okay." He gets to his feet, looking disappointed. "I'll walk you out."

"You don't have to do that. I can see myself out."

"Don't be ridiculous."

We don't speak in the elevator ride down to the lobby. Kent is searching my face, but I keep it blank, revealing nothing. The street outside is quiet, but the second we reach it, Kent's control frays.

"Amber." Kent runs his hands through his hair. "What's going on?" He's standing close to me, too close, and even in my heels, I have to crane my neck to look up at him.

"Nothing." I duck my head, but his hand rises to my chin, and he tilts it back. I blink in embarrassment under his scrutiny.

"Don't lie to me."

A lifetime passes between us. His eyes are warm, filled with concern, and it hurts to look at him.

"You were right," I admit softly.

"About what?"

"It wasn't Erica. It wasn't just you. Back in college," I add hastily, as a look of confusion crosses his face. "I pulled away first. I got involved with Lara, and that stupid crowd, and I lost track of what was important."

He blinks, taken aback by my admission. "You're saying I was important?"

"You were my best friend, Kent. Of course you were. You..." I shake my head, my thoughts in turmoil. So quickly, so easily, we've slipped back into this familiarity, as if the past few years never happened. But they did happen, and Kent – Kent grew up. He grew up into a successful, incredible man, and I was too self-absorbed to notice. I'm the world's biggest idiot.

"What did you mean?" I ask, frantic for a handle on my emotions. "When you said that you dated Erica because she was interested."

"Amber..."

"I want to know." I'm firm because it's been niggling at me since he said it, and I need to know if my suspicions are founded.

His eyes burn into mine. Neither of us looks away. A cab ventures near, but he makes no move to hail it down. My heart starts to beat a little faster in my chest.

"What do you think I meant?" he murmurs eventually, and the resignation in his voice is as good as an admission.

I feel pinpricks of pain in the corners of my eyes. "Why didn't you tell me?"

His sigh is soft and sad. "Would you have cared?"

I don't need to say anything. We both know the answer. I want to apologize, to tell him that I was stupid, and selfish, and blinded to what had been right in front of me, but it's too little too late. And I'm terrified to ruin this fragile new peace between us, to jeopardize the friendship we're so carefully rebuilding.

"I care now," I whisper, so softly I'm not sure he's heard me.

"Amber." My name is a song on his lips. His arms come up, reach for me, and then they fall away. Kent's expression is one of horrified regret. "Amber, there's something you need to know."

I barely register the words which follow. Only that her name is Megan, and they've been seeing each other for a few months. My jaw aches with the effort of keeping my expression neutral, and my heart slows to a dull thud.

"I'm happy for you." I hear myself saying, my voice too high, too bright. "Really, Kent, I am."

A puzzled frown. "Amber, I"

"That all happened a long time ago," I say quickly. "We're different people now. I just wanted you to know that I'm sorry for how I treated you back then, that's all. Mostly, I'm just glad we're back to being friends."

"Can we go back upstairs?" he is pleading. "We can talk about it."

"There's nothing to talk about." I spot a lone cab cruising down the street, and I leap forward to flag it down.

"Amber!" he yells after me.

"Thank you for a wonderful evening," I call back, and then I launch myself into the cab.

I'm not proud of what I do next. Humiliated and heartsore, I text Chase. *What are you up to?*

Nothing right now.

Want to meet for a drink?

His reply is only one word. *Where?*

We meet at a pub just a few blocks down from my apartment. It's tiny, but the jukebox in the corner belts out eighties love songs and drowns out the sound of my phone ringing. Kent has called four times, but I don't answer.

"I must admit, I was surprised to hear from you," Chase says when he arrives. He kisses me full on the mouth in greeting. "I know I wasn't supposed to contact you for another two weeks, but I've never been good with rules, and I certainly didn't expect a reply."

"I'm not particularly good at following rules either, obviously."

He tips his glass toward mine, "To rule breakers."

I force myself not to think of Kent. He's not available, and I'll be damned if I let that come between us now, after we've finally managed to become friends again. The best thing to do is move on, as quickly as possible. Chase is a nice guy. He's successful and funny, and someone I could see myself falling for. So I focus on what's right in front of me. On the present, because there's no point living in the past.

THE FOLLOWING MORNING, I get a text from Kent. *Flying home, something's come up. I'll be back as soon as I can. We need to talk.*

I hope everything's okay. I reply. *We can talk when you're back.*

When he follows that with a phone call, I don't answer it.

I DON'T HEAR from him for two weeks. In that time, I have a platonic date with Basil Mitchell and one of Mandy's other regulars – James Gerber – a giant of a man with a mop of curly hair and the creased face of someone who's spent a lifetime working outdoors. I also have five very non-platonic dates with Chase. The more I spend time with him, the more I start to believe that he could truly be the man who gets me over Kent. I'm aware that I've been avoiding Kate, but she's too nice to comment, and I know that right now I have bigger issues to deal with. Mandy, on the other hand, is not as tolerant. Only two days ago, she'd torn into me on a video call for not keeping in contact. "I'm flying in on Sunday," she'd warned, "and I expect to see your face!"

I don't mention that Saturday is my birthday. I don't tell anyone.

ON SATURDAY AFTERNOON, Chase and I watch a movie at the local theatre, most of which we miss because we're making out in the love seat.

"Can I come back to your place?" he asks as the credits roll, his voice a warm breath in my ear. I stiffen. He hasn't been to my apartment. I haven't been to his, either. We've done a lot of kissing, but our relationship hasn't moved beyond that. To be fair, we've only had eight dates. The old Amber would be laughing her twisted head off. The new Amber is far more conscious of her reputation.

I gaze up into Chase's blue eyes. They're warm and inviting.

"Sure," I say, as his mouth finds mine for another lingering kiss.

Outside my apartment block, he raises both brows and gives a low whistle.

"Business must be good," he teases.

"Well, seeing as I haven't charged you a cent, you should be grateful that someone else is footing the bill." That's another good thing about Chase. He doesn't judge me for what I do. He understands that none of my other dates are any threat to what we have.

He chuckles, his fingers interlaced with mine. His thumb massages the palm of my hand in slow, lazy circles and my pulse spikes. I know what he's expecting, when we get upstairs. I smile at him, trying to slow the frantic beating of my heart as we head for the elevator. Chase seems to sense my unease. He starts kissing me, sweetly, before the doors have opened. I melt against him, feeling his strong hands on my hips, the long, lean length of him pressed up against me. By the time we reach my door, our kisses have become deeper, more urgent, and I fumble behind me, trying to get my key into the lock.

"SURPRISE!" The roar of raised voices sounds the second we tumble through the door. I drop my keys and leap away from Chase, my hand rising to cover my mouth, my shoulders heaving as I gasp for breath. A stunned silence follows as I take in Mandy, Ryan, Kate, Bianca, and my parents standing in the hall of my apartment. I take them in with one quick sweeping glance, but it's the tall, dark-haired man at the end who draws my attention. The man who is gazing at me with a hollow expression, his eyes filled with pain and disappointment. He tears his eyes away from me to look at Chase, and then he shakes his head.

"Kent!" I say as he stalks past us. I don't even bother explaining to

Chase as I rush after him. "Kent!" He's standing at the elevator, jabbing the call button with unnecessary force, his head bowed. "Please look at me."

I don't expect him to obey, so when he does, I'm still trying to find my words. "Where are you going?" I ask lamely.

He laughs, but it's a horrible sound. Dry and bitter.

"What's wrong?"

He doesn't reply, just jabs again at the button. I feel a flare of anger rise in my chest. Sure, having everyone see me and Chase making out isn't ideal, but Kent's reaction is completely irrational. Especially seeing that he has a girlfriend.

When the elevator doors open, I step right in beside him. He jabs the button for the ground floor. "The least you can do is talk to me," I snap.

He rounds on me in disbelief. "Oh, really? Like you've been talking to me the past few weeks?"

I flinch away from the genuine rage on his face. "I wasn't ignoring you. I've just been busy."

"I can see that." The words are cold and ugly.

"That's not fair! This is ridiculous, we're friends. Why are you acting like this?"

"We're not friends, Amber. Not anymore."

"What?"

"Two weeks ago you said things, things that implied you felt something for me. *Two weeks ago*. And I believed you!" That harsh bark of laughter again. "God, I'm an idiot. All these years. People don't change, I don't know why I let myself believe that you had."

"I have changed!"

"Two weeks ago, Amber!" he roars, so loudly that the elevator doors seem to rattle. "You couldn't wait two weeks before you jumped into bed with another man!"

My head jerks up. "Wait? What do you"

"Forget it."

The elevator doors open, and he steps out. "Happy birthday," he sneers, handing me a ribbon-enrobed envelope. I take it, automatically, and gaze up at him, at the muscle going in his jaw, at the cold fury in his green eyes. "Goodbye, Amber."

All the way back up to my floor, I stare at that envelope, wondering what the hell just happened. It doesn't make any sense. I slide my thumbnail under the seal and tear it open, but before I can reach inside, the doors open and the sound of furious voices reaches me.

Mandy and Chase are standing in the hall outside my apartment, clearly involved in a heated argument. There's no sign of anyone else, and I can only pray they're all still inside.

"What's going on?" I say when it becomes obvious that Mandy and Chase haven't noticed me. They both turn to look at me, but Mandy gets there first.

"What the hell are you doing, dating this sack of shit?" Mandy demands.

"I beg your pardon?"

"Chase Crawford!" she seethes. "What's the point of the book if you're going to ignore everything inside it?"

"What are you talking about?" I ask, risking a glance at Chase, He doesn't look angry. In fact, he looks... amused.

"The red list," Mandy says. "This bastard's on it."

"No, he's not," I say, shaking my head in emphasis. "I checked. There's no Chase Crawford on file. He's a new referral..." I trail off as I catch sight of the ugly grin spreading over Chase's face. "You're a new referral," I repeat, but this time I speak directly to him.

"Afraid not, sweetheart."

My blood is thundering in my ears. "I don't understand."

"He's married," Amber spits out, then, giving me an apologetic look, "this is the guy I told you about. The one I broke the rules for. He's a lying, two-timing pig."

"You're married?" I gasp, but Chase isn't listening. He reaches out a hand and brushes his fingers across Mandy's jaw. She slaps it away.

"You girls have your little games," he murmurs, sparing me a wink. "And I have mine."

"Get out," I snarl. "Get out, you son of a bitch, or, I swear to God, I'll rip your fucking dick off."

Chase takes two swaggering steps toward the elevator when I draw back my fist and send it hurtling toward his face. Pain blossoms in my knuckles, but I feel the satisfying crunch of bone beneath it.

"You bitch!" he clutches his bleeding nose.

"Try explaining that to your wife," Mandy drawls.

Chase rounds on her, his arm raised, and for a heart-stopping moment, I think he might hit her.

"Try that, son, and it'll be the last thing you ever do." My father speaks from the now open doorway, the Great White on full display. The predatory look on his face is terrifying. Chase backs up, and I press the call button for the elevator. It opens immediately and swallows Chase whole.

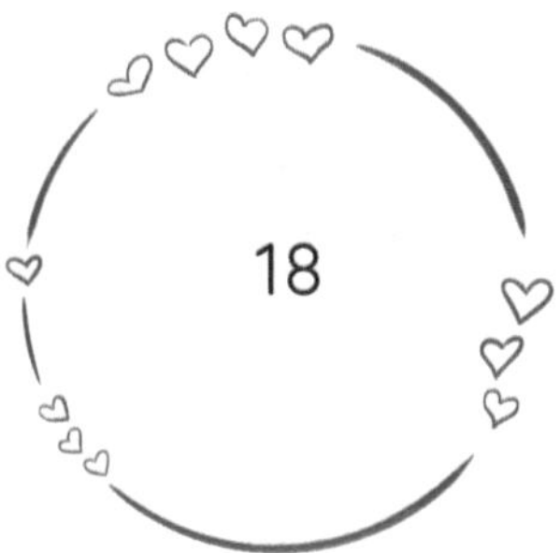

It takes the better part of an hour to explain everything to my parents. There was no lying my way out of it – the apartment speaks for itself – something Mandy forgot to consider when she planned this surprise party. After Chase had left, she took everyone downstairs for a drink so I could speak to my parents in private.

"I don't understand why you'd do it," my dad insists. "If you needed money that badly..."

"Dad, seriously. I'm not a whore. It sounds bad, but it's not like that. And I didn't want your money. Well, I did, in the beginning, but after I started working and cut back on the booze, I started to enjoy the financial freedom. I know this isn't exactly the ideal way for you to be introduced to my life here, but it's been good for me. You were right. It's exactly what I needed."

"Kent told us," my mother says quietly. "That you were flourishing here. He's been keeping us informed."

I try not to wince at the mention of his name. "See? You know Kent wouldn't give me credit if it wasn't due."

Even my father can't fault this reasoning.

"And that man?" he asks. "The one outside. How does he fit into all of this?"

"He's just an asshole who conned me into thinking he was something that he wasn't. Don't look so stressed, dad, we didn't actually sleep together. And even the most responsible people make mistakes. What happened today with Chase doesn't take away from all the good I've achieved here."

He seems about to question me further when his pocket beeps. "It's Kent," he says, reading the incoming text. "He's catching the next flight out of Beijing."

They both look up at me as the blood drains from my face.

"Sweetheart," my mom says softly, "what happened with you two?"

"I don't know. Everything was going well, but then today... he just lost it."

"It can't have been easy for him, seeing you with that man," my dad grunts. "I know it wasn't easy for me."

"Dad, Kent and I are friends, but it's got nothing to do with him who I date!"

"She's right," my mom says, and I give her a grateful smile. "I think your father and I are just confused, Amber. From what Kent was saying, we thought perhaps you two were more than just friends. Or on your way to being more than friends, at least."

"That would be a bit difficult, considering he has a girlfriend."

Their eyes meet, and something passes between them.

"What?" I ask. "What are you not telling me?"

"Honey, Kent doesn't have a girlfriend. He did," she adds quickly, "but he flew home two weeks ago to end things. Megan was devastated, and it took her a few days to accept it, but he explained that his heart belonged to someone else. We were under the impression that *someone* was you."

. . .

I HOLD it together until my parents have retired to my guest room, their jetlag finally catching up with them. Mandy returned about an hour ago, after dispatching all the other guests, including Ryan, home. They're staying in a hotel just a few blocks down. Mandy has barely spoken since the confrontation outside, but once my mom and dad have said their goodnights, we take a seat in the living room.

I heft the book from the side table and dump it on her lap.

"Show me."

Mandy flips through it, the furrows on her brow deepening with each passing page. When she reaches the last divider in the red section, she raises her head and gives me a look of wretched apology.

"I must've thrown it out," she says, in a voice heavy with remorse, "God, Amber, I'm so sorry. I hated him so much. When I found out the truth, I must've ripped it out of the file."

"It's not your fault," I sigh. "He must've known you were gone, and he took a chance. It paid off, obviously. There's no way you could've known."

"I might've, if you'd confided in me," she points out.

I give her a weary smile. "I'm sorry I didn't tell you. I'm sorry I've been quiet. Things have been a bit crazy."

"I know you were upset about Wei leaving. And then something happened with Kent?" It's an educated guess, given what went down earlier.

"Oh God, don't remind me." I cover my face with my hands, briefly, and then force myself to look at her. "I don't even know how this happened. One minute he was the bane of my life, and driving me nuts, and the next..."

"You wanted to jump his bones?"

"Well, yeah."

"I hate to break it to you, Amber, but you've been crazy about that man since the day I met you. I don't know who you thought you were fooling."

"Myself?"

"Good job. You're the only one you managed to convince."

"What am I going to do?"

"You're going to live out the ending of every romcom you've ever watched. You're going to go after him. And," she adds wryly, "you're going to do it without subtitles."

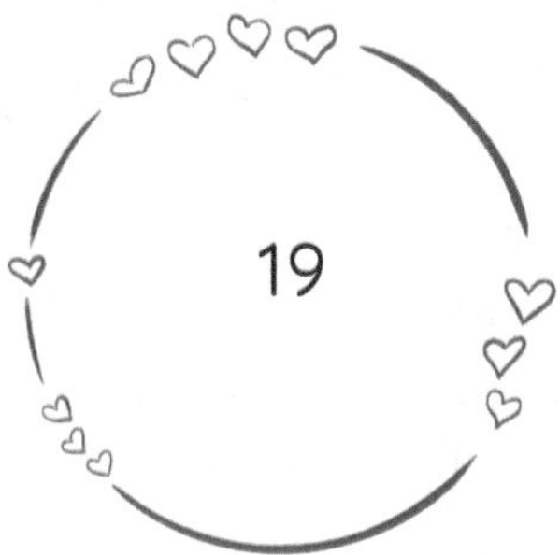

The dry heat of the Santa Ana winds hit me in full force the moment I step off the plane. My father had temporarily lifted his ban on my spending to secure me a first-class ticket home to "sort out my shit," as he so eloquently put it. I know that he only did it because it involves Kent. I could tell by the smug look. Nothing would make him happier than to see me end up with the man he already considers a son. And, for the first time in my life, what he wants and what I want are perfectly aligned. I grabbed the ticket. I didn't even offer to pay for it myself.

Bianca had accepted my excuse that there had been a family emergency, in her stride, but I only had three days. I'd be returning to Beijing, with or without Kent.

The cab ride to his apartment is the longest of my life. I keep my eyes on the road, the miles flashing by in a grey and white blur, while my heart races in my chest.

"Thank you," I say when we finally pull up outside Kent's apartment block. I hand over a few crumpled bills. "Keep the change."

I brought nothing with me, save for my purse. I have enough clothes in my apartment to last a lifetime, let alone a couple of days, and, thanks to Amber and the lucrative second income she passed along, my credit card is good to go.

I stop only when I reach Kent's door. I didn't think to call ahead, and for all I know he's not even here, but I still need a minute to compose myself. What he saw, back in Beijing, isn't going to be easy to explain. The escort business may be innocent, but my relationship with Chase was definitely not.

I'm trying to find the right words to explain it all when the door is yanked open, and Kent bursts from his apartment, in an obvious hurry. Eyes fixed on his cell, oblivious to the fact that I'm standing here, he knocks me clean off my feet, and we go down in a painful heap.

"Jesus, Amber!" he yells, disentangling himself and getting to his feet. "Are you okay?" He offers me his hand and I take it. We face each other and I notice the dark shadows under his eyes, and the empty look within them.

"What the hell are you doing lurking in my doorway? There's a bell, you know."

"I know. I'm sorry, I was about to knock."

His gaze slides over me, from head to toe and back again. "You're sure you're okay?"

I nod.

"What are you doing here?"

"I came to see you. We need to talk."

"Really?" he crosses his arms over his chest. "About what?"

I glance up and down the hallway. "Could we go inside?"

"No. Whatever you have to say to me, you can say it right here."

"Kent."

He doesn't budge.

"Fine! What you saw yesterday, it wasn't what you think. Wait," I add quickly, "it's exactly what you think, but I can explain."

"I'm listening."

"Chase is... was, someone I met before you and I had dinner that night, but we weren't together. Not until after you told me you had a girlfriend."

"Do I look like I was born yesterday?"

"It's the truth! Nothing happened! We haven't even... you know."

"No, I don't know." He is not going to make this easy for me.

"We haven't had sex!" I snap, loud enough that he winces. His eyes travel the length of the hall, and he curses under his breath.

"Get in here," he mutters, holding the door wide. I scuttle inside. We head for the kitchen. Kent starts making a pot of coffee, with unnecessary force. "Explain."

I do, in fits and starts, tripping over my words more than once. I leave nothing out. At some point, Kent hands me a mug of coffee, but he doesn't speak, only stands opposite me over the marble island and listens.

When I'm finally done, I look up at him. Kent's face is unreadable.

"Your coffee's cold," he says.

I blink in confusion. "What?"

"Your coffee," he says simply, reaching over for my mug. "It's cold."

"That's all you have to say?"

"No. I have a lot to say, but I'm trying to get a hold of my..." he trails off, turning away from me so I can't see his face.

"Your temper?" I prompt. "You're trying to get a hold on your temper?"

Only when his shoulders start to shake, do I realize he's laughing.

"What the hell is so funny?" I storm around the island and walk right into his personal space. His eyes are streaming, and he sets down the mugs to wipe at them with the sleeve of his shirt.

"Only you," he says, between gasping breaths. "God, you're a mess."

I don't take it too personally, though, because his arms have come around my waist as he says it. I press my lips together to keep from laughing too.

"It's not funny," I say.

"You're right," he sniffs, composing himself. "And you may be a mess, but you're *my* mess." The possessive pronoun sends a thrill through me.

"You're really not mad at me?"

His face softens. "I'm really not mad at you. I've spent the last few years of my life watching you self-destruct, Amber. What you've done... well, it might not be the most conventional way to do it, but you've stood on your own two feet." He smiles down at me, and his arms tighten, shifting me into the space between them, snug against the length of his body. "When your dad sent you over there, I was convinced you'd be back in a week, broken, and broke. Instead, you not only rose to the challenge, but you embraced it. I couldn't be prouder. I'm sorry I didn't hear you out," he adds, "but seeing you with Chase..." I feel his hands tighten convulsively at the base of my spine and, for a second, his face falls. "You're sure you're not secretly in love with that bastard?"

I rise onto my toes, so our faces are only inches apart.

"The only bastard I'm secretly in love with," I say, speaking slowly and clearly, "is you."

His eyes blaze with triumph. It's a beautiful sight, but I don't have time appreciate it, because his head dips and my eyes close automatically as his lips meet mine.

FIRST CLASS never so looked good as it does now, with Kent lounging in the seat beside me. His hands are constantly seeking me out – they stray to my hair, my thigh, trace small patterns at the nape of my neck.

"My lucky charm," he says, as the air hostess brings us each a complimentary glass of champagne. I grin at him over my glass.

"Is this real?" he asks, and I know exactly what he means. It's all happened so quickly, and yet, taken us a lifetime to reach this point.

"I hope so," I say. "You know, you could've saved us a lot of time and hassle if you'd just admitted you were in love with me back in college."

"You would've run for the hills."

"Lara would've dragged me." Thinking back, I wonder if Lara didn't suspect all along and, fearful of losing her party sponsor, had driven that wedge deeper between us.

"Speaking of Lara. Have you spoken to her at all since you left?"

"Once. She made it crystal clear that I wasn't any use to her without my platinum card."

He gives me a knowing grin. "I hate to say I told you so..."

"Bullshit. You live for it."

He leans over to kiss my nose. "Is it wrong to feel so ridiculously happy after everything that's happened?"

"If it is, I'm just as guilty as you are."

His lips find mine, and he holds the kiss slightly longer than is appropriate, but the flight hostess only gives us a fond smile.

"There are a few things we need to clear up, though," Kent murmurs into my neck.

"Hmm, like what?"

"Well, if you're serious about staying in Beijing and seeing your year out, I'm thinking you should give up that apartment and get a key to mine. Saber has enough invested in Beijing to justify me staying too."

"Give up my apartment?" I fake mock outrage. "After all the work I've put in to get it?"

"Oh, you mean eating at fancy restaurants and drinking all the expensive champagne your heart desires?"

"Yes. That's exactly what I mean. I don't think you appreciate how difficult it's been for me, Mr. James. It's a tough job, but someone's got to do it."

"Well, I guess we better start looking for your replacement. I don't want to tell you how to live your life, but I would prefer that I occupied your evenings from now on." He squeezes my leg and a blaze of heat rockets up my thigh.

"I'm sure we can come to some sort of arrangement," I say, trying to keep my voice light. "I mean, there should be a discount for frequent users."

His low rumble of laughter is music to my ears. "And I plan to use you frequently."

I rest my head on his shoulder and draw the blanket up over us.

"I'm sure there'll be someone to take things over. Mandy's replacement is single, and I caught her eyeing up my Prada boots last week." I tilt my head to breathe in the trace of aftershave on his jaw. "Are you sure you want to stay in China? You've worked so hard. I'd hate to think that you're giving up other opportunities because of me."

"Amber." He shifts so that I have to raise my head to look at him. "I only work so hard because I thought it might get your attention. I only throw my heart and soul into your father's business because I know, ultimately, it's all for you. Trust me," he adds, dropping another kiss on my brow, "I'm never leaving your side again."

"What if my dad decides I need to learn another lesson, and sends me to Siberia?"

"Then I guess I'll have to get a warmer coat."

Of course, my dad wouldn't send me anywhere. He was so thrilled about Kent and I, the only place he wanted us was back home. To his dismay, we refused. I was seeing out my teaching year, come hell or high water. It meant too much to me, this sense of accomplishment, and Gabby Martin had started to show an interest in poetry, of all things. Besides, I couldn't let Bianca down. Amber's replacement, Molly, was only too happy to take over the escort business, but, unlike Amber and I, she resigned from the school within two weeks when she realized how much money she stood to make. I'd handed her the book, with Chase's updated file in the red list. Kent had laughed his handsome head off when Basil Mitchell had called me to tell me he approved.

Now, with less than a week left, we're packing up the apartment which we've come to call home. I have my heart set on a west coast wedding, and Kent's mom has threatened to disown him if we don't get our arses back to the States before Christmas. So, I'm finally headed home. A new Amber. A better Amber. With the man I love by my side. But first, we're making a short pit stop. There's a wedding in Canada that I wouldn't miss for the world.

. . .

END OF BOOK 2.

AWKWARD INFIDELITY

BOOK 3 IN THE AWKWARD SERIES

I never meant to have an affair. I certainly never meant to have one with my own husband, lying, cheating rat that he is. Aaron and I had been separated for almost a year when we bumped into one another at Starbucks. He was seeing Staci at the time – he had been since long before we split – and I'd been dating Blake for almost four months by then. Aaron had run into me. Literally. He'd knocked my Dirty Chai clear out of my hands, spilling it down the front of my new silk blouse. The blouse had been white before the steaming liquid turned it utterly sheer. Eyes fixed on my chest, Aaron had murmured, "you're looking good, Cat." Then he'd lifted those baby blues to fix me with his signature stare, and my stomach had done the conga. Five minutes later we were making out in the backseat of a cab while the driver tried to watch us in the rear-view mirror. Another ten minutes, and we'd collapsed on the crumpled sheets of Aaron's unmade bed, which was still warm. I tried not to think about Staci and the longevity of her hatha yoga body heat.

"This was a mistake," I'd insisted as soon as it was over. Determinedly, I'd donned my still sodden blouse. Then we'd had sex again. Twice.

That was six weeks ago. Now, as I wait in my living room, watching the clock, I can recall every dirty, sexy second of it. The dial of the clock gives off a faint tick as it moves. It has just passed the half-hour mark when I hear a knock on my front door. Two short taps, followed by a pause. Another single tap. I'm opening the door before Aaron can finish the sequence, and I pull him inside by the front of his shirt.

"Easy!" he hisses as a button pops free of its thread and skitters across my hardwood floor. I know what he's thinking – that Staci might notice. Somehow it makes me want him more, rather than less. I throw a mental middle finger at Staci and groan against his lips. His breathing quickens. I know exactly what he likes, and how he likes it. We were together for five years and married for just short of two of those. Three weeks and two days short, if we're counting. I'd spent my second wedding anniversary trying to find myself in the bottom of a bottle of Tequila. All I'd found was the worm. No doubt Aaron had spent the evening plugged into Staci.

I never thought my marriage would end. Nobody does, I suppose, when they're walking down the aisle in that ironically white dress, with baby's breath twined through their hair. Aaron and I met in college, the University of California, Berkeley, during that time in a man's life when he's at his most uninhibited and open to experimentation. We'd been in the same drinking club at UCB. My single, stir-crazy mother, Viola, had raised me in a liberal household and encouraged me to embrace my sexuality. She claimed orgasms were my God-given right. My mother behaves like a bona fide hippy, though she's not yet forty-five. Still, I'd taken her lessons to heart and met Aaron's challenges head-on. The sex had been glorious and, at times, borderline depraved. I know all of Aaron's dirty little secrets, and believe me, some are so dirty that I doubt tree-hugging, yoga-teaching Staci would hang around if she knew half of them.

He's still bothered by the button. I can tell by the set of his jaw, the annoyance flashing in his ice-blue eyes. I twist in his arms and press my backside up against his groin, gyrating slightly. Distracted, his annoyance fades as his strong hands grip my hips, and I smile to myself as he hauls me into the bedroom, all thoughts of Staci blown right out of his mind.

"AM I SEEING YOU ON FRIDAY?" Aaron asks as he buttons up his shirt. It's always like this – the second we're done, he's up and out of the door as quickly as possible. I don't mind. We've never been great conversationalists. He pauses at the missing button. A small frown creases his brow. I bite my lip, knowing my answer isn't going to help his fast-deteriorating mood.

"Actually, I'm meeting Blake on Friday morning. We're having breakfast at *Verdure*." I may be showing off, just a little. *Verdure* is an exclusive new bistro uptown, where you pay a small fortune for a tiny portion of food to be prepared by some of the best chefs in the city. Blake is a surgical resident. He works long hours, but this Friday he has one of his rare days off. Conversely, Staci teaches three back-to-back yoga classes every Friday morning at the community center, which leaves Aaron with way too much free time on his hands. Aaron is a trust-fund baby. Technically, he runs one of his father's subsidiaries, but in reality, I've never known him to work a day in his life.

"Oh." He manages to convey an entire lifetime of disappointment into that one little word. I wish I didn't care.

"I can't cancel, he's already booked. And it's not as if *this*," I wave my hand between us, "is going anywhere."

I try to hide it, but he hears my longing, and his lips twitch upward in smug satisfaction. If I know all of Aaron's secrets, he knows all of mine. He can read me like an open book, and right now he knows that I want him to reconsider the separation. It's no big secret. I've wanted that since the day we split. He crooks his finger at me, and my and I forget how to breathe. *Play it cool, Cat.* My feet ignore my silent plea and slide forward of their own accord until I'm standing right before him. Exactly where he wants me. Aaron runs a long, lean finger down the hollow of my throat.

"Baby, you know I can't leave Staci. You and I, we've got something special, but we don't work the usual way. We've proved it."

"And yet we're not divorced yet," I snap, annoyed by all the '*we*' references when the real reason we didn't work had nothing to do with me and everything to do with him screwing Staci in our marital bed. Aaron's fingers dip under the lace of my bra, and my thoughts scatter.

"You want me to divorce you, Kitty Cat?" he murmurs.

I shake my head, no, as his fingers close around my nipple and squeeze hard enough to hurt.

"I didn't think so." His voice is hoarser now. With expert fingers, he reaches behind me and unhooks my bra. "Well, I guess if I'm not seeing you on Friday, we better make up for it now." I open my mouth to argue that I have work to do, but he's already plunging his hands into my hair and yanking back my head to claim my mouth.

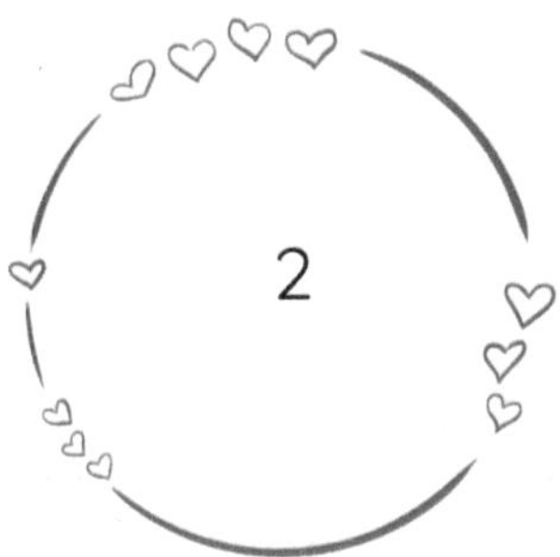

I'm bow-legged by the time Aaron leaves, wishing, as I do every time we part, that he didn't have this hold over me. He's an asshole, but the sex is out of this world. Even better now that it's taboo. There's nothing quite as intoxicating as the risk of getting caught.

When I found out about Aaron's affair with Staci, I was devastated. Kicked in the gut, didn't leave the house for a week, drenched my pillow every night, shattered. There was nothing remarkable about that day, barring the fact that it turned out to be the day my life was turned upside down. It was just an average Monday. I was supposed to be meeting a potential new client, but he'd canceled at the last minute, and it was late enough in the day that I could play hooky, guilt-free. I'd stopped at the deli to get a few of the little pastries Aaron adored, grabbed two bottles of wine to go with them, and headed home, already thinking of new ways to greet him at the door, most of which involved lacy underwear, some of which involved no underwear at all.

I didn't even notice them at first. Thinking back, it's almost laughable how they lay, frozen, on the couch while I'd uncorked the wine and poured myself a glass, taken a long and leisurely sip, and contemplated whether I should call Aaron and let him know I was home early. I'd swilled the wine in my mouth, turned toward the living room, and sprayed it all over the counter. Staci had cowered beneath Aaron while I threw first the bottle and then half a dozen cream-filled pastries at his head.

I'm still not sure if it was my heart or my pride that was most shattered. I'd kicked him out, obviously. It was my name on the lease, and there was no way I was having Staci move into the apartment that I'd spent two years decorating. I'd paint-techniqued the hall myself, with a tiny paintbrush that covered about an inch an hour.

I hadn't seen Aaron for months after that. Secretly, I had hoped he would come crawling back, begging for forgiveness and oozing remorse. In reality, he had moved into a new apartment with Staci less than a month after our split. It had taken me a lot longer to move on. Despite my mother's increasing insistence that I should find myself a new lover, I'd found Aaron harder to shake than the herbs she brewed into her tea. It was, in fact, those herbs that finally got me out of my funk. A few months after the split, I'd gone over to spend an evening with my mother and ended up in the hospital. God knows what she put in that tea, but I was tripping out of my mind when I stumbled into the E.R, one arm draped around her slim shoulders, the other holding a half-eaten hamburger, which I'd refused to relinquish even after I'd started throwing up.

Blake had been on duty. He'd taken one look at me, asked a few questions of my mother, who'd pretended not to be able to speak a word of English, and set up a drip. Two hours later, my mother, who'd recovered her command of the English language well enough to chat up the sister on duty, pushed off to a party and I'd sobered enough for a tidal wave of humiliation to wash over me.

"Your mom's quite something," Blake had said as he removed the drip.

"She's a little wild," I'd admitted. "And she's not Italian, obviously."

"If she were, I'd be worried, seeing as how she was speaking Spanish," he pointed out. "So, your mother is wild. What about you? Do you do this kind of thing often?"

"Do what kind of thing?" I asked, innocently. My mother had taught me well. To my amazement, his face had creased into a smile, and it was glorious. Like watching stone come to life.

"I'm not going to report you, Catrina," he'd said. I'd known a moment of passionate relief before I'd vomited all over his shoes.

"It's Cat," I'd told him before I left. "No one calls me Catrina anymore."

He'd looked at me with an unreadable expression on his face and said, "That's a pity. It's a beautiful name." I'd watched his broad back until it disappeared behind another curtain and found myself hoping the woman on the other side of it wasn't remotely attractive.

I'D CALLED my mom as soon as I got home. Judging by the screaming chaos in the background, the party was still in full swing. For the first few minutes, all she was interested in was whether Nurse Janine's shift had ended yet, and if so, did she mention if she was coming to the party. I answered honestly that I had no idea.

"I bet you fifty bucks that boy calls you," she'd slurred, then. I'd told her she was high. She may well have been, but as it turned out, she was also right.

For a long time, I didn't mention my budding relationship with Blake to any of mine and Aaron's mutual friends. My biggest fear was that he would use it as grounds to finally go through with divorce proceedings which, despite my growing feelings for Blake, wasn't something I was ready to accept. As it turns out, what actually happened was the complete opposite. Not a week after letting it slip, I'd bumped into Aaron at Starbucks. Or rather, he'd bumped into me. The rest, you already know. In rare moments of insanity, I find myself wondering if he'd masterminded the whole thing because he'd realized he might lose *me*. In reality, I know that Aaron simply doesn't like to lose.

I don't take a shower, preferring to keep the scent of him on me for as long as I can. I'm not seeing Blake until much later, so there'll be plenty of time to wash away the guilt. I grab an apple out of the fruit bowl on the counter, shove my laptop in my bag, and head for the coffee shop down the street, which serves as my informal office. I'd studied commerce in college and been smart enough to capitalize on the rise of e-commerce. I now run online stores for a healthy portfolio of customers, including two rapidly emerging brands, and I take a hefty cut of their proceeds in return.

Amy, the regular morning waitress, greets me with a smile. "You want the usual, Cat?"

"Make it a double, please. I have a ton of admin to get through today."

"Coming right up."

I work right through lunch, with Amy refilling my coffee cup every hour. By the time my laptop battery runs low, I've done as much as I can for today.

"You want anything to eat?" Amy asks as she passes by on her way to check on another table. The patron is a slightly creepy-looking man in his early thirties with a mop of blond hair and a fleshy lower lip, who's been casting surreptitious glances my way all morning.

"No, I'm good," I tell Amy. "Just the bill, please."

I leave Amy a generous tip and head home. When the elevator opens on my floor, I'm horrified to find Blake at my door. He's holding a huge bunch of lilies – my favorite, despite the negative connotation – and an unidentifiable DVD. Blake is old-school. He still hires movies the old-fashioned way, even though I have Netflix and unlimited streaming. I'm suddenly acutely aware that my body is coated in all things Aaron.

"What are you doing here?" I ask, mustering a smile. "I thought you were only getting off later tonight."

Blake's eyes crinkle at the corners when he smiles. "It turns out I forgot to log a few shifts. I've exceeded the maximum limit, so they sent me home. Can't have us falling asleep with a scalpel in our hands." He leans in to kiss my cheek, and I duck my head, terrified to get too close.

"Sorry, I reek. I didn't bother showering after gym this morning." The lie rolls easily off my tongue as I quickly unlock my door and step inside. "Make yourself comfortable, I'm going to hop in the shower, and then we can catch up." He gives me a curious look but doesn't argue.

The water is scalding. As it runs over me, I scrub my skin until it's red and angry. God, I am such a bitch. I vow for what must be the twentieth time that I'm going to end things with Aaron. Blake is a good guy – far too good for me if the truth be told. Why the hell am I risking what we have for a man who self-admittedly has no intention of reconciling? *Because he gets you,* the devil on my left shoulder whispers in my ear. *Because you like things a little rough, a little dangerous, and Blake* is *a good guy, but you want a bad one.*

Hair still wet from the shower, I pull on a pair of leggings and an oversized shirt.

"You smell good," Blake murmurs as I cozy up beside him on the couch. He smells of antiseptic and aftershave. It's a wholesome and heady combination. This time when he leans in for a kiss, I turn my face toward him. My stomach disappears. I am most definitely attracted to Blake. He's smart and his sense of humor is just quirky enough to be original. He also overthinks almost everything. I never know what's going on behind those hazel eyes. Hell, in another year he'll be a fully-qualified general surgeon. At least a head taller than Aaron, and twice as broad in the shoulders, I can only imagine how his female patients must fawn over him. I must be crazy.

"How long do I have the pleasure of your company, before your pager interrupts us?" I tease.

"I'm only back after the weekend, so we have four whole days to ourselves. Speaking of which," he says, withdrawing his pager and dropping it into the drawer of the low coffee table.

"Wow, you really are off duty," I say.

He kicks the drawer closed with his foot. "Silence is golden."

"What did you get?" I ask, gesturing at the DVD on the table.

He laughs, a rumble that starts deep in his chest. "*Wedding Crashers*."

I can't help but grin. Blake has a deep and abiding love for Vince Vaughn. I lean forward and kiss him again, letting my mouth linger on his.

"You get it set up, I'll make the popcorn."

"You don't want me to order anything in?" he asks, as my stomach gives a low rumble.

"No, popcorn will be fine. Unless you're hungry?"

He shakes his head. "I grabbed a sandwich at the canteen before I left."

Snuggled up beside Blake on the couch, my feet wedged between his thighs for warmth, my head on his shoulder, it's so easy to forget Aaron. So easy to see a life with Blake – a future filled with marriage, and babies, mortgages and seaside vacations. He's the man for whom your mother would sell her soul to the devil, to see you end up with. Aaron, on the other hand, is the devil who'd claim it.

I'm so lost in thought that I barely pay attention to the movie, until I feel Blake's shoulder shaking under my cheek.

"What is it with you and Vince Vaughn?" I tease, as he lets out another rumble of laughter.

"Oh, come on! He's hilarious. Look at him!" he points at the screen. Admittedly, the sight of Vince trying to blow off Isla Fisher in the bathroom, while she climbs all over him like a rabid monkey, is pretty hysterical.

"We look a bit like them," Blake says, between bursts of laughter. Vince is tall, like Blake, and my hair is long, and red, like Isla's, but other than that, I don't see a resemblance.

"You're better looking," I say. Blake gives me a heart-stopping smile and kisses my hand.

After the movie, he leads me by the hand to my bedroom.

"You must have been in a rush this morning," he says at the doorway. "You didn't even make your bed."

I cringe at the sight of the rumpled sheets, even while my eyes scan the room, searching for any evidence of Aaron. Blake takes a step toward the bed, but I grab his arm, pulling him back.

"Come here," I murmur, backing up until my back hits the cold brick of the hall. Blake smiles, uncertain, so I pull him against me and kiss him deeply. I don't want to make love to him in that bed. He doesn't deserve that.

"What are you doing?" he mumbles as I pull his shirt up and over his head.

"Rewarding you for all those extra shifts you worked," I say, and then I silence him with another kiss.

I watch the suds build up against the washer door with grim satisfaction as all trace of Aaron is washed away. After we'd made love, I'd run Blake a bath and used the opportunity to change the sheets, which assuaged some of my guilt. The next four days will be the longest stretch of time Blake and I have spent together uninterrupted and, to my surprise, I'm looking forward to it.

"Laundry?" Blake asks when he tracks me down. He's wearing only a pair of tracksuit pants, and a towel around his neck. "At this time of night?"

"I spilled my wine," I say, waving the half-full, just poured glass toward him.

I WAKE up early on Thursday to get some work done while he sleeps in. I ignore three texts from Aaron, which had come in late last night, put my phone on silent, and climb back into bed.

The texts start up again that afternoon, detailing every single thing Aaron would do to me the next time we met. With each one, opened in private and deleted as soon as I've read it, my stomach curls in a heady mix of loathing and longing. I don't reply, and the texts become increasingly desperate. I know how Aaron thinks. By ignoring him, I am fanning the flames of his desire. This is a game that I know how to play, and the longer it continues, the more the tension builds. Still, I pay special attention to Blake. I care deeply for him, and what he doesn't know won't hurt him. It's not as if I actually plan to meet Aaron, at least not until Blake is back at work. This is Aaron's punishment for how he's treated me. If it goes on long enough, Aaron might even come to his senses and leave Staci for good. At least, that's what I tell myself as I try to ignore the squirming desire in the pit of my stomach.

Later that night I'm reading in bed when the next text comes through. Horrified, I check to make sure that Blake is asleep before I read it. This one is completely different to the rest. Gone is the flirtatious playfulness, and the coarse language.

I need to see you.

Hastily, I type a response. *I'm busy. We can talk next week.*

I hit send. A moment later another text comes through,

This can't wait.

Blake shifts in his sleep.

It'll have to.

He's already typing, but I switch my phone off and toss it on the nightstand. I snuggle closer to Blake and slip my feet between his legs to warm them, but I register nothing of the pages I read after that.

"I hope you're hungry," Blake teases the following morning as we set out for Verdure. I'd offered to make breakfast for him at home, but he'd insisted we keep our booking.

"I'm starving," I laugh. My hand is dwarfed in his, my palm tingling where our skin touches. We take a cab and are seated by 9.05.

"I need a coffee, the biggest you can rustle up," I tell the smiling waiter.

"Make it two," Blake adds, just as the soft ping of a text sounds from my phone. I pull it from my purse and frown at the screen.

"Everything okay?" Blake asks, his brow furrowed in concern.

"Fine," I reply lightly. I slip the phone back into my purse. "Can you get me the three-cheese omelet? I'm just going to the ladies."

"Sure." He gets to his feet as I stand. I smile at the chivalrous gesture, but my heart is hammering. Aaron's text was only two words. *Bathroom, now.*

I slip into the ladies' room and quickly scan the stalls. They're all empty. For want of something else to do, I wash my hands and splash water onto my face. When I look up into the mirror, Aaron is right behind me.

I barely have time to react when his hands are up my skirt. My conscience screams no, but nothing comes out of my mouth except a startled gasp as Aaron snaps the elastic of my panties clean in two. At the sound, my breath hitches and some primal part of my brain roars to life, driving all reason from my mind. Aaron is already hard, and he flips me around to face him, lifting me off the floor so my thighs are straddling his waist. He carries me to the door and presses me up against it, a barricade for anyone who might try to open it from the outside. His teeth clash against mine as his tongue sweeps into my mouth. He doesn't say a word, but his eyes are furious, glittering with malice and desire. His hands leave my hips, but I clamp my legs more tightly around his waist, keeping myself aloft as he fumbles with his zipper. A guttural moan in my ear is the only warning before he's inside me. His hands squeeze my buttocks, and his lips move to my ear.

"Don't-ever-ignore-me-again." He punctuates each word with a thrust of his hips, and I bite my lip to keep from crying out at the intensity of it.

It's over in a matter of seconds. I collapse against his chest as the dam inside of me bursts, sending spasms through my entire body. Aaron releases his hold, ever so slightly, and lowers me to the floor. His eyes are flint, his lips smeared with my pale rose lip gloss.

I straighten my dress as he pulls up his pants. My panties are bunched tightly in his fist.

"I'm keeping these," he says, shoving them into his pocket. I shrug, not caring in the slightest. As the adrenalin leaves my body, reality is slowly reasserting itself. Blake, waiting just outside. All the progress I've made, gone in an instant. Aaron is never going to come to heel if he keeps getting what he wants so easily.

"You should go." I raise my chin and wipe at my own bruised lips. "This was a mistake."

The smile that spreads across his face is pure malevolence. "So you keep saying, Kitty Cat."

"Yeah well, one of these days I'm going to mean it." I don't wait for him to reply. Instead, I fling open the door, so quickly that he has to hurl himself behind it to avoid being seen by nearby patrons, and stalk back to my table.

"Everything okay?" Blake asks, his eyes searching mine.

"I'm fine, just feeling a bit flushed," I reassure him. Out of the corner of my eye, I see Aaron slip out of the ladies. He has the gall to blow me a kiss.

4

This time, I'm determined to stick to my guns. The high of being with Aaron fades fast, throwing me into a pit of despair and self-loathing. It's the twisted cycle of our toxic relationship. Blake goes back to work on Monday, and I settle into my familiar routine. A week passes, and then another, and I ignore every message Aaron sends me. I send his calls to voicemail and delete them without listening. I make sure to be out of the house first thing in the morning so he'll find an empty apartment if he tries to visit. Surprisingly, my relationship with Blake is improving by the day. Without the distraction of my affair with Aaron, I find it easier to focus on what's right in front of me. In week three, I offer him a key to my apartment, which is the ultimate gesture of commitment, given that its where most of my secret trysts with Aaron take place. Blake is genuinely delighted.

"DON'T FORGET I'm meeting the girls tonight," I tell him one Wednesday morning. We're in bed, snuggling before Blake has to report to the hospital for his shift. Given how close my apartment is to the hospital, he's spending most evenings here, and he's promised to wait up for me. "There's a few frozen pizzas in the freezer, or I could order something for you before I go?"

His arm tightens around my shoulders. "I'm perfectly capable of feeding myself, Cat. You go and enjoy yourself."

Since Aaron and I separated, I spend one evening a month with my two remaining girlfriends. Once, we'd been a huge group, but after the separation, most of our couple friends had chosen Team Aaron. Only Gwen and Bianca have kept in contact with me, but they're by far the best of the lot.

I arrive first and order a bottle of red wine for the table. Then there's the rigmarole of smelling it, swirling it around in the glass, and taking an appreciative sip, all of which is just for show because I wouldn't have a clue. I've only just picked up the menu to browse when Gwen arrives, her coat flapping behind her.

"I'm sorry I'm late, traffic was awful!" she announces at the top of her voice, oblivious of the fact that she's drawn the attention of the entire restaurant. Even if she didn't speak at the decibel level of a small choir, she would have it anyway. A leggy blonde, with chiseled cheekbones and a mega-watt smile, Gwen is one of the nicest people I know. A complete klutz, she's as likely to trip over her own feet as she is to forget her mother-in-law's birthday – which she has, four years straight – but people forgive her because she's too nice not to forgive. Bianca, short, dark, and furious, is the polar opposite of Gwen in every way possible. She arrives only a few minutes later, stalking through the restaurant as if the patrons seated at the tables between her and us exist for no other reason than to inconvenience her.

"Have you heard from Aaron?" Gwen asks. It's her standard opening question. I think that secretly Gwen still harbors hope that Aaron and I will reconcile and bring our circle back together. Gwen's husband, Jason, is one of Aaron's closest friends, and I know that she feels helplessly torn between her loyalty to me, and the pressure Jason puts on her to play nice with Staci.

"No." I give her my standard answer. Gwen and Bianca may be

my best friends, but even they would draw the line at what I've been up to with Aaron.

"I heard he's having trouble with Staci," Bianca announces, throwing her jacket over the back of her chair and slapping an elderly woman at the next table in the face with one sleeve.

I almost drop my glass. "What do you mean, having trouble?"

"She accused him of cheating on her, apparently," Bianca says, oblivious to the dark looks being cast her way by the woman's dinner companion. "Mike says Aaron was pretty pissed about the whole thing, but I told him once a cheater, always a cheater." Mike is Bianca's long-term boyfriend, whom she refuses to marry, despite him having asked at least three times.

Gwen nods in grave agreement and fills her glass. "I heard that too." She doesn't want to say where she heard it, and I don't probe. Neither of us likes to acknowledge that she sees Staci socially.

"Did she have any proof?" I ask carefully, trying to act nonchalant.

"Nothing she can pin down. She claimed she smelled another woman's perfume on his clothes, said it couldn't be hers because she doesn't wear perfume. It's toxic for your skin, apparently."

Bianca grimaces. "I've never understood what he sees in her."

"She's attractive," I offer graciously, while the devil on my left shoulder dances with glee at the thought that Aaron and Staci might be on the outs. There's no point in feeling guilty that I'm the reason – she's the one who had the affair with a married man.

Gwen shrugs. "You're prettier," she says.

"It's true," Bianca adds as I shake my head in mock-humility. I know I am. I was blessed with good genes, although I'm not sure whose. "Anyway, Aaron denied it and last he told Mike, the whole thing seemed to have blown over."

"Oh." I deflate faster than a balloon in a needlestack.

"Enough about Aaron," Gwen moans, taking a massive slug of champagne. "How is that gorgeous man you've been seeing?"

"Blake? He's fine. I gave him a key to my apartment," I confide.

"About time," Bianca sighs. "Why don't you just divorce Aaron and marry the sexy doctor, Cat? God knows you deserve it after what Aaron put you through."

I shake my head so vigorously my hair whips into my eyes. "Hell no. I'm never getting married again."

"Why not? Just because it didn't work out for you the first time doesn't mean you have to give up on the whole idea." Irony isn't Bianca's strong suit.

"You know this whole conversation is pointless, while she's still legally married, right?" Gwen points out. "Why *haven't* you divorced Aaron, anyway?"

I shrug. "I don't know."

"You should do it. It's time to move on with your life, Cat." This time, it's Bianca who nods in solemn agreement.

I raise my glass. Swirl the contents. "Maybe you're right," I concede, and then I chug back the entire glass.

IT TAKES me forever to fit my key into the lock, and when I finally do, I fall inside my apartment. A pair of strong arms catch me before I hit the floor.

"Easy there!" Blake croons, propping me up with an arm around my waist. I squint up at him in the dim light coming from the hall.

"You're beautiful," I say, placing my hand against his cheek.

He grins. "And you're drunk."

"We had wine. At dinner. In fact, I think I had wine *for* dinner," I add, frowning as I try to recall if I ate any of my ravioli.

"Then you need water, and fried eggs."

"That your professional opinion, Doctor Stanton?"

"Nope. Just years of college experience."

He leaves me on the couch with two Alka-Seltzer and a massive glass of water. I doze on and off to the sounds of him cooking in the kitchen, and then he rouses me gently and sets a tray on my lap. Eggs never looked so unappealing, but I try to eat a little, just to appease him. Unfortunately, I manage only two bites before I have to rush to the bathroom. When I emerge, I'm mortified. I've brushed my teeth twice, but I can still taste vomit.

"Sorry," I mumble. Blake leads me to the bed and tucks me in before climbing in beside me. "Believe me, I've seen worse. It goes with the territory."

"If we ever got married, I'd be Doctor Stanton," I say brightly.

Blake laughs, the low, familiar rumble against my ear. "I think you mean *Mrs.* Stanton," he teases, "but I'll take it."

5

The following morning, I wake up to an empty bed. There's a note on the pillow, along with two pills. I recognize Blake's untidy scrawl. *Had to go in early. Take these and sleep it off.*

I swallow down the pills with half a glass of water. Dry-mouthed and head-pounding, I totter into the bathroom to take a cold shower. Slowly the icy blast clears my head. I think about what Gwen and Bianca said last night, and for the first time, the idea of divorcing Aaron doesn't send a wave of panic through me. Aaron wasn't a great husband. In fact, he was a pathological liar and cheat, but for some reason, I've never been able to shake the hold he has over me. The sex is fantastic, obviously, but when you get down to the core, there's not much else. When I check my phone after breakfast, I have two X-rated texts from him, which only prove my point. Aaron only wants me because he can't have me. I can't keep fooling myself that his sudden yearning for me has nothing to do with my growing relationship with Blake. The proof is in the pudding. Every time my relationship with Blake kicks up a notch, Aaron's attention to me rises accordingly. Blake, on the other hand, wants all of me – the good, the bad, and the ugly. And, even if he's not 'the one', deep down, I know

I'll never be truly happy with Aaron. Not now. Not anymore. Hell, I wasn't even that happy before Staci-Gate blew up in my face.

Feeling only marginally more human, I dress in a pair of blue jeans and a white jersey top which leaves one shoulder bare. I take a cab across town to the art gallery where my mom occasionally has paintings on display – when she bothers to paint any. It's a small but upmarket gallery, with stark white walls to offset the vibrant art it favors. The owner knows me well, and she greets me warmly as I step inside.

"Cat! How's my favorite customer?"

"Hey, Trish." I return her hug. "I'm good, thanks."

She gives me a wry smile. "I should've known you'd be in today." She ushers me to the back of the gallery, to where a small oil painting hangs under a white light. "I only hung it this morning. Although, how you always seem to know is beyond me."

"It's a gift," I say, enigmatically, and then walk past her to the far wall.

I recognize my mother's style immediately. Worse, I recognize the face of the nude woman she's painted – it's Janine, the nurse who was on duty the night I met Blake, and who I've met on more than one occasion since. My mother's flirting that night must have paid off after all.

"Gorgeous, isn't it?" Trish murmurs reverently as she comes to stand behind me. Gorgeous isn't the word I would use to describe the painting. Janine's ample flesh is on full-color display, her wrists and ankles bound in a chain mail of dirty needles. I'd recognize the grubby day bed she's spread-eagled over anywhere – it's adorned my mother's studio since before I can remember.

"I knew you'd love it," Trish continues, oblivious. "Every time a new Viola Davis comes in, I think of you. How many of hers do you own now? It must be at least a dozen."

"Twenty-seven," I reply automatically. I can almost hear her brain ticking, trying to work out which other gallery might be her competition. I could tell her, but I won't. My eye falls to the orange sticker. $2600. That's almost three hundred dollars more than the last one. Trish is pushing her luck, but I smother my sigh. "I'll take it."

She gives a delighted tinkle of laughter and claps her hands together. "Wonderful. Let me wrap it for you. Would you like me to have it delivered?"

"No need," I say, pulling out my card. "I'll take it now. And please make sure to mark me down as an anonymous buyer."

She arches her brow but doesn't comment as she lifts the painting down. I think she's let the topic go, but she tries one last time as she rings it up. "I do wish you'd let me tell Viola who you are. She pops in all the time, I'm sure she'd love to meet such a fan of her work."

"Anonymous," I insist, more firmly. Trish lowers her eyes first.

IT TAKES me less than a minute to find a cab. I dump the painting unceremoniously on the seat beside me and rue the fact that I just spent $2600 on yet another of my mother's paintings.

It had all started three years ago. Aaron and I were busy making wedding plans, and my mother, in a rare moment of responsibility, had decided to start painting again. Viola had gone to art school. She'd left before graduating, to have me, having been knocked up by one of her professors. She wouldn't ever tell me his name and, given that he'd known about me and chosen to pretend I didn't exist, I hadn't ever bothered to try to find him.

"You're getting married, Cat," my mom had announced during the one and only dress fitting she'd accompanied me to. "I have to learn how to support myself."

It had been a relief to hear her admit it. I didn't mind helping her out, but when I saw my hard-earned money being blown on booze and recreational drugs, it stung.

I'd supported her decision fully, and I'd even canceled an appointment with my wedding planner to accompany her to a local gallery which we thought might consider showcasing her work.

Unfortunately, the gallery decided that her flamboyant style wasn't quite the right fit for an exhibition. But they were prepared to display one of her paintings, which turned out to be a good thing as my mother, due to a combination of crippling self-doubt and a short-lived relationship with a man she'd met at the dress-fitting, hadn't bothered to paint any others. The painting, a small watercolor which was as abstract as it was intense, was hung the day before my wedding. Aaron and I honeymooned in Thailand, and I gave it little thought during the two weeks we were away. Only once we'd returned, floating back to earth after fourteen blissful nights away, did I learn that the painting had garnered absolutely no interest and my mother had fallen into a pit of drug-fuelled despair.

"It's only been two weeks," I'd told her when she'd sobered up enough to listen. "You have to give it time." She'd told me that hope was indeed a fickle mistress, and then disappeared to the bathroom, where she'd smoked a joint the size of a bratwurst. I'd found her hanging out of the bathroom window singing Chaka Khan while a group of pedestrians gathered on the street below, pleading with her not to jump.

The following morning, I'd marched into the gallery and bought the painting, insisting I be listed as an anonymous buyer. Sadly, no good deed goes unpunished. My mother's gloomy despair was replaced by a fireball of optimism fuelled by a manic desire to sell another painting. When it didn't sell, she slipped back into the dark place I hated. And so began a vicious circle. She would paint, and I would purchase. I'd never told Aaron. I didn't want him to know, didn't want to give him any ammunition to use against her. Aaron was never outright rude about my mother, but I could tell he thought of her as a bit of a joke, and it hurt more than I cared to admit. When she started 'selling' he'd given her a new, albeit begrudging respect, and I didn't want to take that away. My mother's chronic laziness was my saving grace. If she'd painted more frequently, I would probably have gone broke trying to sustain her constant need for validation.

"Miss?" the cab driver's voice brings me back to the present. "This is your stop, yes?"

I blink out of the window at my familiar apartment block.

"Yes, this is it. Thanks." I hand him a crumpled bill and hoist the painting out with me. Safely back inside my apartment, I stash it in the loft, along with twenty-seven others, and then I head back out to meet my mother for lunch.

"DARLING!" she calls as I weave through the busy bistro. She's wearing a floral kaftan, and there's a smudge of burnt orange paint on her cheek, but her eyes are bright and clear, and I breathe a sigh of relief that she's sober.

"You've been working," I say, giving her a brief hug before we take our seats.

"I woke up at five this morning and couldn't get back to sleep. I decided to make the most of it."

The waitress arrives with our menus, but my mom waves them away.

"A black coffee and a cappuccino, with almond milk, if you have," she says. "And bring us two garden salads. No cheese."

"I'll have cheese," I correct, "and regular milk, please." My mother arches her brow, but I ignore her. Despite her frequent attempts to convert me, I refuse to follow her vegan lifestyle.

"Just be grateful I'm not ordering a steak," I say. The waitress hides a smile.

"It's so barbaric," my mother sniffs. "I bet if you visited an abattoir, you'd quickly change your tune."

"I have visited an abattoir, mom," I remind her. "You took me to one on my fifth birthday, remember?" She frowns, trying to recall, but I save her the trouble and change the subject. "How have you been?"

"I'm heartbroken."

"Again?"

"Yes. Dinah left me. It's why I've been battling to sleep."

"Which one is Dinah again?"

"The redhead. Freckles. Legs that go up to here." She lifts a hand to well above her waistline and waits for me to register.

"Ah, yes, Dinah," I say knowingly. "Wasn't she married?"

"Not happily. Her husband doesn't understand her."

"That's what they all say, mom."

"Not all of them. Besides, in Dinah's case, it's true. The husband's a complete dickhead."

"You can't know that for sure," I say, smiling up at the waitress who's arrived back at the table with our coffees. "You've only heard her side of the story."

"Nuh-uh," she says, adding two heaped teaspoons of sugar to her coffee. "I've heard his too. They attended one of Barbara's cooking classes. The bastard spent the entire evening trying to stick his hand up my skirt."

I choke on my coffee. "He what?"

"Well, to be fair, I dated him first."

"Mom!"

"What? Honey, there are a lot of unhappy people out there. And this was before I knew Dinah, obviously." She shakes her head, and I feel as though I've been reprimanded. I should be used to it by now – my mother's warped sense of reasoning.

"Jesus mom, it's no wonder I'm so screwed up."

She gives me a look of utter bewilderment. "Screwed up? What on earth are you going on about, Cat? You're the most well-adjusted person I know." Given the company my mother typically keeps, I can't say I find that very reassuring.

6

I go almost an entire month without seeing Aaron. My routine is my undoing. I'm at the coffee shop, hard at work, when a warm body slides into the booth beside me.

Aaron's lips pull upward. "Hello, stranger."

"What the hell are you doing here?" I hiss, casting a furtive look around.

"We need to talk." For once, he makes no attempt to touch me, folding his hands instead on the table before him, lean fingers steepled. His eyes are bruised, as if he hasn't been getting enough sleep, and he looks younger, somehow – more vulnerable, without the smug smile he normally wears.

"About what?" I ask.

"About us." A plain and simple answer, no snide remark or cocky comeback.

"There is no us, Aaron."

"That's not true, and you know it."

With a sigh, I snap my MacBook shut. "We're separated. It's time we started acting like it."

"I miss you." He says it with a straight face and doesn't back down even when I arch my brows at him, calling his bluff.

"I can't keep doing this, Aaron. I can't be your bit on the side. It's not fair to Blake. Or Staci," I add as an afterthought.

"Do you remember that trip we took to Lake Como?"

It's an abrupt change of subject, but I go along with it. "How could I forget?"

We'd spent ten days in Italy, one Christmas. We'd randomly chosen Lake Como off an ultimate holidays website, and we'd booked tickets that same night. Aaron's parents had been less than thrilled. They preferred us to spend Christmas with them, but given that the invitation was never extended to my mother, I didn't feel half as guilty as I should have about flying off to Italy instead.

"I still can't pass a boat shop without remembering that boat ride."

I arch my brow at him again. The boat ride had hardly been romantic. Out in the middle of the lake, we'd tried to make whoopie, and ended up falling in.

"Oh, come on," he teases, catching sight of my expression. "It was funny."

"It was cold."

"We had good times, Cat."

"We had bad times too. Or, maybe you would still call those good times, given that you were the one having all the fun."

"You know I never meant to hurt you."

"You could've fooled me." I tap my fingers on the table. "Look, I have work to do. And I don't have time for a trip up memory lane. Why are you here, Aaron?"

"I love you."

It comes so completely out of the blue that I can't help the incredulous expression which plasters itself on my face.

"What?"

"I love you."

I shake my head, disarmed by his open gaze. "No you don't. If you loved me, we wouldn't be in this situation."

He exhales a long breath. "Cat, we're different. We don't work the usual way, and I'm not going to bother trying to pretend that we do. But I *do* love you, and I want you in my life."

"You want a booty call," I correct.

His face darkens. "And you don't?"

"What is that supposed to mean?"

"Oh come on, Cat. We're both adults here. Love doesn't always conquer the demon. And we're both just a little bit fucked up. Blame our parents, daddy issues, whatever you want, but don't try to deny that you need me as much as I need you."

I don't even bother to argue. I'm not a hypocrite, and the fact is that I've answered every time he's summoned. I want to call him out on the daddy issues comment, given that his father is a successful businessman named Stan, who just celebrated his thirty-fifth wedding anniversary, but what would be the point? I already know I'm screwed up, and it's likely my mom and absentee father have a lot to do with it.

"Need isn't the same thing as love," I say instead, but I can feel that old magic working. My treacherous heart, responding to his words.

"For us, it is."

I knead my temples as the waitress returns to check if Aaron wants anything. Amy isn't here today, thank the stars.

"I'm okay, thank you. Cat...?" I shake my head, and he waves her away. His hand brushes my shoulder, softly, briefly, and then it's gone. "I know this is messed up," he admits. "I know you've moved on." He swallows as if just speaking the words pains him. "I have too, but I just can't stay away from you. I've tried, but I can't."

I lift my eyes to his. I feel hollow. "Did you ever think maybe there's a reason for that? That maybe we're meant to be together – that we should try to work things out?"

He holds my gaze, doesn't flinch away from the question. The corners of his mouth twitch. He raises his hand to toy with a strand of my hair, and I close my eyes, lost in the moment, forgetting where I am and who might be watching.

"Can you honestly tell me you think that'll work?" he whispers.

"I can honestly tell you that I don't want to hurt anyone else."

He smiles then, finally, but it's still not the cruel smile he usually wears. "Cat, I didn't ever want to hurt you in the first place."

I pull away from him, needing to put some distance between us. I'd been ready to end things, I was tired and angry at being used, but I'm utterly unprepared for this emotional onslaught. To my amazement, he doesn't push it. Instead, he gets to his feet and gazes down at me.

"Come home with me." His voice is barely more than a whisper. "Let me show you how much you mean to me."

Reality snaps back into place, leaving me reeling. "It's Friday," I sneer, giving a bitter laugh. "I should have known."

"That's not what this is about," Aaron snaps. "I want to remind you why we're so good together."

"Go to hell."

He holds my gaze for a few seconds and then lowers his eyes. "This isn't over."

"I want it to be over."

For a second, the smug look flits across his face. "No, you don't."

WHEN HE'S GONE I twitch in agitation, the sense that things have been left unfinished keeping me from concentrating. Hating myself, I pack up my things and hail a cab.

Aaron opens the door almost immediately. His face splits into a smile that is nothing short of dazzling. I open my mouth to speak, but a sob bursts from my chest instead. His strong arms come around me, leading me inside and onto the couch. He holds me until my body stops heaving, and my tears have run dry. Then he lowers his head and kisses me, softly, sweetly, as if I might break apart at any minute.

His lips brush the tears from my eyes, his hands stroke my hair, my shoulders, the small of my back. I've never known him to be so tender, and when his hands reach for my buttons, I don't stop him. When I'm naked from the waist up, he stops, leaning back to admire the view. He cups my chin, lifting it so I have to meet his eyes.

"Are you sure?" he asks. I wish he hadn't. It's easier to play the victim. I nod, my chin rubbing gently against his palm. I know what this means. He's made himself very clear. There will be no reconciliation, not now, at least. But I still feel the thrill of the hold I have over him, the rush of the physical connection between us. And he's right – I *do* need it.

Slowly, leisurely, Aaron torments me with his intimate teasing, caressing me until I'm feverish with desire. When I can't take another second of it, knowing full well I'm going to hate myself later but not giving a damn, I seize hold of his arms and dig my nails in deep. His lips part against mine in a wicked, knowing smile, and his breath quickens. For the first time, he doesn't object when I rake his skin, leaving red marks in my wake. Free to do whatever I want, I meet his passion with abandon.

Two hours later, I stagger from Aaron's apartment, my body tender but absolutely sated. Aaron texts me the next day to say he loves me. And the day after that. And the day after that. I text it back, but I don't break things off with Blake. I'm weak. Weak and gullible. But I'm not stupid.

7

It's a typical Californian spring day – mild and warm and uneventful – when Blake finds my stash of paintings in the loft. Blake had the day off, and I'd had to go see a client who wanted to completely revamp his online store.

"You really should just leave that here," I'd told him that morning, catching sight of the overflowing suitcase at the foot of my bed. "Why don't you clear out some space in my closet and keep some of your stuff here? That way you won't have to live out of a suitcase."

His smile had been worth it. Since I'd reignited my affair with Aaron, I'd been more distant and Blake, intuitive as he is, had noticed. There was a disconnect between us that hadn't been there before. It was ironic because the more time I spent with him, the more my feelings for him grew, but so did my guilt at what I was doing. I'd left him with a lingering kiss and free rein to re-organize my closet. The meeting had gone on longer than I expected, and by the time I got back home, I'd forgotten all about it.

I drop my purse on the kitchen counter to find Blake looking puzzled, and a little perturbed. He's holding the nude I bought last month.

"Please tell me this isn't Janine," he says. I can only imagine how awkward it must be for him to see one of the duty nurses he works with, in all her pink-fleshed glory, but I'm too angry to care. All the insecurities I had when I was with Aaron rear their ugly heads. And it doesn't matter that Blake isn't Aaron, because my embarrassment can't differentiate between the two.

"Where did you find that?"

"In the loft. I figured I'd move your winter stuff up there – I boxed it, but when I went up I found this. And a bunch of others, all with the price tags still attached," he adds meaningfully. "They're your moms, right?" he frowns at the flamboyant signature in the bottom corner to confirm it. "Babe, why are you buying your mother's paintings?"

"That's none of your business."

He flinches at the harsh tone of my voice. "Hey, I wasn't prying. I'm sorry, I just..." His eyes flicker between me and the painting. "I didn't mean to upset you," he finishes softly.

I snatch the painting back and try to rewrap it, but I only end up tearing the brown wrapping paper in half.

Blake halts me with a firm hand on mine. Our gazes lock.

"Stop it," he says.

"I try to wrench my hand away, but he closes his fingers over mine in a vice grip.

"Let me go."

"No."

"I said, let me go!" I yank my hand away so violently he staggers. "You have no right to be snooping through my stuff!" I'm yelling, but I've grown so used to having to defend my mother that *defensive* has become my default setting where she's concerned.

Blake doesn't respond. Calmly, he retrieves the painting with his free hand and sets it on the couch, facing away from us. When he turns back to me, his amber eyes have lost their usual warmth. "I can't do this anymore."

"You can't do what?" I lower my voice as an inkling of dread spiders down my spine.

"Keep chipping away at your walls. What is this, Cat?" He waves his hand between the two of us. "Because I can tell you right now, it's not a relationship."

"People fight, Blake. It's not abnormal."

"We don't fight. You don't care enough to fight. You just shut down and shut me out." In all the time we've spent together, I've never seen this side of him – the unyielding strength, the unwavering confidence.

"Shut you out? You're practically living here, how is that shutting you out?"

He regards me levelly and his question, when it comes, throws me into turmoil.

"When are you going to file for a divorce?" I trip over my next words, and Blake holds up his hand for me to stop talking. "I think that's answer enough. We've been dating almost six months, and yet, you're still married. Don't you think that's just a bit fucked up?"

If only you knew, I find myself thinking hysterically. Still, my heart is thundering in my chest. I don't know what's happening, but I have a sinking sensation that Blake might be about to break up with me. More surprisingly, the thought crucifies me.

"I don't know what you want me to say," I mumble.

"Well then, let me help you." He raises his hands and cups my face. "I love you, Cat. I'm sorry I didn't say it sooner, but I didn't know if you were ready. Now I don't know if you ever will be. This isn't some random fling, not to me. You're the most infuriating woman I've ever met, but I can't help myself." He squeezes his eyes shut for just a moment, and when he opens them, I want to weep with relief that a bit of warmth has seeped back. "I love you," he echoes, "and call me selfish, but I want all of you. I want to help you, to heal you, and to bring you back from the hell that bastard put you through, but I can't do that if you won't let me in. And I can't stay here anymore and watch you self-destruct, because it'll destroy me, too."

I blink up at him, trying to process what this means, to process the bomb he's just dropped on me and the best way to respond. I don't know if I love Blake. I know I don't want to lose him, but does that equate to love?

My hesitation is too much. His face is scrunched in pain and embarrassment as he moves away from me, toward the door. He doesn't even bother to collect his things.

"Blake!"

"No, Cat." He wards me off. "No more. I can't do this. I'm done."

I stare at the door for a full minute after it closes behind him. *What the hell have I done?* I don't even know I've spoken the words aloud, until they ring hollow in my ears. As if in a trance, I slump onto the couch, my thoughts hurtling around my head a mile a minute as I try to imagine my life without Blake in it. It's unimaginably painful. I've been so caught up in my affair with Aaron, I've underestimated how important Blake has become to me, how steadfast and dependable. And let's face it, dependable isn't sexy, but now that he's gone, I'm wracked with regret. I'm also angry – furious that he didn't give me time to explain before he stormed out. *Not that you deserve it,* a snide voice in my head sneers.

I think I'm going to throw up.

No, you're not.

I don't know what to do.

Yes, you do.

"No." I speak the word aloud, determined to ignore the driving need to chase after Blake and beg him to come back. It's better this way. I've treated him appallingly, and it's obvious I don't have the strength to break things off with Aaron, so why should Blake suffer any more than he has. Decision made, I walk slowly to my room to pack up his things.

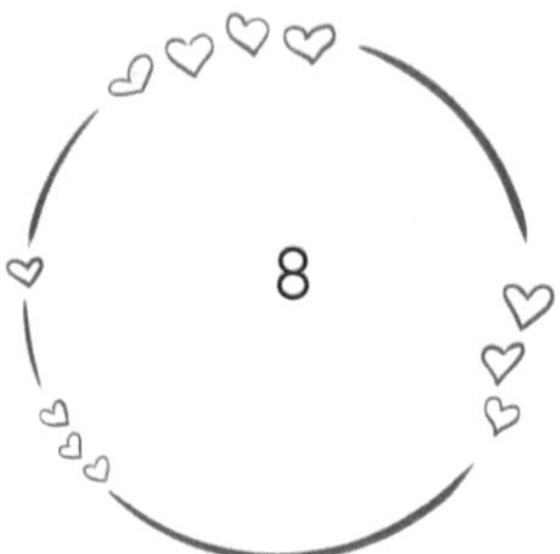

"Why aren't you eating?" My mother demands three days later when I meet her for breakfast. I've barely eaten a thing since Blake walked out, but I don't tell her that. I still can't believe that the same day Blake finally told me he loved me, our relationship ended. It doesn't seem fair, but considering that I only realized just how strongly I felt for him around the same time, I've accepted that my timing is disastrous.

"I had a big breakfast," I lie, curling my hands around my mug for warmth. Living almost exclusively on caffeine is ill-advised, judging by the way my hands are shaking, and I slosh a liberal amount of coffee over the table.

"Cat!" my mother scolds, pulling a grubby looking tissue from her bag to mop it up. A small handful of greenish-brown flutters onto the table. "Oh, shit, I forgot that was in there. It's medicinal," she tells the waiter, as he darts forward to clean up the mess. He gives me a secret wink, but I'm too drained to react. I'm tired of my mother's outlandish behavior – of the shitty example she sets, and the secrets she keeps from me. I don't like the person I've become. Not one bit. And if I'm going to be better, I need answers. It's time for me and

Viola to have a serious conversation. I steel myself and prepare to ask the question that is the entire reason I invited her here in the first place.

"Mom." I make sure I have her undivided attention before I continue. "I want to know who my father is."

Her expression is almost comical. A mixture of shock and bewilderment, with a healthy dose of outrage. Being Viola, however, it doesn't take long for her to recover.

"Why on earth would you care?" she snaps. "He abandoned me the second he heard I was pregnant."

"He abandoned *you*," I point out. "And I get that in doing so he abandoned me too, but I should be allowed to make my own judgment. I can't do that without even knowing who he is." I've thought about this for days. I never wanted to meet my father, or at least, I thought I didn't, but now a part of me suspects my decision may have been my mother's all along. Her influence over me, her insistence that my father is the devil who doesn't deserve us. I never even thought to question it, not until now.

"You don't want to meet him, Cat. He's no good for you."

"Again, that's my decision to make."

"He's dead."

I arch my brow and call her bluff. "Mom."

"Fine, he's not dead, but he may as well be, for all the good he's done you."

I stare her down, and she starts to squirm.

"Please, baby, don't do this. Am I not enough? Because I've dedicated my whole life to you." I want to laugh at the absurdity of that statement, but I don't, because I know that she needs to believe the lie.

"Mom, I love you. This has nothing to do with you and me, but I need to know who he is. I need to know where I came from. I'm not going to be able to truly find myself until I do."

"Find yourself? You're not lost, Cat. You've got a great job, a beautiful home, and you're dating a surgeon. I'd say you're leaps and bounds ahead of most girls your age. Hell, I knew both my parents and I'm far more screwed up than you are."

"Jesus, Mom!" I get to my feet, a wave of anger and helplessness surging through me. "This isn't about *you,* okay? Not everything is about you!"

Now she's playing it right up, her eyes wide and wounded, one hand over her heart, the other surreptitiously reaching for the rolled joint peeking out of her purse like a security blanket. For a second I wonder if she might actually bring it out and light up right here at the table.

"Have I done something wrong, Cat?" she asks in a tiny, breathless voice. It's an act – always the act. "Are you trying to hurt me?"

And just like that, I know that she is never going to tell me. She's never going to take responsibility, never understand how badly I need to know the truth. It will never, ever be about me. Disgusted, I toss enough money on the table to cover our bill, including a generous tip, while my mother sits in stunned silence. "I can't do this right now," I say in a voice like acid.

I make it halfway to the door before I turn back. "Oh, and about that surgeon you love so much? He *left* me. He left me because as much as you hate to admit it, I *am* screwed up." I wait until she raises her eyes to mine. "I guess I really am my mother's daughter."

"Oh, honey"

"No." I cut her off before her sympathy pushes me over the edge. "You don't get to talk to me about it. You don't get to say you're sorry for me, and try to make me feel better, because it's your fault as well as mine." Yes, I screwed up. Yes, Blake was right to leave me. But she's a part of the reason I'm such a mess, and I'll be damned if I let her get away with it any longer. "Don't contact me," I say coldly. "I don't want to hear from you until you're ready to tell me the truth."

I hear her call my name as I walk away but I don't look back. If I'm going to pick up the pieces of my broken life, I'm starting right now.

. . .

OUT ON THE STREET, I suck in a huge breath of air, trying to rid myself of the smell of ketchup and cooking oil. My legs are trembling so badly it takes me a few seconds before I risk stepping up to the curb. Casting quick glances over my shoulder, terrified that my mother might still come after me, I flag down the first taxi I see and launch myself into the back seat. I'm giving the driver directions before I've even closed the door.

Breaking the cardinal rule of mine and Aaron's relationship, I go straight to his apartment. I don't phone first. If Staci is home, I'll just pretend there's been a death in the family. That's a good enough reason for me to contact him. I slump in the backseat of the cab and replay the conversation with my mother. The cab driver gives me a concerned look as I hand over the cash, but says nothing. I stumble into Aaron's building, bolting the two flights of stairs to his floor. He greets me at the door wearing only a pair of faded jeans and a shirt which is unbuttoned, baring his bronzed chest. He probably only pulled it on to answer the door.

"Sweetheart," he croons, the second he lays eyes on me quivering in the hall, "I wasn't expecting you."

"Is she here?"

"No."

I shove past him, into the apartment. The TV is on low, and Aaron's hair is still damp from a recent shower. "Did you just get up?"

He shrugs, then reaches for me. "You know I'm not a morning person. Although, now that you're here, I could definitely become one. To what do I owe the honor?"

I lean into him, letting his hands knead all the tension out of me. When we kiss, he tastes of coffee. Behind him, I see two naked women on the screen, and the scent of incense lingers in the air. I shut my eyes and block it all out, reaching for his straining zipper. I know of one way to numb the pain, and I'm not leaving here until I get it. Quick as a flash, Aaron steps out of my reach.

"What's the hurry, Kitty Cat?" He's teasing now, another game to be played. There's no mistaking the wicked glint in his eyes. I look up at him and burst into tears.

Aaron is at my side in an instant, drawing me to the couch. "What is it?" he asks, confusion etched on his brow. "What's wrong?"

It all comes out; the altercation with my mother, the unanswered questions about my father, Blake leaving me. I tell him how I feel like I'm stuck in an endless spin cycle, getting nowhere. I'm so absorbed in my own grief that I barely notice when his weight shifts, until the arm that was around my shoulders slowly withdraws.

"Baby, you're being too hard on yourself."

I gaze up at him, studying his face. He looks uncomfortable. He looks as though he doesn't want to be here.

"What are you doing?" I ask, as the tears dry on my cheeks.

"What do you mean?"

"I came here because I thought you would understand. Because you're the one person in the world who really knows me. Why are you backpedaling?"

"I'm not backpedaling! I'm right here."

I narrow my eyes at him, trying to pinpoint the source of my unease.

"Oh my God!" I clap a hand to my mouth as it hits me like a ton of bricks. "You son of a bitch!" He gets to his feet the same time I do. "You're actually *upset* that he dumped me, aren't you?"

"What? Of course not!" His eyes tell a different story.

"You really don't give a shit about me, do you? It's all just a sick game to you! You got your rocks off precisely because Blake was in the picture, not because you had feelings for me. This was all a game of fucking one-upmanship."

"That's ridiculous. Are you even listening to yourself?"

I swipe furiously at the tears still drying on my cheeks. "God, I've been such a fool. You don't want me, Aaron, you just don't want anyone else to have me."

"Cat, you need to calm down. I didn't make you any promises, remember? And in case you've forgotten, I didn't seduce you into coming here. You came to me."

This time, the tears that spring to my eyes are tears of shame. "You're right, I did. Because you're an escape, Aaron. A beautiful, twisted escape. But I never escape, do I? I just end up back in the same shitty hole."

When I arrive at the hospital, Blake is in surgery. To my mortification, Janine is the head nurse on duty, but she at least knows who I am, and she offers to let me wait in one of the on-call rooms, which I'm sure isn't really allowed. I wait for over an hour before Blake appears, wearing the tired but triumphant expression I've come to recognize as a sign of a successful surgery. It breaks my heart that his euphoria diminishes when he catches sight of me. He removes his scrub cap and leans back against the door in resignation.

"Janine told me you were here." He says it as though he had tried to convince himself she was lying, and is bitterly disappointed to find that it's true.

"I'm sorry to come while you're working," I begin hesitantly, "but this couldn't wait." His only response is a wave of his hand, letting me know to continue. "Look, I know I messed up. There are *so* many ways I messed up, and so many things I wish I had done differently, but I can't change any of that." I take a breath and two small steps toward him. "I came here to tell you that I love you. Wait, let me finish," I add quickly when he opens his mouth to speak. "I don't want us to get back together. Not yet, anyway. You don't deserve this. I don't deserve you, not the way I am now. You were right about everything – I do shut you out. But I want to be better, I'm *going* to be better. And hopefully, when that time comes, maybe you might consider trying again. If you haven't been swept off your feet by some gorgeous patient who realizes how amazing you are," I add, trying to lighten the mood.

Blake doesn't smile. He regards me thoughtfully. "I'm sorry, Cat, but as much as I appreciate the honesty, I still don't understand why you're here."

"I buy my mother's paintings because when she's working she's sober," I blurt out. "Not for long, but long enough that I get to spend a few hours with her. With the real her – not the junkie who barely notices I'm around."

"Okay, but"

"I'm not done," I say quickly, terrified I'll lose my nerve if I don't get it all out. "I haven't divorced Aaron because deep down I'm afraid no one else would want me."

He doesn't let that one slide. "*I* wanted you. You know I did." The past tense hurts, but I keep going.

"How can you want someone if you don't really know who they are?" I counter.

He lets loose an exasperated sigh. "What exactly is it that you want from me? What more do I need to do to prove myself to you?"

I smile, even as a tear slips over my lashes and down my cheek. "It's not you who needs to prove yourself."

Blake has never seen me cry. More importantly, it's in his nature to care for people in pain. At the sight of my tears, he moves, crossing the distance between us in a single stride, and pulls me against his chest.

"Please don't cry," he murmurs into my hair. "Please. Just tell me what to do, Cat, and I'll do it."

I raise my head. "Please don't leave me. Don't give up on me. Not yet."

His shoulders go rigid. "Cat"

"I mean it. I'm a mess, but I love you, and I'm going to prove it."

"How?"

I give him a watery-eyed smile. "Well, for starters, I'd like you to come with me to see a divorce attorney."

BLAKE COMES over to my apartment straight from work and helps me search for a list of divorce attorneys within a ten-mile radius. I pick one at random and save the number to my phone.

"You're sure about this?" he asks. He's keeping his distance. I'd meant what I said – I won't mess up again. When and if Blake and I get back together, I want it to be for good, and until Aaron is out of my life, I know I can't be one hundred percent honest with him.

"I'm sure. I'll call first thing in the morning. I just want my life back."

"I'm proud of you," he says. He's also promised to help me try to track down my father. We spend the rest of the evening scrolling through the website of the college my mom attended, paying particular attention to the professors who worked there the year before I was born. I examine each and every face, but I can find no trace of myself in any of them.

"It's impossible to tell," Blake sighs, leaning back and rolling his shoulders. "People claim their kids look like them, but honestly, half the time it's bullshit. I can't tell you how many times I've complimented a mother on her kid and how they look just like her, only to discover she's the step-parent." He squints back at the screen, but I shake my head.

"You're right. This isn't going to work."

"Maybe your mom will come clean?" he says hopefully.

"I doubt it. She's had twenty-four years to do that."

"Okay, what about your grandparents? Surely they'd know something."

"Even if they did, I don't know if they'd tell me. They're super-conservative, and terrified of my mother."

"You can only try."

"True." I check my watch. "It's too late to call. I'll do it in the morning."

"You should probably go and see them," he warns. "Something this sensitive... well, you might have better luck in person."

I give him a teasing smile. "How did you get so smart?"

"It's a gift." He grins.

I can tell that Blake is as loath as I am to let the evening end, but I force myself to get to my feet and walk him to the door. He takes one step into the hall and then turns back to face me.

"I don't have to go," he says, the words coming out in a rush. "I have clothes here. I could sleep in the spare room and... or not," he adds, catching sight of the look on my face.

"I wish you could," I moan, and he knows that I mean it. "But if you stay, there's no way I'd be able to leave you alone in the spare room."

A ridiculously smug smile creases his face, and I laugh out loud.

"I miss you," he murmurs when I've recovered.

On a whim, I step forward and kiss his cheek, breathing in the familiar smell of his aftershave. "I miss you too." It would be so easy to reach for him, to bring him back inside and pick up where we left off, but I summon every ounce of my willpower and let him go. Blake is worth waiting for. I won't screw this up again.

FIRST THING THE FOLLOWING MORNING, I call the attorney's office to schedule a meeting. As luck would have it, they have a cancellation in the afternoon, and I take it without hesitation. I text Blake to let him know, but he has a surgery lined up later. I can tell by the tone of his text that he feels bad about it.

You have lives to save, I send back, *I've got this*. Then, without calling first to let them know I'm coming, I drive out to the suburbs to ambush my grandparents.

My mother's parents live in a gorgeous Tudor home with a white picket fence entirely smothered in climbing roses. It's a picture-book house, singularly inappropriate for the woman who grew up here. I arrive to find my grandmother, Francine, alone in the house, my grandfather having already left for his weekly round of golf.

"Catrina, sweetheart, what a lovely surprise!" My grandmother says when she answers the bell to find me standing at the door. "Why didn't you tell me you were coming down? I would've made some scones." My grandmother is the type of woman who would die before presenting a guest with store-bought confectionaries.

"Sorry, Grams." I wipe my boots on the doormat, freeing them of any invisible dirt she might discover. "It was a last minute thing."

"Well, we'll have to make do with some shortbread. I made some yesterday, you know how your grandpa loves it."

Ensconced in the enormous kitchen, armed with a cup of hot, sweet tea and a plate piled high with shortbread, I launch my attack.

"Grams, I need to know who my father is."

Her lips disappear into a disapproving line, and it's a while before she speaks. "May I ask why?"

"I wouldn't think you'd need to," I reply. Grams possesses the reasonable logic my mother lacks. Any child would want to know – it's a measure of how deep my mother's manipulation runs that I haven't until now. Grams locks her fingers around the tear-shaped ruby at her throat, and twists it. "I know it's not an easy subject," I say gently, "but I really need to know. If you won't tell me I'll go to her campus and start asking around, which would be a thousand times worse, but if that's what it takes, then that's what I'll do. Please, Grams, just tell me. I have a right to know."

"Your mother"

"My mother doesn't get to choose for me! I'm a grown woman, I've earned the right to decide for myself. Mom made a mistake not telling me and deep down, I think you know that."

"I know," she sighs, releasing the ruby. "I've told your Pop for years that it was only a matter of time before you came looking for answers, but your mom made us promise to never discuss it with you."

"Why?"

Her eyes are downcast. "Because she's ashamed."

"That she was seduced by a professor? He's the one who should be ashamed. He's the one who took advantage of a vulnerable young girl."

The second I say it, I know it's a lie. Grams' eyes tell me so before her lips even move.

"Sweetheart, your father wasn't a college professor." I hold my breath, not daring to speak in case she changes her mind. Grams gets up and puts the kettle back on even though we've barely touched our tea. "When your mother went off to college, she met another student – a lovely girl from a very respectable family. I was thrilled, obviously. Your mom had already been in some trouble at school and I thought Sophie would be a good influence on her." By her tone, I gather that wasn't the case. No doubt the opposite happened, and poor Sophie was led astray by my feckless mother. "In their second year, the girls had a falling out. I wasn't sure at the time what had happened, and your mother refused to talk about it."

"How very unlike her," I say, barely concealing the sarcasm in my voice. Grams gives a small, dissatisfied sigh, and sets a fresh cup of tea next to my rapidly cooling first cup. "Then we discovered your mother was pregnant."

"Was he Sophie's boyfriend?" I ask, trying to connect the dots. It's nothing less than I'd expect of my mother at this point, to try to hurt her previous friend in the worst way imaginable.

"No," Grams shakes her greying head. "Her younger brother, Stephen."

"Okay," I say, not understanding what all the fuss was about. Grams has already said that Sophie came from a respectable family. "So why wouldn't anyone tell me this?"

It takes her a moment to drum up the courage to speak. "He was only sixteen at the time." All the air seems to drain from my chest, but Grams is on a roll now, a runaway train with no brakes. "I contacted Sophie's parents when I learned the truth, but they wanted nothing to do with it. They even threatened to charge your mother with statutory assault, but that was just a knee-jerk reaction. The Bennetts didn't want the scandal any more than we did, and it was obvious that Stephen had been a willing participant. He admitted later that your mother wasn't his first." She shifts on her chair, uncomfortable at the mention of all this implied sex, but I pay no heed. I'm too busy doing the math in my head. If Stephen was sixteen when I was conceived, that would make him around forty now, forty-one at most.

"I get why this is such a sensitive subject," I say slowly, trying to invoke more understanding than I really feel, "but that doesn't explain why he wanted nothing to do with me."

"Oh Cat," Grams' eyes are starting to water. Her hands are back at her throat, twisting the ruby so tightly I fear the chain might snap. "He never knew you existed. His parents refused to tell him. They paid your mother quite a large sum of money to... well, to take care of things, not that it was necessary, and she dropped out right after."

"They wanted her to terminate the pregnancy? Without even telling him about it?"

"Yes. But your mother never once considered it," she adds quickly, as if that decision alone redeems my mother from a lifetime of shitty parenting.

"And she never thought to let him know? To tell them to hell with their money and tell him anyway?" I find it hard to believe that my mother would follow anyone's instructions, let alone the wealthy parents of a man she'd been involved with. Then again, there was cash involved. I drop my head into my hands, trying to make sense of it.

"Viola wouldn't have told Stephen anyway," she says, and I raise my head. "He'd met someone else, you see, and your mother's never taken rejection kindly. I don't think even Sophie knew the truth.

After that," Gram continues, "your mother went from bad to worse. She was sober throughout her pregnancy," she adds, putting a reassuring hand on my arm, "your Pop and I made sure of that. But once you were born she... well, you know how she is."

"I do," I whisper. On autopilot, I get up and set both cups in the sink, watching as the tannin-colored liquid pools around the drain. "I have to go, Grams."

"Don't leave, Catrina. This must be such a shock. You should stay, I'm happy to answer any questions you might have." There's a new determination in her voice. I want to smile at the tiny act of rebellion against my mother, but my cheeks are frozen.

"I'm fine, Grams. Thank you for telling me, but I really have to go."

"What are you going to do?"

"I don't know," I lie. "I need time to process it all."

"Well, whatever you decide, sweetheart, I'm here for you. And I'm sorry that I didn't tell you before. You're right, you deserve the truth."

I walk out to my car in a daze. I finally have a name. Stephen Bennett.

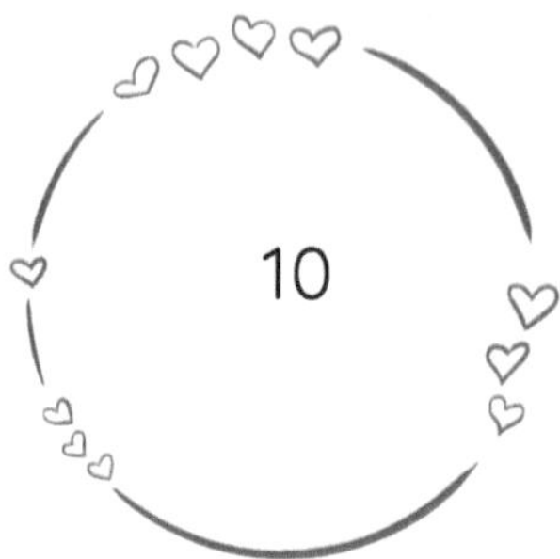

I barely register what the attorney is saying as I sit through the hour-long meeting. I answer his questions on autopilot. My finances, Aaron's finances, the marital property, how and why the marriage ended – nothing is sacrosanct. When the questions finally cease, he gets me to sign the paperwork which will initiate divorce proceedings and promises that Aaron will be served within five business days. I feel like a weight has been lifted off my shoulders, but I'm too numb to appreciate it.

For the rest of the week, I spend my evenings eating junk food, binge-watching Netflix, and stalking Sophie and Stephen Bennett online. I text Blake every time I discover something new, and he replies with enthusiasm. Stephen doesn't have a Facebook page, but Sophie does. She's Sophie Walker now, but her maiden name is still shown on her profile, and I assume it's her because we have a mutual friend in my mother's friend Barbara, who attended the same art school. I scan through the few photographs that are public, but find only a man with an impressive beard and smiling eyes. He's kissing her cheek in one of the pictures, so I figure he's her husband, not her brother. Sophie works at a company called Bennett Communications.

A quick Google search tells me it's been in operation for almost four decades. If it's a family firm, and given the name, I can only assume it is, it's highly possible that my father works there too. I consider contacting Sophie through her Facebook profile, but decide against it. This isn't something I can do on Messenger. The address listed for Bennett Communications is in Long Beach. It's a six-hour drive at least, so I decide to drive up over the weekend, spend some time on my own, and confront Stephen Bennett at his office on Monday morning. When I text Blake to inform him of my plans, he insists on taking the weekend off to come with me.

Do you think that's a good idea? I ask, my heart in my throat at the thought of spending an entire weekend alone with him. His answering text is short and decisive: *You're not doing this on your own.*

ON FRIDAY MORNING, I pack our bags. Now that I've had a few days to get used to the idea, I'm excited about spending a whole weekend alone with Blake, away from everything and everyone, especially Aaron. As if my thoughts had summoned him, I find a text from Aaron on my phone, asking if we can meet. Staci has seriously got to stop working on Fridays. I'm assuming he hasn't received the papers, and I don't reply. It's becoming surprisingly easy to ignore him.

Blake drives a dark blue pick-up. It's very comfortable, far more so than my little run around Volkswagen. We have a six-hour journey ahead, broken only by a brief stop for lunch, and I'm subjected to the sight of Blake's long, lean legs stretched out beside me for far longer than I can bear. My hand itches to touch his denim-clad thigh, so I clench my fists and focus on the road. Blake, meanwhile, makes easy conversation, seemingly unaffected by the close proximity. It doesn't do much for my ego.

We arrive at the Air B&B, aptly named *Step Right Inn*, an hour before check-in. The owner is a sweet, middle-aged woman named Alice, who has the curliest hair I've ever seen. It's frizzed as though she stuck her finger in an electrical outlet, but her smile is warm, and her blue eyes twinkle as she ushers us into the bar for a drink while we wait.

"Your room is almost ready," she promises, offering us a complimentary glass of cheap sherry beside a crackling fire, despite the stifling heat of the day. Being polite, Blake takes one sip while she watches, hides his grimace, and smiles instead. The second she's out of the room, he sets the glass on the counter.

"Jesus, I think I just seared my stomach lining."

I giggle and set my own glass down without taking a single sip. "That bad?"

"Worse." He takes a seat on the couch and whips off his jumper. The temperature in the room seems to go up a few degrees, and it has nothing to do with the fire. Awkwardly, I perch on the opposite edge. As the sound of a Hoover starts up somewhere above us, Blake gives me a lazy smile.

"Are you going to spend the next seventy-two hours curled up like a frightened kitten?" he asks.

"Maybe," I admit. "I'm starting to think this might not have been the best idea."

"Why?" he teases, "because you're worried you won't be able to keep your hands off me?"

"Yes."

It's not the answer he expected. Slowly, he stretches out his arm, inch by inch, until it lies along the top of the couch. Then he curls his finger and beckons me closer. "Come here." I shake my head, but he only smiles and shifts up until he's right beside me. My heart flip-flops in my chest.

"What are we doing, Cat?"

"We're on a mission," I remind him, deliberately ignoring his meaning. "To find my father and get answers." His scent is assaulting my senses. I try to get up, but he grabs my hand, pulling me back.

"Don't," I warn.

"Why?"

"Because," I begin, but then I catch sight of the way that he's looking at me and every argument I could possibly come up with dies on my lips.

"What are we doing?" he repeats.

"I don't know."

"This is ridiculous. You told me you love me."

"I do."

"And you know I'm in love with you?"

I bob my head.

"Then why in God's name are we torturing ourselves?"

My lack of response is all the invitation he needs. When he pulls me onto his lap, I can't help myself. I gasp. Blake's eyes widen, and then narrow almost instantly. I duck my head, not wanting him to see the blush creeping up my neck and across my cheeks.

"There's something I haven't told you yet," I mumble.

"I'm listening."

My voice is small and breathless. "Sometimes I like things a little bit wilder than most women."

His fingers find my chin, tilt my head back. His eyes are hooded, but I feel like he can see into the depths of my soul.

"Wilder?" he asks, still not understanding.

"Sex," I whisper, mortified that I have to explain. "I'm not depraved. Or perverted," I add quickly. "I'm not into threesomes, or porn, or..." I trail off, too embarrassed to vocalize some of the things he might be thinking. "I just like sex. A lot. And sometimes I like to take a few risks..." I can't go on. A hard, dry lump has formed in my throat and I can't get anything else out.

He drops my chin, and I cringe, waiting for the hammer to fall. I knew this would change how he saw me, but there's no going back. I promised myself I would be one hundred percent honest from now on. The reason I'm so drawn to Aaron is that he understands this side of me. I'll never get as close to any other man so long as I keep them in the dark.

Blake is silent for the longest time.

"What kind of risks?" he asks eventually.

"Just risks," I croak. His hand moves to the waistband of my tights, and I hold my breath. He skims the thin fabric, but doesn't stop, moving lower until his hand cups my ass cheek. His grip tightens.

"What risks?" he repeats, his voice low and husky. He breathes the words into my ear, and I shiver, involuntarily.

Blake's eyes rise to the ceiling, where the sound of the Hoover is a distant hum, and I close my own as comprehension dawns on him. When I open them, his lips are curved upward. It's a wicked smile. Still holding me in his lap, he rises from the couch and crosses to the bar. His face is impossible to read as he deposits me onto one of the bar stools and pours himself a scotch. He takes only a small sip. When he offers me the glass, I down it, the amber liquid scorching a trail down my throat.

Blake's fingers slide down my arms and over my thighs, until he reaches my knees. He forces them apart, quickly, deliberately, and steps into the space between them. I'm too terrified to move. I don't know what he's doing, but my pulse quickens. My hands ache to touch him, but when I reach for him, he swats them away.

"What are you doing?" I whisper.

He cocks his head to one side and regards me levelly. "I'm offended, Cat," he says, his eyes homing in on my mouth. He leans forward and runs his tongue across my lower lip before catching it briefly between his teeth. "I studied the human anatomy," he murmurs, his breath filling my mouth. "You should have had a little more faith in me."

With every word, his fingers are circling my thighs, inching upward, and my body unravels just that little bit more. Somewhere in my addled brain, I'm aware that the Hoover is still going, but there's nothing to say that someone won't walk right through the door at any second. Still, I arch my back, exposing my throat and pressing my hips toward his probing fingers.

Blake doesn't hesitate. Lifting me off the chair, setting me down on trembling legs, he whips down my tights and my underwear in one swift movement. He takes a second to release his zipper, then seizes my hips and lifts me clear off the ground. I give a cry of ecstasy as he rams himself into me, my head dropping back, exposing my neck to his mouth. Upstairs, the Hoover falls silent, but it's all over in less than a minute.

I'VE ONLY JUST MANAGED to pull up my pants when Annie walks back into the bar. I turn away so she won't see the liquid desire shimmering in my eyes, or the short gasps I draw in for breath. Blake, however, is utterly relaxed. He barely glances at her over his shoulder and not by a flicker does he betray that anything is amiss, even though I know that beneath the hem of his shirt, hidden from view, his pants are still undone.

"The room's ready!" Annie announces, then, catching sight of the empty glass, "oh, you poured yourself a drink." She's not sure whether to be relieved or annoyed.

"I did," Blake says. "A scotch – the Balcones. You can bill it to our room."

"I'll do that. Would you like another?" She includes me in the offer, but all I can do is shake my head. I'm still trying to catch my breath, while Blake stands there, cool as a cucumber.

"Not right now," he says. "We've been on the road all day, I think we'll just get cleaned up. Do you know if there's anywhere nearby we can get something to eat?"

"Oh, *Café Gitana* is just down the road, you can't miss it. It's not even a five-minute walk."

Blake looks at me, senses I'm bushed, and speaks again. "On second thoughts, any good takeout places? We can try the café tomorrow."

"There's a *Domino's* in town. I'm sure you can order online, and I'll let you know when it's here."

"Great, thanks, Annie." He picks up our discarded bags. "Shall we?" he asks, cocking his head in my direction. I stifle a nervous giggle and follow him out, as Annie leads us up the stairs to our room.

"That was insane," I say, once the sound of Annie's footfalls on the stairs has died away. Blake has dumped our bags by the door and he's leaning against it, watching me closely. Under such intense scrutiny, I find myself feeling inexplicably shy about what just happened.

"Why didn't you tell me?"

I open my arms helplessly. "It's not exactly the kind of thing you tell people."

"I'm not people, Cat."

"I know. I wanted to tell you, but I was scared it might freak you out."

"Freak me out? To find out that my girlfriend has an incredibly high sex drive? That she's not shy to try new things? Are you even listening to yourself? Shit, I feel like I just won the Lasker. It's an award," he adds, catching sight of my confusion. He comes over to sit next to me on the bed and takes both of my hands in his. "The point is, this isn't exactly a bad thing. Not from my perspective, anyway."

"You don't think that I'm some depraved, physical creature who's just using you for sex?" I tease.

"I think you're the woman I fell in love with. An incredible woman. And I have zero problem with you using me for sex, so long as you love me, too. Just so we're clear." He gives me a look that tells me he wouldn't mind me using him again, right now, and I grin.

"I should've told you ages ago."

"You should've," he agrees. "But I'm not surprised you didn't. I blame society – he's a hero, she's a whore, and all that." He stops, and his face turns somber.

"What is it?" I ask, terrified he's changed his mind.

"Your ex," he murmurs, "you and him used to do things like this? Like what we did downstairs?"

Oh shit. "I don't want to"

"But you have to," he interrupts. "No more secrets, Cat. I need to know what I'm up against."

I take a steadying breath. "Yes. We used to do things like that."

"You ever try with anyone else?"

"Not until now."

He squeezes my hand. "Is that why you were so hung up on him?"

I bob my head, trying to swallow the pain and guilt building into a hard lump in my throat.

"I told you, I didn't think anyone would understand."

"You were wrong. I know you don't believe that yet, so I guess it's up to me to prove it to you." He gets to his feet and offers me his hand. "I want to make one thing very clear, though, Catrina. I love you for who you are, for the real you, the person in here." He lays his hand over my heart. "This other stuff," he adds, a twinkle in his eye, "that's just an added bonus."

He leads me to the shower, where he proceeds to wash me gently from head to toe, kneading away the tension in my body with strong, supple fingers. He massages shampoo into my scalp and then uses almost half a bottle of conditioner to comb through my hair. It's almost more intimate than sex, but not once does he try anything more. Goose flesh rises on my arms whenever his fingers skim near my breasts, or over my thighs.

When I finally step out of the cubicle, dripping water all over the floor, I feel cleaner than I've ever felt in my life. It's as if Blake has washed all the ugliness I've been holding onto, away.

He orders two large pizzas, and pays online. Alice brings them up, with a firm warning that boxes are to be disposed of. We eat. We talk. We cuddle. I fall asleep in his arms, feeling safe, and loved, and wondering how I was ever stupid enough to risk losing him.

11

We sleep in on Saturday morning and almost miss breakfast. Two other couples are staying at the *Step Right Inn,* a pair of newlyweds, a few years younger than I am, and one older couple, whose youngest child recently went off to college and who are finally fulfilling their lifelong ambition to visit all fifty states. The younger couple keeps to themselves, cocooned in newly married bliss, but David and Mandy Friedman, the intrepid travelers, seem intent on making new friends along the way. Blake referred to me as his girlfriend when we introduced ourselves, which made me ridiculously happy.

"Where are you folks from?" David asks, once he's given us a play-by-play of their travels.

"Oakland," Blake replies, "Cat's born and bred, but I'm originally from Sacramento. I'm completing my residency. It's my last year, actually."

"Will you stay in Oakland, once you're done?" Mandy asks the question, and it occurs to me that I don't know the answer. Blake has never mentioned anything beyond the end of this final year. I lean forward, as eager for his reply as the Friedmans.

"At this stage, I'm not sure where I'll end up. I've sent out applications to a number of hospitals across the country. I guess it just depends on who offers me a job."

The conversation continues, but I've tuned out. If Blake gets offered a job somewhere else, what does that mean for us?

"YOU'RE AWFULLY QUIET," Blake says as we head out to do some sightseeing. The B&B is comfortable enough, but there's not much to do. Blake has booked a day tour of Universal Studios for tomorrow, but today I'm content to walk along the beach, feeling the sand in my toes and listening to the roaring hiss of the waves breaking against the shore.

I offer him a shy smile. "I'm still trying to process everything that's happened."

He only nods, and slips his hand through mine. It's a small gesture, but it's comforting. Being like this with Blake, open and honest, is like taking off a pair of too-tight shoes after a miserable day.

We pass an ice-cream stand, and Blake gets us each a double-scooped cone, which we eat on the beach, sharing sweet, vanilla kisses and watching the sea, until the sky darkens and ominous thunderheads roll in. Blake gets to his feet before helping me up. We only just make it to a small, seaside diner before the heavens open.

"What can I get you?" The bored-looking waitress asks.

"Two coffees, please," Blake replies, then grins at me as she saunters off to place the order. The coffee is tepid, and the ladies room, when I go to use it, is filthy, but nothing seems to bother me, Nothing can penetrate the cocoon of happiness I'm insulated in. Not even a text message from Aaron, which comes through while Blake is paying the bill, which I delete without reading.

"You sure you're okay?" Blake asks when I get back to the table. "You've been awfully quiet today."

"Actually, I've been thinking about what you said to the Friedmans. About possibly moving when your residency is up."

"Ah," he says knowingly. "I'm sorry, I should've thought that through before I said it."

"What happens if you get a position across the country?"

"Well, that, I have been thinking about. I know your business is taking off, but most of your work is done online, right? And via email?"

"Yes," I draw out the word, sensing where this is headed. "But that doesn't mean I can just pick up and move. What about my apartment? My mom? My whole life is in Oakland."

"Your whole life was in Oakland," he corrects. "When you were with Aaron. No, hear me out," he continues, as my mouth tightens at the mention of Aaron's name. "Your business is moveable, your apartment would be easy to let out. Your mom, I can understand, but to be honest, I think you should focus on yourself. Cat, you're getting divorced. You deserve a fresh start."

The concern that has been building in my chest evaporates when I realize that Blake is not expecting me to uproot my life just because he says so. He wants me to move for me, so that I can truly move on, without the burden of my past.

"If you don't want to move, we will still make this work," he says, with fierce determination. "I'm not losing you. We'll find a way, even if I have to apply to every hospital on the West Coast and sleep on airplanes for the rest of my life."

"You would do that?"

When he smiles at me like that, I would follow him anywhere. "What part of I love you did you not understand?"

"But we've only been together six months. You've wanted to be a surgeon your whole life. I would never ask you to compromise your job for me."

"You're not asking me to. It's called working together," he teases. "We'll find a solution, Cat. Call me crazy, but I'd like to think I can have the job, *and* the girl."

Aaron and I may have been together for five years, but I'd never felt like we were a team. Aaron is selfish by nature, and I'd been too wrapped up in my own issues, anyway. Blake, on the other hand, makes me feel like, together, we could take on the whole world and live to tell the tale.

"I'm going to be sick," I say on Monday morning as Blake and I stand before the revolving glass doors that lead into the Bennett Communications building. Never mind the whole world, right now I can't seem to summon the courage to face one man. The bliss of the past two days made it easy to forget the real reason that we're here.

"No, you're not," Blake says firmly. "Just breathe."

We'd called ahead to check that Stephen Bennett would be in the office today, but standing here, knowing that my father is somewhere beyond these doors, is both overwhelming and terrifying.

Blake gives me only a few seconds before he turns to face me. "You ready?"

"No."

He takes my hand. "Let's go."

I trail behind him, clinging to his hand like a lifeline, and we enter the building together, the revolving doors spitting us out into a classy foyer. Behind the stretch of oak which serves as a reception counter, a middle-aged woman in a black silk shirt gazes up at us.

"May I help you?" she asks politely.

"Stephen Bennett," Blake says brusquely. "Is he here?"

"Do you have an appointment?" She scans her computer screen, a small frown creasing her brow.

"It's a private matter."

"I'm afraid Mr. Bennett has back-to-back meetings this morning. I'd be happy to let him know you popped by"

"I'm sorry, but it really is imperative that we see him," Blake cuts across her gentle dismissal. "Would you tell him that a friend of Viola Davis is here to see him."

Her lips purse. This is not a woman who likes to be told what to do, and particularly on her own turf.

"I really think it would be best if"

"Not to be rude, Ma'am, but your opinion on what's best is not relevant right now. Please could you get Mr. Bennett on the phone. As I said, it's important." Blake's natural self-assertiveness beats her back. Bristling, she lifts the telephone on her desk and dials an extension, all the while casting dark looks at Blake which make her feelings plain. I don't care. My legs have started to tremble, and I think I'm about to hyperventilate. I peek over my shoulder at the doors, wondering if I should make a run for it.

"Breathe," Blake murmurs, reading my thoughts.

After a quick conversation, the receptionist replaces the handset and gets to her feet.

"Mr. Bennett has asked that you take a seat in the boardroom," she says. She can't seem to bring herself to be friendly, even though her boss has obviously deemed us worthy of his time. She leaves us in the vast room, closing the door behind her with a firm click.

"Do you think he's nervous?" I ask Blake. I'm too highly-strung to sit, so I pace the length of the polished oak table.

"Probably. He's married, and no one wants to be reminded of their old flame, especially at work."

"Do you think I should've called first?"

He considers this a moment and then shakes his head. "No. This isn't something you tell someone over the phone. Breathe, Cat. I'm here. I'll be with you the whole time."

I walk the length of the table again, wringing my hands together so tightly they ache.

"I have no idea what I'm going to say to him."

Blake steps in front of me. "You're going to wear down that carpet," he teases, steering me toward one of twelve identical chairs. "Sit."

I do as I'm told, and when he's satisfied that I'm not going to leap up and start pacing again, he busies himself with the coffee machine in the corner of the room.

I take a sip from the cup he offers me and almost spit it out. It's revoltingly sweet.

"You need the sugar," Blake says.

"It's disgusting."

"Drink it. Doctor's orders."

I almost drop the cup when the doors open, and Stephen Bennett walks into the room. He is tall, not as tall as Blake, but somehow more imposing, and he has the air of a man who knows he's vitally important. His hair is dark, so different from my natural red, and silvering at the temples, but his eyes, when they scan the room to rest on me, are the exact hazel of my own. The second they land on me, he gives a visible start, he looks as if he's seen a ghost.

Realizing that fear has struck me dumb, Blake steps forward to extend his hand.

"Mr. Bennett, my name is Blake Stanton. This," he adds, releasing Stephen's hand and gesturing toward me, "is Catrina Davis."

Stephen Bennett's face darkens at the mention of my last name. To be fair, my name now is actually Catrina James, but for the purpose of this exercise, using my maiden name is a smart move.

"You're Viola's daughter?" he asks. It's a fair guess, given that my mother is an only child.

"Yes." I stumble to my feet and extend my hand. Stephen ignores it. Out of the corner of my eye, I see Blake stiffen. "I'm sorry to barge in on you like this, Mr. Bennett. I'm sure you must very busy"

"I am," he snaps, cutting me off. "And no disrespect, Miss Davis, but your mother isn't someone I would consider a friend, so I'm not quite sure what it is you're doing here."

My hand is still outstretched. I snatch it back.

"From what I hear, you were friends, at one time."

He recoils. Darts a glance in Blake's direction and finds only steely resolve there.

"What do you want?"

I breathe in, filling my lungs to bursting. "Mr. Bennett, I think..." I lose my nerve, but Blake steps closer and rests his hand on the small of my back. "I think I'm your daughter," I finish, quietly.

Stephen's response is almost comical. He frowns, then starts to smile, as if he might laugh. He doesn't. Instead, the slight upward tilt of his lips plummets into a furious scowl.

"Is this some kind of joke?" But even as he says it, he's scanning my face. Finding the similarities that lie there – the eyes, the shape of my lips, the point of my chin.

"No," Blake says. "It's not a joke. And I know this must come as a shock, but we've traveled a long way to see you. Catrina only just discovered your identity, and she'd obviously like to find out more about you. I'm sure you also have questions of your own."

"Only one," Stephen corrects. His eyes bore into me, but I have no idea what he's thinking because his face gives nothing away. When he speaks, however, there's no mistaking the venom in his voice. "Who the hell put you up to this?"

HE DOESN'T BELIEVE ME. My father thinks that I'm a fraud. Whether or not he thinks I want money, I can't be sure, because he doesn't directly come out and say it, but I suspect that's exactly what he believes. I can't do anything but swallow down the humiliation as he hurls his outrage toward me, wave after wave of accusatory vitriol.

It doesn't take long for Blake to intervene.

"Enough!" he roars, taking in the tears shimmering in my eyes and the way I'm cowering away from Stephen. "Leave her alone, you son of a bitch! I swear to God, if you don't shut your mouth, I'll do it for you. Can't you see what you're doing to her?"

"What *I'm* doing to *her*?" Stephen sneers. "She arrives here, unannounced, and starts making ludicrous claims, and I'm supposed to feel guilty? I don't know what you people are playing at, but I'm not buying it."

Blake steps right into Stephen's face. "She. Is. Not. People," he growls, slow and menacing, "She is your God-damned blood, you miserable bastard. And you don't deserve her." He raises his hand, and for a second, I think he's going to hit Stephen, but instead, he draws his wallet from his pocket and hands him a card. "Here are my contact details. If you come to your senses and decide to become a decent human being, get in touch. And if Catrina still wants to talk to you, you might just stand a chance of getting to know your daughter. Not that you deserve her," he adds ominously. Then, he offers me his hand. "Come on, baby. Let's get out of here."

WE DON'T SPEAK as Blake leads me outside, his hand clutching mine so tightly that it starts to tingle with lack of blood flow. I barely care. Meek and mute, I follow him, putting one foot in front of the other. Seeing my distress, the receptionist allows herself a small smirk. The second I'm inside the safety of the pick-up and Blake closes the door behind me, I burst into tears. Chest-heaving, bone-breaking sobs, which wrack my body and claw their way up my throat. Blake doesn't console me. Not here, in front of this awful building, in full view of anyone who might choose to look out of a window. Only when we've driven a few blocks, does he pull into a parking lot and haul me into his arms. For a long time, he holds me, until my tears run dry and the ache in my heart hardens, giving way to a quiet fury.

"He doesn't deserve you," Blake murmurs into my hair. He's trying to convince me, but when I test my shattered pride, I find no convincing necessary.

"I know."

Blake raises his head, a small frown creasing between his eyes. This isn't the reaction he was expecting.

I draw in a shaky breath, the remnants of my emotional breakdown wreaking havoc on my breathing. "I'm not stupid. I know I haven't done anything wrong. I know he could've handled that better. I also know that he's probably a world class prick." I wipe the last of the tears from my cheeks and attempt a tentative smile. "But at least now I know."

Blake puts his hand on my leg and gives it a squeeze. "I'm proud of you."

"Thanks for being here. I don't think I could've handled that alone."

He kisses me, and then puts the pick-up into drive.

"Where are we going?" I ask as we pull out of the parking lot.

"Home," Blake replies simply.

We drive six hours straight. Emotionally exhausted, I doze on and off for the last three. I'd tried valiantly to stay awake, to keep Blake company, but eventually, he'd balled up his jacket, shoved it up against my window as a makeshift pillow, and ordered me to sleep.

He wakes me as we approach my apartment block, with a gentle hand on my shoulder. "Good afternoon, beautiful."

I blink the sleep out of my eyes and clear my throat. "We're home already?"

"And not a minute too soon. I don't think I could've taken one more second of your snoring."

"I do not snore!"

"You're right. What you do sounds more like sawing through bone, by hand." He winks at me as he pulls into the underground lot and takes his usual parking space beside my car.

We're both laughing as we get out and stretch our cramped legs. The smiles play about our lips as we cast knowing glances at one another during the elevator ride. I survived. I went through something awful, but I survived. I'm not broken, and we're okay. I brush my hand across the nape of Blake's neck, and then step forward to kiss him, full on the mouth. His lips curve against mine in a knowing smile.

"You seem to be feeling better," he whispers against my lips.

"I know something that will make me feel a lot better," I reply coyly, lowering my hand to grab a fistful of denim-clad backside. Blake laughs, but he mirrors my action.

The elevator doors open and we pull apart. The light, teasing atmosphere vanishes, the second I step out into the hall to find my mother crouched on my doorstep.

"MOM?"

Her head jerks up at the sound of my voice. Her eyes are glittering, never a good sign, and her make-up which, by the heaviness of it, must have been on since last night, is streaked down her face.

"Cat!" she practically yells. "How dare you? How *dare* you!"

There's no doubt in my mind that she knows where I've been and who I've spoken to. Or that she's high as a kite. *Fine, we'll do this now,* I think furiously. I keep my voice flat and tell her to come inside.

"Don't tell me what to do!" she yells back, with all the manic fury of a two-year-old denied a delicate family heirloom.

"Keep your voice down, mom," I hiss, frantically trying to jab my key into the lock. "I have neighbors."

"I don't give a damn about your neighbors!" She turns her head to yell the last words at the apartment door across from mine.

"Inside!" I hiss.

Blake follows us in and then plants himself at the edge of my living room, ready to intervene if he needs to. My mother trips over the couch on her way in, and he catches her arm, keeping her upright. She doesn't even thank him.

"I need you to go," I tell him gently. I appreciate what he's doing, but this is not something I want him to witness. Bad enough that he's seen what happened with Stephen, I don't need him up front and center for the Broadway musical that my mother's about to perform.

"I'm not leaving you."

"Please." I put a hand on his arm. "I need to do this alone." My eyes tell him what my lips cannot – that I'm ashamed – and his expression softens.

"I'll wait in the bedroom," he concedes, "but I'm not leaving this apartment."

"Fair enough."

Without another word, he walks down the hall and leaves me alone with my mother.

"How could you do this to me, Catrina?" she repeats, the second she has my attention.

"Do what to you, mom? I haven't done anything *to* you. This hasn't even got anything to do with you!"

"It's got everything to do with me! How do you think I felt, getting a call from *that* man, after all these years?"

"I'm surprised you even knew who *that* man was, given the state you're in. Don't you dare!" I add, snatching away the joint she's pulled from her bag. "You've had enough." Proving my point, she sways on her feet. "Sit down before you fall over and break something."

"You don't get to speak to me like that. You may not like it, but I'm your mother."

"You want me to speak to you with respect?" I taunt, "then earn it. You're so far gone you can barely stand."

"Barely stand the sight of you, you mean, after what you've done," she slurs, then looks absurdly pleased with herself for being so clever as to come up with it. I know that she's vicious when she's high, but it still hurts.

"Jesus, mom, this is serious. For once in my life, I'd just like to have a normal conversation with you about something that matters. I met my father today! I know it's not what you wanted, but it's what I needed. And he treated me like *shit*." My voice breaks, and I slump onto the couch. My mother hesitates.

"He what?" she blinks, rapidly, as if trying to clear the drug-induced fog from her brain. "What did he do to you, Cat?"

"He all but kicked me out. He didn't believe me." Fresh waves of humiliation redden my cheeks. "He called me a liar."

"That lousy, rotten son of a bitch! I'll rip his throat out with my bare hands! How dare he"

"Mom! Enough! Please." I close my eyes to shut out the sound of her ranting. She falls silent and a moment later I feel the couch dip beside me under her weight.

"Cat?" she asks, in a voice much smaller than I expect. I turn my face to peer up at her with one eye.

"I need you to go, mom."

"Go?" It's as if I just asked her what the square root of pi is.

"Yes, mom. Just go."

"No."

"No?" It's my turn to be outraged.

"No," she repeats. "I'm not leaving. I know that you're upset, but you don't get to turn this around. None of this would have happened if you hadn't gone behind my back."

"I beg your pardon?" I can't believe what I'm hearing. I'd believed, for a nano-second, that she felt sorry for me. That she would comfort me – her daughter – after everything that I'd been through. I should have known better. Viola Davis has only ever cared about Viola Davis.

"I told you to leave it alone, didn't I?" she says, oblivious to the warning look I throw her. "Now look what you've done. That bastard kicked you out, like you were nothing, and he threatened to sue me for about a dozen things that I don't even understand."

"Let me get this straight," I say, speaking slowly and clearly. "You're saying that this is all my fault? That you're an innocent victim?"

"Well, I wouldn't say it in that many words, but there's no doubt that you brought this upon both of us. You've never listened to me, Cat. Maybe now you'll realize that sometimes I actually do know what's best for you."

"Ha!" I bark, my laughter raw and raging. "You know what's best for me, do you?" I launch to my feet and pull down the ladder to the attic. "Tell me, mom, was growing up without a father, or any knowledge of who he was, good for me? Was missing six weeks of my senior year, and failing chemistry, all because you decided we should road trip around the States, good for me? Was getting taken to the emergency room because you spiked my tea, good for me? Was being two hours late for *my own fucking wedding* because you were passed out in the bathroom good for me?" While I'm shrieking, I've ascended the steps and am fumbling around in the dark with my hands. My fingers brush against the edge of a canvas, and I haul it out with a triumphant cry. "Is this good for me, mom?" I say, tossing it down to the ground, where it clatters near her feet. Another painting follows, then another, then another, until I feel strong hands grip my waist.

"Enough, Cat," Blake says, his voice infinitely kind. I whirl to find him standing behind me, his tired eyes reproachful as he shakes his head. "Enough, sweetheart," he whispers. With abject horror, my eyes move past him to find my mother standing amidst a mountain of her own work, her hand pressed to her mouth, her eyes filled with tears. *Oh, God. Oh, God, what have I done?*

BLAKE DRIVES MY MOTHER HOME. We hadn't spoken a word to each other after he carried me off the ladder, past the maelstrom of my living room, and into my room. He'd laid me on the bed, kissed me on the forehead, and promised he'd be right back. I hadn't been able to move, curled on my side, filled with remorse so powerful it edged my vision black. I'd heard him speaking, coaxing my silent mother through the jumble of canvases and out of the front door, and then I'd heard nothing but my own thudding heartbeat, echoing in my ears.

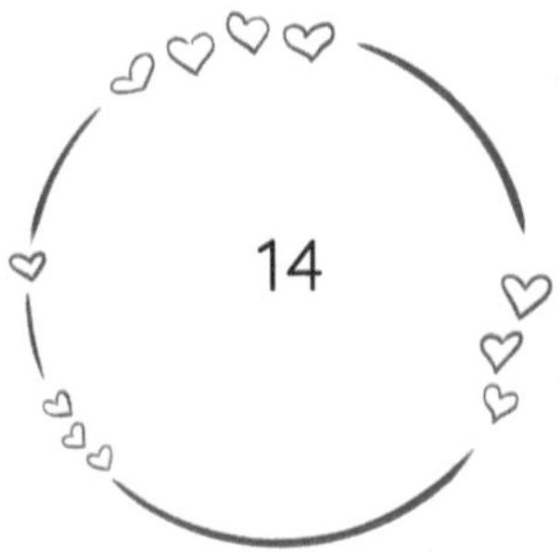

14

I wake up to find Blake in bed beside me, snoring softly, his tanned arm slung over my waist. The memory of everything that happened yesterday hits me like a ton of bricks, and I close my eyes, willing back the oblivion of sleep. Instead, my brain goes into hyperdrive, replaying every awful moment until I slip from the bed and immerse myself under a scalding hot shower.

It's not minutes before Blake's blurred silhouette appears before the frosted glass. He's wearing a pair of tracksuit pants, and nothing else. When he opens the door, his eyes pose a silent question.

"Hi," I say.

"Hi. How are you feeling?"

"Awful."

"I thought you might. Here, give me that." He takes the sponge from my hands and lathers it with soap, as efficiently and thoroughly as if he were prepping for surgery. "You can't blame yourself, Cat," he murmurs, twirling his finger to indicate that I should turn around. I do, and he starts to wash my back.

"I was so cruel to her," I mumble. It's easier to admit now that I don't have to look at him, and I wonder if that's exactly what he intended.

"Yes, but I think you were justified. I heard what she said to you. She was awful first."

"She's not in her right mind," I say as he drops the sponge and starts to knead the tension out of my shoulders with his strong hands. "It's like being cruel to a badly behaved child."

"You make too many excuses for her. We spoke a little, on the way back to her place. She's not as naïve as she'd like you to believe."

I whirl to face him. "What did she say to you?"

"Nothing that would make you feel better. I'm sorry."

"*I'm* sorry. After everything I've put you through, and now having to deal with this mess... it's a wonder you're still here."

He gives me a small smile. "I wouldn't want to be anywhere else, love. Together, remember? We handle it together – the good, and the bad."

I allow myself a moment to forget the horror of yesterday, to forget everything but right here and right now. I lean out of the shower, uncaring of the water streaming onto the floor, and curl my right hand around his neck, drawing him toward me, until he gets the idea. Without dropping his pants, he steps into the cubicle and takes me in his arms. When we kiss, water streams into my mouth, until Blake closes his lips over mine, and then it's just the warmth of his hot mouth on mine, and our breath rising in the steam.

"WHAT DO you think I should do?" I ask Blake later. We're in the kitchen, armed with coffee. The smell of toast still lingers in the air.

"Nothing," Blake replies.

"I can't do nothing. I can't leave things like this."

"You can, for now. You've said your piece, Cat. Maybe not in the most constructive way, but your point needed to be made. Let her stew for a bit. She needs to know you're serious."

He's right. The more I think about it, and even though I'm still cringing at the way I dealt with my mother, it needed to happen. I am tired of caving. I'm tired of being the person who tries, and fails, because the people in my life couldn't give a damn. My mother, Aaron – it's an endless cycle. From now on, things are going to be different, I vow to myself as I kiss Blake goodbye.

"I wish I didn't have to go," he says. "I feel bad leaving you."

"You have work to do," I tell him. "Hell, I have work to do." We'd taken the last three days for ourselves, but the world waits for no one. Life carries on, even when you feel like it's falling apart. Blake has his internship, and I have my business, and both require us to show up.

"Are you going to work down at the coffee shop this morning?"

"Probably. Routine is good in times of trauma, or so I've heard."

He chuckles. "Look at you, getting back on the horse."

I grin up at him. "I have an excellent instructor."

As he leans in for another kiss, his phone rings, He rolls his eyes and pulls it from his pocket, then peers at the screen in confusion.

"Hello?"

I hear a male voice, but I can't make out what he's saying. Blake has gone deadly still. "Yes, Stephen, what can I do for you?"

He listens for a second. "Well, that would be up to Catrina." *He wants to see you,* he tells me. I snatch up my bottom lip between my teeth, considering. Blake comes to a decision. "Let me speak to her. I'll let you know what she decides." Without waiting for an answer, he hangs up.

"What was that about?" I ask.

"He's coming here."

"Here?"

"To Oakland. He wants to take us for dinner – or, rather, take *you* for dinner, tomorrow night."

"Twenty-four hours ago he was throwing me out, and now he wants to take me for dinner?"

Blake smiles. "Is everything out of your mouth going to be a question?"

"Maybe."

"For what it's worth, I think you should go. Yesterday didn't go well, and if you never want to see him again, I'm more than happy to tell him that, but I think you should hear him out. For you," he adds, meaningfully, "not for him."

I nod. "Tell him yes."

THE DIVORCE ATTORNEY had promised that Aaron would be served within five working days. They were a day late. On Wednesday morning, just a few minutes after Blake has left for the hospital, I hear a knock at the door. Caught by surprise, I open it to find Aaron in the doorway, his hair uncharacteristically mussed up, as if he's been running his hands through it all morning. He's holding a sheaf of papers.

"Aaron! What are you doing here?" It's been a little over a week since I last saw him, but he looks awful.

He shoulders his way past me. I grit my teeth and shut the door.

"What the fuck is this?" he asks, hurling the papers at me. They land in a heap at my feet.

"You know exactly what it is."

"A divorce, Cat? You're filing for a divorce?"

Calmly, I retrieve the papers. "It's what people do when they no longer want to be married."

"We both know you don't want to divorce me."

"Actually, I do." To my surprise, he's shaking with emotion. "Come on, Aaron. You don't want to be married to me, either. Why drag this out any longer?"

"It's this new man, isn't it? The doctor? I saw him leave this morning. You got back together with him, didn't you?" he says it as if I've committed a cardinal sin, which is ironic considering he only really wants me when I'm unavailable. "He's put you up to this."

"Are you serious?" my eyes widen with disbelief. "We've been separated for over a year, Aaron! I should've done this twelve months ago, when I found you screwing Staci on our couch!"

"Don't try to turn this on her. You love that I'm with Staci! You've been lusting after me like a bitch on heat since she and I hooked up. She's the best thing that ever happened to us!"

I am at a complete and utter loss for words. "You've lost your mind."

His expression changes, something dark and feral glinting in his eyes.

"Oh really?" he takes a predatory step closer. "Then explain this." He pulls a scrap of lace from his pocket. It's the underwear I was wearing that morning at Verdure. It feels like a lifetime ago, but I still cringe at the sight. "Admit it, Cat, you want me. God knows the sex has never been better. And it was good before, but now..." I stand, mortified, as he brings his hand to his face and inhales deeply. "You don't want to give this up," Aaron croaks thickly. I feel it then – the traitorous tug deep inside of me, the twisted part of me that wants him as badly as he wants me. I draw up a mental image of Blake and brandish it like a shield in my mind.

"I don't want this," I say firmly. "I am *happy*, Aaron. Happier than I ever was with you. Our relationship was toxic, it held us both back from finding something real. You have to know that. Please, just let me go."

Aaron steps closer until we're almost touching. I ball my hands into fists.

"Don't do this, Kitty Cat."

"I won't be your bit on the side, Aaron. Not anymore."

"You want me to leave Staci? Done."

"You're lying."

His hand cups my chin, forcing my face upward. "I am not losing you," he growls. His eyes dip to my chest, where I can feel my nipples pressing through the soft cotton of my nightshirt. His lazy grin infuriates me. I may be strong enough to stand against him, but my traitorous body hasn't caught up yet.

"Who do you think you're fooling, Cat?" he asks.

"Get out."

His long fingers caress the underside of my chin. "Do you remember Verdure?" The heat rises in my cheeks as he raises the hand still holding my ruined panties. "This keepsake reminds me, Cat. It reminds me how I fucked you up against that door while your boyfriend sat just a few feet away. That was only a few weeks ago. You expect me to believe you've had a complete change of heart in just a few weeks?"

The mention of Blake snaps me back to reality. "Get out of my house!" I turn toward the door, intent on forcing him to go, when I stop dead. Blake is standing in the open doorway, his chalk-white face a mask of bleak disgust. He's still holding his key – the one I gave him as a symbol of my commitment. I hadn't even heard him come in. It takes me only a second to realize that Aaron would have seen him enter because he's facing the door.

"Blake!" I stumble over my words. "When did you—"

"A while ago." His voice is curt, clipped, not a trace of warmth in his brown eyes as they slide toward Aaron. "I guess you must be the ex-husband."

Aaron words are flippant. "Husband," he corrects, tapping the papers in my hands. "Nothing ex about it."

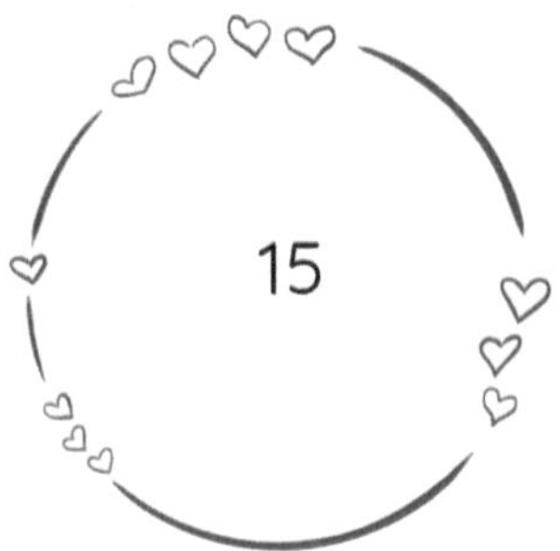

I chase Blake into the hall, leaving Aaron alone in my apartment.

"You have to let me explain!" I sob, stumbling into the elevator after him.

"Explain what?" Blake roars, angrier than I've ever seen him. "Explain how you've been screwing that prick the whole time we've been dating?"

"It's not like that!"

"Oh, really? Then what is it like, Cat? Because from what I just heard, it's exactly like that."

"He said that because he knew you were listening!"

"You're saying it *didn't* happen like that?"

"I'm saying I ended it! I signed the papers! I told you, I don't want to be that person anymore."

"So you finally ended it, after months of cheating on me, and I'm supposed to be impressed? Jesus, Cat, I knew you had issues, but you're something else."

"I didn't plan any of this. I swear, I wasn't seeing him when we met. We bumped into each other a few months ago and it just happened."

"It just happened?" he gives a harsh bark of laughter. "I'm a surgeon, Cat. I have a pretty sound knowledge of the human anatomy, and believe me, it doesn't just happen." He claps his hand to his forehead, covering his eyes, and then drags it down his face. "Verdure, Cat?" The disgust and pain in his voice breaks my heart.

"I'm sorry," I whisper. "I'm so, so sorry. I can explain everything. If you just come back in, we could talk about it"

"I'm not interested. I have *nothing* to say to you."

The elevator reaches the ground floor and the doors open. "Please..."

Blake shakes his head. Unshed tears shimmer in his eyes. "You screwed him while I ordered your eggs. What kind of person does that?"

I don't answer, because the question is rhetorical. We both know the kind of person who does that. A monster.

AARON IS LOUNGING on my couch when I return. Just the sight of him makes me sick to my stomach.

"You need to leave," I snap. I hold the door open to emphasize my urgency.

"Why? Things are just starting to get interesting." He's lost all trace of the desperate man who walked into my apartment. Instead, there's a swagger in his tone. He's amused, I think with disgust. And thrilled with the unexpected turn of events.

I snatch up the papers, which I'd dumped on the table in the hall on my mad dash after Blake.

"Sign them."

Aaron rises from the couch. "I don't think I will."

"You know that I can divorce you, with or without your signature on these papers, right? And I will. All you're doing is delaying the inevitable."

"No, baby. *You're* delaying the inevitable." He comes to stand right before me, and with one lazy flick of his wrist, knocks the papers out of my hands. "You can't fight this, Kitty Cat. Try all you like, but I guarantee we will be seeing each other real soon." His eyes dip to my chest, still heaving with emotion, and his gaze lingers there. "I, for one, am looking forward to it."

I GET NO WORK DONE. After Aaron left, I'd come down to the coffee shop as planned, but I shouldn't have bothered. My vision keeps blurring as unbidden tears slip over my eyelids and track their way down my cheeks. Amy checks on me at first, but after a while she seems to realize I just want to be left alone and goes back to refilling my cup every hour, on the hour, while I stare, unseeing, at a blank screen. I text Blake, telling him again how sorry I am, but hear nothing back. Instead, I receive a message from Stephen Bennett, confirming the time and place of our dinner tonight. Blake must have given him my number, and the thought that he'd done that – that he'd removed himself from this situation with my father, crucifies me. At two o'clock I send him another text message, and then I pay my bill and head home. My apartment feels empty without him in it. My heart feels the same. I lie on my bed with only my dark thoughts for company and try to figure out a way to move past this. There's nothing I can do about Blake. I can't blame him for walking out on me. What I did was unforgivable. But my mother, and Stephen Bennett, I can do something about. Blake may be gone, but I still have the lessons he taught me. To put myself first. To be selfish, if I need to. To speak my truth. And I plan to do all of it.

STEPHEN IS ALREADY SEATED at the table when I arrive. He's staying at the Marriott, but we meet at a restaurant a few blocks away. It's Italian, the walls adorned with chalk paintings of wine bottles, famous landmarks, and fresh tomatoes. Beaded chandeliers hang from the ceilings and the chairs are covered in crushed red velvet. Stephen stands when I reach the table.

"Catrina," he says, by way of greeting. He's outwardly calm, but I can tell by the way his fingers tremble when he gestures toward my seat, that he's not as composed as he'd like to make out. "Thank you for coming."

"I almost didn't," I admit.

"After what happened on Monday, I wouldn't have blamed you. What changed your mind?"

"Blake." It's a simple, honest answer.

"I'll be sure to thank him when I see him next."

I don't think that will ever happen, but I stay silent. I don't want to talk about Blake. It sends a sharp, shooting pain through my chest every time I think of him. Unfortunately, Stephen's next words don't help my cause.

"Will he be joining us this evening?" he asks.

"No." My answer is clipped, I realize, as I say it. "I'm sorry, I don't really want to talk about Blake. We had a fight, and to be honest, I don't actually know where things stand between us right now. It was my fault," I add quickly.

"I'm sorry to hear that," he says, and he sounds sincere. "I hope you manage to work things out. He seems like a good man."

There's an awkward silence as Stephen tries to look encouraging while I fight the urge to burst into tears.

"I wanted to apologize," he says eventually. "For how I behaved. I know it won't excuse the way I treated you, but I am truly sorry for everything I said. And for implying that you were lying."

"You believe me now?" I can't help but wonder what changed his mind so drastically in just twenty-four hours.

He sighs, his fingers toying with the napkin on the table before him. "I knew you were telling the truth the second I walked through the door."

"How?"

A ghost of a smile. "You... you have a sister, Catrina. Her name is Hannah, and she looks just like you." When Stephen had first seen me, he'd balked, as if he'd seen a ghost. Somewhere in my addled brain, this now makes sense, but I'm too stunned to pay attention.

"I have a sister?"

"You do. She's only sixteen."

"Oh my God." I sit back in my chair. I'd never even considered the possibility that I might have siblings. "Oh my God. Can I..." I trail off, realizing that I have no idea whether he's even prepared to tell his family about me. "Do you think I might get to meet her one day?"

"I think she'd like that. Actually," he laughs, low and deep, "she's already told me that if I don't bring her out by next weekend, she's going to steal my car and drive out here herself. And if you ever saw Hannah behind the wheel, you'd know that's a very bad idea."

I'm still reeling, and I don't even register his attempt to lighten the atmosphere. "You told her about me?"

"I did. You're her sister, how could I not? My wife, Lucy, would like to meet you too."

He told his *wife* about me? My surprise must show on my face because Stephen laughs.

"Like I said, we got off on the wrong foot. I know how it must have looked, but I promise I'm not a bad guy. You caught me off guard, and I reacted without thinking. I'll never be able to tell you how sorry I am for that."

"This is a good start," I admit. "I never would have expected you to tell your family about me, especially so soon."

"They're your family too, Catrina," he says. Something warm and beautiful blossoms in my chest. "If you're up to it, I'd like to fly back with them next weekend. I have to leave tomorrow. I wish I could've stayed longer, but I left rather abruptly, and I have commitments at work that I can't get out of at such short notice."

"Next weekend is perfect, or whenever it suits you. Please don't feel you have to upheave your whole life just for me."

"It's hard not to want to," he says. "I have so much time to make up for." He takes a sip of his scotch and shakes his head. "This is so surreal. To think I have a daughter your age, it's going to take some getting used to. I don't know if your grandparents or your mother told you, but I'm only"

"Forty," I finish for him. "I heard. And believe me, it's as weird for me as it is for you." We both pause in embarrassment as we work out that, to the other diners, we are as likely to look like lovers as father and daughter. Stephen clears his throat.

"I should also tell you that I contacted your mother. Shortly after you left my office."

"I heard about that too."

"I wasn't very kind to her either," he admits. "But I'd be lying if I said I'm not furious with her." His fingers drum the table. "She should have told me," he mutters. "I had a right to know that I had fathered a child."

"I know. We both deserved the truth, but my mother wasn't the only one at fault in that regard."

A flash of real anger crosses his face. "She told me. If my parents were still alive, I'd at least be able to take my anger out on someone else. Sadly, your mother was the only available target."

It still feels so strange to hear of family I never knew existed, but I can't say I'm particularly sorry to hear that his parents are deceased. From what little I know of them, I doubt we would have gotten along. Still, they were his parents, so I try to invoke a shred of empathy as I ask, "what happened to them?"

"Car accident, almost three years ago. A drunk driver jumped the light. They were killed instantly."

"I'm sorry." It's really all I can think of to say, as underwhelming as it may be.

"It's okay, it's in the past. I'm more concerned about the fact that I've missed twenty-four years of your life, that I can never get back."

"I know. Me too. But let's look on the bright side. Better late than never, right?"

. . .

TRYING to fit a lifetime's worth of information into one dinner is impossible, but we give it our best shot. Stephen tells me about Lucy and Hannah, the sister I can't seem to hear enough about. I learned that Sophie is married, with two teenaged boys. Not only have I just gained a sister, but two cousins, too. Bennett Communications is, as I'd suspected, a family business, and Stephen and Sophie had taken it over once their parents had died.

"We already had a fifty percent shareholding, and the balance we inherited when they died. Sophie still paints," he adds, "but only as a hobby, thank God. I'm running out of wall space. Sophie likes to gift us one of her paintings every Christmas. She did a portrait of Hannah last year that Hannah refused to let us hang. She said it made her look like a forty-year-old prostitute. Sophie wasn't amused. To be honest, she's never really been very good. Nowhere near your mother's league, at least."

I shrewdly changed the subject, veering it away from my mother. I told him about college, my business, my friends. We bond over the fact that we both like our toast slightly burnt at the edges, and discover we shared a passion for technology. I don't mention Blake. And worse, I don't tell him about Aaron. I don't tell my father that I had been married, or that I'm separated and filing for divorce. I don't want to face the questions that I know he'll ask, and ruin a perfect evening with the ugly truth of my failure.

IT'S past eleven when Stephen pays the bill. We're the last table to leave, and then only because the staff are waiting around at the bar, casting us dirty looks for keeping them so late.

"I feel like there's so much more to say," Stephen tells me as we walk to the door. I know exactly what he means. We hadn't stopped talking for hours, and I still craved so much more.

When we emerge onto the street, I catch sight of a dark blue pick-up parked at the curb. As I meet the eyes of the tall, dark-haired man leaning against it, my heart stutters in my chest.

"Blake?" I don't dare get my hopes up. Beside me, Stephen smiles.

"I'll see you next week, Catrina," he murmurs. We'd made arrangements to have dinner with his wife, Lucy, and my sister, Hannah, next Friday night.

Not taking my eyes off Blake, I reply. "I wouldn't miss it for the world."

Stephen gives Blake a nod, which Blake returns, and then saunters down the street to hunt for a cab. I put one foot in front of the other, trying to remember how to breathe, until I'm standing only a few feet away from Blake.

"How did it go?" he asks. His voice is strained, weary.

"It went really well. He was nice. Nothing like before."

"I suspected as much. He seemed completely different when we spoke on the phone."

I cast around for something else to say. "I have a sister."

His lips tug upward. "You have a sister?"

"Yes. Her name is Hannah. I'm meeting her next weekend."

"That's incredible. I'm really happy for you, Cat." Happy *for* me. Not happy *with* me. We gaze at each other in silent torment.

"What are you doing here?" I ask when I can't take it anymore.

"I needed to see you. To see if you were okay." He rubs his hand over the five o'clock shadow darkening his jaw. I'm too terrified to speak, for fear that he'll leave, but at the same time, I want to beg him to stay. He looks torn. Torn, and angry, and resigned. And I hate that I'm the reason for it.

"I need you to know how sorry I am," I begin cautiously. When he doesn't reply, I gather my courage and proceed. "I know what I did was awful. I know that what I've done is unforgivable. But I also know that I made a decision to be better, and that's exactly what I'm going to do. From the moment I made that decision, I ended things with Aaron. I need you to know that. Even if you don't believe anything else I say, please believe that."

"I do believe you," he seethes, and I can't tell if his anger is directed at me or himself. "I've been replaying that conversation we had at the hospital, over and over in my head, and do you know the one thing that keeps coming back to haunt me?"

"What?" I whisper.

"That you told me I didn't deserve you. That you told me you didn't want to get back together yet, that you weren't ready. How you tried to keep me at arm's length, even at that shitty B&B. And now I understand why."

"I'm sorry."

"Stop saying that!"

"So" I manage to stop myself just in time.

"I should have listened to you. I'm the one who instigated things in that bar. If I'd just listened to you, if I'd given you time..." he trails off, confusion etched in every inch of his face. "I don't even know what to think anymore."

"You didn't do anything wrong."

"I know that, too. But I also can't deny that you tried to set things right. At the end. And that's what makes this so God-damned difficult."

Hope, bright and beautiful, burgeons in my chest.

"What are you saying?"

"I don't know. I just know that I've never been so unhappy in my life. And it's fucking cold out here." He turns to the pick-up and opens the passenger door. "Get in."

I don't need to be told twice. I vault forward and leap inside. A moment later, Blake guns the engine.

We drive in silence for a long while. The smell of his cologne fills the small space and, with it, a pang of longing so fierce I feel dizzy.

"Was it the sex?" Blake says after a time. He winces as he says it. "I need straight answers, Cat," he adds coldly when I don't reply.

"Yes."

He nods. "Are you still in love with him?"

"No. I don't think I ever was. But..." I take a deep breath. This is the time for truth, as painful as it might be. "I don't think he's ever going to let me go. I don't want him, I swear it on my life, but he doesn't believe me."

We pull up to my apartment block, and I want to weep with relief when Blake steers us into the underground lot. He parks in his usual spot, but instead of getting out, he kills the engine and swivels to face me. I can't tell what he's thinking, as I swallow down the lump in my throat.

"I only have two questions," Blake says. "Yes or no, that's all I want to hear from you. Got it?"

I nod my head.

"Is it over?"

"Yes." There's not a trace of doubt in my voice.

"Do you love me?"

"More than you could possibly know." I can't help the raw emotion that surges up and stings my eyes. Blake watches as the tears well, and then gives me a tentative smile.

"That wasn't a yes or a no."

"Yes."

He presses his lips together. Stares at me. Seems to come to a decision, and then opens his door. I hold my breath as he rounds the car and opens mine. When he offers me his hand, a dozen butterflies take flight in my stomach. And as we walk, hand in hand, to the elevator, the world seems to re-align.

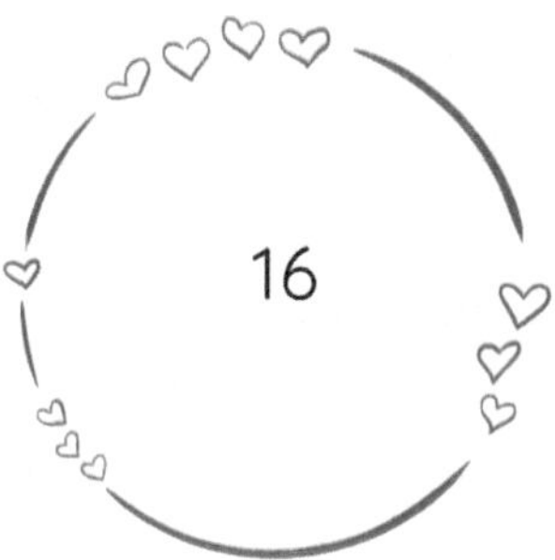

16

"That is the most romantic thing I've ever heard," Gwen sighs, as I relay the story to her and Bianca. We're at 1954, an upmarket, All-American bistro with a fifties flair. I've spent the past hour telling them about mine and Blake's reunion. Of course, I've omitted the part about Aaron. I just told them Blake and I had broken up after a huge fight, but I'd gone into great detail about how we got back together.

"It was," I sigh. It's impossible to put into words how relieved I am that Blake understood that I had chosen him.

"I still can't believe you found your dad," Bianca quips.

"He's flying in on Friday," I say. It's been a week since my dinner with Stephen. A week since Blake brought me home and stayed. Seven long nights, each better than the one before.

"Wipe that look off your face," Bianca says, grinning. "You're making me uncomfortable."

"I can't help it."

"Try. I have news, too, and I'm going to need you to pay attention."

Automatically, Gwen and I both look at her left hand, but her ring finger is bare.

"God no," Bianca whines. "Not that. What is wrong with you two?"

"You can't blame us for hoping," Gwen says.

"How many times do I need to tell you, I don't believe in marriage."

"What's the news, then?" Gwen asks, but I'm focused on Bianca, my brain going a mile a minute. It takes me a second to notice her untouched wine glass, and another to register what it means, but she's already blurted it out.

"I'm pregnant."

The squeal of excitement that follows draws the attention of every diner in the restaurant, but I don't care. I'm already on my feet, Gwen a second behind me, and we're hugging Bianca, who remains seated.

"I kind of wish I'd kept my fat mouth shut," she grumbles.

"This is the best news!" Gwen laughs. "Mike must be over the moon."

"He's got morning sickness," Bianca says. "And he's been strutting around like the cock amidst the chickens since we found out. You'd swear I had nothing to do with it, the way he's behaving."

"Stop it," I chide, still laughing. Mike dotes on Bianca, a miracle, given how she treats him. I glance down at her flat stomach. "I can't actually believe it. How far along are you?"

"Only eight weeks. We just found out. And I've already gained five pounds." She gives a groan off despair. "I'm going to be fat, you guys. I'm going to be one of those women who blows up like a bullfrog and spends the rest of her life battling the bulge."

"You're not going to get fat!" Gwen insists.

"And even if you do," I add, "it'll be worth it. You're having a baby, Biancs! A baby!"

Bianca throws me a filthy look. "I really should have kept my damn mouth shut."

"You're going to have to marry Mike now," I tease, knowing it'll infuriate her even more.

"Catrina, I swear if you don't stop I'm going to punch you in the face."

I feign outraged indignance. "You're with child, Bianca. Remember, the baby will pick up on your emotions, so you should be channeling positivity and light. You should also sing to it, lullabies, preferably, and as often as you can."

Gwen is laughing too hard to comment.

THE REST of the evening is dominated by baby talk, much to Bianca's disgust, but it's inevitable that the subject of Aaron will rear its ugly head. It's Bianca who brings him up, no doubt her way of getting back at me for harping on about all things pre and postnatal.

"He asked after you the other day," she tells me, taking a tiny but defiant sip of her wine. "My gynae said it's fine in moderation," she snaps, as Gwen's eyes widen. "Anyway, Mike was a bit shocked because Aaron doesn't usually mention you, but he wanted to know if you were still seeing Blake."

It's a good feeling, to have Aaron brought up in conversation and not feel a crippling desire to know everything he might have said about me. To be frank, I'd rather be talking about babies.

"I don't really care what Aaron says or does," I reply. "Not anymore. I filed for divorce."

"You *what*?" They chorus.

I shrug. "It's long overdue. Aaron and I aren't getting back together, and I'm tired of living in limbo."

"Wow," Gwen breathes. "I mean, I know you're right, but it just seems so final."

"It was final the day I caught him with Staci. It just took me a while to figure that out."

"I'm not judging you, Cat. I'm proud of you." She steels herself and then declares, "Aaron's an asshole." It's so out of character that Bianca and I are shocked into temporary silence.

Bianca finds her tongue first. "Gwendolyn Jones!" she squawks. "You better not let Jason hear you talking about his bestie like that."

Gwen grins. "It's true, though. He was a bastard to Cat. And if I'm being honest, I can't stand Jason spending time with him. I don't doubt for a second that he's unfaithful to Staci, too, and every time he takes Jason out for a drink I get a sick feeling in my stomach."

"Jason would never cheat on you," I say honestly, even as a kernel of guilt forms in my stomach. Aaron does cheat on Staci – I know, because I've experienced it first-hand.

"I know he wouldn't," Gwen says, "but that doesn't mean I want him hanging around other women through Aaron."

"You should come to dinner with me and Blake. Both of you, with Mike and Jason. They'll like him," I promise. "And maybe, just maybe, we can start our own circle. Blake would never behave like Aaron, he's a good guy. Unless you guys don't want to..." I add, uncertainly, when neither of them respond.

"We totally want to," Bianca clarifies. "We just thought you'd never ask."

"Why do you think we keep coming to dinner?" Bianca says, "and keeping this friendship alive? We've been waiting for you to offer for months."

"I was starting to wonder if Blake really existed, or if he was just someone you made up to make yourself look good," Gwen teases.

"What are you guys talking about? You've met him!"

"Once," she counters. "And for all we know he could've been one of your clients."

I frown. Surely it's been more than that. We had lunch a few months ago, but now that I think about it, I can't recall a single time since then that Blake and my friends were in the same room together. "Really? We've been together over six months."

Bianca gives me a pointed look. "Exactly."

"Right, then, dinner it is. We're starting a new circle. Would the guys go for that?"

"Jason doesn't have a choice," Gwen says. "God knows I have to put up with Staci more often than I care to count."

"Mike will be there," Bianca grins, rubbing at her belly. "Where the baby goes, Mike follows."

17

With all the pieces of my life falling so seamlessly into place, the only dark cloud hanging over my head is the fact that I still haven't spoken to my mother. Blake insists that I should leave it alone, and let her come to me, but the longer we go without speaking, the more I worry about her. Her self-destructive behavior is always worse when she's in an anxious state, and I feel terrible for disclosing that I'm the one who's been buying her paintings. My mother, for all her faults, suffers from crippling self-doubt. I wouldn't be surprised if she never picks up a paintbrush again after this.

My grandparents have seen her, and Grams assures me that she seems fine, but it's hard to believe, considering the source. Grams is a little naïve to my mother's indulgent behavior, and operates on a strict ignorance is bliss policy.

"At least wait until Monday," Blake tells me on Friday night. We're on our way to meet Stephen and his family for dinner, and I'm cradling my phone in my lap, willing it to ring. I've pulled my mother's name up so many times today, but I haven't summoned the courage to hit the call button. "Give her another few days. I know this is eating you up inside, but calling her now and brushing everything that's happened under the rug isn't going to do either of you any favors in the long run."

"I'm worried about her."

He reaches out and gives my knee a squeeze. "I know. But no news is good news, right?"

"True." I shove my phone back into my purse and straighten my shoulders. "It's been this long, what harm could a few more days do?"

We pull up outside the hotel, and a valet steps forward to take care of our parking.

"I can't believe I'm meeting my sister," I tell Blake, as we step into an expensive foyer which smells of orange blossom and money. "What do you think she'll be like?"

"If she's anything like you, she'll be adorable," he says.

IT TURNS out adorable is not a word I'd use to describe Hannah Bennett. We're not even halfway to the table when a streak of red barrels toward me, and a miniature version of myself throws her arms around my neck.

"Catrina!" she shrieks, letting me go for only a second to get a good look at my face, before pinning me in another bear hug. "Oh my God, you look just like me! This is too much, isn't this too much? I can't actually believe it, I swear when dad told me I almost had a shit-fit!" she continues on, but she's speaking so quickly I barely catch a word of it.

"Hannah, language!" a stern voice chides. I look up, to find a slim, attractive woman at Hannah's shoulder. She offers me a smile that doesn't quite meet her eyes. "You must be Catrina," she says, in a practiced voice. "I'm Lucy, Stephen's wife." She holds out her hand, and I disentangle one of my arms to shake it.

"It's really good to meet you, Lucy," I say. Her hand trembles slightly in mine, which I take as a good sign. It means she might be nervous, as opposed to unfriendly.

Hannah releases her vice grip from my neck, but slips her arm through mine and insists on walking beside me. Stephen, on his feet at the table, smiles at the sight.

"You two look even more alike than I thought," he says. He drops a quick kiss on my forehead when I hug him hello, the action as natural as breathing, and then turns to shake Blake's hand. "Nice to see you again, Blake."

"You too, Mr. Bennett."

"Stephen, please. This is my wife, Lucy, and this little firecracker," he adds, ruffling Hannah's hair, "is Hannah."

Hannah ducks away and swats at her middle parting. "Jeez, Dad! Do you mind? I'm sixteen, not six! No, you're not there," she adds, as I start to sit. "You're here, next to me."

"Sweetheart, Catrina can decide where she wants to sit," Lucy says. Hannah gives her an insolent glare.

"Yes, and she wants to sit next to me. Right, Cat?"

I try to stifle my laughter, but Hannah's wicked grin tells me she sees right through me.

"Next to you is perfect," I say. Even Lucy smiles.

IT'S A MAGICAL EVENING. Perhaps it's the sense of family that I've lacked for so long, or just the fact the Bennetts are genuinely nice people, who have embraced me as one of their own, but by the time our main courses arrive, my emotional cup is full. I feel sublimely happy. Until Aaron walks through the door, Staci barnacled to his side.

Blake doesn't notice, or at least, I don't think he does. Aaron's table is behind him and slightly to the left, so unless he turns around the chances are good that he won't. From my seat, however, I have a clear view of them. My euphoria vanishes.

Staci has her back to me. Aaron, on the other hand, looks directly at me as he sits down. For just a second, his face registers shock, and then my stomach clenches as his lips curve upward in a predatory smile. This is exactly the type of situation Aaron gets off on. I did too, not so long ago, but the thought of what's going on inside his head right now makes me sick. Deliberately, I turn my attention back to the others, but I can still feel his eyes boring into me.

I wait until everyone has finished their main course before I make my move.

"Can we trade seats for a bit?" I ask Hannah. "I'd like to talk to Stephen, if that's okay?"

She doesn't bat an eyelid, although Lucy looks slightly alarmed.

"Sure!" Hannah says, getting to her feet so fast she almost upends the table. Then she pauses, a small frown creasing her smooth brow. "Why do you call him that?"

"Who?"

"Dad. You call him Stephen."

The table falls silent, and I feel my cheeks grow hot. I'm sure Stephen doesn't expect me to call him Dad, certainly not so soon, and I'm definitely not comfortable with it either.

"Um..." I trail off, casting a helpless look at Blake, but he seems at a loss for words too. Stephen suddenly develops an intense interest in his own fingernails.

"Hannah, honey," Lucy intervenes gently, "this is all very new, for all of us. Catrina might not be comfortable calling your father Dad just yet."

Or ever, I think to myself, in a panic. It's not that I don't like him, because the opposite is true, but it would feel forced.

Hannah pulls a face, one that I've noticed she uses mostly on her mother. "Whatever. It's weird."

She takes my recently vacated seat and immediately starts bending Blake's ear about surgery, and whether it's anything like you see on *Grey's Anatomy*. Hearing her mention the on-call rooms, I see Blake's ears pink. *Yes*, I could tell her, based on my own experience, *that really does happen*. But I don't, obviously.

"Sorry about that," Stephen says, once he's sure Hannah is fully invested in her conversation and not eavesdropping on ours. "She can be a bit blunt."

"Situation normal for a sixteen-year-old. Trust me, I know. I was impossible at her age."

"Tell me more about your childhood," he says, refilling my glass.

"What do you want to know?" This topic could navigate us into treacherous waters. I answer him as best I can without mentioning my mother, but my answers are superficial at best, and I can tell he's not satisfied.

"I'm just going to use the ladies," I say brightly, needing a reprieve. Stephen and Blake both get to their feet as I do, and I smile at the chivalrous gesture. Hannah makes to follow me, but her mother places a firm hand on her arm.

"Let her at least go to the bathroom in peace," she says firmly.

"I'll be right back," I tell Hannah, and then shoot Lucy a grateful smile.

The bathroom is all white – white tiled floors, white wallpaper with a thin silver foil, and white handtowels, which are disposed of in a white wicker basket beside the sink. I splash some water on my face and dab it dry, careful not to ruin my make-up, and then head back outside. I've only stepped out into the hall when a hand seizes my shoulder and pushes me back up against the wall. It doesn't hurt, but it's rough enough to mean business.

"Aaron!" I gasp, startled out of my wits. "What the hell do you think you're doing?"

"What do you think?" he grins, utterly confident. With his free hand, he pushes open the bathroom door to check if there's anyone inside. I have no doubt that the second he's certain of it, he'll try to maneuver me inside.

I don't give him the opportunity. Wedging both hands between us, I shove at his chest. "Get off me!" Thankfully, the force drives him backward, giving me just enough room to slip past him. I haven't taken two steps when he seizes my wrist.

"Where do you think you're going?" he asks. He strokes the

length of my side with his free hand, from ribs to waist in a playful gesture filled with promise.

"Let me go," I growl, trying to shake him off.

This time, he's genuinely bewildered. Aaron would never hurt me, but he's so used to getting his own way that it would never occur to him that I don't want this. We've played this game for so long my denial may as well be foreplay.

"Get your hands off my daughter." It's a low growl, from not three feet away. We whirl to find Stephen blocking the hall, a menacing look on his face. Aaron drops my hand like a hornet's nest. His head whips from me to Stephen and then back again, in search of answers.

"Your daughter?" he asks, eventually.

"Yes," Stephen says, holding his ground. "My daughter." He offers me his hand, and I snatch hold of it, letting him draw me to the safety of his side. "And who the hell are you?"

Aaron regains a bit of his swagger. "I'm her husband."

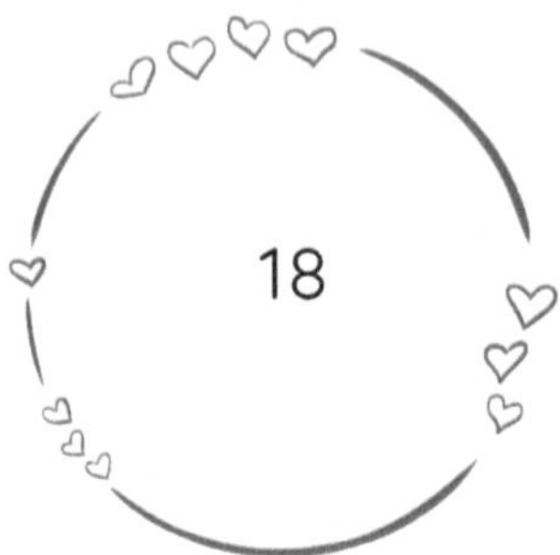

18

Blake is furious. Furious that Aaron was at the restaurant in the first place, furious that he would dare pull such a dirty trick, and mostly, furious that he wasn't there to protect me. Sensing that something was amiss when Stephen and I returned, Lucy had wisely hauled Hannah off to bed right after dessert. Hannah didn't go willingly. Aaron had done the same with Staci, only they'd skipped eating altogether, and Staci didn't put up much of a fight. I don't know what he told her, or if she even knew I was there, not that it matters. By the time Lucy and Hannah had gone, and I'd filled Blake in on what had happened, Aaron had vanished, along with Blake's opportunity to confront him.

"We can't carry on like this," he seethes. His hands are clenched into fists on the table, and I slip my own into them, slowly easing the tension out.

"You're going to need to explain this to me, Cat," Stephen says. His words are gentle, but firm, brooking no room for argument.

I take a deep breath. "Aaron *is* my husband, technically, but I've filed for divorce. We've been separated for over a year." I don't elaborate. There's no way I'm explaining that I was still sleeping with

Aaron up until a few weeks ago. "Aaron had an affair," I say instead, not feeling the least bit guilty that I'm throwing him under the bus. "That's how it ended."

"It didn't look like it had ended," Stephen points out. "At least not from his perspective."

"He's not happy about the divorce. But that doesn't mean he wants us to get back together," I add hastily. "Aaron doesn't want me. He just can't handle the thought of me being with someone else."

"Is he dangerous?" Stephen asks. "I mean, exactly how worried should I be?" The strain in his voice makes me smile. He's acting like a protective dad, and even though this is by far one of the most uncomfortable conversations of my life, it feels nice to be worried about.

"You have nothing to worry about. He's not dangerous, he's just a dick."

"I can handle Aaron," Blake says darkly.

"I'd be more than happy to help," Stephen adds, and they share a look.

"I'm just sorry our evening was ruined," I say sadly. I'm more angry about that than what Aaron did. "I was really enjoying myself."

Stephen manages a small smile. "There'll be plenty more like this. In fact, I've been thinking about a few things. Blake, you mentioned you'll be applying at a number of hospitals? Have you given any thought to California?"

I go rigid in my seat. Stephen must notice because he hastens to explain. "I'm sorry, I'm not telling either of you what to do. I just thought... well, Long Beach is really beautiful in the summer, and to be frank, Cat, I'd love to have you close by. I want to get to know you – to really get to know you, and it'd be a whole lot easier if you weren't four hundred miles away. It's your decision, obviously, but I want you to consider all your options, and know that you have options on the West Coast. You have a family, who would love to have you around." He smiles at me, and it's a smile that tells me how badly he wants this, how desperately he wants me in his life, not only for the occasional weekend, and special occasions, but as a permanent fixture.

So, rather than deny him outright, I find myself saying, "how would Lucy feel about that?"

"DID YOU MEAN WHAT YOU SAID?" Blake asks me on the drive home. "Would you really consider moving to California?"

"I didn't think I would," I admit, "but I'd already decided I'd follow you anywhere, and if anywhere happened to be closer to Stephen, it'd be even better. I don't know," I add, as he gives me a wry look, "I just want to know them. I want to be there, for Hannah especially. I want to be the big sister who offers advice about boys, and who lets her borrow my clothes. I know it sounds corny, but"

"It doesn't sound corny at all," he interrupts. "Family is everything, Cat. You're allowed to want what everyone else takes for granted."

"What about your parents, then?' I challenge. "Shouldn't you be looking for a job in Sacramento?"

"I grew up with my parents," he reminds me, "I haven't missed anything. And it just so happens that two of my hospitals of choice are in California."

"Well in that case," I say, with a surge of delight, "you should definitely apply."

He doesn't bring up Aaron until we're home. I knew he wouldn't let it go for long, but I'm glad he waited until we were curled up on the couch in our pajamas, because I have a plan of my own to get rid of Aaron once and for all, and I know he's not going to like it.

His response is as predictable as it is vehement. "No way. There's no way I'm letting you do that. I'll talk to him. Trust me, when I'm done he'll leave you alone."

I don't doubt that Blake could intimidate Aaron, but the problem is, that I don't. I'm the one who Aaron feels he can push around, and until he learns otherwise, this will never be over.

"You can't be with me twenty-four-seven," I say. "He'll find a way to get me on my own. That's what he does. *I* need to do this. I need to take back my life, not have my boyfriend do it for me."

"You shouldn't have to do anything. You've told him it's over. It should be enough."

"It's more complicated than that." I cringe, because what I mean is that I've told Aaron numerous times that it's over, only to go crawling back to him. It's not surprising that he doesn't believe me now - I'm like the little boy who cried wolf. Blake's scowl assures me that he knows exactly what I mean, but he holds his tongue.

"I *want* to do this, Blake. I'm *going* to do it. For me, not for you," I add meaningfully. "I'm not asking for your permission, but I would like your approval."

He exhales a resigned breath. "So long as we're clear, I don't like it."

I poke him between the ribs. "Oh come on. You like it a little bit."

He gives me an arch look. "I really don't."

"It's nothing less than he deserves," I say. "It's high time Aaron had a taste of his own medicine."

I HAVE to wait a week to put my plan into action. Now that I've made the decision, I want to get it over with as soon as possible, especially after the two text messages that I get from Aaron over the weekend, which I don't tell Blake about. I meant what I said to Blake, about taking my life back, but he has no idea just how deep my resolve lies. He could never fully understand how much Aaron has taken from me over the years – how he chipped away at my self-confidence, at my sense of self-worth. How he played on my vulnerability and my desperate need to feel loved. Aaron didn't give a damn about how my mother treated me, it only made me that much more malleable, like putty in his hands. And his affection was my reward for good behavior, the sick bastard. Aaron twisted me into something ugly, but now that Blake has shown me that I'm worthy of being loved, I'm learning to love myself again. I am no longer Aaron's plaything. He's taken too much, and, in just a few days, I get to take it all back. To be free of him once and for all.

ON MONDAY MORNING, just as I'm bracing myself for the dreaded phone call to my mother, I get a call from Trish at the gallery.

"Catrina, you're an extremely valued client," she begins, after the pleasantries are over. "I thought long and hard about making this call, but I realized I have no choice."

"What is it?" I ask with a sigh. "Did another Viola Davis painting come in?"

"Actually, more than one," Trish says, but before I can express my surprise, she's talking again. "I am so very sorry to have to tell you this, but Viola has issued strict instruction that you are not permitted to buy any more of her work. I don't know how she found out," she adds quickly, defending her gallery, and her reputation, "I can promise you I would never disclose an anonymous buyer's information."

"It's okay," I say, letting her off the hook. "I know you didn't tell her."

"I can't think why she would want to exclude such a fan of her work," Trish tuts. I'm pretty sure her disappointment has more to do with the commission she's going to lose, than my lack of access to Viola's paintings, but it's sincere, nonetheless. "Such a pity, too," Trish sighs, "as the showcase opened today. I just wanted to let you know before you read about it in the papers."

"What are you talking about? What showcase?"

"The Viola Davis exhibition. I assumed you'd have heard, given what a huge fan you are of her work."

"You're exhibiting her work? Like, a full exhibition, not just a single painting?"

"Yes. She brought them in a few weeks ago and we signed her up immediately. Even I have to admit, they're incredible. So different from her usual work, but utterly captivating. Perhaps if I spoke to her again"

But I don't wait to hear what Trish proposes, and I end the call without another word. I'm already walking out of my apartment, snatching up my purse as I go. I catch a cab and bite agonizingly at my nails as we get stuck behind one slow-moving vehicle after another. I tap my foot impatiently, cursing my bad luck. Eventually, when we're only a few blocks away, I tell the cabbie to stop, and I hand over the fare. It'll be quicker to walk the rest of the way.

A GORGEOUS SIGNBOARD sits outside the gallery entrance, heralding the exhibition of incredible local talent, Viola Davis. Seeing my mother's name in print, validated by such a respected establishment, brings tears of pride to my eyes. I slip inside behind a tall, bespectacled man carrying a camera bag. A press pass hangs from the lanyard around his neck. Trish is busy with a customer, and another is waiting in line. I keep my head down and turn my back to her, while surreptitiously scanning the walls.

"Holy shit," I breathe, forgetting that I'm supposed to be hiding from Trish. I turn a full 360 degrees, my eyes feasting on the riot of color which adorns the walls. A bunch of lilies in full bloom, in a cracked bottle-green vase. A pink buckled bicycle, with streamers made of old newspaper, rippling in the wind. A rusted swing set, with an apricot silk scarf where the chain should be. An overgrown lawn, rampant with sunflowers. A silver station wagon, the fender dented. And in every single one, a redheaded child. I'm watering the lilies with an ancient, rusted watering can. Riding the bicycle, in a white broderie anglaise dress, red braids flying behind me, parallel to the makeshift streamers. I'm on the swing, feet pointed toward the sky, reaching higher than ever. I know that not five minutes later, the apricot scarf will rip, and I will crash to the ground in a heap, my wrist broken. I'm walking between the sunflowers, my eyes alight with wonder as I peer up at them, my hand brushing the green stalks.

In the station wagon, I'm kissing a boy. He has blond hair and glasses, and I recognize him even though his face is in shadow. Neil O'Donnell, my first kiss.

My mother has painted my entire childhood, in frenzied, vibrant strokes. My life in color, a poignant reminder of details I'd long forgotten. I turn again, taking in every painting. I grow older, holding the hand of a man with a brittle smile and cold eyes. I marry him. The dress is beautiful, my face is not. Instead, I wear a halo of tears, and an expression of pain. I'm in a hospital bed, pale against the stark white sheets, but beautiful now. I'm smiling up at a man with a stethoscope around his neck. I turn on the spot, rotating slowly as I take in every exquisite detail, every truth my mother has laid bare on canvas, and my legs start to tremble beneath me.

"Catrina?" Trish's voice seems to be coming from far away. My head begins to pound, dark spots flickering in my peripheral vision. The girl in the paintings is smiling. Then she's not. My knees hit the hardwood floor. "Catrina!" Trish is at my side, frantic. My shoulders heave, wracking sobs consuming everything. "Call an ambulance!" Trish yells.

"No," I croak, shaking my head. Tears flow freely down my cheeks, blurring the sight of those beautiful, beautiful paintings. *She remembers.*

"Catrina, I need you to talk to me," Trish insists, her hands on my face, pulling it toward her. Through my tears, I smile, and then, as the beast which has been sitting on my chest, crushing me for years, unfurls itself, my tears give way to laughter.

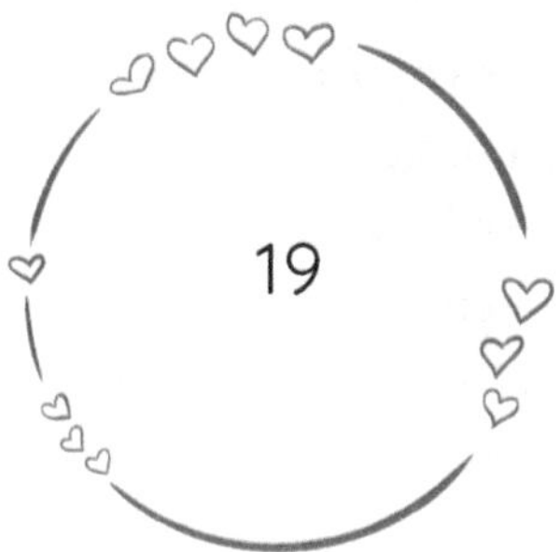

19

"Cat!" Blake bellows, when he sees me being wheeled into the E.R on a stretcher. "What the hell happened?" I'm laughing, and crying, and far too hysterical to answer, so the kind-faced paramedic named Paul, who'd held my hand in the ambulance while I poured my heart out, does it for me.

"She's fine, she's just had a bit of an emotional breakdown."

Blake is at my side, his face assessing mine. "Let's get her into a bed." He leads the way to a private room, then lifts me off the stretcher and onto the bed. "Thanks for your help," he tells the paramedics.

"Just doing our job," Paul replies. His associate leaves without a word, but before he goes, Paul gives me a brief pat on the leg. "You look after yourself, Miss."

"I'll be right back," Blake tells me. He steps into the hall to speak to the nurse on duty in a low voice. I hear her raised protests, but Blake cuts her off. "I need ten minutes." He's back almost immediately, closing the door behind him. He stands over me, his eyes filled with concern. "What happened?" he murmurs softly. "Is it Aaron? Did something happen?"

I shake my head, no.

"Your mom?"

I nod, and promptly burst into fresh tears, which galvanize Blake into action. He opens a cabinet on the far side of the room and roots around for a minute before withdrawing a syringe and a small vial.

"I'm going to give you something, okay? To calm you down."

I manage another bob of my head.

"I'm sorry Cat, but I need your verbal consent."

"Yes." My voice is hoarse, and barely audible, but it's all he needs. He rolls me gently onto my side and I feel the prick of the needle in my backside.

The effect is instantaneous. A warm, fuzziness spreads from the source of the jab to envelop my whole body, and I slump back on the bed. I feel as though I've just woken up, or am just about to fall asleep. It's a heady calm.

"Wow. That's lovely."

"It packs quite a punch," Blake agrees. He disposes of the needle and comes to sit beside me on the bed. I scoot over to make room, but my movements feel sluggish and uncoordinated.

"Tell me what happened," he says. And this time, I do. It takes some time, and I shed a few more tears, but I get it out eventually.

"What do you think it means?" he asks gently when I'm done. I think he already knows the answer, but he wants me to say it.

"I think, in her own way, my mother loves me."

His smile is dazzling. "I think she does, too," he says, pulling me against his chest. I bury my face in his scrubs. "Do you remember that night I drove her home?"

"Mmmm," I murmur.

"I lied to you. I told you that nothing she said would make you feel better, but that wasn't true. I just didn't want to tell you because I thought it would be best if you heard it from her."

I lift my face to meet his gaze. "What did she say?"

"A lot. But in a nutshell, that the real reason she didn't want you to meet your father, was because she was terrified of losing you."

I think about how quickly I'd been ready to pack up and move to Long Beach. "She wasn't wrong. After everything she's done, Stephen seemed like a knight in shining armor."

"He's your father, Cat. He cares about you. It's not an act. And I do still think it would be good for you to get out of this place. To leave all the bullshit behind and start afresh."

"But?"

His chest rises and falls beneath my hand. "But I think it would destroy you to abandon Viola. No matter what she's done."

"You're saying I should stay?"

"I'm saying we should figure out what's best for both of us before we make any decisions."

He's right, as usual.

THE VIOLA DAVIS exhibition sold out in under a week. Trish, having finally discovered my true identity, texted me to let me know that the gallery was planning another in the fall. I still haven't spoken to my mother, but Grams let me know that she'd asked to move back home, just for a couple of months, to "get her stuff together" as Grams so eloquently put it. I'd decided to give her space. If she wanted to talk to me, she would. Even after the revelation of seeing her paintings, I didn't reach out. I was working through my demons, and she needed to work through hers. I could only hope that she'd be ready to talk when she had. I suspected she would. It's what I would do, and I was, after all, my mother's child. For now, I was just taking things one day at a time. And today, it just so happens that I face my final hurdle. The final barrier between me and my new life. I'd waited longer than a week, but as I had so recently learned, late was always better than never.

I CLIMB the steps to Aaron's apartment with a clear head and a clear conscience. He started texting me again after the night he'd seen me with my father. I'd read every single one, letting his words fuel the flame of my determination. He'd also fired back a legal letter to my attorneys. He was contesting the divorce. That had been the final nail in his coffin.

I lift my hand to the door to knock. Two short taps, followed by a pause. Another single tap. Our secret code. Aaron's face blazes triumphant as he jerks open the door.

"Kitty Cat," he croons. "What took you so long?"

I don't make it easy for him. He'd see through that. I stride inside and fix him with the most furious look I can muster.

"This has gone on long enough, Aaron," I snap, dumping my purse on the dining table. "You need to sign the papers. I'm not going to ask you again."

"How's your doctor friend?" he asks, blatantly ignoring me. "I do hope I didn't cause too much trouble when last we met."

I cock my head and regard him levelly.

"Actually, you didn't. Blake moved in last weekend."

The spark flares in his eyes. Anger, because Blake has moved in on his territory. Lust, because Blake still wants me.

"You really shouldn't lead him on like that, Cat." His eyes are roaming the length of my body. My outfit, so carefully selected, for the tightness of the blouse and the short length of the skirt, is taking effect.

"Just sign the God-damned papers, Aaron."

"Fine," he says. I stand rooted to the spot. This wasn't what I'd anticipated. "If," Aaron croons, and I exhale in relief, "you give me one last kiss."

"I'm not playing this game."

"Aw, come on. What harm could it do? If you're so obviously over me, and you really want this divorce, what difference would one little kiss make? We could call it a goodbye."

"Fine," I snap. "If that's what it takes, what the hell. But you swear you'll sign the papers?"

He holds up his hand. "Scout's honor."

"You could never be a boy scout, Aaron." I take a steadying breath and walk toward him. He stays where he is, lounging against the back of the couch, his hands in his pockets. Bastard. When I'm only inches away, I lean forward and kiss him chastely on the cheek.

"There. Happy now?"

"Not a chance, sweetheart." He's really enjoying himself now. "I know your boyfriend's probably as vanilla as they come, but surely you haven't forgotten everything I taught you."

"Aaron."

"A deal's a deal, Cat. Unless deep down, you don't really want me to sign those papers?"

Furiously, I reach up and seize him around the neck, before sliding my fingers up into his hair. I yank a fistful, hard enough that it brings tears to his eyes, and Aaron hisses.

"That's better," he sneers. "Perhaps you haven't forgot"

I don't let him finish. I'm already pressing my lips to his, parting them instantly as his tongue darts out to sweep my mouth. Aaron groans, low and deep in his throat, and then his arms come around me. I can feel his need, straining against his zipper. Without warning, he shoves his hands beneath the waistband of my skirt and slides them over my backside, lower and lower, until his fingers brush my core. I leap back, shoving at his chest so hard he almost falls backward over the couch.

"What the hell, Cat?" he thunders.

I give him a pained look, my chest heaving. "Stay away from me," I croak.

Comprehension dawns on his face and his own lips curve upward. "Why? Are you struggling to keep your hands to yourself, sweetheart? Where's all that fiery determination now?"

"Just sign the papers, Aaron." But it's useless. He knows he's got me exactly where he wants me, and he stalks toward me like a predator advancing on its prey.

I try one last time. "Please let me go."

"Not a chance. You belong to *me*." His eyes are liquid with desire, and my pulse is racing frantically as I try to find an escape route.

"There's nowhere to run," Aaron taunts, drawing so close that I can smell his cologne. "And even if there was, what are you running from? You'll never find this with anyone else. Let me love you, Cat. You know how good it'll be." At that, he reaches for me, his big hands lifting me clear off my feet before he traps me against his chest. "What are you going to do now?" he asks, his eyes probing mine. Beneath the challenge glimmering in the blue depths, there's tenderness too. In his own twisted way, Aaron does love me, but it's not the love I need. Not anymore.

"I don't know," I whisper. "What am I going to do now, Aaron?" My chest is still heaving, rubbing against his own with every inhalation. His mouth crashes down onto mine, and I resist for only a second before I melt against him. I arch my body against his, our tongues engaged in frantic swordplay. I fumble for his shirt and pull it over his head. The brief moment our lips are parted is too long, and he claims my mouth again immediately, even as he kicks off his pants.

My groan is his undoing. He yanks at my clothing, his hands warm against my bare skin.

"Slowly," I breathe into his mouth. His answering groan is pained. I kiss his neck, then trace circles with my tongue, moving lazily lower, down his neck, over the hollow of his throat. His hands are everywhere, touching every inch of me he can reach, but I twist away, playing coy, making him work for it. He's becoming frantic, his fingers biting into my soft skin, and I'm starting to worry that it will all be over too quickly, when finally, mercifully, I hear the door open behind me.

Aaron's expression, as he catches sight of Staci, is priceless. It's Friday, after all. She shouldn't be back for hours. But it had taken just one call from me, half an hour ago, for her to hurry home.

I don't wait for Staci's wrath. With a small smile up at Aaron, I scoop up my clothes, wrap my coat around myself, and retrieve my purse from the table.

"Aaron refuses to give me a divorce," I tell Staci as I pass her on my way to the door. I pluck the letter from his attorney from my purse and hand it to her. She doesn't look at it. She only has eyes for Aaron, naked and guilty, standing immobile with shock.

"I was so sure you were lying." Her voice is small, and filled with pain.

"I'm sorry," I say. And I am. Not that she had to find out, but because I know she loves him.

"You bitch!" Aaron yells, regaining his voice only slightly too late, as I step out into the hall.

I EMERGE ONTO THE STREET, the weight of Aaron's hold over me gone. He will never hurt me again, never make me feel inferior, or that I'm not worthy of being loved for anything beyond my body and the things that I can do with it. He knows now, the lengths I will go to if he tries to force my hand again. As if on cue, Blake pushes off the pick-up and comes toward me, his eyes scanning me for any sign of ill-treatment.

"How did it go?" he asks. I know how badly it hurts him to know that Aaron has touched me, so I keep my distance, planting my heels a few feet away. It'll take a bit of time for him to be okay, but I'm not going anywhere. We have all the time in the world. Blake didn't want me to do this - hated that I was doing it, but ultimately, he understood that it wasn't just about Aaron getting caught. It was about humiliating him the way he had me for so long, and reclaiming my sense of self.

"He won't be bothering us anymore," I say.

Blake releases a slow breath and then a smile, honest and beautiful, creases his face. He takes in the crumpled ball of clothing in my hands, and his gaze lowers to the buttons of my coat. The knot in my stomach unravels under the intensity of that gaze as he reaches out his hands and loops them through the belt of my coat, pulling me toward him. So much for my theory that he'd take some time to get over it, I think wildly, as he pulls me in for a long, lingering kiss.

"Let's go home," he says when we break apart. His voice is hoarse. A sign just ahead catches my eye, and I lean over and toss my clothes into the front seat of the car. We're both acutely aware that I'm wearing nothing beneath the cream cashmere.

"I've got a better idea," I say, taking his hand. "Let's go get a drink."

END OF BOOK 3.

AWKWARD IN TROUBLE

BOOK 4 OF THE AWKWARD SERIES

"Chloe is such a slut!" Megan announces, dropping into the chair beside me and taking a huge swig of champagne. I follow the line of her narrowed gaze to where the company secretary is dancing on a black-boxed speaker, her hands roving all over her body, while most of the IT department gather eagerly around to watch.

"I wouldn't talk if I were you, Megs. She's not the one banging the boss."

"Shhhh!" Megan casts a furious glance around, checking that no-one is within earshot. "I've put an end to all that crap!"

"Since when?"

"I made a resolution yesterday morning."

"It's been a whole forty-eight hours? I'm impressed."

"This time I mean it," she insists and, although I know better, I find myself hoping that she does. Megan and I have been inseparable, ever since we both joined the sales department for Focus Media four years ago. Focus is an advertising company and, between us, Megan and I handle public relations, advertising, and media marketing for some of the biggest firms in the country. Megs is the complete opposite of me, and not only in character. She is dark where I am fair, and her blue-black hair is long and sleek, a shiny curtain that falls halfway down her back, whereas my hair is white-blonde and cut in a messy bob. I was going for get-up-and-go, but most days my hair gets up and goes without me. I've been trying to grow it out.

Megan's eyes are the color of chocolate – the real dark stuff, not the cheap kind. My own are a dirty Smurf blue, and, given that they dominate most of my face, could really afford to be a bit more impressive.

We both gaze across at Chloe as her performance increases in tempo.

"Dave the whizz-kid has the most enormous hard-on," Megan remarks drily, and I give a screech of laughter. Dave looks a bit like Steve Carrell in the *40-year-old Virgin,* and he has the personality to match. I don't think he's ever had a girlfriend. Megan laughs along with me until Jack Pendleton enters the room. Then she sobers instantly, leaving me cackling alone like a maniacal hyena. I give her a kick under the table but miss, stubbing my toe on the table leg instead.

Jack is the Company Director, young for the position at thirty-seven, married with two children – aged seven and nine – and too handsome for his own good. He glances around the room, shakes his head at Chloe, who has progressed to a spectacularly uncoordinated floss, and then his eyes come to rest on Megan.

"Don't do it," I murmur, thinking that if the heat in Jack's gaze is anything to go by, Megan's resolution is about to go up in flames.

"Oh God, I can't help it, Emma!" she sounds forlorn as Jack looks away. "I mean, *look* at him."

"He's married, Megs," I point out.

"Not happily."

"They all say that when they want leg-over. Ask him to leave his wife."

"He can't. He says he couldn't bear to leave the kids, at least not while they're so young."

"God, what a cliché." I take a slug of champagne. It's not that I don't respect my boss. Jack is an extremely astute businessman, and he is fair and pays us well. I do respect him, I just don't like him very much, and I hate that he has this hold over Megan. I can understand the physical attraction, given that Jack looks like a young Benedict Cumberbatch, but I know it's not going to end well.

"Hey, new guy!" Megan shrieks, and I turn my head to see the new sales executive who joined the company last week, making his way toward us. He hasn't been assigned to a team yet, so the jury's still out as to which Accounts Manager he will be reporting to.

"Hi Megan, Emma," he nods at each of us in turn and then pulls up a chair.

I return his smile. "It's Oliver, right?"

"At least one of you remembers." His hazel eyes crinkle at the corners when he smiles.

"New guy has a nice ring to it, I think," Megan teases. "But if you insist, Oliver it is."

Oliver chuckles as he leans over and refills our glasses. He's probably only a year or two older than I am, twenty-nine, thirty at most. He has nice hands, I note, as he sets the champagne bottle back in the ice bucket. I notice hands. Hands and eyes. And Oliver has a nice pair of both.

"Are office functions always like this?" he asks, gesturing over his shoulder at Chloe, who is now weaving around Dave like a Siamese cat on poppers.

"With *her*, it's always like this," Megan says. "I suggest you keep your head down, Oliver. Chloe loves fresh meat."

"Thanks for the warning." He grins again, and I find myself smiling too.

Megan has stopped paying attention. Once again, I follow the line of her gaze and I'm not surprised to find Jack at the end of it. He inclines his head discreetly toward the door and without waiting for confirmation, walks through it. I've barely opened my mouth when Megan is on her feet.

"Do me a favor and keep Emma company," she tells Oliver, swooping up the half-empty champagne bottle. "There's something I need to take care of." She winks conspiratorially at me and heads for the door.

Oliver watches her leave, a bemused expression on his face. "What was that about?"

I shake my head, draining my glass. "It's safer not to ask."

"Right." He flags down a passing waiter and orders another bottle of champagne and a light beer.

"So, are you married?" he asks, but it sounds more as though he is simply making pleasant conversation than prying.

"Divorced." I hold up my bare left hand as proof.

"Ah," he holds up his own. "Snap."

"What happened?" I ask.

"She left me for someone like Chloe." His face is deadpan, and I choke back my laughter until I see the amusement in his eyes.

"I'm sorry." I don't really know how to respond, but he just shrugs.

"I'm not, although I was a little jealous at first. Her girlfriend had the most incredible boobs."

"They could've at least given you a preview."

"That's what I said."

"Do you have any children?" I ask.

"No, thank God." His eyes widen as the obvious thought occurs to him. "You?" he asks, far more somber.

"One. A little girl – Alyssa. She's four."

"Beautiful name," he says, accepting the bottle from the waiter and setting it in the empty bucket.

"Thank you. It suits her."

"What happened?"

I take a moment to consider the question. My standard response is a simple, "it didn't work out" but the champagne has loosened my tongue.

"He drank too much."

"Ah," he nods thoughtfully, although there is no fake pity in his honest, open gaze. "My dad was an alcoholic. It's a disease, they can't really help themselves."

"I know, but when you have a child to consider, your tolerance goes out the window."

"Understandably." He raises his beer. "Well, here's to new beginnings for both of us."

"I'll drink to that."

An hour later, with the buzz of the champagne still warming my body, I cast a quick glance around for Megan. She's still missing – as is Jack. So much for Megan's resolution. I check my watch. It's time I checked on Alyssa. "I need to fetch my purse," I say.

Oliver gets to his feet a second before I do, old-school manners on full display. "I'll walk with you."

"No need. I need to make a call anyway. I'll be right back."

My office is down the hall, only a few doors down from Jack's, and I tiptoe toward it, praying I don't meet Megan and Jack on the way out. Jack's door is closed, his blinds drawn, and I heave a sigh as I retrieve my purse from under my desk. I'm bent over, my ass to the door when I hear a throat being cleared.

"Emma."

I whirl around to find Jack standing behind me, with an extremely attractive man at his side. Taking only a second to appreciate his tall, athletic build, mussed up blond hair and tanned face, and a few more to accept that he no doubt got an eyeful of my ass, I quickly turn my attention back to my boss. He looks agitated, and a small muscle is going in his cheek. I daren't ask him where Megan is, not with this stranger standing here.

"Yes, Jack?" I ask politely.

"Emma, this is Gregory Daniels. Greg, this is Emma Johnson. Emma handles the Nanosec account." He gives me a look that I assume is supposed to mean something important, but the champagne has addled my brain. Jack raises his eyebrows at me. "Mr. Daniel's company, Trivia, has just bought out Nanosec."

Oh! The penny drops. The new CEO of Nanosec, a company that spends over four million dollars a year with Focus. Nanosec is one of my key accounts which means that this man is now my biggest customer. What the hell is he doing at a private Focus function?

"I invited Greg to stop by and enjoy the festivities," Jack tells me, as if reading the question from my mind, "and I thought I'd introduce you."

I drop my purse on my desk, smile warmly and I extend my hand. "It's lovely to meet you, Mr. Daniels."

"Greg, please." He takes my hand, still cold from clutching my champagne glass, in his own, and it warms instantly. His green eyes hold my gaze for slightly longer than what I would deem appropriate and then dip almost imperceptibly to my chest.

"Greg," I correct, withdrawing my hand and feeling flustered. "I was actually going to give you a call tomorrow to set up an introductory meeting for next week."

"Next week sounds good," he nods, but his eyes are dancing with amusement. "Just give my secretary a call, and she'll set it up."

"Absolutely." I keep the smile plastered on my face. "I'll do that."

He gives me the ghost of a wink. "I look forward to it." He shakes my hand once more and then he excuses himself. As soon as he's out of earshot, Jack turns back to me.

"Emma," he begins, sounding sterner than usual, "there's something else I wanted to discuss with you. I'm afraid Megan Harris has been dismissed, her employment with Focus terminated with immediate effect. I am only telling you this now, *in confidence*," he continues as I open my mouth to interrupt, "because I know that you two are close." That's the understatement of the century – Megan is my best friend. "I do not want a scene," Jack warns, "and I expect you to handle this situation in the professional manner that you would display were it any other employee here at Focus."

"Why is she being let go?" I demand, keeping my voice low. Jack will not meet my eyes, and suddenly, I know. "Your wife found out, didn't she?" I hiss.

That gets his attention. "Emma," he warns, his voice low and threatening. "This has nothing to do with you. I am only telling you because I understand that your relationship with Megan may result in her confiding in you. However," he draws himself up to his full height, "you would do well to remember that I am your boss. And you will conduct yourself accordingly, or you will be charged with insubordination."

"This is bullshit!" I snap, knowing that there is not a damn thing I can do about it. "Megan is damned good at her job, and you know it!"

I'm surprised to see a flash of regret cross his features before his mask slips back into place.

"She is," he concedes, "and I'm not a monster, Emma. I have found Megan another position, she'll be on the same package, have the same benefits. In fact, she's been put on a higher commission structure, so this move will be good for her."

"Good for her?" I gape at him. "Really? How is losing her job good for her? And commission means nothing if you don't have any clients. She's worked her ass off to build up a base, and you're taking it away from her."

"Like you said, she's good at her job. She'll recover quickly," he insists. "And her salary won't change."

I can't even formulate a response, so I simply glare at him.

"I didn't want things to end up this way," he sighs. "But I have no choice."

"That didn't stop you before. You chose to have an affair without any scruples, so why let your conscience lead you now."

"Emma." It's my second warning, but I'm too angry to care.

"No, Jack, you know that I'm right. If Susan needs proof that it's over between you and Megan, why don't you leave instead?"

"That's not how things work."

"Really? And your wife dictating who you fire – is that how it works?"

"I never meant for it to end this way," he says, "but I will not sacrifice my marriage for a random fling."

I shake my head. "You're disgusting. You used Megan, and now she's paying the price."

"Megan was a mistake." He sounds as though he's trying to convince himself. "And this conversation is over. I will see you tomorrow." Before I can say another word, he turns on his heel and strides out of my office.

Fuming, I snatch up my purse and follow suit. I need to find Megan. I'm barely out of the door when I run straight into Oliver, who is holding two half-full glasses of champagne, the front of his shirt dripping with the balance.

"Oh my God, I'm so sorry!" I clap a hand to my mouth.

"That's okay," he shrugs, "I needed a hosing down, it's pretty hot in here."

"Seriously, Oliver, I'm really sorry," I stammer, grabbing a pack of wipes from my purse and pressing one against his sodden shirt.

"You keep those in your purse?" he asks lazily, his eyes crinkling again.

"I'm a mom, remember," I say, dabbing at his chest. "There, that's the best I can do."

He holds up the glasses. "I guess we'll need to refill these."

"I'm sorry, I can't. I have to go."

"Right now?" he asks, raising his eyebrows in surprise.

"Right now," I nod, stuffing the wipes back into my purse. "I'll see you on Monday."

I LET myself into Megan's apartment with the key she gave me two years ago when she got tired of letting me in, and dump my purse unceremoniously on the table in the hall. The smell of champagne hits me as the sodden wipes tumble out of it. Muffled sobs come from Megan's bedroom.

Her dress has hitched up over her thighs, black lace panties on clear display. They're the kind you wear to be seen.

"He's a miserable son of a bitch," I say as I climb onto the double bed beside her and stroke her hair. Her body is wracked with sobs, her pillow soaked through. "You can take him to court, you know."

"No," she mumbles, wiping her face on the pillow and raising her head to look at me. Her brown eyes are bloodshot and her make up is smeared all down her face. I get up and cross to the vanity, soaking a cotton pad with cleansing cream.

"Sit," I instruct, and she gets up, crossing her legs beneath her and closing her eyes as I clean her face.

"I can't do that," she admits eventually.

"Why not?"

"Because it's not his fault."

"Oh, so it's yours?" I ask, anger flaring in my chest.

"No. Maybe. I don't know. I should have listened to you, Em. You told me this was going to happen."

"What did happen, exactly?"

"Susan found an old email I sent him. It was..." she pauses, trying to find the right word before she settles on "colorful." I can only imagine. "Apparently she went berserk, threw a stack of dinner plates at him and then demanded he get rid of me or she would take him to the cleaners."

"So, what, now he thinks she's just going to forgive him?" I snort with derision. "That if he does what she says they're just going to go back to playing happy family? That's never going to happen."

"You really think so?" Her face lights up with hope, and I toss the cotton pad aside.

"Megs!" I wail, "You're still hung up on him? Even after this!" I can't believe her. Jack just fired her, and she would still have him back in a heartbeat. She buries her face back in her pillow.

"I think I'm in love with him," she says in a small voice.

"Oh, Megan!" I feel helpless, unable to find the words to ease her pain.

"Where's he sending you?" I ask, after a long silence.

"Carter & Boyd." She lies down and stares at the ceiling. I do the same, and we lie side by side.

"Carter & Boyd are direct opposition to Focus," I say. "Why would he do that? Why would he risk you taking business away from his own company?"

"He wants what's best for me," she sniffs. "I know you think he's awful, Em, and I don't blame you, but you didn't see him. He was devastated. He blames himself, says he's screwed up my career. He wants me to have the same opportunities I would have had if this hadn't happened."

I contemplate this for a while, saying nothing. It's a pretty grand gesture for Jack to make. He's hurting himself by sending someone as good as Megan into the opposition's hands. Maybe he's not as cruel as I thought. At the very least I might be able to tolerate being in the same room as him, which is not something I could avoid if I want to keep my job. And I really love my job.

It's after midnight when I finally feel that Megan has calmed down enough for me to leave her. I promise to check on her first thing tomorrow, and then I wearily descend the stairs from her apartment and hail a cab to take me home. I pay the sitter, pull on my old comfy sleep shirt, and climb into bed beside Alyssa. I pull her tiny warm body against mine and breath in her sweet scent – a mix of talcum powder, fabric softener and pure innocence. As always, it calms me, cementing me in this moment and overriding all the stress of my day. I kiss her cheek before closing my eyes, and then I drift off to sleep.

"Coffee," Oliver announces the following morning as he sets a Starbucks-emblazoned paper cup on my desk.

"You are a saint," I reach for it and scald my tongue with the first sip. "Who's bright idea was it to have the party right in the middle of the week, anyway?"

"You left in a hurry. Did you take the party elsewhere?"

I shake my head. "I wish. I had to leave for another reason. Girlfriend in need."

"Ah," he waves his own coffee in the air. "My ex-wife had that problem often. Although in her case, it was a little more literal." He heads out the door to his own office, and I smile despite myself.

I check my emails, and I am surprised to see one from Greg Daniels, sent at six this morning.

EMMA,

Further to our conversation last night, I propose we meet tomorrow (Friday) at 10.00 am. Please advise if this is acceptable to you.

Regards

Greg Daniels
CEO
Nanosec Technologies

Tomorrow? I thought we had agreed to meet next week. I quickly check my diary. I'm supposed to be an at internal sales meeting at 11, but I know Jack won't mind if I miss it.

Dear Greg,
10.00 am is perfect, thank you for setting aside the time to see me.
Regards,
Emma Johnson
Key Accounts Executive
Focus Media International

I HIT send and check the rest of my emails, replying to each and making notes on those that I need to give more thought to. I wait a few minutes, but nothing new comes through, and so I pencil the meeting in my diary and pick up the telephone to make two calls. The first is to let Jack know that I won't be at the meeting tomorrow. The second is to check on Megs.

"Hey." Her voice is hoarse from crying.

"Hey," I reply, as brightly as I can manage, "how are you feeling?"

"Like crap."

"I'm sorry." It seems like such an insignificant thing to say.

"It gets worse," she sighs, "Jack's wife called me."

"Susan? What did she say?"

"She wants to meet me."

"Oh God, Megs. What did you tell her?"

"That I don't think that's a good idea," she sighs again, and my heart hurts for her. Megan is one of the happiest people I know. Usually.

"Have you spoken to Jack about it?"

"I can't. I'm terrified to call him in case she's around or sees the call register."

"Why don't you call the office?"

"No, I'm paranoid now. She could have spies anywhere. What if she's spoken to Chloe? Chloe hates me anyway, and even if Susan hasn't got her clutches in there, Chloe would think it's weird me calling, particularly after being fired. She'd probably tell the whole office."

"You're right," I admit. That's exactly what Chloe would do.

"Maybe you could...?" Megan lets the question hang, and I shake my head, even though she can't see me.

"No, Megs! I can't. Please, I don't want to get in the middle of this."

"I know it's difficult for you, but I just really need to ask his advice on how to handle it." Megan knows exactly how to push my buttons and play on my sympathy.

"I'll see what I can do." I concede, knowing I'm going to regret it.

"Thanks, Em. I really appreciate it."

"I'll chat to you later." I hang up and get back to work, wondering how on earth I am going to keep my promise to Megan as well as my own job.

Determined to research Greg Daniels as thoroughly as possible before our meeting tomorrow, I open a new browser window. It takes me less than a minute to sign into my Facebook account and another twenty seconds to find Greg's profile. It's set to private, so I can't see much, but I zoom in on his profile picture. He's on a mountain bike, covered in mud, and he's giving the cameraman two thumbs up. I click on the photos tab and a handful of images come up. A group of people in a white-water raft, one toppling out of the side as a wave of water hits the prow. A photo of Greg skydiving, his cheeks oddly distorted by the updraft. More cycling pictures, one where he is surrounded by a group of smiling women each wearing a matching pink shirt. I zoom in on the photo to read the words emblazoned on their shirt pockets: *Dirty Angels*. What the hell?

The more I look, the more I realize that I have nothing in common with Greg Daniels. He's a super-fit, super-competitive, over-achiever. I prefer my achievers moderately adequate, and my idea of exercise is leaping over discarded Lego while cleaning the house.

Green tea, I think wryly. I bet he drinks green tea and snacks on Goji berries. In an act of defiance, I take a huge gulp of my coffee. It's ice cold.

I'm so absorbed in my stalking that I almost miss it when my phone pings. It's a text from Megan: *Did you speak to him?* I gaze dejectedly out of the window, then I push back my chair and head out of the door, taking a sharp left turn.

"Come in," Jack barks when I knock on his office door. I push it open and stand uncertainly in the doorway. Jack is at his desk, bent over a stack of paperwork and scribbling furiously, but he glances up when I enter and peers at me over his reading glasses.

"What is it?" He asks suspiciously. Usually, I just buzz him from my office like I had earlier.

"Um..." I take a few steps into the office, closer to his desk, "Jack, I was wondering if I could ask you a question. It's about Megan."

"I thought I made this clear to you last night, Emma," Jack interrupts furiously. "Megan is no longer employed by the Focus Group, and I have no wish to discuss this matter any further."

"It's not that – I mean, I'm not here to try and get her job back or anything." I wave my hands helplessly in the air. "She asked me to come," I say eventually. "Your wife called her."

Jack gets up without a word and closes the door. He takes off his glasses and pinches the bridge of his nose. "Susan called her?"

"Yes. She wants Megan to meet with her, and Megan obviously doesn't know what to do. She doesn't want to cause any more trouble."

"How is she holding up?" His voice has lost all trace of irritation. Now, he sounds weary and concerned.

"She's your wife, you'd know better than I."

"Not Susan. Megan. How is Megan doing?"

The question is so unexpected it throws me for a loop. "She's okay," I reply. "She just wants to speak to you. I think she'd want that even if Susan wasn't hounding her for a meeting, though," I say pointedly, my message crystal clear. Jack smiles, and it's the saddest thing I've ever seen.

"Tell her to go ahead and meet Susan," he says, to my utter surprise. "I know my wife," he explains, "she won't leave Megan alone until she gets what she wants."

"What should Megan tell her?"

"The truth," he says simply, "I don't expect Megan to lie for me, Emma."

I nod and let myself out of his office, mulling over his unexpected thoughtfulness. This is the second time that I have been witness to Jack's feelings, and I'm starting to think that Megan is not the only one who was so affected by their relationship. It doesn't make me feel any better to suspect that Jack may care far more deeply for Megan than he's letting on.

I text Megan to let her know what happened, omitting my suspicions about Jack's feelings, which would only add fuel to the fire, and then I get back to work.

AFTER A BUSY DAY, I weave my way through traffic. My parents' house is only a few blocks away from my own, a sweet little two-story house with a grey roof and a blue front door.

When Alyssa was born, Max and I had stayed in an apartment in the city, but after the divorce, I'd moved out to the suburbs. It was well worth the extra half hour of traveling every day to see Alyssa playing outdoors, and I'd wanted to be closer to my support base. My mom and dad are a huge help; they fetch Alyssa from preschool, take her to the park, play with her in the garden, and do all sorts of fun things that I don't always have the time to do. My mom invariably almost always cooks dinner for the both of us, although sometimes I take mine to go.

"It's me!" I call as I enter through the kitchen door. My mother is standing over the stove, waiting for the kettle to boil. "Hi, mom." I kiss her cheek.

"Do you want some tea?" she asks.

"No, I'm good, thanks. I grabbed a coffee on the way home."

"How was your day?"

"Long." I grin. "Where's Ally?"

"They're in there." She points in the direction of the sitting room, where I find Alyssa and my dad playing dominoes.

"Mom!" Alyssa leaps up at the sight of me, knocking half the dominoes across the table.

"Hey, baby!" I scoop her up and twirl her in the air, kissing her neck until she squirms in my arms. "Did you eat?" I ask her, as I bend down to kiss my dad on the cheek.

"I did. Grandma made broccoli." She sticks out her tongue in disgust.

"Broccoli is good for you." I tap her on the nose and set her back down.

"I drawed a picture of us," she says coyly, trying to distract me.

"Drew," I correct automatically. "Oh wow!" I take it from her and can't stop the warmth that suffuses my cheeks as I look down at it. She's holding my hand under a wax-yellow sun. My parents stand beside us, their dark hair such a contrast to mine and Alyssa's. My mom meets my eyes over the drawing.

"We spent all afternoon on that," she says.

"It's beautiful. Definitely one for the pinboard."

"Your supper's in the warmer."

"I'm not staying, I've got a big meeting in the morning."

"Give me a second, I'll decant it for you." She disappears back into the kitchen.

"You okay, pumpkin?" my dad asks. "You look tired?"

"Long day," I reply. "Nothing a good night's sleep won't fix."

Mom comes back holding a plastic container, and I accept it gratefully before giving her a hug and my dad a farewell kiss on the cheek. I grab Alyssa's bag and head for the door. "We'll see you guys tomorrow!" I call over my shoulder. Alyssa trails along happily behind me.

An hour later Alyssa is bathed and ready for bed, and I manage to put my feet up for the first time today.

"You didn't eat all your broccoli," my daughter reprimands, glaring over my shoulder at the plate on the coffee table.

"Don't tell Grandma." I smile, and she narrows her eyes, sensing weakness.

"Can I have ice-cream before I go to bed?"

I pull her over the sofa and onto my lap. "Tell you what. Why don't we *both* have ice-cream before we go to bed?"

"Don't tell Grandma?" she asks, her dimples prominent as she smiles slyly.

"Don't tell Grandma," I agree, kissing her nose.

Twenty minutes later, I read her a bedtime story and tuck her into bed. She clutches 'Raffy' tightly to her chest and closes her eyes, utterly content, and my heart swells at how far she's come. After the divorce, it took months before she would sleep in her own room. Raffy is a stuffed toy giraffe that I bought for her as a baby. He is worn and faded, but she cannot bear to be separated from him, even now. I smile as I remember the time one of his legs fell off, and how I had to sew it back on while frantically trying to console her. When she'd finally calmed down, she had examined my stitchery, narrowed her eyes and announced that grandma would've done a better job. She hadn't asked my mother, though, and my uneven stitches remained.

At about nine o'clock my phone pings beside me. I frown as I reach for it. Who would be messaging me so late? A second later my question is answered. It's my ex-husband, Max.

Can I pick Alyssa up tomorrow night? I have tickets to see Cinderella at the Play Theatre.

I quickly type my reply: *I don't think that's a good idea. Let's stick to the arrangement. You can collect her on Saturday morning.*

I see him typing almost immediately. *I got great seats. The tickets cost me a fortune.*

I heave a sigh and feel the familiar fatigue settle over me. *Why did you buy them in the first place? You know you are only permitted day visits with A?*

There's a short pause, and then a new message comes through. *I didn't think it would be a big deal. She's my daughter too, Emma.*

Always Emma when he's taking me to task. I fight the urge to scream at how quickly the conversation took a turn for the worse. Instead, I hit the call button.

Max answers almost immediately. "Hi, Em."

I keep my voice calm. "Hey. Listen, I'm sorry about the tickets, but the judge did say we should stick to the agreement."

"Yeah, Emma, I hear you, but it's just one damn night."

"Max, please, let's not get into an argument."

"Who's arguing?" he counters, and I'm relieved to hear that he sounds sober. "I have really great tickets. For *Cinderella*," he emphasizes as if I don't know who that is. As if I didn't buy Alyssa the whole dress-up outfit for Christmas last year. "Ally will love it, what's the big deal?"

"The big deal is that I don't want you having her overnight. And I don't need to explain why, you know my reasons. They're the same reasons the judge decided on no overnight visitation to begin with."

Max is silent for a long moment and I cringe, expecting his temper to flare, as it always does. Surprisingly, when he replies, he sounds calm and amiable. "Okay, point taken. How about this. How about I fetch her at six, take her to watch the show, and then drop her straight back home after? The show is two hours plus an interval, so we won't be later than nine."

I consider this for a moment. Alyssa *would* love it – she's crazy about Disney princesses, and despite everything that happened between Max and I, she adores her father. And he has been trying, he spends as much time with her as he can and in the year since the divorce, I have never known him to be anything but sober when he's with her.

"I won't even get her an ice-cream on our way back," Max coaxes. "Straight home."

I cave. "Okay, that sounds fair. I'll let her know in the morning. You'll fetch her from my folks, then? At six?"

"Perfect," he says, and I can hear the delight in his voice. The knot in my stomach eases ever so slightly. Max has his faults, but he's a good dad.

"Great, I'll see you tomorrow."

"Tomorrow," he confirms. "And Em, thank you."

I hang up the phone and stretch my arms. It's getting late, and I have a busy day tomorrow. I pack Alyssa's bag, carefully folding her Cinderella dress, and feeling grateful that I opted for one size up last Christmas. It still fits perfectly. I pack her lunch for school, stowing it in the refrigerator before I switch off the lights, and pad down the hall to my room.

Sleep eludes me. I just can't relax. A part of me is furious that I agreed to Max going against the court order, and the other part of me is berating that part for being such a cynical bitch. I try to read to distract myself, but the words blur, running into one as my eyes droop. I give up, slamming the book down on my bedside table and reaching for the switch on my nightlight. My gaze falls on the frames on my bedside table.

In the first, Alyssa is laughing outright at the camera. It's not the best photo of her, her hair is a tangled mess and she has paint on her clothes, but I love it. The second photograph is of me with my parents. I'm riding my dad's shoulders and my mom is smiling up at me. It was taken only a few months after they adopted me, and mom says it's her favorite because it was taken the first time they heard me laugh. I avoid looking at the third photograph. The silver-framed image shows a pretty blonde woman on the beach, shielding her eyes from the sun, her curls blowing in the breeze. I can't face it tonight.

Instead, I switch off the light without looking at it, and whisper softly, *Goodnight Mom*.

"Mr. Daniels will see you now," the platinum blonde at reception announces. She eyes me with cold indifference as I get to my feet.

I glance at my wristwatch as I make my way to the large double doors at the end of the hall. It's 10.00 am, on the dot. At least Greg Daniels is punctual. As I reach the doors, they open from the inside, and Greg smiles down at me, his blue eyes warm.

"Miss Johnson, welcome. Tracey, two coffees, please." He steps aside and gestures me in. I have been in this office plenty of times before, when the previous CEO was in residence, and I am struck by the changes in decor. Gone are the Persian rugs and the dark mahogany furniture. Instead, the walls are painted a dove-grey, and an enormous white shag-pile rug covers most of the floor. Greg's desk is enormous, but he directs me to a plush white leather sofa instead. I perch primly on one end, and he takes a seat beside me, lounging gracefully, his arm resting along the back.

"Thank you for taking the time to see me," I say, feeling strangely awkward at the informal setting.

“It’s my pleasure,” he replies, “I’ve heard only good things about your services.”

“That’s nice to hear.”

He drums his long fingers on the sofa near my hair and regards me curiously.

“Look,” I say, rising to the silent challenge, “I know why I’m here. I know that a new broom sweeps clean, and all that. I’m sure you want to explore all avenues and possibly make some radical changes here at Nanosec – it shows that you’re actually doing something. I also know that you no doubt have a few weak spots in your expense budget, but I’m here to prove that I’m not one of them.” I pause, and he nods his head, an invitation for me to continue. “Mr. Daniels, I *know* Nanosec, I know your policies, I know your systems, and more importantly – I know your people. I’ve done a fantastic job with your advertising and marketing over the past two years and, more importantly, I’ve hugely increased your brand recognition.” He’s smiling at me, but I’m not sure if it’s encouragement or simple amusement. I shake my head, “What I’m trying to say, very inarticulately, is that you should give me a chance to prove myself before you start requesting comparatives.” I stop, eyeing him patiently. “I’m done,” I add when I realize he’s still waiting.

“You think I asked you here to tell you I would be shopping around?” he muses, a small smile still playing around the corners of his lips.

I blink in confusion, feeling more and more out of my professional comfort zone. “It’s what I would do,” I say.

“What if I told you that I asked you here because I wanted to see you again?” he asks boldly, just as the door opens and Tracey enters holding a tray. Her eyes shoot daggers at me, and I flush to the roots of my hair as I realize that she heard his last comment. Greg, on the other hand, is completely unfazed, grinning down at me and not even glancing away when Tracey puts the coffees down on the table, with far more force than necessary.

“Thank you, Tracey.” He waves her airily away. He waits until the door closes behind her before he speaks again. "Believe it or not, Miss Johnson, I did my research *before* we purchased the majority stock in Nanosec. I've seen the figures, and I already have a fairly good idea of who's not pulling their weight. I also know which of our service providers are worth their weight in gold, and you most definitely fall into that category. So, no, I didn't call you in to let you know that I would be seeking out comparatives. I called you in because I wanted to see you again and this was the easiest way to do that."

I regard him steadily. "Please," I say teasingly, "tell me how you really feel."

He laughs out loud. "What are you doing this evening?"

"I have no plans." I take a sip of my coffee, a part of me dreading where this conversation is headed and the other part ecstatic.

"I'd like to take you to dinner."

"I really don't think that's a good idea. After all, you are my client, and this could potentially cause a problem down the line."

"You mean once I've had my wicked way with you and moved on, and you have fallen completely and utterly in love with me?" He remarks, deadpan.

I really like this man. He has my sense of humor. I adopt a suitably solemn expression.

"Yes, then."

"That's understandable." He takes a sip of his coffee and pretends to ponder this dilemma. "Let's say, for argument's sake, that we find we don't enjoy one another's company. I'm not one to let my personal life interfere with my professional life, and I don't believe you are either. If it makes you feel any better, you could bring a briefcase full of reports, and we could treat it as a business meeting?"

"Why on earth would you want to take me out?" I ask. "We don't even know one another."

"I know what I want, and I didn't get to where I am by being hesitant. You might think I'm forward, but I prefer to think of it as being decisive."

"I actually like decisive," I admit, thinking of Max, and how much easier things would have been if I had followed my gut instinct. "Decisive is good."

There's a knock at the door. Tracey is back. "I'm sorry to interrupt, Mr. Daniels, but there's an urgent call from Tokyo on line two."

He gets to his feet. "I'm sorry, Emma, but I have to take this." I'm happy to note that he really does look sorry.

"Of course." I snatch up my things and follow him back to the door.

"Email me your address," he murmurs as I breeze past him. "I'll pick you up at 7."

By the time I get back to the Focus building, almost everyone else is on lunch. I head into my own office, shutting the door behind me, and wonder how I had taken such leave of my sanity. I agreed to go out with Greg – a client. How had that happened? I open a new email document, determined to cancel, but my fingers hover over the keyboard. What if I offend him? And truthfully, what harm is there in going? He's a client, and I've taken plenty to dinner. I have an entertainment allowance for that exact purpose. Besides, I *want* to go. I haven't dated since the divorce and Greg is the first man I've met that makes me want to consider it. Plus, it'll take my mind off Max taking Alyssa to the theatre and save me an evening of stressing about it. I hastily type up my address and hit send before I can change my mind, and then I get down to work.

I work hard. It's a big part of the reason I've been so successful and why my clients stick with me. I am so immersed in paperwork that, at first, I don't hear the knock at my door. When it becomes a firm rapping, I glance up from my notes.

"Come in!" I call, turning the page and highlighting Nanosec's new product range, which will directly affect their advertising portfolio.

"Hey, Emma!" Oliver grins, handing me yet another Starbucks coffee. Jack finally announced that Oliver will be reporting to Harvey, one of the other account executives. My initial dismay that he wouldn't be on my team was quickly replaced by relief that we could become friends, given that I'm not his direct boss.

"You are in serious danger of becoming my replacement Megan," I say, putting down my pen and stretching my neck from side to side. Oliver slouches into the chair across from me, looking at ease as he sips his own coffee.

"Just don't ask me to braid your hair," he teases.

"Not much to braid."

"True, but I could probably style you an awesome bed-head. What are you working on?"

"The Nanosec account. They've got an entire new range coming in, I'm going to have to completely rewrite their current proposal."

He's already halfway to his feet. "I didn't mean to interrupt."

"Please, sit. I could use the break."

He drops back into the chair. "What are you up to tonight?" he asks. He sounds only mildly curious.

"I actually have a date." I drop my voice conspiratorially, "with a *very* attractive, *very* powerful man."

"Ah," he nods knowingly, "I'm in the same boat. Except my date is female. And not very powerful. If I'm being honest, she's not even that attractive," he adds.

I laugh at his quirky sense of humor. "I hope it goes well."

"Ditto to you." He tosses his paper cup into the wastepaper bin. "I better go, Jack's got me reading through last year's reports to get me up to speed."

"Sucks to be the new guy," I tease.

"Tell me about it. Well, if you're at a loose end over the weekend, let me know. I'm always up for a coffee."

"Sure," I answer half-heartedly, my mind already on other things.

By 6.45 pm I'm dressed and ready. It's amazing how much quicker everything goes when you have the house to yourself and aren't being bombarded with questions from a four-year-old wannabe chaperone. I smile indulgently at the thought and then call my mother. Max fetched Alyssa right on time.

"Are you sure you don't mind waiting up for her?" I ask, for the hundredth time. In light of my date with Greg, I've arranged for Max to drop Alyssa back at my parents' place after the show, and they had agreed to have her sleep over. It means I won't have to rush and can let my hair down a bit.

At seven o'clock, on the dot, a dark blue Mercedes pulls up in front of my house. I hurry to the bathroom to do one final check of my appearance. My hair is clean and silky, if still too short, and my blue eyes look even bigger than usual, thanks to a new silver eye-shadow and at least three coats of mascara. I adjust the thin straps of my dress, which is a gorgeous aquamarine color. I bought it for last year's awards ceremony – the biggest Focus function of the year – but chickened out of wearing it at the last minute. A thin diamante belt fastens around the waist, and the skirt falls softly around my thighs and ends just above my knees.

A sharp rap reminds me that Greg is here, and I hasten back to the front door, switching off the lights behind me.

"Hi!" I smile up at him as I open the door. He really is gorgeous – possibly the most attractive man I have ever laid eyes on. His blonde hair is still in its deliberately mussed up style, and his strong jaw is clean-shaven. This close I realize that there are tiny flecks of green in his blue eyes, those wicked blue eyes that take in every inch of me, from head to toe, before he gives an almost imperceptible nod of approval.

"Shall we?" He asks, offering his arm.

"Let's." I smile, pulling the front door shut as I slip my arm through his.

GREG TAKES me to Luigi's. The risotto cakes are out of this world, the angel-hair-wrapped prawns even better. As we move on to the main course, the red wine loosens my tongue, and the conversation flows. Greg is surprisingly easy to talk to. As I suspected, he's incredibly competitive and very athletic – doing everything from mountaineering to cycling.

"What do *you* do for fun?" he asks, filling up my glass and signaling the waiter. "A bottle of mineral water, please," he says, before turning his attention back to me.

"You're not having any more wine?" I ask, narrowing my eyes.

"I'm driving," he points out wryly. "So, fun?" he reminds me of his original question, and I wrack my brain. God, I don't do anything. My life revolves around work and Alyssa and trying to fit in the occasional leg wax, but I can't say 'nothing', and I hardly think that getting drunk at home with Megan while we burn the brownies for Alyssa's Baker Day will count.

"I swim," I hear myself saying. Sure, it's not the most exciting sport in the world, but at least I can pull it off. No fancy terminology or high-tech equipment. He never has to know that my version of a good swim is lounging on an air mattress, without wetting so much as a single toe, while drinking Pina Coladas and gossiping with Megs. To my relief, we're interrupted by the waiter, who sets down our main course.

As the evening progresses, I find myself becoming more and more attracted to this man. He is handsome, smart, successful, wealthy, athletic. He's almost too perfect. But I also realize that he is fiercely competitive, jealous by nature, and more than a little arrogant. He knows he's good looking and multi-talented. Somehow it only adds to his appeal.

We order coffee and I cave and order an exquisite Crème Brûlée. Greg declines pudding. No wonder he's in such good shape.

"Alyssa loves this stuff," I comment, as I take a spoonful. It literally melts in my mouth, and I close my eyes, savoring the smooth, creamy texture.

"Your daughter?" Greg prompts.

"Yes, she's four."

"My son is five," he states calmly, and I almost choke on my dessert.

"You have kids?" I hide my surprise behind a pleasant smile. Greg is at least 35, so I suppose it makes sense that he would have a child, and possibly have been married before.

"Just Jesse," he corrects.

"So, you're divorced?"

"Not exactly." He looks uncomfortable for the first time since I met him.

"What?" I ask, trying to stay calm. I'm sure there's a logical explanation. Maybe he's widowed. Oh God, that's it, he's a widow. I'm so insensitive, why did I bring it up?

"I'm still married," he admits bluntly.

"To your dead wife?" I blurt out.

He laughs, his eyes widening incredulously. "To my what?"

"Are you a widow?" I prompt, feeling confused and hurt.

"My wife isn't dead, Emma." He places his hand over my own on the table, and I realize that this has all been a set-up. He wants me to be his bit on the side, just like Jack with Megan. Tears of anger prick at my eyes and I set aside my plate, reaching for my purse. "Let me explain," his voice is low and inviting. I meet his gaze levelly.

"Greg, you ask me here on, for all intents and purposes, a date, and it turns out you're married. What explanation could possibly make that okay?"

"The one where I tell you that my wife and I have been separated for over two years and she's living with someone else?" he ventures.

I close my mouth. "Oh. Well, that might work, I guess." I purse my lips trying not to smile, but the effort is too much, and I grin unabashedly at him. "I'm sorry," I say, sounding anything but.

"Don't be," he shakes his head, signaling for the bill.

By the time we arrive back at my place, it's well after nine. Greg walks me to the door, and I lean back against it. I don't know if it's the wine or his presence that's making me feel a little unsteady on my feet.

"Thank you so much, I had a great time," I murmur, peering up at him and feeling ridiculously shy.

"Me too." He takes a step closer so that our bodies are almost touching. It's such an invasion of my personal space, but I'll be damned if I back away from a challenge.

"Well, I guess I'll see you this week?" I smile, and his gaze moves from my eyes to my lips. He doesn't say anything, but he lifts his hand and brushes my hair out of my face. My breath catches in my throat, a warm feeling spreading from deep in my belly through the rest of my body.

When his lips touch mine it's like an explosion. Feelings that I haven't felt in a very long time burst out of me, and my head feels fuzzy with longing. I hang almost limply from Greg's neck, barely able to stand my knees are so weak. He kisses my nose, grinning at the devastating effect he's having on me.

"You better get inside before I really take advantage of you," he murmurs, his voice heavy with the unspoken question. He doesn't want to go anywhere. I take a deep breath, throwing caution to the wind.

"Would you like to come in?" I manage, as his mouth comes crashing back down onto mine.

The moment is heating up fast and furious when my mobile phone rings. I pull away from Greg, using every ounce of my willpower, and reach into the depths of my purse. My mother's number flashes on the screen, and all thoughts of Greg are forgotten. I lift the phone to my ear.

"Mom?" She would never phone me this late unless there was an emergency.

"She's not home, Emma." She is trying to keep calm, but I can hear the underlying panic in her voice, "He hasn't brought her home and that bastard's not answering our calls."

"I'll call you back." I end the call and immediately dial Max's number. The phone just rings until it diverts to voicemail. "Son of a bitch!" I curse, immediately dialing again. "I'll kill him," I murmur under my breath and then, realizing that Greg is still standing here, I shake my head apologetically. "I'm sorry, my daughter isn't home yet, and my ex isn't answering his phone. You should go. Thank you for a lovely evening." I open the door and swing it wide, only half-paying attention. I'm already calling again, and I pace up and down as I listen to the dial tone.

To my relief, Max answers. To my dismay, he is slurring.

"Where is Alyssa?" I demand, grabbing my purse and heading out the door. I hesitate as I realize Greg is standing there, a hard expression on his handsome face. His jaw is twitching, and he hasn't moved an inch.

"She's with me," Max mumbles, "I figured there was no point driving her all the way back there and then fetching her again tomorrow."

"You don't get to change the plans, you bastard. And you've been drinking," I add, disgusted and terrified.

"Ah, that's not fair, Em. I only had a few beers."

"She's got no bag with her, no pajamas, no toothbrush." I snap.

"Stop being such a bore. She's fine, she's in one of my T-shirts."

"Whatever. Where are you?"

"We're at home. Chill out, everything's fine. I'll bring Ally back in the morning." His tone is final, as though the matter is settled.

"I'm coming to fetch her," I snarl, ending the call and tossing my phone into my bag. It immediately starts ringing.

"Dammit!" I check the caller ID and lift it to my ear. "Sorry, mom, I found her. She's at Max's."

"Do you need us to...?"

"No, don't stress, I'm headed over there now."

"Sweetheart if you prefer, your father can come with you."

"No, mom, thanks but that's not necessary. I'll call you when I'm on my way back."

"Where to?" Greg asks as I shove the phone back into my purse. His eyes are flashing. I hesitate for only a moment. I really don't want him caught up in this mess, but Max can be less than co-operative when he's been drinking, and I could use the support. I make my decision and nod at him, rounding the Mercedes and getting back into the passenger seat. Getting Alyssa home safely is my top priority right now, and if I never see Greg again because of this drama, well, it's a small price to pay.

The half-hour journey is tense, and we barely speak to each other, other than me issuing directions every now and again. We pull up outside of Max's apartment block, and I quickly climb the stairs and press the intercom button for 4C. I keep pressing it, over and over. It takes forever before I see finally get a response.

"Mmm?" Max's voice is thick and heavy with sleep. He must have passed out.

"Max, it's Emma. Open the door."

"Emma? What in Gods name are you doing down here?" He sounds so confused, and I still can't quite believe that he thought that his drunken explanation earlier would be the end of it.

"Max!" I yell, slapping the intercom unit as my anger boils over, "you open this door right now, or I'm calling the cops."

"You're making a scene, Emma! I told you she's fine. *We're* fine."

"Open the door!" My tone turns pleading as my desperate need to see Ally, to see for myself that she is okay, rears its head.

"I told you, I'll see you tomorrow," Max's voice is tight-lipped and menacing. "Now do us all a favor and fuck off." The connection goes dead. I blink in embarrassment and bite my lip, trying not to give in to the tears that are pricking at my eyelids.

I've already got my phone in my hands, intending to call the cops after all, when Greg steps forward, his face a mask of fury. As I watch, he presses the call button for 4B. The name tag reads 'Holloway'. After a short time, a woman's voice comes through the intercom, sounding half-asleep.

"Hello?"

"Ms. H?" Greg injects just the right pitch and slurring speech to sound convincingly like Max. "It's Max from 4C, I can't seem to find my keys, could you be a sweetheart and open up for me?" I can sense her shudder of contempt even from down here, but a second later the door clicks open. I am about to step through the doorway, but Greg bounds up the stairs ahead of me. I hasten after him, suddenly wondering if this might not have been the best idea.

By the time I get up the stairs, Greg is banging on the door of Max's apartment. I'm about to intervene when Max yanks the door open. Before he can even register his shock, Greg slams his fist into Max's nose. Max staggers back, tripping over a side table and falling heavily to the floor, his hand clutching his nose and covering his face. I don't waste any time. I rush into the apartment and down the passage to Ally's room. I find her awake in her bed, wide-eyed and shivering.

"Mommy?" She sits up as soon as she sees me. I pick her up off the bed, throwing the blanket around her, and scoop up her clothes and shoes. "I want Raffy," she moans, her lip quivering.

"We'll go get him, baby," I promise. Raffy is with her overnight bag at my parents.

I make my way back into the hall, where Greg is standing over Max as if daring him to get up. I think he's giving Max far too much credit, he looks incapable of standing. I shudder as I think of him driving Ally in that state.

"Who's the bodyguard?" Max stares at me through one glazed eye. Greg takes a step closer to me, and I give a tiny shake of my head. "I'll pick her up tomorrow," Max inclines his head at Ally, who has dropped her head onto my shoulder, her wide eyes taking everything in.

"No, Max, you won't." I declare, walking out the door. I don't look back.

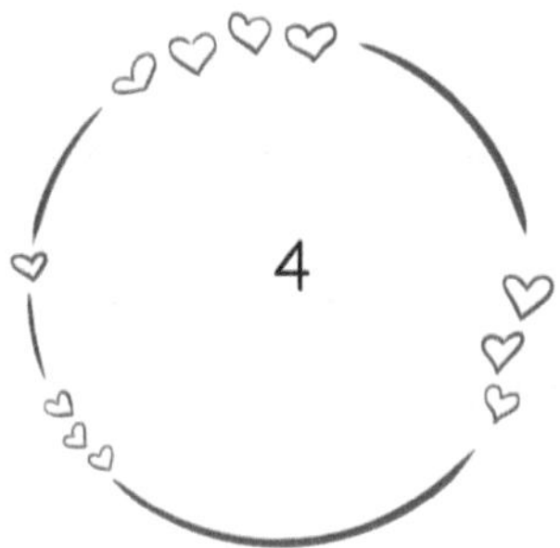

"If you wouldn't mind, I just need to pick up something from my parents' house," I tell Greg, keeping my voice low so as not to wake Ally. The interior of the car is warmer now – he had turned the heat up while I deposited her on the back seat.

"No problem." His voice is surprisingly gentle after the cold anger he displayed earlier. I call my mom on the way, and she is relieved to hear we are both safe. I explain that I'm going to just take Ally home, but that I need to stop and collect Raffy first. I hang up and direct Greg, leaving him in the car to watch over the now sleeping Alyssa while I run in to fetch the stuffed toy and the small Frozen backpack filled with Ally's overnight kit. I feel Raffy's matted fur beneath my palm. It's no wonder Ally couldn't settle. Max really doesn't know his daughter at all. I take a deep breath, determined to stay calm. Max is an asshole, that's why I divorced him. He can't hurt me anymore, or Alyssa. I went against my better judgment letting him take her out at night, but it won't happen again. Back in the Mercedes, I give Greg a tentative smile.

"Got it," I hold up the tattered toy and his lips pull up at the corners. When we pull up in front of my house, I open the back door and lift Ally into my arms. I maneuver the keys in my left hand, as I do so often when she falls asleep in the car. I hear Greg chuckle beside me as I fumble with the lock. He takes the keys from me and opens the door in three seconds flat.

"Thank you," I mouth, kicking off my shoes and padding down the hall to tuck Ally into bed. I slip Raffy between her arms and she clutches him to her chest with a small sigh. After five minutes, she still hasn't stirred, so I kiss her cheek and leave her to sleep. I find Greg in the kitchen making coffee.

"Thanks." I take the proffered mug gratefully and raise it to my lips, meeting his gaze over the rim. "So, I guess our date turned out to be a bit of a disaster?"

He comes to stand beside me and leans back against the counter. I can feel the warmth of his body at my side.

"Was his drinking the reason you got divorced?" he asks gently.

"Yes and no. We were very different, it probably would have ended eventually anyway. But if he wasn't drinking I might have hung in a little longer – the marriage may have limped along a few more years."

"He ever hit you?" It's such a personal question, I flinch, but I won't lie. I have nothing to be embarrassed about, or so my therapist told me.

"Only once."

He nods slowly, then turns and puts his cup in the sink.

"I should go." He clears his throat and turns to face me, then without warning, he puts his warm hands around my neck and pulls me to him. He tastes of coffee and I kiss him back, my head swimming with desire.

As the kiss deepens, he runs one hand down my left thigh and lifts my knee, cupping our bodies even closer together. I groan as his teeth graze my bottom lip, and his breath fills my mouth.

"You should go," I murmur. He nods, but neither of us makes any move to break apart. When he kisses me again, I rake my nails down his back. Greg groans and the sound only fans the flame of my passion. "Or, you could stay," I add, my voice hoarse with longing. After the stress of this evening, I crave the oblivion of sex. It's all the invitation that he needs. He picks me up and carries me, my legs wrapped tightly around his waist, all the way to my bedroom.

I WAKE in the morning and give a start. Greg is sleeping soundly beside me, and as I grab my phone to check the time, I hear Ally's bed creaking – a sound symbolic of her waking up.

"Greg!" I hiss, shaking him frantically.

"What?" He opens one eye. A lazy smile parts his lips.

"You have to go!" He gives me a look of pure astonishment. "I'm sorry, but Alyssa is waking up, and I don't want her to see you." I blush furiously – I can't believe I am asking him to do the walk of shame. I can only assume it's because he has a child of his own that he understands.

He eases himself out from under the covers and stretches uninhibitedly. I admire the view for a moment before he reaches for his clothes and pulls them on. I get up, pull on my robe, and slip my feet into my well-worn snoopy slippers. I open the door and peer through the crack. Ally is nowhere in sight. Praying she's still in her room, we hastily make our way down the hall and to the front door. "I'll call you later." He kisses my nose, grins, and turns for the door. His hand has curled around the handle when I hear Ally's voice right behind us.

"Mom?"

I freeze, wondering how I'm going to explain this, when Greg suddenly shuts the door, turning to face me and announcing in a loud voice. "Thank you for letting me in, Miss. As I said, my car ran out of gas just outside and I need to use your phone, if you don't mind?"

I gape at him, until his foot brushes my own.

"No problem at all," I say, playing along. "I'll get my mobile. This is my daughter, Ally," I add, smiling down at her. Ally narrows her eyes suspiciously. "Ally, this is..." I trail off, and he takes his cue.

"Greg," he extends his hand, and I shake it, "Greg Daniels."

Ten minutes later Ally is back upstairs in her room playing, and Greg and I are settled in the kitchen with coffee, supposedly waiting for a gas-wielding friend of his to arrive.

"That was some pretty quick thinking," I concede, still laughing over the morning's events.

"I took an acting class in college," he boasts, then, checking his watch. "I guess it's about time my friend arrived with the gas."

I watch as he quickly rinses his mug and sets it in the drying rack.

"About last night..." I say to the broad span of his back. He turns to face me, waiting.

"Yes?" he prompts when I say nothing further.

"I'm not quite sure what to say," I admit. "It's not exactly something I normally do."

"Which part? Taking your dates to your ex's apartment, or jumping into bed with them on the first night?"

I pretend to ponder the question. "Both, I guess."

He chuckles and then fixes me in that blue-eyed stare. "I want to see you again."

"Well, as long as you keep using Focus for all your advertising, you'll see me at least every fortnight, for sure," I tease.

He smiles lazily. "I was thinking maybe a little more often than that."

"How often?" I pretend to be contemplating.

"Often," he states simply, the word filled with meaning.

"I'll have to check my diary and see if I can carve out some extra time."

"I'm away until Tuesday, I'm competing in a cycling challenge. Could you come by my office on Thursday, say ten, and we can discuss it?"

"That sounds good."

He cocks his head, listening for the sound of Alyssa, still playing upstairs. Convinced, he crosses the kitchen to kiss me.

"I'll see you on Thursday."

I'm still grinning when I hear the BMW start up outside.

NOT FIVE MINUTES after he has left, the doorbell rings, and I open it without thinking.

"Did you forget something?" My smile falters as I gaze up into the cold, bloodshot eyes of my ex-husband. He's sporting a spectacular blue bruise around his left eye, and his nose is swollen above the grim line of his mouth.

"Max," I stutter, stepping forward into the doorway, barring him entry. Ally is still upstairs. "What are you doing here?"

"How dare you," he spits, his voice ominously low. "How dare you come into my home and take my child?"

"I beg your pardon?" I snap, my ire outweighing my fear. "You were dead drunk, and you had *our* daughter. What did you think I was going to do – leave her there?"

"I certainly didn't expect you to have me assaulted."

"Assaulted?" I smile sweetly, "I have no idea what you are talking about. You were hammered. For all I know, you tripped over your own feet."

"You think you've got this all neatly wrapped up?" he sneers, uncharacteristically aggressive considering he is sober. Max has always been a nice guy, save for when he drinks – it brings out the devil in him. "You will not keep me from my child." He takes a big step forward so that we are almost touching.

"Max," I press my hand firmly against his chest, trying to calm him down. "Don't make a scene. Please. You know I would never keep you from her unless I thought she was in danger. You were drunk, and in violation of the court order," I add, firmly but with no accusation. "She was cold and she had no clothes with her. I did the right thing." He hesitates, and a shadow of guilt passes over his face, which softens slightly.

"Yeah," he relents, "I guess that was pretty dumb. But you drove me to it, Emma. You're too damn uncompromising. She's my daughter too. I need to see her." That was the gist of it, right there. Max may have been a terrible husband, but he does love Alyssa and, despite everything, she loves him. I have never denied that fact.

"Then *earn* it, Max. Your behavior last night is proof that I can't trust you with her."

"Who was the guy?" he changes the subject abruptly. "The one you brought with you?"

"Just a friend."

"I don't want to see him again, Em. You bring him near me, I'm going to return the favor – you got that?"

"Got it," I agree – anything to have him gone. I am immensely relieved that Greg left when he did. Who knows what might have happened if he had still been here when Max showed up. "Look, Max, I know technically today is your day, but she's still a little shaken up about last night. Please, just leave it for today, until we've both calmed down. I'll drop her at your place next Saturday." I have no intention of ever leaving Alyssa alone with him again, but I need to buy myself some time to get the court involved. In the meantime, I need to keep Max calm, and not invoke his temper.

"Where is she?"

"Upstairs, playing."

He glances toward the stairs, deliberating. "Okay," he agrees finally, and I expel the deep breath I have been holding.

"Thank you," I say, meaning it. "And I'm sorry about your eye," I add, gesturing toward his face.

"Like I said," he replies, "don't let me catch him sniffing around here."

I WAKE up late the following morning, as is my custom on a Sunday. Alyssa is curled up in the small of my back, her warm body acting as a natural hot water bottle. She must have come to cuddle and fallen back asleep. I ease myself out of bed and tiptoe downstairs, retrieving the paper from the front porch and settling down on the sofa, a steaming cup of coffee in hand.

By mid-morning Alyssa is climbing the walls and desperate to go out. On a whim, I call Megan.

"Hello," she croaks.

"Hey," I chuckle. Megan would sleep until noon if she could. The joys of not having children. "How are you holding up?"

"Not good," she replies, sounding oddly stilted. "I met Susan last night."

"Oh shit. How did it go?"

"It was awful." She groans.

"Well, I have just the thing to cheer you up. We're going to the park. Get up, get dressed, and meet me there in an hour."

"Seriously?"

"Yes. Alyssa says she's missing you."

"Liar."

"Well, no, she didn't, but that's probably because she's forgotten who you are."

"I saw her at her ballet recital."

"That was over a month ago. Now get up."

"I'd rather just curl up and die."

"No, you wouldn't. You're Megan Harris, young, gorgeous, marketing-wizard extraordinaire. Oh, and you're going to be late – get moving. We'll see you in an hour."

"I hate you," she intones grumpily.

"I hate you more. Move your ass."

By noon Alyssa is playing on the playground and Megan and I are stretched out on the grass, enjoying the midday sun.

"It was awful," Megan moans, after relating her meeting with Susan. "She was just so devastated. I always thought of her as a cold-hearted bitch who didn't understand Jack, you know? But she adores him. Her heart is broken."

"Was she angry with you?"

"No," she shakes her head, her dark hair trailing over the grass behind her. "That's the worst part. She was so nice. She said she doesn't blame me – that he is ultimately responsible and the person she expected loyalty from."

"Ouch. So, does that mean she's going to leave him?"

"She says she can't because, despite everything, she still loves him."

"Shit."

"I know." She slumps forward, head in her hands. "Am I an awful person for wishing he'd call?"

"No," I console, squeezing her shoulder. "But I wish you'd told me things were this serious."

"I didn't expect them to be. It started out as a fling – the best casual sex I'd ever had."

"Too much information," I groan.

"Well, it was!" She smiles. "But then, I don't know, somewhere along the line it became something more."

"Have you heard from him?"

"Not a word. Has he said anything to you?" She is trying to be nonchalant, but she can't hide the desperate hope in her voice.

"Nothing, Megs, I'm sorry. But it's only Sunday."

"Yeah. They're probably having family time as we speak."

"Don't do that. Don't obsess over it. You need to move on with your life."

"You're right." She sits up straighter. "Tomorrow I start at Carter & Boyd. And my first item of business will be to screw every available man in the office."

"Not the best way to impress the boss," I laugh.

"I'll screw him too," she teases, "he'll give me a raise."

5

Monday flies by, and I'm slightly disappointed that I haven't heard from Greg, but I figure if he's out in the wilderness on his bike, he probably doesn't have the best reception. I pencil in our appointment for Thursday in my diary and log it into the electronic system for good measure. I contact my solicitor, who promises he will send through a court order application immediately, pressing for supervised visits only between Max and Alyssa. I feel a twinge of regret that it has come to this, but Max is spinning out of control, and I cannot allow Alyssa to get caught in the cross-hairs of his emotional issues.

"How was your date?" Oliver asks, appearing at my door after lunch, his auburn hair standing up at all ends.

"It was good," I smile, glancing up at him. "Yours?"

"Disastrous. She was at least forty, if a day, although God knows she did her best to hide it. I think she takes her make-up off with a chisel." He takes my smile as an invitation and comes into the room, lounging on the chair opposite my desk. "Oh, and she deliberately chose the most expensive items on the menu," he adds, outraged.

"Ah, one of those," I nod knowingly. "I suppose she gave you only a motherly peck on the cheek to express her gratitude.

"I wish," he slumps further down in his chair. "She grabbed hold of me like a sumo wrestler and sucked like a Hoover. I thought she might suck out my soul," he adds shakily. I burst out laughing.

"Well, I guess then I forgive you for not bringing me coffee this morning. You've been scarred. How did you escape?"

"I said I was going to get some Champagne and ran like hell."

"She could find you," I point out. "Did you tell her where you worked?"

"Yes," he sounds woeful. "Couldn't you maybe just tell her I died?"

"We'll figure something out," I chuckle. "What was her name?"

"Simone."

"Well if Simone calls and I happen to answer I'll make sure to let her down easy. So long as you promise never to forget coffee again. Deal?"

"Deal." He grins, getting to his feet, and then, almost as an afterthought. "Hey, you didn't tell me about *your* date?"

"We'll chat later, I have a few calls to make."

ON TUESDAY I seek Jack out, determined to have something to tell Megan when I meet her tonight for drinks. I know she's going to drill me and, given that I work only a few doors down from our Director, I may as well try and glean some information out of him.

"Jack," I knock softly.

"Come in!"

"I'm sorry to intrude," I begin, and then I trail off when I see Susan sitting opposite him, dabbing at her face with a tissue. "I'm sorry," I start backing up, "I'll come back later."

"No, no, come in," Jack looks grey with exhaustion, and I wonder at the emotional toll this whole thing must be taking on him. "Susan was just leaving." As she turns away from him, I notice a flash of anger cross her face, before she quickly composes her features and gets up to kiss him goodbye. She scowls at me as we cross paths and then shuts the door quietly behind her.

"What can I do for you, Emma?" Jack asks politely, resting on the edge of his enormous desk.

"Really, it's not the time," I mutter, wishing I had never come in here. Jack regards me steadily, waiting, and eventually, I cave under his scrutiny. "It's Megan. I'm so sorry to bring it up, but I'm meeting her tonight, and I know she's going to ask me about you. I know it's completely inappropriate, but I thought maybe you had a message I could give her. Something that will make her heart hurt just a little bit less?"

"You're meeting her tonight?" he asks.

"Yes. For drinks."

"Where?"

"*Buccaneers*, but that's not the point... wait, you aren't thinking about joining us, are you?" The look on his face makes it clear that he was thinking just that, but, as I watch, his expression changes into one of determined acceptance.

"No," he replies, "of course not. I'm sorry, Emma, that you've gotten caught up in this whole mess. Not to mention the pain I've caused my wife, and Megan."

"Was it worth it?" I can't help but ask him. There is something in the way he looks every time he mentions Megan's name. He doesn't answer me for the longest time. I'm just wondering if I should get up and leave when he focuses on me again, his face pained.

"Yes and no," he says. "If I hadn't started it, I wouldn't have to deal with these mixed emotions. I love my wife, but I can't seem to get Megan out of my head."

"You have to," I point out, feeling incredibly sorry for him. I can see now how hard this is on him, the toll it's taking, and my heart goes out to him almost as much as Megan. "You can't possibly carry it on, and Megan deserves to be happy. You need to let her move on with her life."

"I know," he agrees. "And I won't leave my wife, or my kids. I would regret it forever, I know I would, no matter how Megan makes me feel. Tell her that," he adds, pushing away from the desk and crossing the room to sit behind his computer. His expression changes. "I see you have a meeting with Gregory Daniels on Thursday?" he asks and I take it that the 'Megan' portion of our conversation is over.

"Yes," I reply.

"How do you feel about our retaining the Nanosec account?"

"Oh, very positive," I answer honestly. "Trust me – Nanosec is not going anywhere."

"Good," he nods. "In that case, I'll be coming with you on Thursday."

"With me? Why?" I ask. Jack almost never accompanies me to any client meetings. He trusts me implicitly. I'm just that good at my job.

"Because I'm the Company Director," he retorts snappily, "and Nanosec is one of our biggest clients. I'd like to touch base, unless you have a problem with that?"

"Of course not." I smile, cursing the fact that I scheduled the meeting into our electronic system. "Well, I have work to do, so, if there's nothing else?" Jack waves airily at the door, dismissing me, and I wonder how someone can be so personal one minute, and such a dickhead the next.

"SO THAT'S ALL HE SAID?" Megan asks, hungry for information.

"Yes," I admit, "he has feelings for you, but he won't leave her, Megs. Ever."

"So, he won't even call me?"

"It's better if you have no contact."

"That son of a bitch!"

"He's struggling," I try to explain. "This whole fiasco has taken a lot out of him. He looks exhausted, and I think Susan's giving him a harder time than he's letting on."

"What, so you want me to feel sorry for him now?"

"No, it's not that. But I kind of do."

"Oh my God. Are you crushing on Jack?"

"What?" I gasp, "Are you insane? He's my boss!" She pulls a face, and I quickly change tack. "What I mean is no. Not at all. I don't see him that way."

"He's an asshole." She shakes her head angrily. "An utter, bloody asshole."

"I don't think he meant to hurt you." I'm trying to calm her down, but it only riles her more.

"Well he *did*, Em, and, as my friend, I would expect you to be on my side."

"I'm not on anyone's side!" I exclaim. "I feel sorry for all of you, it's a terrible situation!" She doesn't look appeased.

"Are you sure you don't have feelings for him?" she asks, eyes narrowed suspiciously.

"I am *so* sure. Besides, I've met someone."

"What? And why are you only telling me this now?"

A part of me is wondering why I am telling her at all. I don't even know what's happening between Greg and I but I'm so desperate to convince her that there is nothing going on between Jack and I, that I blurt out the whole story.

"I don't believe it," she breathes when I'm done. "Who would've thought you had it in you. Go, Emma! Was he good in bed?"

"Marvellous," I grin, taking a slug of my Martini.

"Well, at least you know Nanosec isn't going anywhere."

"Not if I can help it. Jack would throw a shit fit if I lost their account."

Just for a second, a flash of something sinister crosses her face. "You won't." She says. "Not as long as Greg Daniels is in charge. When are you seeing him again?"

"Thursday. He's out of town, competing in some cycle race."

"Has he called you?"

"No," I shake my head, signaling to the waitress to bring me another drink. "But he's probably busy."

"Um-hmm," she raises a skeptical eyebrow. "Sure he is. When is he due back?"

"Today, actually."

"So why is he only seeing you on Thursday and not tomorrow?"

I get the sense that Megan's man-hating frenzy is spilling over to encompass the entire male population.

"Let's talk about something else, okay?" I say. "I don't want to jinx it."

"Okay, how about how I'm going to make Jack suffer?" She proposes, and I laugh. It relieves the tension slightly, but it is still there, lingering between us, for the remainder of our evening.

The court order comes through on Wednesday morning, far faster than I expected. I'm on lunch when my mobile rings and Max's name appears on the screen. I cringe, bracing myself as I answer.

"Hi."

"How dare you, Emma?" he sounds incandescent with rage. "How fucking dare you do this?"

"Max, calm down." I'm relieved that I sound calmer than I feel.

"Don't tell me to calm down. How the hell can you do this to me?"

"You gave me no choice after last weekend."

"That's bullshit!" he retorts. "It was a one-off, Emma, and now you want to keep me from my own daughter? You've gone too far!"

"I'm not keeping you from her!" I snap back, just as Oliver steps into my office, a perplexed frown on his handsome face. I lower my voice and turn away from him, my hands shaking. "You can still see her just as often."

"With supervision!" he roars. "So, I have to contend with your ugly mug every time I want to spend time with my daughter?"

"Essentially, yes," I reply, forcing a confidence I don't feel. Max has always had this effect on me – making me doubt myself – making me question whether I am doing what's best for Alyssa.

"Well, I think I'm going to report you, too," he threatens, "for the assault that you orchestrated."

"You deserved it," I point out.

"Possibly," his voice is ominously low, "but it should spark some doubt as to your apparent perfect parenting. You're no saint, Emma. In fact, the secrets I have on you would probably get social services very concerned over Alyssa's safety. After all, violence tends to be inherited. Maybe you're more like your old man than I ever gave you credit for."

"You leave my parents out of this, you son of a bitch!" I hiss, then, realizing that me losing my temper is exactly what he wants, I take a deep, steadying breath. "Do you really think that having Alyssa removed from my custody is best for her? To be taken into social services and shuffled from foster home to foster home until the truth prevails and they determine I am a fit mother?"

"You're going to pay for this," he replies, not answering my question.

"I'm doing what's best for Ally!" I yell into the receiver, "why can't you see that?"

The line goes dead as he hangs up on me, and I fling the phone across my desk, tears pricking at my eyes.

"Emma," Oliver's voice is low, "are you okay?"

I had all but forgotten that he was in the room. Embarrassed, I sniff loudly and clear my throat, forcing a smile.

"I'm fine," I insist. "Ex-husband problems."

"You want to talk about it?" he asks gently.

"Not really." He nods his head and turns for the door, but before he reaches it, he stops.

"I have a friend who works at social services," he announces, turning back to face me. "I heard you mention... well, if there's anything I can do to help, I'd be happy to give him a call." I hesitate, my pride battling my good sense. I need an ally, and some advice on how to handle things should Max make good on his threat.

"Actually, that might be very helpful," I admit, taking a deep breath. If I'm going to accept Oliver's help, he needs to know the truth. He takes a seat opposite me, his amber eyes warm and trustworthy.

"My ex took my daughter home without permission on Friday night. He was supposed to drop her at my parents, but he had a few drinks and decided to take matters into his own hands," I add, and Oliver's eyes widen in understanding. "Anyway, I applied for a court order so that he no longer gets unsupervised visitation."

"Ah," Oliver nods. "And I assume he's not taking it lying down?"

"No," I sigh, rubbing at my temples.

"Well, if the court has issued the order, I don't see that he can do much to oppose it."

"He wants to plant doubt that I'm a fit parent."

"Do you think he would do that? That's not going to do Alyssa any good."

"Max can be a bastard," I reply simply, by way of explanation. "Right now, all he wants is to hurt me. He won't think any further than that."

"But surely the court will realize this is just his way of lashing out at you?"

"Hopefully," I admit, "but there's more to it than that."

Oliver says nothing, waiting for me to find the right words, which of course, is impossible. There are no words to explain what happened.

"My father murdered my mother," I blurt out eventually. I hear his shocked intake of breath. There was no way he saw that one coming. "They were really happy for the longest time – he was the most amazing man, and we were very close. Then he lost his job when I was about twelve, and he started drinking. My mother had to go out and find work, and I think he really struggled with that. She must have met someone at the office, because she started coming home late, and they started arguing a lot. It spiraled out of control pretty quickly. She was always out, and he was always drinking, and when they came head to head, it got really ugly." I close my eyes briefly as I recall just how ugly. I can still hear the echoes of their fighting, like ghosts in my head that I can't shut out.

"Emma," Oliver murmurs tentatively, a world of compassion in that one little word.

"My mother eventually announced we were leaving," I state, opening my eyes and smiling sadly at him. "She had met someone, at work, just as we suspected. I'll never forget my father's response. He said 'You try, and I'll put you six feet under'."

"Jesus," Oliver murmurs.

"Two days later I came home from school with a friend. Their bedroom door was closed, and I figured my dad had passed out. By the time my friend left and it started to get dark, I was getting concerned that if my mother didn't get home soon there would be another epic row."

"Did your dad...?"

"He wasn't there," I interrupt, needing to get it out while I still can. It's been years since I've spoken about this to anyone, barring my therapist, after Max and I got divorced. "She was. It got to the point that my concern for her safety overthrew my fear of an argument and I went to wake him up so that we could go looking for her. She was on the bed, surrounded by half-packed suitcases. Her face was blue, and her body was cold, but I tried to revive her anyway." I pause, the memory becoming so clear that for a moment I can't go on. Oliver makes to stand, but I stop him. "I'm fine," I gesture him to remain seated. "The police arrived shortly after. My father had turned himself in. I wish they had been an hour earlier, though. I wouldn't have found her if they had."

At this, despite my protests, he makes his way around the desk, pulling me to my feet and taking me in his arms. He pulls me against his chest and for a moment I let the sound of his heartbeat, steady and solid, comfort me.

"I'm sorry," I mutter, feeling embarrassed.

"For what?" he asks, incredulous. I step away, smoothing my hair nervously and trying to regain control over my emotions.

"It was a long time ago," I stammer, pulling myself together, "and I ended up in foster care with the most amazing couple, who treated me as their own. They adopted me and gave me an amazing life. My mom still cooks me dinner most nights." I force a laugh. I can't believe I just told him all of that, and then I remember his friend in social services and why I started telling him in the first place. "Anyway, Max knows, obviously, and he's threatening to use it to cast doubt over my character and cause trouble."

"I'll call my friend right now," Oliver promises. "He'll clear it all up. You don't need to worry about anything."

"Thank you," I take his hand and squeeze it, not knowing how else to express my gratitude. Oliver glances down at my hand and I quickly let go. A small silence follows and then he moves away from me, toward the door.

"Emma," he calls, when he reaches it.

"Hmmm?" I glance up to find him regarding me intently, as if not sure how to voice what he is thinking.

"Your father...?" he lets the question hang in the space between us and I smile reassuringly, letting him know that the question doesn't offend me.

"He's in a federal prison, serving a double life sentence for murder in the first degree."

"The first?" he frowns, and I can understand his confusion. Ordinarily, my father would have been tried for a crime of passion.

"I testified that he had threatened to kill her," I explain sadly, "it was enough to try him for premeditated murder."

ONLY WHEN OLIVER is gone and my office door closed firmly behind him, do I collapse back on my chair, my legs shaking. I haven't seen my father since the day they led him away in court. I was thirteen years old. Although fifteen years have passed, it still feels like yesterday, and the haunted, hollow-eyed look he gave me as they led him away is crystal clear in my mind.

Determined not to dwell on it any further, I turn my attention to my computer and check my emails. I find a message from Greg, which would make me feel better if it weren't just a short note to postpone tomorrow's meeting.

Emma,

Something has come up that I need to attend to. It can't wait. Can we reschedule for Monday afternoon?

I slump back in my chair, my whole body deflating. Even though he hadn't called yesterday when he arrived back, I had still been holding out hope that he would, at least before our appointment tomorrow. Now, the very first correspondence that we have since he left my house on Saturday morning is to delay our next meeting. It doesn't inspire much confidence that he wants to see me again.

I set my personal feelings aside and type up a response.

Greg,

No problem at all, Monday will be perfect.

I trust you had a wonderful trip.

I stay at my desk for the next half hour, hitting the refresh button every few minutes, but no reply is forthcoming and I have meetings scheduled this afternoon. I type up a quick email to Jack to let him know of the postponement and then I shove my chair back and stride from the room.

6

"Hello!" I call as I push open the front door.

"Mom!" Ally comes rocketing down the stairs and vaults into my open arms just as my mom emerges from the kitchen. She has flour on her nose.

"You've been baking again, mama?" I ask, chuckling, just as the smell of her famous shortbread reaches me. "I hope I get to take some of that home?"

"Obviously," she says.

"You ruin all our fun," my dad grumbles as he descends the stairs, looking forlorn. "I waited for ages!" he adds, scooping Alyssa up as she shrieks with laughter. "You didn't find me!"

"I found you now," she points out happily.

"True," he acknowledges, leaning over and kissing my cheek. "How was work, sweetheart?"

"Busy." I follow my mom into the kitchen.

"I keep telling you, you work too hard," she admonishes, opening the oven and setting a tray of golden shortbread onto a board on the kitchen table. I grab a piece and pop it into my mouth, savoring the warm, heavenly crumbliness.

"Good?" Mom asks with a smile.

"Divine," I reply, through a mouth filled with shortbread.

My mother, Janet, and my father, Reggie, fostered me after my mother's death. I had been a withdrawn, troubled teenager, and yet, somehow, they had managed to see past the walls I had built up and had coaxed me out of my protective fortress. "Life is for the living," they'd reminded me gently, never pressing me, but slowly smothering all my anger and despair with kindness. They had been unable to have children of their own and had fostered several, of various ages, but for some reason, they had chosen me to adopt permanently. They had never fostered again, preferring to dedicate all their love and devotion to me instead, and give me as normal an upbringing as possible. Somewhere along the way, Janet and Reggie had become my parents – become mom and dad – and I loved them both just as much as I had my biological parents. Their greatest delight is Ally, who is the apple of their eyes, and who has them both wrapped around her little finger.

"Are you staying for dinner?" My mom asks, and I smile across at her.

"Dinner would be great."

We get home a little later than I'd planned, and I carry Ally to the house, careful not to wake her. I leave the front door open as I carry her to her room, needing to go back to the car to fetch my purse. Tucked up in bed, she snuggles Raffy, smiling in her sleep, and I gaze down at her in wonder. Sometimes the love I feel for her seems like it might overwhelm me – this beautiful, fragile child, who completely and utterly captivates me. It's still hard to believe that after all the terrible ugliness in my life, I was rewarded with something so exquisitely beautiful. Kissing her cheek, I brush her blonde hair off her face and make my way quietly from the room, pulling the door shut behind me.

The smile still lingers on my face as I descend the stairs, my mind slowly shifting back into work mode. Determined to spend at least an hour on a new campaign I've been working on, I move toward the door and give a screech of fright as a tall figure looms over me.

"Oh my God, Max!" I gasp, my hand clutching my chest. "You scared the crap out of me. What the hell are you doing here?"

"I want to talk to you about this." He waves a stack of documentation under my nose, no doubt the court order papers, and I catch the sour ferment of beer on his breath.

"You've been drinking."

"Oh please. Don't start your shit with me."

"You need to go," I walk past him to stand at the still open door. "We can talk about this when you're sober." Max doesn't move, and I see the spiteful glint of satisfaction in his eyes. He loves to antagonize me when he's been drinking – to prove what a big man he is. Forcing myself to stay calm, I try to focus on the good times we shared, before he started drinking so heavily. Max had been a good husband, and he had loved me unconditionally. I had accepted long ago that he wasn't the same man anymore, but it was still a tragedy that he had become this awful person.

"Please, Max. I don't want to fight with you."

"You started it," he retorts, throwing the papers toward me. I watch as they flutter to the floor.

"I'm sorry, but I did what I had to do. One day you'll thank me – when you realize that I kept Ally safe."

"I would never harm a hair on her head!" He moves closer to me, trampling the discarded papers underfoot.

"Not intentionally," I admit, digging in my heels. "Don't you think I *know* that? But you're not the same when you drink, Max. You promised you'd never hurt me either, remember?" He hesitates, a flash of guilt crossing his angry features. He *had* promised. When the drinking had started to get out of hand and I began to fear the worst, he had assured me that he would never, ever hurt me. That I was his whole world. He had been sober at the time, and he had meant it. But just two weeks later he had come home drunk and spoiling for a fight. Our argument had escalated rapidly, and before I knew it, he'd dealt a brutal left hook to my cheek. I had suffered a black eye and a fractured cheekbone, which was agonizing but fortunately required no surgery.

I hadn't given Max a second chance. I refused to be one of those women who didn't learn the first time. I had seen first-hand what alcohol could do to a man, had watched my kind, gentle father become a monster, and I had watched my mother hesitate before leaving him. If she had just left, she might still be alive today. So, I didn't hesitate. I left Max the very next day and filed for divorce. He had begged and pleaded, sworn that he would never do it again. Eventually my quiet, earnest, "I will not become my mother," had silenced him, and he'd signed the divorce papers.

Without Ally and I there to curb his drinking, Max had spiraled out of control faster than I would have thought possible. My concern for his safety was tempered by the fact that Alyssa's safety came first, and in his defense, he was always sober on the days he had visitation with her. I had never smelt so much as a whiff of alcohol on his breath when he returned her in the evenings, and for a long time, he had often stayed after dropping her and had dinner with us.

It was only recently that things had started to change. At first, it was barely noticeable, and I might have missed it if I hadn't been paying such close attention. Max had dropped Alyssa home one Sunday afternoon, and his eyes were slightly redder than usual. He was also too careful with his words, and speaking in a stilted, formal manner. I had gone berserk, threatening him with legal action, and berating him mercilessly for driving our daughter, even if only mildly intoxicated.

He had taken it gracefully, and for a few weeks, things had gone back to normal. Convinced it was an isolated slip, I eased up on him, trying to give him the benefit of the doubt. It turned out to be my undoing because less than a month later he made the same mistake. That had been three weeks ago, and then last weekend had been the sleepover incident. It was enough. Three strikes and you're out, in my opinion. I would not let empathy cloud my judgment.

Max sways slightly as he peers at me, and I take advantage of his temporary guilt to set the record straight.

"The order stays," I announce, "not because I want to hurt you, but because I cannot allow you to hurt Alyssa. I'm doing this for you, too. You would never live with yourself if something happened to her. If you can't be responsible enough to make that call, then I have to make it for you."

He says nothing, just gazes at me with an unreadable expression on his face. He doesn't seem angry, but a muscle is going in his jaw, and his hands are balled into fists at his sides.

"You want to talk about responsibility?" he murmurs eventually, his voice so low I can barely hear him. "What about yours? You had a responsibility to me, to our marriage and the vows we made. You broke up our family, Emma. I could've stopped... I would've stopped."

"When?" I cry. His twisted reasoning infuriates me. Max refuses to be held accountable for his own actions. "When you broke another bone? When I ended up in a hospital? I gave you so many chances, I begged you! We were a family, Max, and *you* fucked it up! You wouldn't stop! You *couldn't* stop!"

A dark shadow crosses over his face. For a long moment, he simply stares at me, the monster inside him barely leashed. Then he releases a shuddering breath. "Well I guess now I have no reason to," he murmurs, and just like that he stalks past me and out into the night.

I shut the door and rest my back against the warm wood. Sinking to the floor, I pull my knees up against my chest and drop my head. I had mourned the loss of my marriage a long time ago, but when I catch glimpses of the man I had once loved so deeply, it still makes my heart hurt.

AT TEN AM the following morning, I am staring unseeingly at my computer screen, all too aware that right now I should be walking into Greg's office. I'm far more hurt by the fact that he hasn't called than I want to admit. My budding relationship with Greg had been the silver lining in a sky full of grey – something bright and colorful, the euphoria of possibility.

"You up for a visit?" Oliver's dark head peeps around the door frame.

"So long as you have coffee in those hands you're hiding." He steps around the door frame and into my office, bearing two steaming mugs.

"Have I told you I'd be lost without you?" I ask, perking up considerably.

"I have a hidden agenda," he admits, setting the coffee down on my desk and curling his long frame into one of the stiff chairs opposite me.

"Oh, really? And what is that?"

"I'm hiding," he grins, "Simone's called my cell twice, and I haven't answered. She's bound to call here next."

"You want me to screen her?" I laugh, picking up my mug and blowing on the coffee to cool it.

"No, just give me sanctuary for a while. She's stalking me. And I'm far too nice a guy to tell her off." The fact that he's right makes me smile, but his next words make me laugh out loud. "By the way, you can't purse those lips like that and expect me to keep a handle on things." I almost choke on my coffee, and as I try to swallow it down, he grins goofily.

"Your knack for innocent flirtation is a gift, you know."

His phone starts to ring, and he winces, showing me the screen. "She's not going to give up."

Lifting my handset, I dial reception. "Chloe," I say as she answers, "Oliver's in my office, he'll be here a while. Please forward all his calls to my extension."

"Sure," Chloe answers breezily, and I hang up.

"You are a lifesaver," Oliver sighs, lifting his legs up onto the desk and getting comfortable.

"So are you," I reply dryly, tipping my mug at him.

"What are you up to this weekend? Any plans?" Oliver asks as we both watch the phone expectantly.

"No," I shake my head. If Greg wanted to see me, he would've mentioned it in his email. I gathered from his curt message that I would only see him again on Monday. I haven't even bothered to tell him that Jack will be coming with me, it hardly seems to matter considering the meeting will no doubt be all business.

"Ah," Oliver frowns sympathetically, "your date didn't work out either?"

"Not exactly."

He regards me steadily for a while and then his face lights up.

"Let's go out!" he proposes. "We can console each other over the pitiful state of our social lives. We'll drink to our singlehood, long may it last! I propose Saturday – do you think you could get a sitter for Ally?" The fact that his first thought is consideration for my single motherhood status is so startlingly kind that, for a second, I simply stare at him, barely noticing the phone, which has started ringing. Oliver cringes, clapping his hands dramatically over his eyes, groaning, and I snap back to the task at hand.

"I've got this," I laugh, holding up my hand for him to be quiet.

"Hello, Emma Johnson speaking."

"Hello?" A breathless voice murmurs nervously, "Is Oliver there, please?" Simone sounds far younger than she must be.

"May I ask who's calling?"

"My name is Simone."

"Simone, I'm so sorry, but Oliver had to fly upstate for a few days to negotiate a new contract. He'll only be back mid next week." Oliver is pressing his lips together to keep from chuckling. "Next week?" her deceptively youthful voice squeaks.

"I'm afraid so," I reply curtly. "Is there anything I could perhaps help you with?"

"N... no," she stammers, "that's okay, I'll call him next week." Without another word, she hangs up.

"Well yes, actually I do have his direct line number," I speak into the handset, and all the blood rushes from Oliver's face. "It's five five one..." I continue as he shakes his hands frantically, signaling me to stop. I place the phone back into its cradle, chuckling. "She's gone," I concede, and he slumps back into the chair in relief. "She hung up. She's going to call you next week."

"Well, at least I don't have to worry about her for a few days," he sounds ridiculously pleased.

"You can't avoid her forever – you know that, right?"

"Yes, but maybe if I avoid her just long enough, she'll get the message and find a new victim to sink her claws into."

"I wouldn't bank on it. She doesn't sound forty, by the way."

"Right? She's a practiced predator." I burst out laughing, and Oliver joins in. "So, about this weekend," he continues eventually. "Think you could get someone to watch Ally?"

"My folks would do it, I don't even have to ask."

"Well then, no excuses. Shall I pick you up at seven?"

I shift in my seat. For him to fetch me feels too much like a date.

"I'll meet you there," I say. "And I'll ask Megs to join us. She could use a night out." His face falls for just a fraction of a second, so fast I might have imagined it.

"Awesome!" he declares, getting to his feet. "*Zack's* at seven?" He is already making his way toward the door. "It's where all the cool peeps hang out these days. Or so I've been told."

"We'll be there."

"Hey, new guy!" Megs kisses Oliver when we arrive at the bar, leaving a flaming red lipstick mark on his cheek.

"Hi," I say, wiping it off with my thumb after I give him a quick hug. "Sorry we're late, it took forever to catch a cab."

"No problem, I took the liberty of ordering you a drink," he gestures at the table where two Martinis lie in wait.

"Dirty, just the way I like it," Megan croons, swooping her's up and taking a huge slug.

"Why am I not surprised?" Oliver grins. Megs waggles her eyebrows at him. Megan has always been a flirt, but for the first time, I find myself a little irritated by it. Throughout the evening she never misses an opportunity to lay her red-taloned hands on Oliver, giggling at his jokes and giving him long lingering eye-meets.

As a result of their endless conversation, I drink more than either of them. Listeners always drink more, I think stupidly, my head buzzing as I raise my hand at the nearest waiter and signal for a refill.

"Maybe you should take it easy?" Oliver murmurs, his eyes meeting mine.

"What are you, my mother?" I chuckle, pushing his shoulder and almost unseating myself.

"Emma's a big girl," Megan interjects, drawing Oliver's attention back to herself.

"I guess," he shrugs, turning away, but I am all too conscious of his concerned glances back at me.

"I'm going to dance," I announce, feeling a little embarrassed. I *have* had far too much to drink. The stress of these past few weeks is catching up with me. Swaying, I move toward the pulsating dance floor, which is filled with shiny, beautiful people. Oliver and Megan join me a moment later, and we form a crude triangle, laughing and spinning as we move in time to the up-tempo music.

Oliver takes it in turns to spin us, his hands remarkably steady. Megan is writhing around him, rubbing her body against his and lifting her arms above her head in that sexy, slutty way that I've never been able to master. My moves are far less coordinated, but I shuffle around like a baby elephant, having just as much of a good time. Most surprising is the fact that Oliver is not responding to Megan's advances. In fact, he deliberately moves closer to me, raising his eyebrows in fear. I stifle a laugh as I step closer to murmur in his ear. "It'll be okay. She's not Simone, and she's not as scary as she seems."

The next thing I know, his head shifts to the left and our mouths meet. I'm not sure who initiated the kiss, but the sensation is warm, heady, and familiar all at once. It lasts only the briefest of moments, and then Oliver pulls away, his hand catching me by the elbow as I stumble backward.

"I'm sorry," he apologizes over the loud music, his hazel eyes searching my face. "Are you okay?"

"I'm fine," I smile, embarrassed.

"I didn't mean to..."

"It's okay," I insist, brushing it off. "Really, Oliver, it's fine."

Megan's face is a priceless mask of indignant outrage, but she quickly composes herself, shrugging nonchalantly.

The evening continues without incident, and I share a cab with

Megs on the ride home. Oliver is charming as ever, and there is no awkwardness after our impromptu kiss. He bustles us into the waiting cab, unfazed.

"What was that about?" Megan whirls on me the second the cab door closes on us.

"What was what?"

"Oh please, don't you 'what was what' me! That kiss!"

"That was a simple case of far too many Martinis."

"Oliver didn't have too many Martinis," she points out wryly.

"What is that supposed to mean?"

"I don't know if you were paying attention, but he hardly drank a thing all night."

"He must have," I insist, but now that I think about it, I wasn't really paying attention.

"A couple of beers at best," Megs confirms.

"Well, it was nothing," I insist. "A mistake. It won't happen again."

"What about Greg? Are you guys still a thing?"

"I have no idea," I admit.

MY DOORBELL RINGS the following morning, and I moan, clutching my head as a stabbing pain shoots through my skull. Ally spent the night at my parents, so I'm alone in the house, and not particularly in the mood for company.

"Go away!" I groan as I descend the stairs to another chiming ring of the bell. I yank open the door, and the sunlight hits my eyes like needles. Blinking against the bright light, I find Oliver standing on my porch, holding two enormous coffees. He looks revoltingly refreshed.

"Morning," he grins. Wordlessly I take a coffee and pad back inside. "How are you feeling?" he asks as he follows me through to the living room. I slump onto the sofa, cradling my coffee against my chest like a lifeline.

"Hungover."

"I figured you might be."

"Aren't you?" I ask, narrowing my eyes slightly as I recall Megan's words from last night.

"I feel like someone put me in the drier overnight on spin cycle," he counters. "Listen, I'm not going to stay, I just wanted to apologize, again, for what happened last night. I don't know what got into me, but I blame it on the alcohol."

"Me too," I agree. As far as I can remember, it wasn't as if Oliver forced himself upon me. I don't think either of us initiated that kiss – it just kind of happened.

"As long as things aren't going to be weird between us-" he begins, but I cut him off.

"Oh God, no. You're like, the only person I even talk to at work – you're my person, my Christina Yang." The fact that he laughs at this and understands the *Greys Anatomy* reference only proves that we're destined to be friends. "Besides, who else is going to bring me my daily caffeine fix?"

"Who indeed," he replies, looking relieved but not entirely convinced.

"You want to stay for a bit?" I ask. "I only have to fetch Alyssa this afternoon. We could watch a movie?"

He hesitates, trying to decipher whether I really want him here, or whether I'm just being polite. I give him my most sincere smile. "Okay, sure," he says eventually, taking a seat opposite me. "What are we watching?"

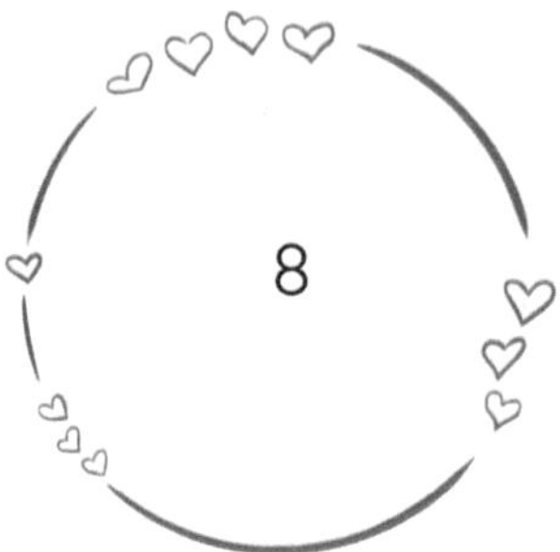

8

By Monday afternoon I'm angry enough that I feel no nerves walking into the Nanosec building. Greg's complete lack of communication has made it clear that our relationship was a non-starter and I will not allow my personal feelings to jeopardize my career. I know that my work is unparalleled, and I'm ready to prove it. I spent the whole of Saturday developing a cast-iron marketing proposal that not even Jack could punch any holes in.

Tracey ushers us to the soft leather sofas across from her desk, far more friendly now that I have a handsome man in tow. "Mr. Daniels will be with you shortly. May I offer you anything to drink while you wait?"

"No, thank you," I reply, while Jack simply shakes his head. We spent most of the morning closeted together in my office and, mercifully, Megan didn't come up once. I think it is safe to say they are both moving forward with their lives, although my relationship with Megan seems to have taken the brunt of the damage this whole mess has caused. There is something up with her that I can't quite put my finger on. Vowing to pop in on her after work and see how she's doing,

I get to my feet as Greg's office door opens and the sound of laughter reaches us.

Jack's astonished intake of breath beside me is completely justified, and my own polite smile vanishes as I recognize Megan's voice a second before she appears in the doorway. What is she doing here? I rack my brain, trying to remember if she mentioned having any reason to call on Nanosec, but I come up blank. A sick feeling settles in the pit of my stomach. Greg's arctic blue eyes meet mine over her dark head, and his own mouth hardens into a grim, determined line.

"Thank you for your time, Ms. Harris," he drawls charmingly, "I'll be in touch." Megan pirouettes toward us, her high heel hitting the ground before she registers Jack and I, standing directly in her path. Shock and worse, hurt, flash across her face as she meets Jack's gaze, but she quickly composes herself.

"Jack, Emma," she nods curtly, refusing to meet my eyes, and then she sweeps past, her heels clicking on the expensive marble floor. Jack is visibly stunned, whether from seeing Megan again, or specifically, from seeing her *here*, I cannot tell, but I smooth down my skirt and pull at his elbow as we follow Greg into his office.

Greg is professional and courteous, but there is an ugly set to his jaw, and the greeting he bestows upon Jack is noticeably warmer than the perfunctory nod he offers me.

My presentation takes twenty minutes, during which I offer a non-stop dialogue as to the advantages of my new proposal, which is a good thing because it keeps me distracted and allows me the opportunity to compose himself. Greg watches me intently, but I refuse to be flustered, and I answer all the questions he fires at me afterward with confidence. Inside, I am seething. How dare he contact the opposition when he promised me that Nanosec would continue to do business only with Focus. *And after he slept with you*, a little voice in my head adds.

"Thank you both for coming," Greg says, after we have concluded the business at hand. "I'll need some time to mull things over, but your proposition seems sound enough. I'll try to get back to you before the week is out."

That's it? I want to scream, *that's all you have to say*?

"Thank you for your time, Greg," Jack shakes his hand warmly, but I can tell that his calm exterior is feigned. Not surprising when I assured him that the Nanosec account was secure, only to find Megan here upon our arrival and Greg deciding he needs time to mull things over. I concentrate on packing up my things, shoving diagrams and paperwork roughly into my presentation folder. Eventually, I can avoid it no longer, and I turn to find Greg standing right behind me. He extends his hand, and I take it, finally looking up at him. I can't hide the hurt that I know is reflected on my face. His eyes widen in surprise, but I retrieve my bag and hoist it over my shoulder.

We are almost at the elevator when he catches up to us.

"If you don't mind, Jack," he calls, "I'd like to speak to Miss Johnson alone. I have a few more questions I'd like her to answer."

Jack seizes the opportunity as a positive sign and nods his head exuberantly.

"Absolutely, take all the time you need. I'll meet you back at the office," he adds meaningfully.

Greg doesn't look at me once as we walk back toward his office, but as we pass Tracey's expansive desk, he calls out to her. "Tracey, two coffees, please." Only when we are finally alone, and he has shut the door behind us, does he take a deep breath and turn to face me.

"How could you?" I can't help the blatant accusation in my tone. I don't know if I'm more hurt by his personal rejection or his professional one, but I decide to focus on the latter. "How could you set up a meeting with Carter & Boyd before you'd even given me the chance to present? I've worked my ass off for this company, for four years. Since signing with Focus, Nanosec's revenue has increased threefold. I didn't deserve this!"

"On the contrary, you *asked* for this," he replies cruelly, his jaw clenched so tightly it's a wonder he can get the words out.

"I beg your pardon?"

"You had the account!" he's almost yelling now, "you had it to begin with, and there was no way I was going to move it anywhere. I know how hard you've worked, and your service speaks for itself, but you left me no choice! How do you expect me to be taken seriously as the new CEO if I'm seen to be making decisions based on my personal life?"

"What?" I have no idea what he's talking about.

"You went and blabbed about us to your *opposition*, Emma! How arrogant are you? Telling Carter & Boyd they would never shift Nanosec's business because you were sleeping with the boss?" He is so insanely angry that I take an automatic step back, my mind whirling as I try to comprehend what he's saying. "If you screwed me to retain this account, I don't even want to know what you do for all your other clients!"

"What are you talking about?" I stammer, as the door opens and a highly excited Tracey steps through it with a tray.

"On the table," Greg barks, and she quickly deposits the tray. "That will be all," he adds menacingly. Her face falls, but she darts from the room, closing the doors behind her.

Greg runs a hand over his clean-shaven jaw and takes a deep breath before continuing. "I'm talking about getting a call from Carter & Boyd on Wednesday morning accusing me of exercising nepotism in the running of a fortune five hundred company. And seeing as I certainly didn't kiss and tell, that information could only have come from you." He throws me another look of utter disgust. "Did you get some sort of kick out of telling everyone you're screwing the new CEO, Emma? Does it give you some sort of twisted power trip?"

"I didn't tell everyone!" I retort, outraged, "I told one person! My best friend! Oh my God." I trail off as it hits me, "Megs must have let it slip – someone at Carter & Boyd must have found out, and they sent her here to try and secure your contract."

"Megs?" he asks, forgetting to look terrifying for a second, "you mean Megan Harris?"

"The girl you just met with, yes."

"She's your best friend?"

"Yes. Well, she was. She worked with me at Focus for four years, until just a few weeks ago. Why?"

His expression is unreadable. "Some friends you have, Emma. Megan's the one who called me in the first place."

IT ALL COMES CRASHING down around me, too fast for me to process, and I collapse onto the white sofa. Greg only arrived back on Tuesday and Megan had called him on Wednesday morning. She hadn't wasted any time. The shock of my best friend's betrayal is mind-numbing, but through my confusion, something else dawns on me.

"Is that why you rescheduled?" I ask, glancing up at him hollowly. "Is that why you didn't call?"

"I prefer not to be used to further someone's career, Emma," he replies coldly, "no matter how pleasurable the experience may be."

"I didn't use you, you asshole! I confided in a friend – someone I trusted." My righteous indignation takes him aback. "Megan is – was – my only confidant. There must be some mistake. She wouldn't do this to me."

"There's no mistake." His tone is softer now, but only marginally.

I shake my head, trying to make sense of it all. "Megan wouldn't throw away our friendship for the sake of one account."

"It's a big account," he points out.

"It doesn't matter. She wouldn't do this. Not to me... Oh, God." I drop my head into my hands.

"What?"

"Jack," I groan, mumbling into my palms. I feel the sofa dip under his weight as he takes a seat beside me. I turn my head to peer at him. He deserves an explanation. "Megan and Jack were having an affair," I sigh, knowing that this admission could very well cost me my job. "Jack ended it and fired Megan, but not before he found her a position at Carter & Boyd. Megan swore she was going to destroy him, but I didn't think she'd actually go through with it."

"Let me get this straight," he says, sounding dubious. "Megan did all of this just to get back at Jack, even if it meant ruining your reputation?"

An ugly black rage rears in my chest. "Apparently."

"So, you didn't believe that sleeping with me would secure my business?"

"I hate to break it to you, but last week I didn't give a damn about your business," I retort. "I was more concerned about when I would see you again."

He takes time to process this, and I drop my head back into my hands. I feel ill. I still can't believe that Megan would do this to me – that she would turn on me so viciously. I know she's been upset about Jack, and taking away our biggest account would hurt him, but it hurts me far more.

"I can't believe she'd stoop this low," I mutter, reaching automatically for the coffee on the table before me.

Greg doesn't say a word. He just sits there, staring at me as if trying to figure out if I'm telling the truth. I set my cup down and get to my feet.

"I'm going to talk to her."

He stands too. "You're not going anywhere until we've figured this out."

"You figure it out," I snap. "You believed that I was capable of this, that I would stoop so low. You obviously don't know me at all, and I'm not about to try to convince you otherwise."

"How was I to know your opposition is your best friend?" he counters.

"You could have asked me! You could have talked to me instead of cutting me off and making a fool of me in front of my boss. But instead, you immediately jumped to the worst possible conclusion. Get out of my way," I add, trying to shove past him.

"No," he grabs my arms and pushes me back. "We're going to talk about this."

"Screw you."

That stops him in his tracks, and a blaze of righteous anger crosses his face.

"You walk out of that door, and I will give this contract to Carter & Boyd."

"You're threatening me now?" His silence speaks volumes. My eyes widen, incredulously. "You know what, Greg," I say, snatching up my bag. "You can go to hell." I stride toward the doors and don't look back.

I HEAD STRAIGHT for Megan's apartment. She won't be home yet, but I'll wait all night if I have to. I'm not leaving without answers. During the short cab ride over, I make two calls. The first is to Jack, explaining I will only be in tomorrow and we can debrief then, and one to my parents to say I might be a little late fetching Ally. Unsurprisingly, when I arrive at Megan's, I find that my key no longer works. She must have changed the locks. I settle down on the carpet outside her apartment to wait.

Megan gets home just before six, and I scramble to my feet as she gets out of the elevator.

I don't even bother hiding my anger. "How could you, Megan?"

"How could I what?" she replies coolly.

"You're going to destroy my career!"

"No, I'm going to destroy Jack's," she corrects.

"If I lose Nanosec I'm going to be out on my ass!"

"Carter & Boyd will take you on," she justifies. "You know the Nanosec account – they'll need you." She's so calm, so carelessly unapologetic it feels like a punch to the gut.

"You betrayed me! How could you use what I told you in confidence against me? All that time you and Jack were carrying on, and I never told a soul."

She shrugs. "Maybe you should have." Then she notices the tears welling in my eyes, and she heaves a sigh. "He's only a client, Em. You said yourself you're not even sure you guys are a thing. Besides, from what I saw on Saturday night, you've clearly moved on."

"Oh my God, are you for real? That was nothing, I told you that! Oliver and I are just friends."

"You seem to have a lot of those," she sneers.

"Not as many as I thought," I reply pointedly.

"Look, Emma, it's not personal. I have a job to do and targets to meet, and Nanosec will go a long way to meeting those targets. I still have to prove myself at C&B, it's not like Focus."

I gape at her. "Not personal? You're my *best* friend! You're trying to steal my biggest client, and worse, you used my private affairs to do it! How is that not personal?"

"Firstly, I'm not trying." She allows herself a small smile. "I'm ninety-nine percent certain that Nanosec will be signing with Carter & Boyd in the next quarter. Secondly, once you've calmed down, you'll realize that I've done you a favor."

"A favor?"

"Yes. Jack's a dick, Emma. Focus is going to fall. You're better off deserting the ship before it's sunk."

"You're insane. This isn't a movie, this is my life we're talking about. My job, my reputation!"

She pulls a face. "You're just pissed that after all these years of living in your shadow I'm finally going to be the hottest property in advertising."

I open my mouth but nothing comes out, because this accusation is so absurd, I have no words to respond. I have never seen Megs as my competition, we've always worked as a team. Apparently, she doesn't share this view. I wonder if she ever did. I never suspected the extent of her professional jealousy. Yes, I am better at my job than she is, but that's only because I work harder. Megan is lazy by nature and does the bare minimum.

"Don't you find it ironic," I sneer eventually, losing my fragile grip on my temper, "that the very thing you've accused me of is the one thing that ensured you kept your job for the past four years?"

"What?" she snaps.

"Well, if you hadn't been screwing the boss, you probably would've been fired years ago," I smile spitefully. Tossing my useless key at her, I turn on my heel.

"You are going to fall very far, princess," she calls at my retreating figure. "I'm going to take every single client you have left – Nanosec is just the beginning."

"Do your worst, Megan," I scoff, barely flinching as her apartment door slams violently behind me.

By the time I've settled Alyssa into bed and opened an expensive bottle of red wine, my black rage has settled into a dull, vengeful anger. There is no point mourning the end of a friendship that obviously meant nothing to Megan, and I am nothing if not fiercely competitive in business. Paging through my customer files, deliberately avoiding Nanosec's, I barely notice the doorbell ringing. Glancing at my watch, a sickening dread settles in the pit of my stomach. It's after ten, and there's only one person I know who would come around this late.

PEERING THROUGH THE PEEPHOLE, I am so relieved that it is not a drunken Max on the other side that I open the door.

"Greg! What are you doing here?"

"You left."

I raise my chin defiantly, recalling his ultimatum. "Yes. I left."

He has the good grace to lower his eyes first. "I shouldn't have threatened to give Carter and Boyd the account."

"It was a dick move," I concede.

"I know."

I cross my arms over my chest and lean against the door frame until he finally realizes he's not done.

"I'm sorry."

"Good."

"You understand that this isn't entirely my fault," he muses. I get the sense that he's used to getting his own way and isn't quite sure how to handle this situation.

"I know."

His blue eyes crinkle at the corners. "You're really not going to make this easy for me, are you?"

"It's been a long day."

"Did you speak to Megan?"

"I did. I think it's safe to say that friendship is over."

"Are you okay?" I blink up at him, surprised at the genuine concern in his voice. I've been so angry, it hasn't even occurred to me that I've lost my best friend.

"I will be."

He nods, slow and thoughtful.

"I should get to bed," I say, glancing at my watch.

"If you're up to it, I'd like to take you to dinner tomorrow night."

I arch my brow. "Really. And why would you possibly want to do that?"

"Because I've been a prize prick and I'd like to make it up to you?" I can't help but chuckle. "Seriously," he continues, more somber, "I'm sorry. I'd really like a second chance to prove it."

"I need to spend some time with Ally tomorrow," I say, "but Wednesday could work."

The smile he gives me is dazzling. "I'll pick you up at eight."

"No." I'm not letting him off that easy.

"No?"

"I'll make my own way and meet you there. Just let me know where."

He gives me an arch look. "Are you always this stubborn?"

I start to close the door, not giving him an answer. "Text me the address," I say, before I close it completely.

I watch him through the keyhole. A small smile plays about his lips and he shakes his head, as if he can't quite figure out what just happened, before he turns away and strides back down the path to his car.

"EMMA!" Jack snaps the second I exit the elevator the following morning. "What the hell is going on? I tried to call you a dozen times yesterday!"

"I know, I'm sorry, Jack. I did tell Chloe to let you know I wouldn't be coming back in and that I'd brief you this morning."

He's not appeased. "She told me. I don't appreciate being kept in the dark."

"I know," I echo. "But I promise it was necessary. I had to do some major damage control." That stops him in his tracks.

"Why was Megan at Nanosec? You told me this account was in the bag."

I see Oliver's head appear in the doorway behind him, but he quickly retreats, and I focus on Jack. I've never seen him this wound up.

"It is," I soothe. "That's why I needed time. Megan tried to outplay us – she's pissed – at you actually, and she did her best to pull the account away, but she failed. Nanosec is secure."

"How sure are you?"

"Ninety-nine percent sure."

He deliberates this for a second and then runs his hands through his hair, his relief palpable.

"Why would Megan do that?"

"Why do you think? You broke her heart, Jack. She wants revenge."

"She's not that petty."

I give a scornful laugh. "Apparently, neither of us knows her as well as we thought we did. And you should know, it won't end with Nanosec. She's going after all of our accounts."

Jack opens his mouth to question me and then notices one of the other executives, lurking in his open doorway. "Into my office," Jack murmurs. I follow him inside, and he shuts the door behind us. "Explain."

I collapse onto the black leather chair opposite his desk. "Megan tried to use something I'd told her in confidence against me. She went behind my back and tried to get Nanosec to jump ship. And before you ask, no, I'm not going to tell you what it was."

"I wasn't going to ask."

"Good."

"Why would she do that? I get that she's mad at me, but why would she do that to you?"

"I have no idea." I don't mention Megan's comment that I should join Carter & Boyd. It might just send Jack over the edge, and besides, I could never work in the same company as her again. Not now, not after this. "Megan is not who I thought she was."

"I can't believe she would do something like this."

"Believe it, Jack. Hell hath no fury like a woman scorned."

He cringes. "For what it's worth, I'm sorry that you got dragged into all of this."

"Me too."

"You did a good job yesterday." It's high praise, coming from Jack.

"I did. Nice of you to notice."

He lets my sarcasm slide. "You're sure the account is secure?"

"I said so didn't I?"

"You said you were ninety-nine percent sure."

"So?"

"Be a hundred percent sure. Both our asses depend on it."

THE SECOND I'm back in my office, Oliver ducks inside, emitting a low whistle.

"What was that about?"

"You wouldn't believe me if I told you." Being Oliver, he doesn't press me, but I find myself telling him most of it anyway – how Megan betrayed me and tried to steal Nanosec's account from right under my nose. Oliver is righteously outraged on my behalf, but he doesn't look as surprised as I expect him to be and I say as much.

"Yeah, well, she didn't strike me as being a very good friend," he admits.

"Why do you say that?"

His cheeks redden. "She, um, well, she propositioned me on Saturday night when I came out of the men's room."

"Oh God, what did she say?" Megan had thrown herself at Oliver most of Saturday night, but I wasn't aware she'd voiced her intentions.

"It doesn't matter." The fact that he doesn't want to tell me is a clear indication that whatever Megan said to him wasn't complimentary as far as I am concerned.

"What did she say?" I repeat, locking gazes with him.

"She might have mentioned that I should take her home because she wasn't as prim and proper as you were, and that she would do things to me that you could only," he raises his hands and puts air quotes around the rest, "dream about."

"She didn't!"

"She did!" He is half-laughing, half-disgusted. "It scared the shit out of me!"

"Well, it's hardly an insult."

"Agreed. It was more that she felt she needed to make the comparative, you know. As if it was some competition between the two of you. Anyway, in my opinion, friends don't do that."

"No, they don't," I agree. "Which is why I'm so happy that I found a new and improved bestie to take her place."

"You and Jack getting cozy?" he teases, and I throw a pad of Post-Its at him.

He catches them lazily. "Any exciting plans this week?"

"I have a date," I admit.

"A date?" he grins without a trace of awkwardness. "How exciting. Who's the lucky man?"

I don't want anyone to know about Greg yet. I'm pretty sure Jack wouldn't like it. Not that he has any say in my personal life, but with everything that's happened with Megan and Nanosec, it'll raise a red flag. "Just a guy," I tell Oliver.

He gets to his feet and walks toward the door. "Well, have fun," he teases, eyes sparkling with ill-concealed mirth.

"I will," I call back, smiling to myself.

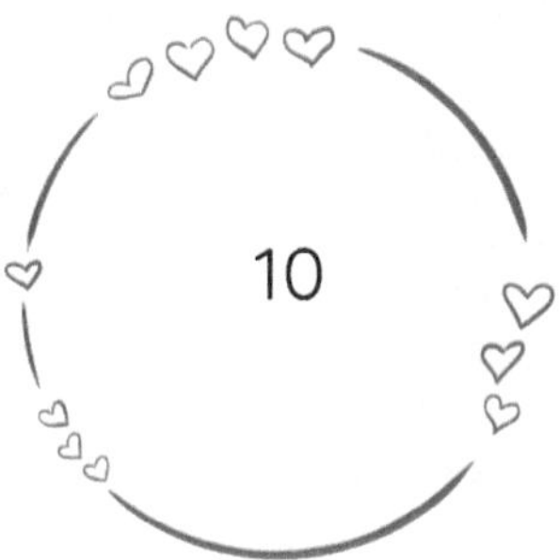

Alyssa and I head for the movies right after work. It's a school night so we catch the early show. She's been withdrawn since last weekend when I had to fetch her from Max's, and he hadn't bothered to show up for his visit this past Saturday. After the movie, I treat her to ice-cream, and she slowly comes out of her shell.

"I miss daddy," she admits guiltily.

"Of course you do, angel. It's okay to miss him," I add, trying to reassure her. "But daddy's going to come and see you on Sunday." As I say it, I vow to make it happen whether Max likes it or not. "We can go to the park, if you like?"

She brightens instantly. "All of us?"

"All of us," I promise. She nods her head in excitement at the very thought, and I suppress a sigh. All I ever wanted for Alyssa was for her to grow up in a safe, stable environment. To feel loved and adored by her parents and never experience even a token of what I felt as a child. But Max screwed that all up, and yet I'm the one who has to deal with the consequences.

She falls asleep on the drive home with chocolate ice-cream all over her face. Not wanting to wake her, I wipe her down with a warm cloth and tuck her into bed.

Ten minutes later, armed with a scalding cup of tea, I dial Max's number.

"Hello?" he answers immediately.

"Hi. I'm sorry to call so late, we just got back from the movies."

"That's okay. What did you guys go see?" To my surprise, he sounds completely sober. He doesn't bring up the missed visit, and I find myself not wanting to either.

"The new Dumbo."

He laughs. "Was it any better than the old one?"

"Not particularly."

"Did Ally enjoy herself?"

"She had ice-cream. Need I say more?"

I hate to ruin this fragile peace, but I have to bring it up for Ally's sake. "You missed your visit on Saturday," I say. I hear him exhale a shuddery breath. "Max?"

"I'm sorry. I..." he trails off, and I bite my lip to stop from filling the silence. "I have a lot to tell you," he says eventually. "But I'd rather do it in person."

"Okay," I draw out the word. "Should I be worried?"

"No. Can I come over this Saturday?"

"Actually, that's why I was calling. Ally wants to go to the park. I thought maybe we could have a picnic." I cringe, waiting for him to snap, to insist that I'm not only insisting on supervised visits, but now dictating what we do during those visits. To my utter astonishment, Max agrees.

"Sounds good. Can I bring anything?"

"No, I'll pack a basket. Can you meet us there at ten? The one on the corner of Madison and Sixth."

"Sure. I'll see you then."

"See you then." I hang up, not quite sure what just happened. It feels oddly surreal. I've never denied that when Max is sober, he is one of the nicest people I know. Buried within the depths of his alcoholism is the man I fell in love with – the man I was prepared to spend the rest of my life with. It is nothing short of tragic that his disease was stronger than his love for his family, but I have come to accept that's exactly what it is – a disease. Max is ill, and there is nothing anybody can do to heal him. I can only hope that one day he finds the strength and the courage to heal himself.

THE FOLLOWING EVENING, I have the house to myself. Alyssa is sleeping at my parents. My dad fetched her straight from school, and he'll drop her off in the morning, so I'm officially off duty for twenty-four hours. I shave my legs, paint my toenails, and even give myself a mini-facial, which includes a bentonite clay mask that makes me look like something out of a horror movie. When I wash it off, I see no visible difference. Go figure.

I pull the tag off the dress I bought during my lunch break. It's coral, high at the neck and plunging at the back. The soft fabric clings to my body in all the right places. I'm meeting Greg at eight, but with so much time on my hands, I arrive early.

"Would you like me to show you to your table?" the waiter asks. I decline and opt to wait at the bar. By the time Greg arrives ten minutes later, I'm halfway through my first Martini.

"You look..." Greg trails off, his eyes roaming the entire length of my body. He doesn't finish the sentence.

"You too," I murmur shyly. His athletic frame would make anything look good, but the dark grey chinos and open-collared white shirt is the perfect balance of smart-casual.

"Have you forgiven me yet?" he asks.

"I haven't decided."

A low chuckle and his arm brushes against mine. "Should we go sit down? I'm starving."

The waiter darts forward to show us to our table. Greg pulls out my chair, leaving the poor man hovering with one arm outstretched. Greg orders a bottle of red, giving him something to do.

"I assume your daughter is safe and sound tonight, and we won't need to be paying any surprise visits to your ex?"

"She is," I nod, "she's at my folks. And Max is actually being pretty agreeable." He doesn't comment, but I can see the hard, unforgiving doubt in his blue eyes.

"I never asked about your race," I say, changing the subject. "How did you do?"

"We did well."

"We?"

"It was a team event. Eight of us participated."

"Oh, nice." I shut my mouth because I have no idea what the correct response is. I know nothing about cycling.

As if reading my thoughts, he gives me a wicked grin. "How's the swimming going?" *Oh shit.* I'd forgotten about that. I'm supposed to be a swimmer. Obviously, I haven't done any swimming lately, other than an awkward doggy paddle around my parent's pool with Alyssa on the occasional hot day.

"I did a few laps this morning at the gym," I reply airily. His gaze flickers up from the bread roll he's smearing with butter, and he raises a skeptical eyebrow.

"Which gym?"

I open my mouth and realize I have no idea where the closest gym is. In fact, I have no idea where any gym is. Greg is still staring at me, an amused expression on his face.

"Okay fine, I don't go to the gym. In fact, I don't swim – well, not the way you think. I'm more of a professional floater. The thing is, work keeps me pretty busy, and I have a four-year-old daughter who takes up every minute of my life not spent working, so I don't really do much in the way of exercise."

He hands me the roll, liberally buttered, his eyes never leaving my face.

"You think I'm a slob, don't you?"

"No. I think you're adorable."

I blush crimson at the blatant desire on his face. Then he winces.

"What?" I ask.

"Nothing," he says, but he shifts uncomfortably on his chair. I lower my gaze and comprehension dawns.

"Oh!"

"Do you have this effect on all men, or am I just powerless to your charms?"

"I think it might just be you."

"I think you don't give yourself enough credit."

Now that I know he's horny, I find I can't concentrate on anything else. A sleeping beast in my chest opens one eye and purrs.

Our conversation is interrupted by the waiter, who returns to take our order. We settle on a seafood platter for two, but the second the waiter leaves, Greg drops his napkin and moves around the table to sit beside me. His arm trails along the back of the seat, his fingers brushing the ends of my hair. It's intimate and unnerving, having him so close, but I shift so that my hip presses up against his. I meet the challenge in his gaze. Hidden by the starched table cloth, his other hand clamps over my thigh. His thumb traces a lazy circle, setting my skin on fire.

I snatch up the glass of water on the table and drink deeply.

"Is it hot in here, or is it just me?" I ask, flashing Greg a grin and trying to break the mounting tension. He doesn't respond. Instead, his forefinger joins his thumb, inching upward with every lazy circle. When his hand finally cups that most sensitive part of me, I bite my tongue to stifle the gasp of pleasure which threatens to claw its way out of my throat. This is so surreal, so primal, and reckless, but I raise my hips, returning the pressure of his hand. Greg's eyes are glittering, his pupils dilated. Beneath the skirt of my dress, my thighs open of their own accord and his fingers slip inside my pants.

By the time the waiter returns, my breathing is coming in short, sharp gasps. He gives me a strange look as he deposits an enormous tray before us, but one narrow-eyed look from Greg is all the warning he needs to make himself scarce.

The pressure building between my legs is almost at breaking point. I clamp my hand onto Greg's thigh, needing to ground myself, and my nails dig in. It takes everything in me to keep my expression neutral, to act as though this entire restaurant hasn't been reduced to the blazing heat of my very core. I reach the brink and start to topple over and, just as quickly as he started, Greg whips his hand away, abandoning his merciless assault on my body.

I exhale in a wave of despair as tiny shockwaves ripple through me, fading with every passing second.

"What are you doing?" I breathe. My head feels too heavy for my neck. At least when he speaks, he sounds just as affected as I am, his voice hoarse.

"I think it's called foreplay," he says. He picks a juicy pink prawn from the plate, his deft fingers peeling it expertly before he hands it to me. It's dripping in lemon butter.

"My cardiologist thanks you," I manage to joke before I pop it into my mouth. It's heavenly. I take a small sip of wine, wipe my fingers on my napkin and meet Greg's gaze. His eyes are dancing.

"You're trouble with a capital T," I say.

Without missing a beat, he leans forward and puts his lips on mine, his tongue sweeping mine so quickly I might have imagined it as he savors the lingering taste in my mouth. My blood sings, rushing to my head and thundering in my ears.

"Enough."

"Enough?" he asks, his brow raised in challenge. I have no doubt he'd go on all night if I let him, but quite frankly my body cannot take another second of his teasing.

I lean forward, my lips pulling up at the corners, and boldly place my hand over the front of his pants. Greg almost lurches out of his seat as his hand flies into the air.

"Cheque please," he gasps.

We don't make it home. We barely even make it to his car, before I'm tearing at his clothes. In one swift movement, he hikes my dress over my hips, which is all he can manage in the confined space. I spare a fleeting moment of gratitude for the darkly tinted windows before his mouth claims mine, and all I know is oblivion.

11

During the drive home, I keep bursting into fits of giggles. Even Greg can't keep the smile off his face, although his is far smugger, no doubt as a result of the three orgasms he coaxed out of me, despite the cramped space and an awkward pause when an elderly couple ventured too close to the window, and he'd almost castrated himself on the gearstick.

Despite it all, I'm still not satisfied.

"Ally is sleeping over at my folks tonight," I say pointedly as we turn into my street. His teeth flash in the dim light of the car.

"Had this all planned, did you?"

"Believe me, what happened tonight wasn't premeditated."

He pulls up outside my house and rounds the car to open my door, then retrieves a small black overnight bag from the trunk.

"Who's presumptuous now?" I tease, but my heart stutters in anticipation. He holds my hand as we walk up the path, and it's so easy, so comfortable. Once inside, I head straight for my room and into the en suite to turn on the shower. I stick my head out of the door and give him a lingering look. "You coming?"

He doesn't need to be asked twice.

Later, we lie on sheets still damp from our after-shower tussle. I nestle in the crook of Greg's shoulder while his fingers trail over my arm. My stomach growls, and we both laugh, thinking of the wasted seafood platter.

"I have my son next weekend," Greg says after a time. "How about we go bike riding? Alyssa would love it." I blink in the dark. I really, really like him, but I balk at the thought of spending a whole day with him and his son so soon. I don't want Alyssa meeting anyone I date until I'm sure that they are going to become a part of my life.

"She doesn't really know how to ride a bike," I say, cringing at the flimsy excuse. "She still has training wheels."

"Even better, we can teach her."

"She's only four."

"Jesse's been riding without them since he was three. She'll pick it up in no time, I promise."

"I just don't think..."

"That we should meet each other's kids?" he finishes my sentence.

"Well, yeah."

"We don't need to make a big deal out of it. We're just friends, spending the day together. Our kids don't need to know any more than that. Unless you don't trust yourself to keep your hands off me, which would be perfectly understandable." His grin is infectious.

"It sounds fun," I concede, throwing caution to the wind. "But we'll have to make it Sunday. Saturday is Max's day with Ally."

"Sunday is perfect." My stomach rumbles again, and Greg gets to his feet. He rummages in the black bag and pulls out a pair of sleeping shorts, which he pulls on before offering me his hand. I eye it, bemused. "I'm going to make you a sandwich," he says, by way of explanation. "There's no way I'm going to get any sleep with that noise."

I sit at the kitchen table while he smears peanut butter on two slices of bread. He slaps them together and cuts four perfect triangles before pushing the plate toward me.

"You're not even going to cut off my crusts?" I tease.

"Eat your crusts, they're good for you."

I take a bite while he fetches the milk from the fridge and pours me a generous glass. Only once he's taken the seat opposite me do I stop eating. This is easily one of the best evenings I've spent in a long time. Greg is confident, cocky, and surprisingly funny for someone who is so ruthless in business.

"How are you single?" I blurt out. He doesn't seem surprised by the question.

"Work takes up a lot of my time."

"I don't buy that. All men say that, but it doesn't stop them taking care of their physical needs."

He shrugs. "You didn't ask about my physical needs. You asked why I was single."

"Oh," I say. I wish hadn't asked.

"I'm not promiscuous," he says, his eyes holding mine, "but I certainly haven't been celibate since the separation."

"And this?" I ask, waving a sandwich triangle between us. "Is this something you might have time for?"

He gives me an arch look. "Are you asking me if we're dating?" I feel the heat rise in my cheeks, but I stand my ground.

"I'm asking if this is just a physical needs arrangement, or if it's something more."

His blue eyes soften. "It's definitely something more."

"I'm honored." I grin. "What with you being so busy and all."

"What about you? Have you dated much since your divorce?"

"No. And before you ask, I haven't really taken care of my physical need either."

"Anytime you need help in that department, I'd be happy to oblige."

"How generous of you."

He spreads his arms. "What can I say? I'm a generous guy."

"And so humble."

He laughs at that and then stands to take my empty plate to the sink.

"We should get some sleep. I have an early start."

"Have you had time to review my proposal?"

"Yes, actually. There are a few things I'd like to change, but all in all, it's sound."

My professional pride protests. "What changes?"

"Why don't you swing by my office tomorrow afternoon and we can go through it."

"Okay, sure." We walk down the hall, and something else occurs to me. "Have you heard from Megan at all?"

"Yes, actually. She called me this morning to set up a follow-up appointment."

I feel my hackles rise as we climb into bed. "What did you tell her?"

"I told her to come see me on Monday."

"What? Why?"

He pulls my head onto his chest. "So that I can tell her in person that Nanosec will not now, or ever, have any interest in doing business with Carter & Boyd," he replies, eerily calm.

"Why didn't you just tell her over the phone?"

"Because I want to tell her in front of her boss. I asked that she bring him along."

"What?"

"Megan crossed a line. He needs to know what kind of employee he's brought into his company."

"But she'll be fired! You can't do that!" This is yet another glimpse into the fact that below all his charm lurks a ruthless businessman.

"I can, and I will," Greg counters. "Nobody manipulates me, Emma. Megan Harris's career in advertising is over."

It is the first time I become aware that he is capable of cruelty. His ego, however, in no way diminishes his sex appeal. If anything, it only makes him that much more attractive. Max was weak, which is why he couldn't fight his addiction. It's also no less than Megan deserves. Setting aside how she treated me, the way she conducted herself was appalling and utterly unprofessional. And yet, as angry as I am with her, I don't want her to lose her job.

"I don't think you should do it," I murmur quietly.

"Emma, this isn't personal, and it has nothing to do with me and you. I'm not that petty. Megan's actions were unprofessional, and she deserves to be disciplined."

"I guess."

"But?" he can sense that I am biting my tongue.

"It just seems a bit cruel."

"I can be cruel," he says matter-of-factly and without the slightest bit of contrition. "Does that bother you?"

"I don't know," I admit.

He sighs and raises himself onto his elbow, head propped in his hand. "Look, Emma, I like you. A lot, if I'm being honest. But this is how I do things. I didn't get to where I am by being nice, so unless you can give me a very good reason why I shouldn't bring Megan's misdemeanors to light, I'm not changing my mind."

12

Come Saturday, Ally is in one of her rare, overly-excited moods.

"Calm down!" I say, for what feels like the twentieth time, as we pull into the parking lot. The sound of children playing reaches me instantly. Ignoring me completely, Ally opens her door and leaps down from her seat, making a beeline for the playground.

"Alyssa!" I scream in horror, as a white station wagon pulls into the lot. Ally streaks directly toward its approaching path. She either doesn't hear me, or she is too buoyed up to listen, and I am too far away to do anything about it, but I dart forward anyway, my heart in my throat.

A strong pair of arms grab her at the last minute and pull her out of the path of the oncoming car. My legs buckle in relief.

"Max!" I gasp as I reach them, clutching my chest. "Oh, thank God." Max holds an unsuspecting Alyssa tightly, his mouth a hard, grim line.

"How could you let her run across the lot on her own?" he thunders angrily.

"I didn't! She ran off!" I place my hand on her shoulder, desperate to reassure myself that she's okay.

"That's not good enough, Em! That car could have hit her!"

"I know!" Tears prick at my eyelids. Being taken to task by the worst parent in the world is humiliating and grossly unfair, but he's right. "I'll put the child-locks on," I promise, trying to diffuse the situation. "You take her to the playground, I'll fetch our stuff." He turns on his heel without another word, and I head back to the car to retrieve our bags, my heart still thudding violently in my chest.

Our morning is not off to a great start, but soon Alyssa's infectious delight perks both Max and I up.

"How are things at work?" he asks placatingly after about an hour of disapproving silence.

"Good." I wave at Ally on the swings, "Megan has left. She's gone over to Carter & Boyd."

"Isn't Carter & Boyd your opposition? That's got to be tough on the friendship," he whistles sympathetically.

"To say the least. We're not really friends anymore."

"You didn't let work come between you, did you?"

"No," I shake my head. "I have no problem with professional rivalry. She just... well, let's just say she betrayed me in a very dirty, underhanded way."

"I'm sorry to hear that," he says, sounding as though he means it.

"Thanks."

Max wanders off to play with Ally, and I lie back on the blue-and-white checked blanket, closing my eyes and letting the sun warm my skin. The sound of laughter and a healthy dose of vitamin D is far better than any therapy, I think lazily. Dozing lightly between sleep and wakefulness, I give a humph of surprise when Alyssa jumps onto my belly a short while later, driving all the air from my lungs.

"Daddy's getting us ice-cream," she announces, her cheeks flushed with excitement. A moment later Max hands me a lolly – raspberry, my favorite.

"You know me too well," I remark drily, without really thinking.

In times like these, it's easy to forget the horror of our divorce and the events leading up to it.

"Better than you know yourself." It was his standard response when we were together, and the familiar teasing makes me feel both nostalgic and irritated.

After we've packed up, Max walks us to the car. With Alyssa strapped safely in her seat, he makes a point of checking that the child-lock is on before closing her door and turning to face me.

"Look, Emma, about the court order."

"Please," I hold up my hand to stop him, "let's not get into this now. I'm not trying to hurt you—"

"I know that," he cuts me off. "I just wanted to say that I'm sorry. I'm disgusted with myself for how I acted that night – for how I behaved. I don't want to lose her..." he trails off as he gazes through the window. Alyssa is smiling up at us, oblivious to our tense conversation. "Anyway, I wanted you to be the first to know that I've joined A.A."

It takes me a full minute for the words to register, and when they do, the impact they have is remarkable.

"Really?" I feel like I might burst into tears.

"Really," he nods. "I don't want to end up being a deadbeat dad with nothing to show for my life. I've already ruined the best thing I ever had."

"Max, that's wonderful. I'm so proud of you." Stepping forward, I hug him properly for the first time in years. His arms come around me naturally, and another wave of nostalgia washes over me. "If there is anything I can do to help, just let me know."

"Actually," he releases me and looks slightly sheepish, "there's a meeting in a few weeks. They want us to bring someone along – someone directly affected by our drinking. I think it's part of the healing process and taking responsibility for the damage we've caused."

"I'm there," I say without hesitation. "Just let me know when and where, and I'm there." I smile up at him, seeing him in a new light.

There is no possibility that Max and I will ever reconcile, but this could mean so much for his relationship with our daughter. And if he stops drinking, I might be able to trust him again. I could revoke the court order, and everything could go back to the way it was.

"Thanks, Em," he murmurs.

"You're very welcome." I give him a quick hug and climb into the driver's seat. Max waves as we pull out of the lot.

"I'm five minutes away," Greg says when I answer his call the following morning.

"We're almost ready," I say, a smile in my voice. I've been up since dawn, packing a picnic.

Exactly five minutes later Greg pulls up to my curb in a flashy black SUV. I'm already locking the front door as he gets out to greet us. He doesn't try to kiss my cheek as he usually does, keeping to his word in front of Alyssa.

I smile up at him, grateful that she can't read my expression. "Where's your car?"

"This is my car. I have more than one," he admits sheepishly, catching sight of my arch look. "And in my defense, the bikes won't fit in the Beemer."

He loads Alyssa's bicycle in the back and I strap her in beside a cherubic-looking little boy with Greg's green eyes and dimples he could only have inherited from his mother.

"You must be Jesse," I say, smiling at him. He doesn't reply, but the dimples deepen shyly.

"He sure is," Greg announces, settling into the driver's seat and swiveling to face his son. "Jess, this is my friend Emma who I was telling you about, and that's Alyssa, her daughter." Jesse and Ally give each other an appraising once-over before turning back to face us.

"Maybe we should just get going," I tell Greg, trying not to laugh.

The park he takes us to is surrounded by a broad bicycle track which means that I'm able to lay down a blanket and set up our picnic without ever losing sight of Alyssa. I settle down to watch as she pedals furiously after Jesse, who, by the look of it, has been riding since birth.

"We should get those training wheels off," Greg tells me after a time.

I frown. "I don't know. If she falls, she might lose all her confidence."

"And if she doesn't, she'll gain a whole lot more," he counters.

I'm still not convinced. "Let me ask her."

Ally is hesitant but willing to try. Within minutes, Greg has the trainers off, and I find myself jogging alongside her as she wobbles on the bike. Greg joins me on the second lap, a secretive smile plastered on his handsome face.

"Don't," I warn, conscious of my jiggling backside and the fact that my bra is far more sexy than supportive.

"I wasn't going to say anything," he lies, and then, lowering his voice so Alyssa won't hear, "let her go, she's got it."

Slowly, I ease my firm grip on Ally's seat. I jog beside her for at least fifteen meters before she wobbles, and I grab hold of her again. "Well done!" I yell, triumphantly, "you were riding all by yourself!"

"Don't let go, mommy!" she shrieks, but I can hear the euphoria beneath her fear. As soon as she's stable, I let go again. After four more laps, I'm drenched in perspiration and gasping for breath, but Alyssa is riding on her own.

"Mommy needs a break," I pant, conscious of Greg jogging along beside me, barely breaking a sweat.

"Here, let me take over," he offers. Gratefully, I accept and head back to the picnic blanket.

Five minutes later, Greg joins me, while Ally and Jesse race around the track. Ally is nowhere near as fast as Jesse, but that doesn't stop her from trying her best to catch up with him.

"I can't believe she's riding on her own," I breathe in awe.

"She's a fast learner," Greg concedes, with the smug charm of a man who's been proved right.

"Thanks for doing this. It's nice to have a man around who knows how to handle this kind of thing."

"This kind of thing, as in cardio?" he teases.

I throw a grape at him. He catches it easily and pops it in his mouth. "You should come out with me one day – on the bikes, I mean. I think you'd enjoy it."

"Hmm-mmm," I mumble, non-committal. "I'll think about it."

When they drop us off around midday, Greg and Jesse come inside. The kids disappear into Alyssa's bedroom and soon the familiar sound of games on her iPad floats down the hall. Greg steps up behind me as I fill two glasses with ice, his hard body pressed up against mine. I ignore him and set about making two cups, while my heart flip-flops in my chest. When his hand steals up my shorts, encountering bare thigh, I almost slosh soda all over the counter.

"It sounds like they'll be occupied for a while," Greg croons in my ear, his voice low and inviting as his fingers creep northward. I lean back into him, feeling the hard nudge of him against my backside, and my head droops back onto his shoulder. The ice is melted by the time we're done.

"You are incorrigible," I tell him later when we settle onto the sofa, drinks in hand.

He gives me a devilish grin. "I didn't hear you complaining, although I did hear a few noises I wouldn't mind hearing again."

"You're making me blush."

"I should hope so." He sets his glass down. "When do I get to see you alone again, so we can finish what we started?"

. . .

THE PROBLEM with dating when you have small children and are trying to keep it secret, I realize as the weeks go by, is that you never feel fully satisfied. Stolen moments, fast and furious sex, fully-clothed, all add to the thrill of it, but I'm starting to look forward to having our relationship out in the open. I do love the long, lazy nights on the rare occasion we get the house to ourselves. Greg is insatiable, and an expert lover. I'm surprised I'm not bow-legged every time he leaves. I've spent a few evenings at his place, too, although it took me a few visits before I could get used to the opulence of it. "You live like a Kardashian," I'd told him. He'd laughed and admitted he'd always had a thing for Kourtney.

I don't see or hear from Megan for almost three months, so my gasp of astonishment, when she barges into my office one Thursday morning, is completely genuine. Between Alyssa, work, and my relationship with Greg, I've been too busy to even think about her. I'd heard through Greg that she'd received a warning once her boss had heard about her unprofessional conduct, but as far as I knew, she was still working at Carter and Boyd.

"What are you doing here?" I demand. Unruffled, she drapes herself over the visitor's chair opposite my desk and examines her fingernails.

"Word has it you have your eye on the Greaves account," she announces. "I'm here to tell you not to waste your time."

Greaves Dawson is an international conglomerate that manufactures a range of health foods and spends millions of dollars a year on advertising. They're also one of Carter & Boyd's biggest accounts.

"They reached out," I tell Megan, feeling my hackles rise. It's true – only last week I got the call from their head of marketing, calling for a meeting.

"Bullshit!" Megan hisses, losing some of her sass.

I shrug. "I guess they're not happy with how Carter & Boyd are handling their portfolio."

"You mean how *I'm* handling it."

"Your words, not mine," I counter.

"Is that how you're going to play this now, Emma? Poaching clients?"

"Like I said, they approached me. And in case you've forgotten, Megan, you started this by going after Nanosec."

She jumps on the name like a cat. "Speaking of Nanosec. I believe Greg Daniels is quite close with Greaves' head of marketing. Joanna, I think her name is." She waits for a response, but I remain silent, refusing to be baited. "*Very* close, if my sources are correct."

"Get out."

"Are you still seeing him?"

"That's none of your business."

"Oh," she feigns sympathy, "you are. Poor thing. Well, I guess so long as the work's coming in, there's no need not to share. Who knows, maybe he'll get his new friend to sign you on when our contract expires."

I get to my feet. "I told you to leave. I won't ask again." For a second, her face falls, and I catch a glimpse of the old Megan, but it's gone before I can blink. "What happened to you?" I ask before I can help myself. "We were friends. Why are you doing this?"

She gives me a pitiful look. "We were never friends, Emma. You were a means to an end – an alibi, nothing more."

I nod. "Well, then I guess there's nothing more to say."

I SHOULD HAVE KNOWN she wasn't here for me. The second Megan steps into the hall, her eyes cut to Jack's office.

"Don't even think about it," I begin, but it's too late. His door opens and Jack steps out into the hall. It takes him three seconds to notice Megan's presence. Megan flashes him a smile and then she swivels on her inch-high heels and sashays toward the elevator.

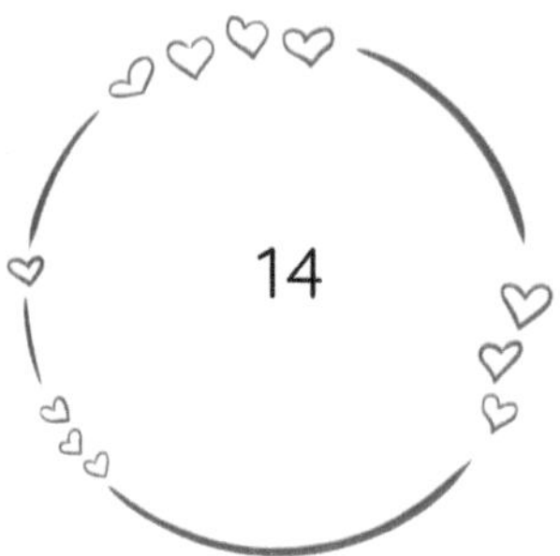

"I can't believe she barged into your office like that," Oliver says. We're in my car, I'm driving, and I've been catching him up with what's happened. Oliver was away on conference this past week, so he missed the entire episode. I'd missed him. Over the past few months, he has cemented himself well and truly as my person at Focus – my work-husband, as Greg likes to call him. I tell him everything, although I omit the details about Jack and Megan. That's not my secret to tell.

"She was so brazen," I tell him, indicating left. "She just walked in as if she owned the place."

"How did the meeting with Greaves go?"

I sigh. "Well. Very well, actually."

"And yet you don't sound happy about it?"

"I'm ninety-nine percent certain they're jumping ship."

"You know this is a good thing, right? Greaves are almost as big as Nanosec."

"I know. I'm just not looking forward to Megan's reaction."

He gazes out of the window, watching suburbia fall away. "Do you think she's mentally stable?"

I frown. Three months ago I would've laughed at the question, but now I'm not so sure. Oliver seems to sense my distress because he changes the subject.

"How're things with Max?"

That brings a genuine smile to my face. "He's doing so well. Ally is with him today, I'm picking her up later."

Max had been true to his word. He recently celebrated his ninetieth day of sobriety. I went with him to the meeting. I even brought a cake.

"That's good. I'm glad he's getting his shit together."

I glance across at him. "You don't sound so sure."

"I just don't think you should get your hopes up. It's a lifelong struggle."

"I know. Thanks for that, Debbie Downer."

We pull onto the dirt road that leads to the beginning of the cycle trail.

"I can't believe you're making me do this," Oliver grumbles as we emerge from his car.

"Oh, come on, it'll be fun. And just think of the women you might meet."

"I've sworn off women, remember." It had taken weeks before Simone had finally stopped harassing him.

"Until the next crazy lady who bats her eyelashes at you," I tease. "Besides, you're owning those pants." The cycling tights he's wearing leave nothing to the imagination.

"You made it!" Greg's voice reaches us as soon as I switch off the engine, and I turn to see him striding over, fully kitted out in tights, form-fitting shirt, and cycling shoes. Only Greg could make that ridiculous helmet look sexy, I think, my stomach flip-flopping at the sight of him. We've been dating for months, and yet he still has this effect on me. I still haven't asked him about the infamous Joanna. We haven't spent any time alone since Megan mentioned her, but with Ally sleeping out we have the house to ourselves this evening. I vow to bring it up later. Oliver averts his eyes as Greg kisses me hello. I can see my reflection in his sunglasses.

"We did," I reply, feigning a confidence I don't feel.

"Well, saddle up, we're leaving in five." Greg squeezes my ass before making his way back to a small group nearby. I pout as I realize the group is predominantly made up of women, who have eyes only for him.

"When are you just going to come clean and admit you'd rather be on the sofa watching tv?" Oliver asks.

"I wouldn't!" I argue, and then, seeing the knowing smirk on his face, I relent. "Okay, I so would, but he loves it. I'm being *supportive.*"

"You're being a dork. Why don't we just leave now and save ourselves the hassle?"

"We are doing this, Mr. James. Now saddle up – you heard the man."

DESPITE MY BRAVADO, I am terrified. I finally bowed to Greg's subliminal pressure and started cycling a month ago, but it is completely out of my comfort zone. I also dragged an unwilling Oliver into my mess, needing someone who feels the same to sympathize with me. Watching the lady cyclists fawning over my boyfriend wasn't really my idea of fun, but I never let that on to Greg. Only Oliver knows how I truly feel about it

"Do you really think I'm being naïve about Max?" I ask him as we don our helmets.

"There's nothing wrong with giving him the benefit of the doubt. I just don't want you to be disappointed if it doesn't work out."

"He's really trying. And it's important for Alyssa to have a relationship with her dad."

Oliver is struggling with his helmet clip, and I reach forward to help him.

"That is not true. My dad was an asshole, and I turned out just fine," he quips.

"According to who?" I grin.

"You guys ready?" Greg calls, mounting his bike.

"Absolutely!" I reply brightly.

Half an hour later, my legs are burning, and my shirt is drenched in sweat as we pedal over dirt paths and tree roots. The terrain is even rougher than I expected, and my heart rate is going through the roof. Oliver and I have fallen behind, but no matter how hard I push myself, we don't seem to be catching up. Peals of laughter and muted conversation carry back to me on the wind.

"At least they're having fun," Oliver pants behind me. "I can't believe you forced me into this," he adds petulantly.

"It's good for us," I huff back.

"I'm going to have a heart attack. I'm pretty sure that's not good for me."

"Stop moaning and pedal."

We finally catch up to the others at a small, rickety wooden bridge that can only accommodate one rider at a time. I watch in trepidation as one by one, the cyclists cross over. It's not a long drop, but the bridge is narrower than anything I've had to traverse before.

"Can we go around?" Oliver asks, echoing my sentiments.

"You'll be fine," Greg reassures us. "But maybe it's better if I help you over, Em. I'll come back and take your bike over – you walk across."

I sense rather than see the smug smiles of the women cyclists.

"No, I'm fine," I snap, gritting my teeth.

"Emma."

"I said I'm fine."

He hesitates a moment but then slowly pedals onto the bridge.

"You're a stubborn ass," Oliver murmurs behind me. "And why didn't he offer to take my bike over?" I burst out laughing.

"Right," I say, once everyone else has crossed. "Let's do this."

"Let's not," Oliver grumbles, but I place my foot firmly on the pedal and push off onto the bridge.

. . .

I WAKE up to the sound of frantic voices and a ringing in my ears. Greg's face looms over me, filled with concern. When he sees my eyes open, he sags in relief.

"What happened?" I croak.

Oliver's face appears behind Greg's. "You fell on your ass," he says, not even trying to hide his smile. "Well, technically, you fell on your head."

Oh, God. I pull myself into a seated position and take in the sea of faces. "I fell?"

Greg is still tight-lipped. "You fell," he confirms. "You caught the railing on the way down and knocked yourself out."

"How's my bike?"

A tiny tug at the corner of his mouth. "Your bike is fine. Still, you shouldn't ride after that hit, you might be concussed. I've called for an emergency collection, they should be here in a few minutes."

"Okay." I'm mortified.

"You guys keep going," Greg tells the others. "We'll see you back at the start."

A chorus of disappointment rises up. "You should go," I tell him. "I can wait on my own."

"I'll wait with her," Oliver offers.

Greg isn't happy. I can tell by the set of his jaw, the way his eyes flicker from my face to the group behind me. Torn.

"Go," I repeat.

He gives Oliver a long, appraising look. "You sure?" he asks me.

I swallow down the knot of disappointment which has formed in my throat. "I'm sure."

Abruptly, he comes to a decision. "Okay. We're not far from the end, I won't be long. If you need me, call me. Joanna knows the way, she can guide the others if I need to bail."

His lips brush my temple. I blink rapidly as he gets to his feet and walks away. *Did he just say, Joanna?*

15

It's not long before we hear the rumble of the powerful 4x4 engine. Our bikes are loaded up, and Oliver and I are driven back to where we started. The medic gives me a thorough examination and concludes that I'm not concussed, but that I will have a thumping headache. I swallow down the pills he gives me and slump on the ground, pressing an ice pack to the impressive egg-shaped swelling on my forehead.

"Why so glum?" Oliver asks, taking a seat on the loamy soil beside me. He takes the ice pack and holds it for me.

"He did say, Joanna, right? I wasn't imagining it?"

"You weren't. Why, is that important?"

"Megan implied that something was going on between Greg and a woman named Joanna."

He winces. "Shit."

"Yeah."

"Do you want me to take you home?"

My head is throbbing, and I feel weepy enough that I might burst into tears. "Yes, please."

I ask the medic to let Greg know that I wasn't feeling well and decided to go home.

"You better come in, I'll call you a cab," I tell Oliver when we pull up in front of my house. There's no way I'll be able to drive him home.

"You go lie down, I can do it."

I nod gratefully and sink onto the sofa. Every time I close my eyes, my head spins. Oliver sets a cup of tea on the table before me, and I smile gratefully.

"You feeling okay?" he asks.

"No."

"If it helps, it was a spectacular fall. Really impressive. It was like you'd practiced."

I throw a cushion at him. "Do you think he'd cheat on me?"

Oliver's lips tighten. "I'd like to say no," he begins hesitantly, "but I honestly don't know. I barely know the guy, Em."

"You know him well enough," I point out, but Oliver refuses to say anything further. It's all the confirmation I need.

"Are you sure you're going to be okay? I can stay. I don't like the thought of leaving you here on your own."

"I'm fine. My pride's bruised more than anything."

"Okay, well at least me fetch Ally for you."

"Would you mind?" I smile gratefully.

"Of course not. Besides, I might even snag some of Mrs. J's shortbread while I'm there."

I laugh at that. My parents adored Oliver at first meeting, and since he demolished an entire tray of my mother's shortbread, she's constantly sending me into the office with baked goods for him."

"No doubt," I say. "Thanks, Oliver."

He leans in and kisses my cheek. He smells of sweat and soap. It's a nice smell. "I'll see you in a bit, Em," he says. Only once I hear the front door close behind him do I let the tears fall.

I'm finally dozing off when Greg erupts into the house like a tornado.

"Emma!" I can hear him calling for me the second he crosses the threshold.

"I'm in here!" I call back. He's beside me almost immediately.

"You left," he says. His voice is laced with anger and accusation.

"I'm sorry. I wasn't feeling well, and I figured it'd be easier if I just got out of the way."

His head jerks up. "Out of the way?"

"Yeah, well, there were a lot of people there, and I didn't want to be a killjoy."

"Are you being serious?" he's building up steam and I feel my own hackles rising.

"Who is Joanna?"

That throws him. "What?"

"Joanna. Who is she?"

His brow creases in confusion. "Joanna Meadon?"

"I have no idea what her last name is."

"She's a friend. She was there today – you met her."

"No, actually, I didn't. You didn't introduce me to anyone."

"Jesus, Emma, I'm sorry. There were over twenty cyclists out there today, it must have slipped my mind. I can't keep track of who knows who."

"I'm not just one of your cyclist friends! I'm your girlfriend!"

"I know that! I just don't understand where you're going with this."

My head is pounding. I take a deep breath and start again. "Megan came to see me this week. She implied that something was going on between you and a woman named Joanna."

"And you believed her?" He's incredulous.

"I'm asking you."

"Let me get this straight. Megan – a proven liar – tells you that I'm involved with someone else and you actually considered there might be some truth in it?"

"I don't know what to think. I want to trust you, but I've been burned before. I won't be naïve."

When he speaks again, his voice is so low I have to strain to hear him. "You're comparing me to Max?"

Too late, I realize my mistake. "No!" I grab his hand. "Greg, no! That's not what I meant." This is all spinning out of control, and I force myself to lower my voice. "Megan came to see me on Thursday. That was two days ago, and I haven't even mentioned anything until now. I didn't think it was true, but I had to ask."

"Okay, then, while we're on the topic, how about we talk about Oliver."

I blink in confusion. "Oliver?"

"Yes, Oliver! You told me to leave, and you chose him to stay with you. Do you have any idea how that made me feel?"

"I didn't choose him over you. You had a group of people relying on you."

"I don't give a shit about those people! You were hurt! Don't you think I wanted to be with you?"

"I didn't mean it like that." It's all I can say. I didn't choose Oliver over Greg, I just didn't want to inconvenience him. Not once did I consider how it might look – how Greg would feel, or how it would embarrass him in front of the others that his own girlfriend would shun him.

Greg's eyes don't leave my face, but the fire inside of them dims slightly. For a second, he squeezes my hand back. "I'm not sleeping with Joanna," he sighs. "She's a friend, nothing more."

I believe him, but somehow nothing is fixed. Greg gets to his feet. "I should go."

"Please don't. Ally's on her way back – we can have some dinner and talk about this."

His eyes narrow as he considers it. Then they darken. "Who's bringing her home?"

"Oliver," I admit, and I know what he's going to say before he even says it.

"I can't stay right now, Emma.

"Yes, you can. I want you to stay."

He doesn't meet my eyes. "You need to get some rest. I'll call you tomorrow."

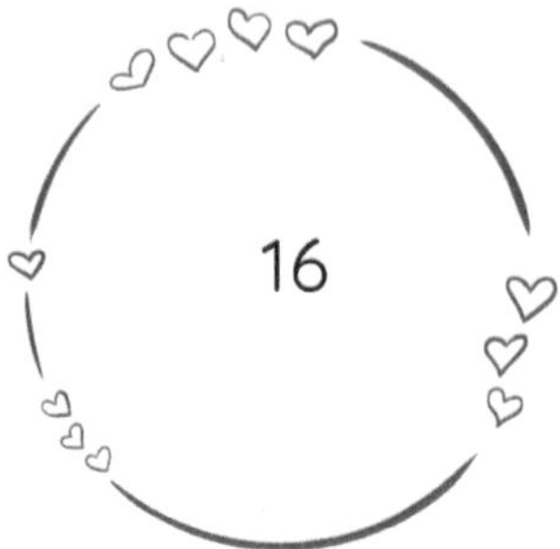

16

"It's a double," Oliver announces on Monday morning, setting an enormous paper cup on my desk. "I figured you might need it."

"You have no idea." I take a sip and burn the roof of my mouth.

"It's hot." Oliver is laughing, but I can't seem to locate my sense of humor. Greg didn't call yesterday. I'd spent the day on the sofa with Ally, watching cartoons and checking my phone every five minutes, but other than a few texts from Oliver to check if I was feeling better, the screen remained depressingly black.

"Do you want to grab lunch today?"

"I can't. I have a meeting with Greaves Dawson's at eleven."

He gives a low whistle. "Good luck."

"Thanks." I'm already rifling through my notes, and I barely notice when he gets up and leaves.

AT FIVE MINUTES TO ELEVEN, I'm ushered into a boardroom which is as impressive as it is intimidating. The table is twice the size of our own at Focus, and the marble floor is polished to a high sheen. I take a seat at the end of the table and pull out the proposal I've spent almost a week working on. When the door opens, an austere woman in a tailored two-piece suit stalks in. Her face is slightly familiar.

"Miss Johnson, I'm Joanna Meadon. I hope you don't mind, but I hijacked your meeting. Ultimately the decision is mine, so I let my associates off the hook." She extends her arm as I rise for the chair. "How's your head? That was quite a fall you had on Saturday."

I cringe, mortified that she witnessed it. I catch sight of her muscular calves, the sign of a true cyclist. She looks only a few years older than me, but her face is harder.

"I'm fine, thank you for asking. I guess cycling just isn't for me."

"It's not for everyone," she concedes drily. "Look, I'm going to level with you. The reason we reached out, is because you came highly recommended by Nanosec. By Greg," she adds meaningfully. "I know that the two of you have been seeing one another, but I've also known him long enough to know that he doesn't mix business and pleasure. He wouldn't recommend you if you weren't the best."

"I like to think I know what I'm doing," I reply. "I've had a look through your account history and I'm almost certain I could cut your expenditure by twenty percent, while still retaining your current rate of return."

"That's a very bold statement."

I raise my chin. I don't care if Greg referred me, he wasn't wrong. I'm good at my job, and I know what I can do.

"I can talk you through it, if I may?" Joanna lowers her eyes first.

It takes the better part of two hours before we are done.

"I'm impressed," Joanna admits. Despite the rocky start, I'm surprised to find that I like her. She's direct, but she's smart, and she doesn't mince her words. I hold my breath as she considers, her perfectly manicured fingers drumming on the smooth table top. Finally, she comes to a decision.

"We'll sign on with Focus. A six-month trial, with a possible two-year extension."

"Thank you. You won't be sorry. Although the projections I've made were based on a two-year period, I'm confident you'll see immediate results."

"I want to be very clear about one thing," she continues as if I haven't spoken. "We are signing on with *you*, specifically."

"I'm not sure I understand what you mean?"

"It's come to my attention that Oliver James was recently employed in your sales department."

"Yes...?" I draw out the word, not understanding where this is heading.

"Under no circumstances do I want Mr. James involved in our portfolio. I trust that won't present a problem?"

My mind reels. No sooner has she issued the instruction when it hits me. *Greg.* I can't believe he would stoop this low.

"Miss Meadon, I'm not sure what you have been told, but Oliver is a very valuable member of our team. To exclude him from a project of this magnitude—"

She cuts across me. "Despite what you may think, I don't base my decisions based on hearsay. I have my own reasons for not wanting Oliver James anywhere near my account." This time, I look away first. "Now," Joanna continues, "is this going to be a problem?"

"No," I admit, stifling the guilt that racks my chest. "I'll take care of it."

JACK IS EUPHORIC. Landing this account is the largest feather in Focus's cap since Nanosec came on board. Joanna and two of her directors visit Focus on Wednesday to sign the contract and the second they are out the door, he calls for champagne.

"Well done, Emma," he toasts. Most of the sales department is crammed into the boardroom, including Oliver, who gives me a high-five. I haven't told Jack about Joanna's condition yet, and my stomach is in knots. To top it off, I still haven't heard from Greg. Despite Joanna's insistence that it has nothing to do with him, I can't help but think that he somehow sabotaged Oliver out of spite. I've been so busy negotiating the final terms of this contract that I haven't had a moment to get in touch with him about it, but now that it's wrapped up, the sense of urgency to do so is overwhelming.

"I just need to make a quick call," I tell Jack.

"Nonsense! This is your victory party, everything else can wait!"

"I just need to check on Alyssa," I say, pulling the concerned parent card. "I won't be long."

I closet myself in my office and dial Greg's number. It almost rings off, and for a dreaded heartbeat I think he's not going to answer, but he does.

"Emma?"

"Hi." Now that I've got him on the line, I can't seem to find the right words.

"I just got off the phone with Joanna," Greg tells me, "I believe congratulations are in order."

The mention of her brings me back to the issue at hand. "We need to talk."

"You're damn right we do, but I was under the impression you didn't want to talk to me."

What? "I just... look, I really need to see you. Could I swing by after work?"

"I don't think this can wait. Can you come past my office?"

"Of course."

"I'll see you shortly." he disconnects, and I quickly send a text to my mom to let her know that I'll be late fetching Alyssa.

I've just hit send when Oliver's head appears around my door. "Everything okay?"

"Actually, no. Can you come in here for a second? There's something I need to tell you."

"She didn't say why?" Oliver's eyes are wide, and he shifts uncomfortably in his seat. He's taken the news badly, but I can't blame him. Finding out that one of the biggest brands in the country has specifically requested you be excluded from their account is a bitter pill to swallow, especially when you're trying to build a reputation in corporate advertising.

"I'm going to sort this out," I promise. "I don't know for sure, but I think that maybe Greg... well, he and Joanna are friends, and he's not your biggest fan."

"You think Greg did this?" His voice is low and furious.

"I don't know for sure. I'm heading over to see him, and I promise I'll get to the bottom of this. I'll sort it out. If it is him, I mean."

"What else could it be, Emma?" he's yelling now.

"Oliver, calm down!"

He runs his hands through his hair. "I'm sorry. It's just, well, this is a lot, you know?"

"I know." I nod in sympathy. "Look, before I head out, is there any reason that Joanna Meadon would want you excluded. Anything you can think of? You came from SalesCom, right? Did you ever have any dealings with Greaves before?"

"No. SalesCom is a tiny fish in a very large pond. They didn't have the resources to handle an account this size."

"She was insistent that this was her decision. Think, Oliver."

"I am thinking!" his eyes dart around the room before settling on my face. "Do you think I did this?"

"I'm not saying that."

"Well, you're certainly not saying that your boyfriend is the villain here. Does Jack know?"

"No, I haven't told him yet."

"This could ruin my career, Emma."

I knead my temples. "Look, let's not panic just yet." I glance at my watch. "I'm going to see Greg now, this can't wait. Let me go and tell Jack – I'll tell him there's an emergency at home. I'll be right back."

He sinks onto the chair opposite my desk and nods bleakly. As I pass, I place my hand on his shoulder. "It's going to be okay, Oliver."

When I return for my things, he's still slumped in the chair.

"What did Jack say?"

"That we'll pick this up tomorrow. Look, go home. Try to relax. I'll call you as soon as I leave Nanosec."

"You're going to his office?"

"Yes."

"And you'll call me?"

"Of course. Just as soon as I'm done." I feel terrible, leaving him in this state, but the best way to help him is to get to the bottom of this.

GREG IS in a meeting when I arrive, so I wait in reception while Tracey casts dark glances in my direction.

"I'm not sure how long Mr. Daniels will be," she says pointedly. "And without an appointment..."

"He's expecting me," I fire back.

As if on cue, Greg's office doors open. He gestures me in while Tracey walks his guests to the elevators.

"That will be all, Tracey," he tells her on his way back. "You can pack up and head home."

I wait until the doors are closed before I begin.

"I saw Joanna."

"I heard." He walks around his desk and focuses on his laptop. "She was very impressed."

There's no easy way to have this conversation, so I dive right in.

"She asked me to exclude Oliver from all dealings with Greaves."

His eyes meet mine over the laptop. "And you were surprised?"

His words stop me in my tracks. "Did you have something to do with this?"

"Emma, I don't know what's going on with you, but I'd think, given the information I sent you, that you'd have taken some action yourself. I get that you're angry with me, but—"

"What information?"

His head jerks up. "You didn't get my emails?"

"Greg, I haven't heard from you since you walked out on Saturday."

"Jesus, Emma, you're not serious."

I take a step back. "Why don't you just tell me what is going on?"

"I did some digging over the weekend. It seems your friend Oliver has had a number of near-misses with the law over the past three years."

"What?"

"Several women have laid charges of assault against him. One even claimed he was stalking her." He scans his screen. "A Juliana Reynolds – has he ever mentioned that name to you?"

"No." My addled brain doesn't seem to be firing on all cylinders. "Oliver would never… if he'd committed a criminal offense, personnel would have picked it up."

"That's the thing, he was never convicted. All charges were withdrawn."

"This can't be true. Oliver's a good guy. How do you know these women weren't just trying to blackmail him, or..." I trail off, unable to think of a single reason why anyone would do that.

"I tracked down his ex-wife, Simone James."

"Simone?" I shake my head. "No, that can't be right. Simone is some woman he dated, she's been stalking him, not the other way around."

"Simone was with Oliver for five years, and married only one of those. She says he's mentally unstable. He's harassed her for years since their divorce, but in the past few months he's left her alone. She was concerned – she thought perhaps he'd turned his attention to someone new." He gives me a pointed look.

"This is crazy. He's never done anything to raise any flags. He's my *friend*, Greg."

"I know he is. Which is why I didn't report this to Jack, or the authorities, not without concrete proof." He frowns at his screen. "That's why I sent it to you instead."

"I haven't received anything from you."

"It's right here!" he swivels his laptop to show me the screen. Three emails, all in his outbox, addressed to me.

"I've been busy, maybe I missed them." It's a hollow claim. I wouldn't miss an email from Greg. But I had been away from my desk for hours at a time, working through the Greaves contract. My stomach contracts. "Someone must've deleted them."

"Did someone screen my calls, too?"

"What?"

"I've been trying to call you for three days, Emma."

"That's impossible. I would've seen missed calls from you." I don't add that I'd been checking for his name every five minutes.

"Check your register."

I do, to find dozens of calls from Greg's number.

"What the hell?" Greg is already dialing. He puts his phone on speaker, and we both listen to the sound of dialed ringing. My phone stays silent.

"He must've blocked my number." Greg is on his feet. "Emma, this is serious. If he's tampered with your phone and your emails, we need to go to the police. And we need to alert Jack, too."

I nod, struck dumb with the revelation that Oliver might really be who Greg says he is.

"I need to check in with my parents – to let them know what's happening."

"You can call on the way."

We're already in the elevator when my mom answers. "Hey love, are you done already?"

"No, not yet. Mom, something's happened. My friend Oliver – he's, well, he might be dangerous. I need you to keep Alyssa tonight, can you do that?"

"Alyssa?" her voice is a horrified whimper. "Emma, Oliver picked Alyssa up a few minutes ago. You texted me to let me know he was coming!"

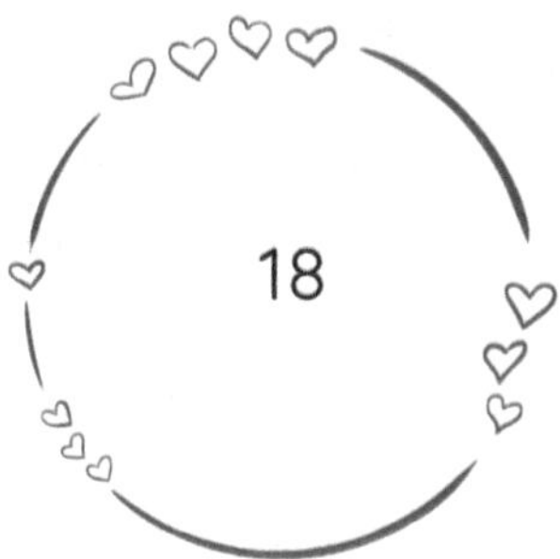

18

Someone must be looking over me because every light is green as we race toward Oliver's apartment. Greg is on the phone to the cops, explaining what's happened. I've tried Oliver's cell, but he's switched it off. Jack says that nobody has seen him since I left, but he's alerted security and that if Oliver tries to enter the building, he'll be detained.

"What else can I do?" he asks before I disconnect.

"Could you pull his files, try to find any alternate address?"

"I'm on it. I'll call you if I find anything."

Greg finishes up his call at the same time. "They've put out an alert. They're sending someone over to the house too, we'll meet them there." He falls silent and then slams his hands on the wheel. "Dammit! I should've just come to see you."

"Why didn't you?"

He hangs his head. "Male pride? I don't know, Emma. I had suspicions but nothing concrete. I thought you were avoiding me. I was pissed off. Put it down to a number of stupid reasons."

"You did try to warn me." It's little consolation, but it's all I can offer. A strange calm has settled over me. Inside, I am spinning out of control, my fear for Alyssa threatening to overwhelm me, but a combination of adrenalin and determination is keeping me going.

"I didn't think it was this serious," Greg says, apology in every word.

"I'm going to kill him," I say softly. "If we find them, I am going to kill him with my bare hands."

"*When* we find them," he corrects, "I'll help you."

The police arrive at Oliver's apartment first. They go in ahead of us, but I already know he's not here. I've visited only a few times in the past few months, but I always thought it was a happy apartment. Now, something heavy hangs in the air. A sense of wrongness. How could I have been so blind? Like a film reel, I keep playing all our interactions over and over in my head, trying to pinpoint where I went wrong. There was the odd look, gesture, a flash of anger that seemed out of place but that I could explain away at the time.

"Where the hell is my daughter!" Max's voice penetrates my dark musing, and I rush back into the hall to find him grappling with a police officer who is trying to stop him from coming inside.

"Let him go!" I yell, skidding a halt beside them. Greg pulls me back, just in time to avoid getting an elbow in the face. "That's my ex-husband – he's Alyssa's father!" I yell at the policeman. He releases Max immediately.

"Where is she, Emma?" Max's eyes are frantic and fearful, but there's no trace of the redness which accompanies his drinking.

"I don't know, Max. Oliver fetched her from my folks – he sent a text from my phone when I wasn't looking – but I have no idea where he could've taken her."

"How did this happen? How did he get your phone in the first place, and why in God's name would your parents let her go off with some stranger?"

"He's not a stranger. He's picked her up for me a few times when I've run late, and my parents have met him multiple times. As for my phone, I have no idea. He must've texted when I left him alone in my office just before I left."

"This is your fault!"

I open my mouth to deny it, but no words come out.

"I'm sorry," I manage, before Greg intercepts.

"I'm calling Simone," he says. "She's Oliver's ex-wife," he explains to Max. "She might know where he would go."

My phone rings. I snatch it up and almost pass out with relief when I see Oliver's number.

"Oliver!"

"Hey, Emma." He sounds so normal, so unconcerned, that for a second I wonder if this has all been a terrible misunderstanding.

"Where's Alyssa?" Greg and Max have frozen beside me, hanging on every word. I watch as Greg gestures the nearest policeman over and signs to him that Oliver is on the phone.

"I should've left when I saw his emails," Oliver says, and I hear it then, the touch of madness lurking below the cool exterior. "I wanted to, but I thought I'd have more time to make you see."

"Make me see what, Oliver? Where is my daughter?" Through the crippling terror, I hear a sound in the background that seems amplified because I know it so well. My eyes widen as I turn to Greg. *Southside Mall,* I mouth. I'd know the sound of that arcade game anywhere, Alyssa plays it every time we go shopping.

Max is already moving. Keeping my voice calm, I follow him down the stairs while Greg hastily explains to the cops what's going on.

"Where is she?" I say into the phone, keeping up pretenses. "Why did you take her? Please, Oliver, she's only a little girl. She has nothing to do with this. Please bring her back. I won't tell anyone, I promise." I raise my voice at the end, trying to mask the sound of the car door closing.

Max already has the engine running when Greg tears out of the lobby. I hit the mute button as he leaps into the back seat.

"I'm not going to hurt her, Emma. I only wanted you to hear me out."

"I'm listening! I'll come to you, we can sit down and have a drink. You can explain it all, but please let me get Alyssa home first."

"Not until you promise you won't call the cops."

"Why would I do that? You're my friend, Oliver."

"What about the lies your boyfriend told you about me?"

"Greg?" I force as much disdain into my voice as I can. "I didn't even give him the chance. He admitted that he's been seeing Joanna, would you believe it. As far as I'm concerned, he can go to hell."

Max gives Greg a confused look over his shoulder, but Greg just shakes his head and gestures for me to keep going.

"Why did you take Ally?" I ask. "Were you trying to help me out? I know you expected I might be late?"

I've given him an easy out, and he seizes it. "You know I'd do anything for you, Emma."

"I know." I force a laugh. "God knows I'd never survive at the office without your daily coffee delivery. I don't know what Greg is trying to do, but he's not going to succeed."

"He really slept with her?"

I lower my voice. "He really did."

"God, Em, that sucks. I'm sorry."

It blows my mind how quickly he's slipped back into the old familiarity. The son of a bitch has taken my daughter and yet he's talking to me as if we're still the best of friends.

"Tell me about it. My taste in men sucks." The irony of that statement, given that two of those choices are currently in the car with me, on a mission to save my daughter, is almost laughable.

"Where are you, Oliver? I'll come to you and we can sit down and talk about it. I need a shoulder to cry on."

We've arrived at the mall and my adrenalin spikes. There are loads of people here, he'll hear it if I get out of the car. In the background on Oliver's side, I hear Alyssa's voice and my chest constricts.

"Can I speak to her?"

"She's fine."

"I know she is. I know you'd never hurt her. I just want to hear her voice – I've been so worried."

He gives no indication that he's going to do it, but the second Ally's breathless voice comes down the line, I'm moving, launching out of the car and sprinting toward the arcade, Greg and Max right beside me.

"Mommy," Alyssa whines.

"Hey, baby! Are you having fun?"

"I want to come ho-"

"There, are you happy?" Oliver demands. I cringe as a group of teenagers rushes past, gossiping at the top of their voices. Oliver gives a bellow of rage and cuts the call.

"He knows!" I yell, pushing my body even faster. "He knows we're here!"

Greg bolts through the crowd, cutting a path for me and Max. I keep my head down and sprint after him, scanning the sea of faces.

Greg gets there first. Oliver is trying to drag Alyssa out of one of the back exits when Greg's fist thunders toward his face. He spins a full 360 degrees and drops Ally. I snatch her up, cradling her to my chest. She's crying, and I cover her face as Greg hits Oliver again. Then Max is there, leaping on top of Oliver as he goes down and landing blow after blow every place he can reach.

It happens so quickly I can barely keep up. I'm stroking Alyssa's back, her hair, and smothering her with kisses, desperate to reassure myself that she's unharmed. The police arrive and haul Greg and Max off Oliver, who is whimpering in pain and fear.

His eyes meet mine, and I wonder how it's possible to hate someone as much as I hate him right now. He sees it and his bloody mouth opens.

"Emma." It's a plea. Over Alyssa's head, I mouth three words so only he can see. *Go fuck yourself.*

It's a long night. My parents meet us at the police station where we all have our statements taken. I'm sitting in the waiting room with Alyssa on my knee while Greg finishes up giving his account of events when a mousy-haired, long-legged woman walks in. Her doe-eyes are wide and fearful. I know instinctively who she is.

"Mom, take Ally for me, please." I get to my feet and walk forward to meet her. "You must be Simone." She can't seem to focus on anything, her eyes scanning the room. "I'm Emma," I say, holding out my hand.

Her eyes find mine. "Are you her?"

"I am."

She exhales a sigh of relief. "I wanted to warn you, but he wouldn't tell me who you were. And he wouldn't take any of my calls."

It strikes me that I, myself, helped Oliver's cause. I helped him screen this woman when all she wanted to do was help me.

"Everything happened so quickly," I say. "One minute he was fine, the next..." I swallow down the lump in my throat. "He took my daughter."

She follows the line of my arm to see Alyssa snuggling into my mother's chest. Her eyes look more, rather than less terrified.

"That's how it is with him," she whispers. "Sometimes I used to think I was the crazy one. He's an amazing man, but then..." she pauses, gathering herself. "His medication helped, but he refused to stay on it."

I take her hand. "It's okay. You don't have to talk about it."

"Where is he?"

"He's been taken into custody. The officer in charge says he'll be convicted unless there's a medical reason to have him committed. Either way, he's not going to hurt anyone, ever again."

Her legs are trembling. "He's sick. He doesn't mean it, but when he's off his meds, he can't control himself. I tried to help him, I..." she takes a deep breath. "I tried."

"Like you said, he's sick."

"He wouldn't hurt anyone if he could help it."

I stare up at her, at the compassion and sadness reflected in her brown eyes.

"My mother used to say that," I say.

EPILOGUE

It's been three months since Oliver was arrested. He's currently undergoing treatment for his mental health issues. I don't know how long he'll be there, or whether he'll serve jail time after, and I don't care. Simone was right – he is sick, but he's also a coward. He won't come near me or my family again, and, if he does, I'll be ready for him.

That said, he'd need to get through Greg's security system first. Ally and I moved in with Greg six weeks ago. It'll take some getting used to. I haven't sold my house yet. I did, however, sell the bicycle. Greg's quite content with my new creed to keep the cardio in the bedroom.

Max is still sober. He brought his new girlfriend around for a barbecue last weekend. She's nice enough to treat Ally well, but not nice enough to take any nonsense. She'll keep Max on the straight and narrow, not that I think he needs it.

I haven't seen or heard from Megan. She didn't even make contact after what happened. Last I heard, she'd been dismissed from Carter & Boyd for inappropriate conduct. I'm not sure what she did, but I have my suspicions.

. . .

THE END

ABOUT THE AUTHOR

Rachel Rhodes is a pseudonym for award-winning author, copywriter, and lover of the written word, Melissa Delport. She is published in both S.A and the U.S.A and offers professional copywriting services and author coaching.

For ten years she owned and operated her own specialized logistics company until she woke up one morning and decided it was time to put her English degree to good use.

Melissa lives with her husband and three teenagers, none of whom take her seriously.

She also writes romantic suspense as Lissa Del and contemporary romance as Rachel Rhodes.

For more information, visit www.melissadelport.com

ALSO BY RACHEL RHODES

ROMANCE & ROMANTIC COMEDY (as Rachel Rhodes)

Awkward in Print

Awkward Abroad

Awkward Infidelity

Awkward in Trouble

CONTEMPORARY WOMENS FICTION (as Lissa Del)

Rainfall

Riven

A Life Made of Lava

URBAN FANTASY

GUARDIANS OF SUMMERFELD SERIES

The Cathedral of Cliffdale (Book 1)

The Fight of the Fallen (Book 2)

The Hope of Hawkstone (Book 3)

The Balance of the Blood (Book 4)

Full Series Boxed Set (Books 1-4)

SHADOW MAGIC SERIES

The Witchborn Curse (Book 1)

The Shadow Huntress (Book 2)

The Charmed Quarter (Book 3)

The Rogue Coven (Book 4)

The Darkest Realm (Book 5)

The Hybrid's Fate (Book 6)

Full Series Boxed Set (Books 1-6)

THE TRAVELER DUOLOGY

The Traveler (Book 1)

The Survivor (Book 1.5)

The Saviour (Book 2)

TIME TRAVEL FANTASY

The Clock Keeper

DYSTOPIAN

THE LEGACY TRILOGY

The Legacy (Legacy Trilogy Book 1)

The Legion (Legacy Trilogy Book 2)

The Legend (Legacy Trilogy Book 3)

ANTHOLOGIES

The Space Between Dreams & Chaos

The Space Between Magic & Mayhem

www.ingramcontent.com/pod-product-compliance
Lightning Source LLC
Chambersburg PA
CBHW020918310726
48980CB00011B/940/J

* 9 7 8 0 6 3 9 8 4 4 8 9 3 *